J.C. Gemmell was born in Fɛ
B.A. in Computer Studies anu a ivɪaster s Degree in Applied Science from the University of Portsmouth. Before turning to science fiction, he worked as a software engineer for a number of multinational organisations. He lives with his partner on the south coast of England.

Find out more about the author at jcgemmell.com

J.C. Gemmell

Tionsphere

Tion Book 1

For The Stibster

This story incorporates the cultures of Earth's many nations, and it is proper for it to include a few foreign words into its standard English. Much as we would be comfortable eating *enchiladas* in an *alfresco café*, these people have adopted words to suit their needs. Indeed, in a massively-populated world, having several terms for people is crucial.

Most of these foreign words are easily pronounced; however, Icelandic (used in terms related to men, women and so forth) includes two less-familiar letters.

The first is 'eth' (Ð, ð), typically pronounced 'th' as in 'the'. The second is 'thorn' (Þ, þ), typically pronounced 'th' as in 'think'.

Readers should not need to look up these foreign words to understand and enjoy the story; they are deliberately placed to imply context. However, for those who really need to know, a glossary is included for your reference.

Please enjoy and perhaps leave a review rating,

J.C. Gemmell.

CONTENTS

CHAPTER ONE
Jovana
বর্তমানে

SHU-FEN AND Danesh waited hand-in-hand. It had been fifteen years since their conception, and they were almost adults, about to become *fullorðnir*. They had spent their whole lives together; neither could recall a time when they were apart. Shu-fen thought they were incredibly similar, and they were somehow associated. Danesh maintained she was indistinguishable from all other new women, that everyone looked alike, so Shu-fen refused to have sex with him, quoting archaic taboo, just in case.

Their entire existence had been in school, preparing to become data capitalists. Neither had a spectacular record, but neither failed to qualify. As with physical appearances, they were average, just new people starting their new lives. Each was extremely nervous, but Danesh was also excited because he wanted to see the world. They were ascending to their Kilometre-Four work assignments. Miraculously, their allocated cells were in adjacent K4 districts, but it would be the first time either had been alone. Shu-fen was scared and quietly wanted to remain home.

Other adult children, other *ný-fólkið*, surrounded the pair, each dressed in white trousers and shoes, shirts and caps.

Danesh is correct, Shu-fen thought, we do all look alike. She estimated they were over halfway to the departure door, maybe ten minutes until it was their turn to leave. Shu-fen had barred all of her messaging, only seeing the white walls and hundreds of others who were patiently waiting. An empty canvas. She had no idea where the phrase came from, unbidden into her consciousness. Shu-fen had never truly offlined, although once she had received self-access, she had installed an adaptive algorithm to restrict her feed to only the things she could see. Danesh regularly teased her about her limited interaction, but she did not mind. One of the new men behind her was reciting from the annals, and as Shu-fen listened to the chaunter sing and watched the comforting words drift above his head, she wondered if his future life would have more meaning than hers.

Shu-fen squeezed Danesh's hand as they edged forward. He did not reciprocate because he was immersed in Sodality, entirely distracted by his virtual experiences in online, allowing his agitation to be washed away by users who did not know him. Danesh was fulfilling his base need to hunt for data and gather information. It gave him purpose. She imagined he was painting his own landscape on their white surroundings, fields and trees, birds in a blue sky. Clouds. These things existed solely in imaginings and were delusions for children, for *börnin*.

Together, they surged closer to the doors. Shu-fen turned to face Danesh, and his interrupts kicked in, distracting him from his quantum immersion. He raised an eyebrow.

'Are you all set?'

'I think so,' she said, 'after all, we can't go back.'

He smiled. 'For as long as I remember we've been getting ready for today. Everything we've done. Do you remember when we overrode the lockdown and escaped, and the outside was full of people and places and sensation?'

'It wasn't real, Danesh.' She gave him a slightly condescending look. 'Everything we've ever experienced isn't real. It's a fantasy. Make-believe to keep *börnin* happy.' There was just a handful of new people in front of them, and they would soon be entering their car.

'But it was nothing like this,' Danesh ventured. 'We're empty and unmarked. When we step through those doors, the world will burst into a million colours, and we'll be right in the middle of it, shining like two brand new sunstars circling each other. We'll be awesome.'

'You've never seen the sunstar,' she pouted, 'let alone two. So how do you know? Anyway, you can't look at the sunstar because if you're really, really outside and there's no air to filter out all the violence so it could blind you. Everyone knows that. It kills people. And it's too bright to look at, and there's so much contrast you can just see all-light or no-light. Binary vision, I guess. And I expect you'd melt or burst into flames or something. Not unless you're an essential maintainer wearing a *kostym* to shield you, ensuring the empyrealodes send us heat and light, and you're protected, and anyway, we're not going to do that—'

Danesh stopped listening to her chatter. The *ný-fólkið* in front of them had left, hurtled into their futures, leaving him to face the automatic doors. Shu-fen finally realised and fell quiet. The youths surrounding them were also silent, remaining motionless, as if they had already abandoned their old lives. The doors opened slowly, and the brilliant light dazzled them. Danesh didn't understand why he hadn't noticed the glare before. Six children stepped forward.

'Tion unique identifiers.' Danesh listened to the names, three new men, three new women. Both those girls are Zayins, he thought. Rightsiders. A single moji in their names enough to entice disdain throughout their lives. They look like the same new woman, perhaps sisters. Twins. The word came deliciously to him, uninvited. He checked their public names: Humaira, Zara. He had already forgotten their TUIDs but refused to replay the moment like an infant. He would track them down for himself. Danesh pondered the number of Humairas in the world. No more than a billion, he surmised. He wanted to divine the answer, the way an adult would, not pose a question and wait for a response. He stared at the girls, visualising Zara upon Zara queuing up before him. Each one unique and special in her way.

'Keep your thoughts to yourself,' Shu-fen interjected spitefully.

'I was running numbers,' he protested.

'I see.'

The six new people filed into the carriage, sitting opposite one another, segregated by gender. They were mute and blank-faced, waiting for the Pallium to confirm their entry to adulthood. Danesh and Shu-fen were going to live a mere thirty-five seconds of arc apart and could probably walk a thousand metres to see one another. The car hurtled into vast corridors, passing through the vacuum silently to deposit them at their future. He knew people could circumnavigate the tionsphere in ninety minutes, although no one would ever want to. The vehicle data feed indicated they would arrive in just over one-third of that time. Danesh inspected the colourless features of the capsule; his eyes eventually flicking between the two unfamiliar, familiar girls. They were both quite ordinary-looking and similar, their skin was flawless, their hairstyles identical and their faces devoid of any emotion. Do not disturb, they read. It had been three minutes since the car crossed into the Lacuna, the world's airless arteries. Danesh continued to resist the welcoming glow of Sodality in an attempt to demonstrate his independence. After a few minutes, he realised no one was paying him any attention, so he submitted. He watched a woman gaze at him. She wore white feather-fur, and her blond curls danced in the virtual breeze. She was entirely opaque.

Shu-fen studied Danesh silently. He was the sole person she had ever thought stood out. She used to think he was not the same as the other boys, but now she was not so sure. He will have these two girls, or girls like them, instead of having me. I messed things up. She stared at him with her eyes locked on his, yet he was unaware. Perhaps his world had already burst into millions of colours, she thought, though, in reality, they are all the same.

There was a jolt of intense deceleration, accompanied by a tremendous noise as compressed air rushed from the car's motor. The domain inside their vehicle collapsed into information darkness so that everywhere Shu-fen looked was void. The two girls and three boys were instantly *börnin* again and looked at her as if she was responsible. Shu-fen felt her stomach reel as the capsule's speed varied, her mouth watered so much she thought she might vomit. There were several loud bangs accompanied by long, grating noises. The module was scraping across the walls, and as it slowed the lights flickered and dimmed. A straightforward message appeared before them in bold, no-nonsense letters.

Reserve power sufficient to arrest motion. Standby.

The lights went out, and Shu-fen was not the first to be sick. The passengers lurched from their seats, and one of the boys started to moan, clearly in pain. The pod rolled about its central axis, spinning with alarming speed, while the rasping continued as air cushions attempted to protect the delicate vehicle. Shu-fen was aware of a hand on her leg, sharply clutching with nails that dug in. As the grip tightened, she started to whimper, pawing at the fingers. The pod continued to lurch for the longest time but eventually came to came to a halt.

The power failed in a brilliant electric spark, and a pale orange glow enveloped the interior. The two boys were on the floor, one with his legs at impossible angles, his breathing shallow. They had no way to deposit him at a cacherie to be processed nor had any skills to tend to him. Shu-fen looked away. Humaira and Zara clung together, their heads buried in each other's shoulders. Feeling flooded into Shu-fen's thigh as Danesh reached across to help the uninjured boy up from the floor. The pain in her leg was awful. She looked down at the damp, black spots where his fingers had been.

'You hurt me,' she said.

Standby.

They faltered, hopeful that the one feed they had would offer something more.

'What have you done?'

Shu-fen stared at the boy with dismay. She couldn't identify him because they were all offline. 'Are you all okay? What are you called?'

'Ahmad.'

'Humaira. And Zara.'

'We're Danesh and Shu-fen.'

'His name is Haziq Lla-Four-Ne-Te. Is he dead?'

'No, he's still alive,' Shu-fen sobbed. 'I don't know what to do.'

They were isolated from the real world and unsure without connection. Shu-fen tried to exclude Haziq from her eyesight, but the Pallium did not handle the request, and he remained before her. His cap was near Shu-fen's feet, so she picked it up and dumped it over his face.

Standby.

'Someone will come,' Danesh promised. 'When we don't show up, someone will look for us.' He tried to sound reassuring, but his voice betrayed his fear of being punished. 'We can't leave the transport because there's no atmosphere in the Lacuna and they can't leave us here because the capsule will block the transit system. They will have to come.'

'We have to try to get out.'

'We can't.'

Ahmad started to grope around in the dim glow, using his fingers to search for a compartment or a storage bin. 'There'll be something to help us, maybe a tool, or something to breathe with, surely.'

'It says to wait.'

'But what if no one comes? It's getting cold. We have to do something.' He continued to look around the capsule, but there were only the seats, the door and six frightened children. Their panting and occasional groans dispersed the silence. Then, a muffled clink on the outside of the pod and tapping across the exterior shell. A clunk, a scratching noise and metal turning on metal. There was a swerve as something dragged the vehicle along the artery wall.

Salvage. Standby.

One of the two girls started to giggle, but Danesh could not remember which one was which. He presumed it was a nervous response and edged away. He moved closer to Shu-fen and took her hand. 'I'm here,' he said.

She looked into his eyes and felt a connection that had nothing to do with technology. After a while, they became accustomed to the motion and waited in silence.

'You shouldn't have covered him,' Ahmad said eventually. 'He's my friend.' He took the hat away, touched Haziq's face and nudged him. There was no response. 'I hope he will be all right.'

The car stopped moving, and the lights came on to dazzle them. They felt the rush of connection flowing over them. There was loud, mechanical moan and the doors were prised open. Three men crowded into the small enclosure, bringing with them a strong smell of sweat. One pushed Haziq aside with his foot, ignoring the boy's yelp, and seized Danesh by the neck.

'Out.' The men took hold of the four undamaged children and roughly propelled them from the transport.

Danesh raced through directories, desperate to summon enforcing assizes to rescue them, but the data pathways collapsed. The sound was overwhelming, and his corrupt imagery swamped his eyesight. It forced him to offline.

'What are you doing?' he cried, and the man tightened his grip on his throat.

'Quiet.'

The man viciously thrust Danesh through the doors, and someone pulled his hair from behind, spraying foam into his mouth. Rough hands covered his eyes and taped them shut. His arms were shoved behind him, drawn together and his wrists bound. There was a blow to the back of his knees, and he buckled to the groundplate.

'What a fucking pain in the arse,' one of the men remarked.

'Enough,' Miyu said and rubbed her eyes.

The five women sat in a loose group, blinking in the ambient light. Jovana got up and poured water for them. She sighed and smoothed Miyu's thick, black hair as she handed her a glass. 'You'll be fine in a moment. Some days are just—' She made a guttural noise, and Caitlyn laughed.

Miyu closed her eyes and fished the ice out of her water. 'I wish we could go out there.' It was their favourite discussion, one that consumed their spare time. The women had joined their elucidarium at the start of their adult lives and already spent five years confined together solving other people's problems, with no option to venture outside.

'Come on, Miyu, it's dirty and unpleasant. It's dangerous.' Kavya was the appointed diffuser and worked hard to maintain harmony in the group. 'What shall we do to unwind?'

'Food,' Caitlyn and Jovana chorused, forgetting the moment. They were fifteen years post-conception when they met, and each had prominent scores and substantial prospects. After they arrived in their apartment and maintainers had removed the door, their prearranged hierarchy gave way to Jovana. She was not the most accomplished in the group, but she had a drive the others could not match and gradually assumed authority. The others called her Head Girl behind her back but were content with their situation.

Jovana made her evening promenade around the room. It was a pleasing, broad circle with individual sleeping chambers buried in the walls. She brushed past the wardrobes and private places, the areas to exercise, work and eat. The entire space was a uniform deep beige into which incidental light disappeared, but Jovana was dressed in pastel colours and created a joyous contrast to their allotted surroundings. She sang softly to herself and touched some of the hanging pictures, sculptures and small furnishings as she walked. Of course, she had found all of these things outside and had discretely bartered for delivery to their home. Salvage was Jovana's favourite task because it gave her access to Tion's past. Kavya and Freja were sought-after design engineers, while Caitlyn was their principal problem solver. Miyu was the quietest of the group, a mathematician, but her passion was for online fantasies.

Freja cut up some fruit, examined each one and proclaimed its nearest ancestor. 'Mango. Kiwi. Lime.' She called up images of each as she identified them and shared the pictures with the women who were listening. She popped a segment of a lemon into her mouth and savoured the sugary flavour.

'All fruit taste of fruit,' Miyu said and took a segment from her. 'You try to over-complicate things.'

Jovana stopped behind Kavya. 'Tell me what you're working on.' Sometimes talking helped.

'First topsky transparency. It's a ridiculous problem. People want to see beyond the world, as if anything is interesting there. They want to do so without being exposed or whatever. I don't understand it. The cost is immense, just for a view any of us can summon with a wish. They want to experience it. At least I'm only working on re-routeing external services across level Zero, gas exchangers, radioactive waste ports, and so forth. I can't believe the technicians will be able to create anything robust enough to be a clear skyplate to protect privileged *fólkið*. Working on something I don't enjoy is utterly boring.'

'That's because you want to ascend.'

'Don't be ridiculous,' Kavya said and smiled.

'I'm estimating populations by level again.' The others groaned. 'This is my last time. Do you think your assignment is stupid? People hatch, people are cached, and a few die—one in, one out, more or less. The Pallium, the FMP,' she emphasised, 'maintains balance. They've got me proving harmony exists through checking its bloody processing systems are accurate.'

'Sweetie,' Jovana said to Miyu, 'you are the numbers girl.' There was laughter all around. 'You forget the offliners.'

'There's a record of every disconnection, and they can't do anything unobservable. The Pallium knows where each one is. Most offliners reconnect eventually. It's not an issue.' Miyu yawned.

'I'm on cataloguing duty,' Caitlyn complained. 'There's a bunch of regeneration going on deep in the Eights, giving the level a new lease of life. There's very little worth saving, I'm afraid.'

'I'll trade with you next shift,' Jovana offered. 'I think someone switched our assignments. They've given me a cooling failure to work through. I hate being an engineer. There are only so many times I can ask why.' More laughter. 'I'm hoping you found something nice.'

Caitlyn nodded. 'There was a small Tanzanite ring, set in platinum. Very pretty.' A reference number appeared in Jovana's eyesight. 'I can order you one up.'

'It's not the same.'

'It was filthy.'

'What about you, Freja?'

'I don't want to talk about it.'

There was silence for a while. Kavya stared blankly into space and Jovana circled some more until she stopped at an image of the five of them taken years before.

'The door,' Miyu said. 'That's where it was.' The five *konurnar* had barely spoken about it because their contracts made no provision for them to leave. 'I wonder how they will take our bodies out when we're cached,' she murmured. There was almost no discussion before they slept.

'I find immense pleasure in it,' Milagrosa declared, 'it's what the *forfeður* made me for.'

'It's what we were all made for,' Bailey said. Approval rang out across the farm.

Milagrosa saw herself as an ancient hag, hovering in front of her. 'Cut that out,' she hollered, not knowing who had created the epitome.

They worked a grass farm. Bright glass columns encased the sturdy plants, reaching sixty metres to the skyplate. Milagrosa deftly hooked a seed head through a small opening in the tube, so it could ripen for a few days before falling to the decking for the dumpers to collect.

When the plant stopped producing, the grass workers would wind it down at its base, recycling as much as sixty metres into clearfibre. Then it would grow again. In all directions the grasses were tended by lithe people, simply clothed in the harnesses that tethered them to the plants. The farm was warm, and the air intoxicating. Milagrosa never tired of it.

She pulled the last seed head through with her grass blade, consulted their schedule and selected her next specimen, far from the group. She threw a line between transparent bars, trusted its hold while cutting loose and enjoyed the cooling air as she swung. She climbed up to the sky and peered into the pipe to inspect the grass. The tube was a pillar of diffuse light, scattered by a pale mist within. Milagrosa clasped the ceiling mesh and intently stared while she hung motionless.

'*Lýðirnir*, we've got another one,' she proclaimed.

The grass was torn away at its top, and the fine blades were an oozing pulp. Something had smudged the dew on the surface of the cylinder, and on one side there was a single, tiny handprint. Milagrosa took a small hammer from her harness and rapped the glass sharply.

'Buffy,' she called.

Shrill calls from across the farm answered her, long piercing animal sounds that were expertly mimicked by her friends. She saw Hyun-jun work his way towards her and waited while he leapt from column to column unaided. She looked away and tried to conceal her amusement.

'Can you see it? Is it there?'

'You're the only man I have ever known who in all of his fifteen years has never seen a marmoset. What did you do as a young *drengar*? Spend your entire boyhood on the ground?'

'I tasted one once.'

She laughed. 'Is that what they told you?' She leant across and stretched over to spank him, but he danced out of the way, his smooth body disappearing between the grasses.

'You'll have to do better than that,' he cried, and the old hag appeared again.

'I knew it was you!'

Milagrosa opened the glass casing, took her grass blade and made a lengthwise cut in the woody plant. Its interior was dusty white, and a stale, fungal odour wafted out. She closed the inspection hatch and unhooked, so that she could slowly slide down the column, pausing to block each seed hole with tape from her harness. Occasionally, she struck the shaft, and a chime rang out across the farm.

The other workers picked up the note, adding octave, fifth, octave, major third: overtones that built on the unique sound of the grass tube. Their funeral song was simple in the lower register but became discordant with each new tone. Other fundamentals sounded as the farmers used their tools to strike the columns. Milagrosa dropped to the floor. There was silence.

'Today, we end this magnificent grass and are thankful for the life it has given us through its grain.' The pillar darkened, and she grasped it with both hands and howled as the cold bit into her. She felt the violent force of air blast the remains of the plant from the vibrating shaft and then the searing heat of its sterilisation. 'Tomorrow, I will reseed you,' she whispered.

There were *fólkið* around her, placing rough fingertips on her skin. One of the women took her hands and inspected them, cleaning them with kisses.

'You protect the buffies yet do this to yourself? It achieves nothing.'

'They show us infested plants. We need them.'

'Hyun-jun. Make sure she rests.'

They returned home with arms around each other's waist while Hyun-jun improvised notes from their threnody. They reached a clearing, one of several across the grass farm used for sleeping. Thick mats woven from the grasses covered the mesh groundplate, and furniture crafted from sturdy culms waited for them. Hyun-jun passed Milagrosa a cup of water and searched for a blanket.

'I remember the first time I saw one. It had pressed its face up against the tubing, and it was staring right at me. I was about five. I couldn't believe this tiny thing was a whole being. "What are you for?" I asked, but it couldn't reply. One of the old workers said the buffy-headers were pests, but I knew he was wrong. When I opened the pipe, it disappeared into the ground while its warning chirps echoed back to me. They are attracted to the fungus that sometimes grows up from the base of the grasses. If the marmos are there, the plant is unlikely to survive. We have no clue as to where they come from.'

Hyun-jun sat close to her, and their bodies touched. He felt her warmth. 'Do you remember the first time you saw me?'

'Of course. You were almost as tiny as the buffies, with such a mop of black hair. There were lots of babies that year, passed from mother to mother. I don't know whose you were. You were just another little infant, but I remember nursing you in particular.'

'You don't,' he retorted. 'Everyone knows you can't resist coddling all the *börnin*. You loved each of us.'

'Babies and men are two different things,' she reminded him. Hyun-jun leant in and nuzzled Milagrosa's collarbone. She rested her wrist on his head with her sore hand propped in the air. They were still for some time, breathing together, his young body felt taut, and he was hard against her. She waited.

'Our world is so small,' he ventured.

'Nonsense, it takes several days to haul from end to end. We are a compact group yet, with plenty of space and plenty of seed to reap.'

'What happens to it? Other than what we eat.'

'The world is vast, Hyun-jun. Beyond this grass farm are many others, feeding the countless *þjóðirnir* in the tionsphere. Who can guess how those people live? We ask the FMP, and it answers in riddles, although it does teach us to be thankful for our part in it.'

'Then how do you know?' He glided up her body until they were eye-to-eye. 'Have you seen it?'

She welcomed him gently. 'When I was young, I also wanted more. I have been to other farms, Hyun-jun. There are ways. But it was a long time ago, before your conception.'

He was still, intent. 'How?'

Milagrosa knew there would not be peace until she sated him. 'Where does the grain go? How do we summon heat and light? Who tends the Pallium? These are such childish questions. There was a stretch of grasses that weren't producing well. When we investigated, there were beetles, like tiny brown phalluses, swarming inside the plants. The lament went on for hours. We ended the plants and cleansed the tubes with fire. It's the only time I've seen it. The columns were blackened and destroyed and needed replacing. People came, and they said they were a maintenance crew. I was terrified of the strangers and hid for days, but the adult farmers knew where I was and weren't concerned. One morning, after they headed out, I spied on the outsiders. They were removing the sky with special tools so they could take out the pillars and did the same at the ground. There are great spaces above and below us, where *þjóðirnir* could hide. Later in the day, I saw my chance. The maintainers were resting with their equipment scattered around them. I spotted their sky tool and took it.'

She could feel his excitement grow until it would burst from him, and he would be lost. 'I still have it, and it is safe from you, Hyun-jun.'

He screwed his eyes shut and with great determination remained calm. 'Please, Milagrosa. Don't keep this from me. That is not our way.' He held his breath and tried to relax.

They eventually heard their people returning from the grass fields. The bustle grew as the men and women arrived, dropping their harnesses to the ground. Some checked their equipment for damage while they settled down, and waved as the children started to appear from amongst the glass columns. It was their duty to feed and tend to their seniors, but they were always reluctant to get started. Lior, one of the other new men, pointed at Milagrosa and Hyun-jun, saying something they didn't quite hear before he ran off.

'He needs putting in his place,' she said and pushed Hyun-jun up. 'Go.'

She watched him skip away as Bailey sat beside her. He looked carefully at each of her hands.

'He's still a boy, Milagrosa. You shouldn't tease him.'

'He asks too many questions. He'll outgrow us. He needs to be distracted.'

'Let the young *fólkið* do that. Hyun-jun can experiment with them. You're overly generous.' He clasped her hands in his. 'You'll be fine in the morning.'

'I don't know what to tell him.'

Bailey slowly rose from his seat. 'I'm too old for this. I need to rest.'

The clearing was full of people, talking, stretching and making themselves comfortable. Several of the older children passed between the adults with jugs of *sato*, sometimes stealing sips when they thought no one was looking. The farmers formed a large seated circle and helped themselves to food. The chatter was composed of projections, images and text, as well as vocalisation: Milagrosa thought it was a nice mix. She drank from her mug, savouring the wine as it blossomed on her tongue. Hyun-jun sat among a group of new men, and she watched as they laughed and slapped each other on their backs and thighs. Milagrosa delighted in their youth.

After the meal, when the storytelling was over, and the children had fallen asleep in clumps, the *fullorðnir* talked. Riley Khar pulled himself up. 'For generations, we have worked in these fields, supporting each other. We have grown prosperous because our world is kind to us. We have everything we need, but the *lýðirnir* are restless.'

'We are too many,' Riley Sampi proclaimed. 'There are not enough grasses for us to all tend. The new men and women do not have enough work, and they have become idle.'

Hyun-jun yawned as he got up. 'That's unfair. I work my share; we all do.' The young adults sent messages of affirmation.

'We require a new farm for our *ný-mennirnir* and *ný-konurnar*. We can't remain as we are,' Riley Sampi continued. 'There will be unrest. We must request disseveration for these new men and women.'

'I have asked,' Riley Khar said. 'It was denied. We are to remain here and must limit ourselves.'

'I am expecting,' one of the women said.

Milagrosa held up a hand. 'For now, yours will be the last child welcomed by our group. Let us be thankful for all that we have and restrain ourselves.'

The conversation died down, and the people prepared to sleep. Milagrosa sat apart and watched the *tánin-fólkið* set overnight alarms to ensure they didn't miss updates on their newsfeeds. Riley Khar moved between the young *lýðirnir* and quietly told them to sleep.

There are always options, she subvocalised.

What will you do? Set our children aside?

Let them go. Another farm will welcome them. Give me access and let me make enquiries.

It's too dangerous. Assizes might come to punish us. Balance will return in time.

Once she was sure that everyone was asleep, Milagrosa slipped back among the grasses. She knew her way in the darkness, having returned to the site of the burning many times. She found the groundplate she had released all those years ago. No one could know that it was merely resting in the dirt, waiting for her. She grunted at its weight and with one tender hand, reached for the sky tool. Milagrosa returned to the clearing, located Hyun-jun and shook him awake. She smiled and pointed to the implement left at his feet before returning to her bedding.

In the morning, he was gone.

The elucidarium did not have any windows, yet even if it did, they would not reveal the passing of the hours. Inside, daytime was a perfect cadence and the night's duration sufficient for restorative sleep. Each evening, the colour gradually faded away, the twilight encouraging the women to retire, and the dawn was a measured return to the working optimum.

Freja was the first to rise. She was online, sifting through job details, and trading with colleagues and other workgroups. Unseen opportunities danced in front of her closed eyes; Freja had shut out the actual world. She made initial assessments and assigned tones to each. Soon she was immersed in a richly textured soundscape in which she re-evaluated the data by adding harmonies and counter-melodies. From within the song, various themes developed. Some were familiar, against which she tagged pictures of people, places, problems to solve and let them sink into the background. Others she kept in view and waited for a moment in a different song, swapping tasks with more willing parties.

A pleasing note began to swell in her ears. She ignored it and waited for it to evolve the subtle polyphony of detail. Freja relaxed, knowing she had the Pallium's attention, confident that it would solve her problem. While she floated, she was aware that Kavya had arrived. They traded greetings, and Freja described what she had found.

'I don't know,' Kavya said. 'It's been an awfully long time since we've collaborated on a project. We'd end up bickering.'

'We know each other well enough to get along,' Freja suggested. They both watched the song build until it hung between them as a challenge.

'I expect something significant in return.'

'It isn't marked. Do you know what I think? I think we get to set the price.'

'Please get the others.'

Freja placed a hold and closed the feed. Jovana and Caitlyn came to sit with them, both mentioning that Miyu was still fast asleep. One of the women reconfigured the wall to display a rainbow of fish darting amongst brilliant coral.

'I'll wake her.'

Jovana ordered hot chocolate and pastries and waited for them to arrive. Caitlyn sat as she carried them to the table. 'Tell us what you've found.'

'*Fólkið* used to think the world was a great disc, floating on the ocean,' Kavya said, 'or on the back of a monstrous animal. It took aeons for them to discover the truth.'

'Little has changed since then,' Caitlyn mused.

'People still make assumptions.'

'Freja's found a job,' Kavya said. 'It's not regular, but it could answer some of Miyu's esoteric questions. It might give us a way out.'

Freja nervously rifled through virtual files that none of the other women could see. 'There's a catch. If we proceed, we won't be allowed to return to missing persons. We could be left in here and almost certainly offlined if we fail.'

The girls looked at one another and inspected each other's faces. They slowly entered the vestibule, cautiously sharing their thoughts. Kavya affirmed she had closed her feeds, ensuring no one outside the vestibule could reference their discussion. Jovana nodded and did the same.

'I don't think the FMP is in control,' Freja suggested. 'I think people like us make the big decisions. And I think they're running out of ideas.'

'Go on,' Caitlyn said, affirming her exclusivity.

'Will you affirm, Miyu? I've said more than I should. Thank you. Ladies, there's a job on the lists, buried far deeper than anything I've seen before. It was Miyu that got me looking for something more challenging. I'm still not certain what it is because it's bound up by heavy security. It's like an invitation for the smart *fólkið*. Figure out there's something there and sign up.'

'Which you've now done,' Caitlyn said acidly, 'but you should have discussed it with us. You had no right.' She summoned the exit button, but Kavya waved it away.

'Tell Caitlyn what's on offer.'

'Unfettered access to the Pallium. The principal task is an investigation into its system status, or possibly a precaution in case the FMP fails. I've bargained hard. We can ascend to First topsky if that's what we want.'

Caitlyn tutted. 'You aspire to a life in Tion's premier level, and to be stationed above the majority of the elite. It's delusional.'

'If it were possible, we would have to deliver before any of the other elucidaria,' Jovana warned.

'No job is worth enough for us all to end up in K1.'

'Not necessarily,' Kavya ventured. 'The Pallium is densely packed components, all parts and machine. Think about what this means. The FMP is vast: it encircles the world.'

'Everyone knows that,' Miyu laughed.

'Yet it's failing. We need to figure out the reason and stop it. Reverse the damage.'

'Who's the client?' Jovana asked.

'It is,' Freja said.

The barracks were never absolutely dark. None of the workers wasted their staters on privacy filters, whatever they followed danced freely in the space above their bunks; often running throughout the night while no one watched. The only sounds came from those that slept, their mumblings and moans synchronised with their dreams. For most, it was their single source of genuine excitement and how they spent their earnings.

Connor was part of this unaligned workforce. Just from his paltry life experience working as a regenerator, he believed what people said: there was no end to the citizens who were willing to work, all of them equally unskilled. He was glad to have his current contract, and he saw no reason why it couldn't last a lifetime unless there was someone else who was quicker than him, someone who was more affordable, preferable in some way, or different. Connor spent his off-hours attempting to learn new skills to better himself.

Most of the independent labourers were men. They were all the same, homogeneous. He smiled bitterly: the women have an easier option if they're fit for nothing else. Those *konurnar* called the men homos, saying all they were good for was each other. Connor had been with a woman three times in his life. The first time was in a workers' dorm in front of two hundred men. The foreman said it was an initiation and passed around an applet to collect their staters. He felt a flush of embarrassment as he remembered and realised the distant memory still hurt: his co-workers had paid for him to enter manhood. A few months later, he had met Erica Ini-Rayanna-Di-Ban, one of the few female workers. She had been kind for a day but left that evening for a new contract. He didn't know where she went. He had not asked the name of his third conquest—he had been drunk, and she hadn't talked. Three loves, he thought, what an empty life.

Today was Connor's first of ten shifts, with pay and a two-day break at the end. He had always been one of the first men to wake because he always struggled in the crush. This dorm was like all the others, bunks stacked on bunks in row after row, divided by public stations for tubing, eating and dressing. Some of the men twitched as their sleepercise apps came to an end. Connor eased himself upright from his bed, slipping down the ladder to the floor. It remained quiet enough, but as workers rose, the clamour would be unbearable. He padded into a cleantube and on to his breakfast. Around him, there were movements from some of the cots. The workers' food was a pale mush and body-temperature, like the air. Connor chewed the dough slowly because he liked to pretend his meals delighted the senses, the way things had been for his ancestors, the *forfeður*.

He was sitting within a multitude of bleary-faced strangers, but Connor didn't waste his hard-earned staters on useless information. While he ate, he ran arithmetic in his head, enjoying the simple progression that numbed his disconnection. It was how Connor maintained his balance, using numbers to calm his data withdrawal. He walked to the clothery and dressed for the day in a thick jumpsuit, heavy boots and gloves. The garments were new, but the fibres had been recycled cheaply and not broken into their molecules. They retained the smell of a thousand previous wearers and the echo of their labour. He shrugged because nothing ever changed.

It was only a short walk from the dormitory to the coalface. Each time the coalface moved forward, the living quarters progressed efficiently with it. Some of the men talked about mining as if its legend inspired them and gave them comfort. Connor recognised the truth: the world had exploited men for their muscle and ingenuity throughout time, they were cheaper to maintain than machines, and there was a steady supply. Over three thousand men worked on this regeneration project. This small part of Kilometre-Eight, Tion's eighth level, would be torn down to erase the back streets and alleyways, the stench of continual sprawling passageways and endless rooms, packed with vagrants. The people would be scooped up for recycling along with everything else, assuming they were already dead. Connor used to be uncomfortable with his work, but he was good at it.

Behind us, reconstruction crews are creating a paradise for a better *fólkið*, he thought, ceaselessly regenerating Tion due to the imperfect Forming. Connor knew it was only a matter of years before the lower levels, kilometres below, were filled with affluent citizens who had descended out of desperation. It was not a world he comprehended, or he would ever be a part of it, but he was aware. His limited access meant he had no way to know how many individuals were waiting for this opportunity. Some claimed their work was a deception, replacing the decay with cleanliness at the expense of the unjoined, unconnected population, but Connor wasn't sure.

Huge gantries lit the coalface, each lamp too bright for his unprotected eyes. There were layer-upon-layer of dwellings, communal areas and public interchanges. Most were under three metres high; hundreds packed into the entire kay. They were torn open on a heroic scale, a sheer, thousand-metre high cliff of devastated living space. Alchemists were growing boron fibres to bind the fullerene pillars and support the tionsphere above, while the workforce suspended just six skyplates. In the distance behind him, Connor could see workers divide the space between each plate into apartments, open areas and gardens for those who were alive. Tion segregates *fólkið* into two communities, he thought, those that catch a glimpse of the world and trust its uniformity, and those who know that all things are not the same. He wished he was among the ignorant.

Connor logged onto the scheduler. He was early and required to work but would not be compensated for the twenty-four minutes before his shift started. Connor pursued an improved image of himself; this was his routine. As usual, he was part of the search team. Its roots were humanitarian, as it would be unfortunate if a fellow *persónan* were resequenced from person to useful elements and recycled into soil. Still, the actual task was to seek out things that had value beyond their chemistry. Connor didn't have much in the way of training. He inspected the items inhabitants had left behind, to allow the Pallium to determine their worth, and to wait for a deliverer to collect them. I don't understand, he thought, it's just stuff—easily recreated.

He stepped onto a lifter plate and gripped the handrails. It sprang forward at an exhilarating speed, the air tugging at his clothing. Moments later, it came to a halt at the edge of a torn-open room, just like one in the dolls' house he once found. He stepped in, careful to avoid the edge, in case it was unsupported. The text in his eyesight identified the unit as an abandoned jewellery shop. There were several overturned display cases, and looters had shattered the glass storefront from the street outside. He already knew there was nothing of value there.

Connor liked to be methodical. He started on the left side of the room, straightening the counters and opening all of the drawers and compartments. Thieves had stripped the shop of anything of worth, and nothing registered a response from the FMP. He was diligent in his work and was unexpectedly rewarded with a small, blue stone, set in a metal band, tucked between the broken glass and front panel of a display case. He wiped it clean and looked intently at it until he received a response: *discard*. Connor considered hiding it in his jumpsuit, keeping it as a future gift, but he had no woman to give it to, nowhere to hide it and the risk was significant. He flicked it onto the floor, where it landed with a bright note.

'Pretty,' Youssef remarked, 'but you're not going to take it.'

Connor grunted, sifting through some papers. 'You're late.'

Youssef picked the ring up and slipped it onto a finger; it stuck at the second joint. He extended his hand out to Connor with a flourish.

'They know it's here. The silver will show up.' Connor crossed the room, kicking at the debris on the floor.

'They don't know I'm here though.' Youssef shrugged and let the ring fall to the floor. 'Smoke?'

Connor finally smiled. Youssef was as good a friend as he had, decent in most ways. The two men crossed the room to the cliff edge and sat with their feet dangling. No one would notice them. The view of the newly built district was magnificent. It was growing out of the destruction the men had wrought, filling their field of view. Connor had once heard they worked in a cubic kilometre of space in the densest part of the world, slowly eating through squalor and shitting gold. He knew it was a sparse approximation, often the coalface was three or four kilometres wide, depending on the size of the workforce and the rate at which they could build the pillars.

'If I just stand still and wait, I will become a new resident. I will be able to give my women diamonds.'

'If you stand still they'll fire your arse.'

They flicked their virtual-cigarettes into the abyss and watched them wink out. Their banter continued as they sifted through what remained of the front of the store. The oppressed, enclosed street outside was deserted. They walked back towards a lifter plate, sent to take them to their next assignment. As Youssef crossed the room, he looked for the ring. It was not there.

Connor's day continued in similar places, vacant units and communal homes, nothing of interest to their supervisors. In the afternoon, they joined a larger search team in a disused production facility, and they tried to guess what it manufactured. There was a processing delay as he submitted items for evaluation and Connor complained that it was putting them behind schedule.

'Makes no difference to me,' one of the men retorted, and the others agreed.

'Which is why you'll never get out of this shit hole, Tāne,' Youssef said, punching the big man in the arm. 'You'll still be here in twenty years. I have no desire to remember any of this.'

Connor struggled with a large piece of machinery. 'You *mennirnir*, give me a hand. I can't get a good view of this for assessment.' A few of the men gathered round to help. There were lots of loose items, bits of metal and some rubble. Tāne pulled back a sodden tarpaulin. A rank odour bubbled up, and some of the men retched.

'One for you, Connor.'

It was the body of a young woman, naked and bruised. 'Can't have happened more than a day ago.' Connor looked away. He knew what the other men were thinking.

'Come on, get this one logged and covered up. No cacherie for this little *kona*. This poor woman's missed her chance to live on in the Pallium.' Youssef looked at Connor with kindness in his eyes, which the other workers did not see.

He stared at the body and submitted various images to the FMP. She was slight, almost under-developed, with narrow hips, like a boy's. Her hair was a golden blond but matted with dried blood, and her face was slightly puffy with a peculiar colour. One inert, brown eye was open. Connor leant over to close it. 'She might have had enough staters to pay to be cached,' he said without conviction.

Identity unconfirmed. Connor did not receive a text or audio response, but he knew. With a sigh, he tore a clump of hair from her head, tucked it into his pocket and pulled the tarp back over. The other men had long since moved away.

'Why do you always deal with the bodies, Connor?'

'I'm not sure. Maybe it started with the live ones because I thought I could help by talking to them. I guess that makes me the people guy. I don't know.'

'Shift's nearly done. Let's go.'

The two men took a roundabout route back to the dorm and arrived with the main surge of workers. They had to queue for the amenities, which set Connor on edge. After they had eaten, there was nothing to do except talk.

'You should have given her that ring,' Youssef said.

'It wasn't mine to give.'

'Did the Pallium ID her?'

'A possible name, which is no use on its own. What does it matter who she was? She's no one now. Just remnants.'

'You're not responsible.'

'Nobody will miss her.'

'Get some rest.'

Youssef looked for Connor in the morning, and throughout the remaining nine days of their shift.

Jovana sat apart from the rest of the group and pretended to study quantum entanglement. She placed a text call to Joaquín, one of the boys she grew up with, and explained she was supposed to be working and didn't want any fuss.

He said he'd not stopped thinking about her, and they exchanged pleasantries about their nonage in Sixth. She said she had been fond of him, as she had of all of the boys from their childhood. He told her he was contracted just a week after her and worked in a sizeable group of men, which could easily be close to her home. He reminded her they could meet up in almost every way.

She reminded him they couldn't meet up in a way that might count.

Joaquín asked why she had decided to call, so many years after they had ascended.

She explained that her group had a job offer, which they had accepted. It was a risk for them, as it was outside their area of expertise. No, she wasn't looking for an external party, just someone trustworthy to bounce ideas off.

He said he was probably unable to help, as she was probably still somewhat smarter than him.

Jovana said she wanted someone to keep an eye on her, in case things became complicated.

Joaquín said he didn't understand.

When Jovana finished the call, she felt frustrated and wasn't ready to sleep. Miyu was also awake and sat by herself in her sleeping area, dressed in a thin robe. She had some bread and cheese on a napkin and was trying to keep crumbs off the bed while she reviewed the daily logs.

'Did you find what you were looking for?'

'Of course.'

'Figure out the EPR paradox?'

'Huh?'

'What were you really doing, Jovana?'

A pause and Jovana sat down on the side of Miyu's bed. 'I just wanted to talk to someone else. About all this,' she said. 'Nothing stupid. Not like your farm boy.' She sent a copy of her conversation with Joaquín to Miyu. 'I want someone outside to be keeping an eye on us, that's all.'

Miyu reviewed the log. 'Tell me something about him.'

'I liked him a lot. We were almost adults when I last saw him, but I think he will have grown into his looks. I've not pulled any recent pictures of him because they wouldn't be genuine. I don't know him now, but I trusted him before. I think that's enough.'

'You should tell Caitlyn and the others.'

'What's the harm? I only want him to call me now and then, isn't that what guys do?'

'I hate secrets.'

They were all enjoying the routine, particularly having a long-term contract. Jovana frequently said she found peace in their new stability. Freja reminded her she should work more and eat less; otherwise, she would be fat, finding peace in unemployment and eventually queuing up at a cacherie.

Caitlyn had resumed leadership of the group and Jovana was relieved. She had teamed up with Kavya to review the Pallium's infrastructure while the others were researching its barely measurable degradation. Kavya kept saying she could do a better job digging up information if she were allowed outside.

'I need to rest,' Freja complained.

'Where do you think the answers come from when you gaze at the ceiling?' Caitlyn remarked. 'They're from the very the system we're trying to restore. The longer you take, the more you'll have to do for yourself.'

'Who made you Head Girl?' Kavya asked with a nod.

For the third time that day, Jovana failed to place a full-service call to Joaquín. She was annoyed because he had become a welcome distraction when the others weren't paying attention.

CHAPTER TWO
Youssef
বর্তমানে

IT WASN'T UNPLEASANT; it was nasty, an obnoxious odour that ballooned from the bundle of rags in the corner of the rank room. It seeped into Youssef's clothing, crawled up from the floor and nestled around his collar as a constant reminder of the wretchedness in which these people chose to languish. If he had squandered his bursary, he might also have become unjoined, living in some pocket of a disused factory, sleeping rough and eating rotting waste, but he made his choices a long time ago. The smell burrowed into his skin and became a part of him, beckoning him to rest in its noisome embrace. It should have made him violently gag in protest, but it was almost familiar. He wondered how he could have had become used to it; he remembered nothing. The air tasted of death.

Someone had occupied the bed minutes before. In the twilight, the heat signature was a vibrant dance of colour and flared as Youssef turned the scraps of cloth over. In amongst the swirling patterns were brilliant pinpricks of life, bugs and worms and things that lived off the *hðirnir* who slept there. He assumed that in turn, these unjoined people fed on them in a symbiosis where neither was victorious. The bedding was damp with sweat, and Youssef wanted to burn it all away. He was unashamed of his passion for fiery destruction, and he preferred its living splendour to the clinical deconstruction technology provided. He would be able to clear Tion's lowest levels of everything, given enough latitude. He could make the world pure again.

Youssef held himself perfectly still and allowed his heart to slow and his breathing to stop. He would only need a few moments of solitude to confirm the unjoined had fled and then quickly resume his work. Youssef applied a filter to dampen the rush of blood through his ears and switched in processing to detect the footfalls fleeing the chamber. He was alone.

As he looked around, Youssef thought these last pre-Forming remnants of a forgotten lifestyle should be set apart as echoes of a better world. He already knew the facility had no purpose other than to be enjoyed. The crews called them *valse huise* and delighted in tearing them down. The words had no meaning beyond Bodem, and he reluctantly thought they meant little here at the interface. These places were not real, in the sense they were created to represent something they were not and were a rendering of something irrevocably lost. Youssef remembered it like it was yesterday.

His new shift-partner, Walloppong, had whooped with joy when he discovered the rails. The two parallel steel pipes twisted and turned throughout the structure. 'Touch the bricks,' he said. 'They're made from polymers. This was an intricate façade designed to cover the industrial guts of the building. I once visited a genuine ancient building and walked through its halls before we resequenced it as support pillars. Look at these.' Walloppong pointed at a pair of parallel rails suspended above them. 'In some places, they are missing, ripped away in the distant past, but you can trace the endless circuit of loops and turns. It served no purpose I can fathom. It's just one more in the catalogue of countless mysteries from the pre-Forming.'

Youssef wished that Connor was there to see what Walloppong saw. He was already struggling to recall how his friend reacted to new experiences. The iron would be readily extracted with auto-eaters, programmed to pick away at the ferrous element an atom at a time. They would also shit out perfect nodules of manganese and cobalt and nickel in smaller quantities, together with whatever else they could find, which would be rolled away into Tion's foundries to become tomorrow's unicabs and furniture. It was the nature of things. In some small way, Youssef helped keep the cycle alive, but it was not enough to fulfil him. He recalled that thrill-seeking people used to ride the rails for fun.

Youssef doubted that Connor had ever had any fun. He was concerned for his friend and didn't want to think of him lost in a pile of fetid textiles, suffocating in an unknown man's musk. Connor had such an empty life and spent his days afraid of failure, without realising what he had already achieved. In some way, Youssef was pleased: whatever Connor was now doing, he wasn't wasting his life identifying discarded *māsadā-sarīra*, the bodies of forgotten *fólkið*, and trying to find meaning, he was out in the world discovering his future. Or that was what Youssef hoped, that Connor chose to escape his wearisome existence, even though he had no funds, limited access and no one beyond the construction gang to assist him. Anything but elective caching, because Connor was not despairing enough for that.

Youssef eventually finished preparing the area for disassembly and watched as the eaters started their work. Connor had always enjoyed guessing what metal the compact machines would deposit first. He often collected the miniature spheres when he thought no one was watching and lodged them in conspicuous spaces in the barracks. Connor called them art. Sometimes he would be chastised by Rabindra, their latest supervisor, sometimes not.

When Connor didn't show for his shift, there were no questions from the foreman. Occasionally, a worker was not fit enough and would sit the day out without pay, but it was rare for a man to be absent for two days, and never more. Youssef knew there was something wrong because Connor played by the rules. He wanted advancement and a better life, and he wasn't the sort to run away. There was little likelihood he would have given up and enjoyed a day of empty indulgence, or chosen to languish in perpetual nothingness. There was no one else in the crew who cared that Connor was missing, and the men continued with their days, making the best of their own opportunities. In death, Connor would have nothing of value to leave his friends, and his only generosity was his way with people. The few *mennirnir* that knew him spoke kindly of him, even though they would tease him and laugh at his sensitivities. He would have told Youssef where he was going.

Youssef had signed up for Connor's vacant shifts and rationalised his choice as protecting his friend's livelihood. He did not have Connor's gifts, and the additional effort left him agitated. There was a two-day-old note in his dailies about a sleeping woman. Her hysterical, piercing screams had driven him to strike her, over and over, and when he had finished, she was another body they were required to clear away. He was glad there had been no one there to see it.

Walloppong was sweeping the metal pellets away from the suspended rail as they fell to the ground. He said that keeping the path clear was essential and would mean no one would slip, but he couldn't keep up with the efficiency of the machines. Now and then they fell into his black, unruly hair, which caused him to shake his head vigorously in a way that made Youssef smile. One of the auto-eaters stopped in its tracks, and Walloppong stopped too and reviewed its log files. The refiner was grappling with a section of scandium-aluminium alloy and couldn't decide if it should separate the atoms. He reminded it of its place the grand hierarchy of things and sent it on its way.

Walloppong was aware someone was observing him while he worked. He wondered if Rabindra had sent Youssef explicitly, or if the foreman was looking for another worker to remove from the gang. It was evident that Rabindra must have dismissed Connor, probably due to information Youssef provided to their supervisor. He would have told Rabindra that Connor liked to steal artefacts. It was plain that very few of the men would stand by him if required, and he probably didn't have too many contacts outside of this K8 crew. Walloppong needed to be careful of Youssef. He had drifted into their section a few years ago and hadn't made acquaintances easily, but fortunately, no one cared much for him. Walloppong had no idea why Connor asked to work with him in the first place. Then again, he didn't understand much about *fólkið* who chose to live in this artificial hell. *Lýðirnir* like himself.

Youssef had been asking about Connor for two days now, probably for the bragging rights or some other claim to status. Walloppong found it hard to interpret other people's behaviours, he knew it was not compassion for a missing *maður*, so maybe they were friends, although they probably weren't. Perhaps someone had looked out for Youssef in his past, and now he felt he needed to repay that kindness. Perhaps he had a terrible life before he came to the coalface and this was a better place for him, but he struggled to find allies. Perhaps he was an assize, a behaviour regulator, who had come to spy on them or was here to uncover someone hiding in their midst. Walloppong decided he didn't care, hurried along the tunnel, checking the eaters as they gnawed away at the rail.

Ahead of Youssef, the hallway was awash with the tiny, metallic balls. Many rolled away when they landed, particularly the ones that were around the width of his thumb. Anything larger would be pretty painful, Youssef thought. Walloppong had constrained the eaters' safeties, but now he was gone, Youssef had no concerns about increasing the nodule size and programmed a ridiculous upper limit. The rain petered out and was replaced by the irregular drumming of fist-sized globes against the hard ground until the metal was finally too large for the eaters to hold and they fell with their progeny. Youssef delighted in the chaos and returned the fallen machines to the rail.

There was a low cry somewhere in front of him. An unkempt man staggered forward and his greying beard jutted in Youssef's direction. His movements were jagged, and he had obviously been hit by one of the nodules when he lay hidden, but something about his general coordination was disturbing. One arm flailed behind his back, as if he was losing control of his body. Youssef could see the distress on the man's face, but the falling metal did not cause it. Another hit him squarely on the back of his neck, and yet another bounced from the *maður*'s forehead. The sight transfixed Youssef, a person who did not understand what was happening, a *persónan* struggling to keep his balance while his body betrayed him, while dense, heavy shrapnel barraged him. Youssef knew if he did nothing, the man would die, and no one was going to miss him. He hoped Connor had left the coalface behind and had found a way to better himself, instead of lying spent and forgotten in an obsolete building.

Youssef added a proximity routine to the eaters to ensure his own comfort. It was time to stop worrying about what had happened to Connor; instead, Youssef needed to find him and make sure he was safe. Youssef had stashed away a variety of pre-Forming searches that might be suitable. He would, however, have to be prudent to avoid attracting attention because no one used such software any more. Like most workers, Youssef had an economical, high compression, low-grade data allowance, so he needed to persuade the foreman to provide him with access. Rabindra was an arrogant man, a self-important kind of bureaucratic *maður* who liked to break the rules when it suited him but hated it when others did the same. Enticing him to assist would be a challenge because he would be as disinterested in Connor's whereabouts as he would be in who Youssef might have once been. The workforce was inherently transient, and Tion homed billions who were waiting to take their place. Rabindra was only concerned with his compensation and his status and lacked any interest in the *lýðirnir* who made up the workforce.

Rabindra's position gave him access to the processing capacity Youssef required, and Youssef had extensive knowledge of the intricacies protecting Tion's quantum-currency. He had access to many lifetimes' worth of staters and could reassign some to his supervisor's TUID, once he updated the audit trail. They would both benefit once their initial discussion had taken place, although Youssef would have to move on quickly because forensic data analysts would eventually trace the transfer. He decided it didn't matter as it was probably time to start over before too many people noticed his stagnation. Youssef was excited by the prospect.

The farm was still dark when Hyun-jun felt someone shake him. Even before he opened his eyes, he knew it was Milagrosa. She placed her hand lightly over his mouth, urging him to remain quiet. When he tried to touch her, she pulled away, but her burnt fingers lingered on his lips. Something was resting on his legs, and when he reached down, it was cold, and its intricate edges were sharp.

He knew exactly what it was.

Once Milagrosa had gone, Hyun-jun gathered his few possessions together, rolled up his small blanket and stuffed it into his harness which he secured around his waist. He grabbed some food from Lior's satchel and set off into the columns. Night flattened his eyesight into a two-dimensional enhanced image, and he could see perfectly well.

As he walked, he considered the food hastily stuffed into his pack. The community only tended one crop and, apart from the marmos, there were no animals on the farm. He supposed meat came from another place, somewhere outside. Why hadn't he thought about this before? If the food came from beyond their plantation, there must be other *lýðirnir* who grew and processed it, and many disparate things besides. He queried the Pallium, but the response was vague and seemed evasive. He headed towards the far edge of the farm and an area that the grass workers had not tended for some months. It would be light in under an hour, and Hyun-jun wanted to be away before the *fólkið* started their day.

He chose a grass adjacent to the farm wall and climbed its entire height in a fluid motion. At the top, he hooked onto the mesh above him and looked at the regular pattern in the panels. After a few minutes' reflection, he took out the tool Milagrosa had given him and held it against the grid. It was about the length of his forearm and hand combined, with a small bend at the wrist and its fingers were fused, ending in a curious set of uneven teeth. Hyun-jun turned it over and over as he hung from the skyplate and looked for clues to its use. For a while, he jammed it at various parts of the grid, hoping he would chance upon a solution until in frustration he threw an inquiry at the FMP. There was a momentary delay in its response, almost like it was seeking permission to share a secret. Then with one motion, Hyun-jun unlocked a tile, and it fell, knocking the sky tool from his hands.

He counted three heartbeats before the crash rang out across the farm.

Hyun-jun knew he had little time to move forward. He briefly considered climbing back down to retrieve the panel but supposed it would not be necessary. The workers would realise he had chosen to leave and was not missing among the glass columns. Milagrosa would help the others understand why he needed to go and discourage his foolhardy brothers and sisters from following.

He popped his head back through the skyplate. It was dark and cold, and his augmented vision revealed little detail. He pulled himself through in a clumsy fashion, grateful that there was no one there to criticise his technique, and sat with his feet dangling over the farm. He unhooked the line, checked the void above his head, and stepped away from the gap. Hyun-jun could see the comparative warmth of the mighty plants below, but not how much clearance there was. There were no distinctive features in this space covering the farm's sky. He peered back through the opening to orientate himself and edged to one side. At his feet, the grid changed to a solid floor, just before a partition, which he presumed was over the farm wall itself. Hyun-jun decided to follow the boundary.

He was aware of the slight breeze from the farm long before he noticed it was becoming light. It toyed with his hair as it flowed, and soon he could hear the air moving along the wall. The featureless vastness offered itself up as the dawn blossomed. The bright azure walls absorbed the light into their smooth expanse, arching to form a false sky maybe a hundred metres overhead. The sound of the wind became a series of moans as gusts battered the wall. Hyun-jun could see pieces of detritus coming up through the grid as the farm air below expanded and sought means of escape. This is a massive lung, he thought, breathing in the morning. Daylight poured from plump pouches suspended in the sky. Hyun-jun was reminded of water skins, burst with a keen knife, but although they swayed in the breeze, they did not diminish. A rush of warm air pushed him hard against the wall, forcing him to turn to face one of the radiant sacks. The light was dazzling, and he dropped to the floor with his eyes tightly shut.

Hyun-jun lay still for some time, with one arm flung over his face as protection from the ever-warming wall. The wind had died back, and the air was silent. The heat on his body was unlike anything he had ever experienced, even heat from the cooks' fire, and it washed over him. He realised he was not sweating and the dry atmosphere was stealing his moisture. He had to keep moving but despaired because he did not know where to go. Hyun-jun considered returning to the grass farm and nonchalantly joining the adults as if he'd been working in the pre-light. Milagrosa would clasp him against her firm body and not ask where he had been. He slowly turned until his back touched the vertical surface and, with his eyes tightly shut, sat upright. He requested an eyesight overlay for the Pallium so he could retrace his steps. Again, there was a slight delay while the FMP considered his request, but a few seconds later, his vision stopped swimming and adjusted to his orientation. It reminded Hyun-jun of nonage games, of spinning around a glass column and the slight nausea of being dizzy.

Through his closed eyes he saw neon directions running towards the hatch, set against a series of markers spreading away from the wall. Hyun-jun decided the empty green circles were a reference to the columns below. He clambered to his feet and took a step into the scorching air, and as he did so, he became aware of the beyond-periphery indicators that only the FMP could create. Hyun-jun had forgotten to look behind him, and the Pallium offered him an alternative.

Flags hovered near the wall at regular intervals, and the closest stated he was just over a kilometre from an exit. Keeping his eyes shut and breathing through his nose to protect his dry mouth, Hyun-jun strode towards the doorway. When he arrived, he complied with the red *Press Here* ve-label and stumbled through.

He stepped into a service corridor, identified by a jumbled assortment of mojis in the FMP tagging. A uniform, yellowish light filled the passageway, crisp and laden with moisture. He waited motionlessly, enjoying the simple comfort of the air and considered what he should do next. Hyun-jun needed a strategy, something that had not occurred to him when he had picked up his harness. He had enough to eat for three days but no water, and other than his knife, a blanket and grass-tending tools, had nothing to help him survive. There were two options ahead of him, the familiarity of another grass farm, or the daunting mysteries that lay beyond. He had begun to recognise how little he knew of the tionsphere, of its inhabitants and potential hazards.

The floor of the corridor was slightly concave and dark marks ran parallel to its edges, perhaps something had been dragged along its length. The data from the FMP was unintelligible, and he did not know the direction to take as he began to walk. Hyun-jun needed water, and he knew he would struggle to find it on his own. The crux of his problem was the Pallium's refusal to accept that he, a grass worker, was accessing areas which it reassured him were only attainable by maintainers. He assumed these were the same people that Milagrosa spoke about, the strangers who cleared the grasswork after the burning. What were the crew like, and where did they live? Hyun-jun began to feel his control slip away, yet continued to pry at the edges of the system.

Describe Hyun-jun Ezh-Wynn-Rr-S.

Hyun-jun Ezh-Wynn-Rr-S, 15, grass worker [K6 location].
Appointment: grass worker. Late-nonage education: waived.
  Where is Hyun-jun Ezh-Wynn-Rr-S?
  [K6 location].
  The grass farm, Hyun-jun thought. *Where am I?*
  [K6 location].
  Then call Hyun-jun Ezh-Wynn-Rr-S.
  Cannot selfref.
  So where is Hyun-jun Ezh-Wynn-Rr-S?
  Error.

He wasn't particularly surprised by the responses. They were not the sort of queries that would provide him with the information he wanted. The Pallium seldom coped well with inconsistent data. Children learnt this in their formative years and would often submit contradictions to hide their intentions from the *fullorðnir* around them. As Hyun-jun grew older, he realised the truth was almost the reverse: the FMP actively prevented access to off-limit knowledge.

He continued to poke the Pallium as he moved along the featureless passageway, and ran his fingers over the curved wall. He almost missed the doorway, only noticing it with his light touch. It was unlike the entrance he had used several hours before; instead, it was discrete and unused. Hyun-jun took out his grass blade and ran it along one edge, hoping to trigger an opening mechanism, but the FMP was unyielding and refused to identify the portal. In frustration, he banged it repeatedly with the edge of his fists until his hands ached. Finally, he slumped with his bare back sweating against the structure.

Hyun-jun was astonished, and then overwhelmingly excited, to hear a responding knock. He bounced up to face the door, smoothed his hair and settled his harness about his waist. He picked up the knife from the floor and tucked it away, then took it out and held it behind him. They might not welcome me, he realised, but what is one grass blade against a new community? He sheathed it.

With a clunk and a slight hiss of air, the doorway revealed itself, the panel slowly sinking into the groundplate. Hyun-jun saw familiar glass columns disappearing into the familiar, blue horizon and caught the comforting smell of life.

'Why are you here?'

Three people, poised and intent, were waiting for him, two men and an *eldri-kona*. The old woman studied him carefully, but Hyun-jun did not know how to answer.

'We have no use for you. Leave us.'

The panel rose from the floor as they turned from him. Hyun-jun did not know why he needed to follow them, but he jumped up as the door filled half the entrance. With his arms and head leaning over the top, he pulled himself up, critically aware he had little time to clear it. One of the young men turned towards him and raised his half-staff. The *hanbō* hit Hyun-jun smartly across the face, and he fell back into the empty corridor.

Joaquín was busy administering a Lacuna passage across nine degrees of arc and nearing the end of his shift. Most of the capsules had a twelve-minute scheduled transit time, but occasionally he received a priority directive. The day's fastest movement was one hundred and twenty-one seconds, close to his personal record, which caused no end of chaos for the vehicles he had to clear. It also gave him a delay penalty he didn't want to consider. Eight kilometres per second: who could justify the expense?

He had much preferred the sedate dance of subsonic unicabs. He liked to sort them by colour or occupants or some other arbitrary system and would shuffle them so that one passenger might have an unexpectedly rapid journey at the slight expense of a few others. At slow speeds, commuters had some insight into their prioritisation, and Joaquín made it his mission to delight at least one faceless citizen each day. Not that they cared. *Lýðirnir* assumed the Pallium handled the insignificant details of their lives.

He had trained as a router since mid-nonage and spent the subsequent years in simulations. He did not know when he started handling real traffic. The FMP switched him in at some point before he was fifteen and newed, finally an adult, and he only knew he had measured up because he was still controlling. Unless his entire adult life was an unfathomable deception. It didn't do to think about it.

Joaquín accepted his last movement and closed his request socket. He would handle the final vehicle and then log off, and leave his successor to manage the traffic held a few seconds behind. He considered rushing this job through, but he didn't have much of a margin to play with, and things would back up elsewhere in the pipe. He checked off each unit as it cleared his route and hurried the stragglers as much as he could. He was looking forward to a cold beer.

His fourteen-man crew handled four modes, and each *maður* was qualified for any assignment. From trawling Sodality, he knew his group was large, but a large team meant it was easy for him to trade for Lacuna at the start of a shift. Joaquín found private routeing dull, was baffled by the quantum nuances of point-to-point transfers and assumed he had scraped through his final beltway module. He liked working general traffic because there was something pure about it: one cab in, one cab out.

You nearly done?

A message from Friedrich, his closest friend. He couldn't risk another reprimand on his file, so he remained silent, but he was pleased there would be someone to unwind with, someone who would happily listen to the dramas of his day. Most of the time, he would seek solace online, sometimes taking full-service calls from strangers or passing acquaintances. He knew Pallial algorithms were stimulating him, but a man needed some kind of release.

Joaquín barked a series of commands as he handed his final transport off. The Pallium updated his licence for his total movements before forcibly disconnecting him. He was alone in the controllers' suite and assumed the others were either online or resting. A substantial crew meant their accommodation comprised several separate areas, which was the main reason he had requested this assignment. He cleantubed and entered the kitchen to grab some food.

'I didn't think you knew how to tube.'

'You might learn something, Friedrich.'

They idly chatted while preparing food and drank a couple of beers each. Friedrich teased Joaquín about his latest virtual conquests, but he was merely fishing for dating tips. The conversation ambled round to work, and inevitably, they talked about Tion's level Zero. The world's ultimate surface, constructed kilometres above Bodem, was a source of constant fascination to the routers.

'It doesn't make sense,' Friedrich said. 'The majority of the infrastructure is already in place. The shafts used to force water out of the trenches still exist. There are great, empty conduits that rise vertically from Bodem. Open them up for general routeing via the surface.'

'There's no point because it wouldn't be as efficient as the Lacuna. I'm sure the Definitive Sitting wouldn't allow it or at least permit routeing for anyone who wasn't an assize. Anyway, there is still residual water in the Pretermissions, in the Sixteens, Seventeens and Eighteens. What if it needed to be ejected by the Pallium?'

'There has to be a way, Quín. Can you imagine how impressive it would be? Countless comets fired at other planets. It would be amazing.'

Joaquín threw some video on the wall. 'Don't have to imagine. All that waste. At least some of the minerals were extracted first, it's what makes up Tion. It must have been an incredible time when the *forfeður* were constructing the world. I wish I could have been part of that and had the opportunity to build something magnificent.' He submitted a series of short queries. 'The FMP is clear. There's no cost-benefit in reusing the water mines for transport.'

'It doesn't want us escaping its control.'

'That's ridiculous. You talk about the Pallium as if it has an objective. Long before Tion, people surrounded themselves with alternate processors but barely utilised them. *Fólkið* wanted data capacity, not processing power, and turned to innumerate services to meet their needs. As conglomerates swallowed corporations and demand increased, only a handful of providers remained, until the *forfeður* commandeered their holdings as part of the Forming. They unified the technology and ensured the FMP would be permanently available to all. It's an it, not a who. Do you want another beer?'

Friedrich shrugged and continued to argue for the development of the water mines, using all of the available surfaces to sprawl supporting equations. Joaquín countered each assertion with contrasting formulae, and they laughed as their arguments became more outrageous.

'Come on; you can't mean that. It's not geometrically possible.'

Their debate was interrupted by a flash message. It summoned them to the vestibule, where they devoured the situation report—an incident. Eighty-one officers in attendance, although it was probable assizes had sequestered the accountable controller, subject to investigation. A twenty-ex freight craft had burst through the Lacuna sleeve and exploded across forty seconds of arc. Fortunately, the vacuum claimed a lot of the damage, and Joaquín assumed the transit corridor would be sealed off, rather than cleared.

Joaquín's reality dissolved without his consent, leaving him deep in a numerical representation of the Lacuna tunnel, its ports and maintenance walkways, and the surviving transport vehicles. He took charge of twenty-one unicabs and assessed their survivability. Joaquín was amazed so many withstood the event and started to look for ways to extract them from the Lacuna. His instructions were clear. The salvage team's priority was the main conduit and its maintenance runs; the surrounding services were expendable. The occupants were irrelevant, and Joaquín should not consider them. He assumed a rogue driver had caused the accident and wished that manual overrides were not permitted. He classified each craft by the damage it had incurred and how difficult it would be to release it from the void, dutifully ignoring any data about the occupants or their net value. He wondered if he could somehow claim caching fees, but didn't know how to register as a cachier. He had no path to riches, to way to escape his lot because Tion had trapped him forever in a secure apartment, which meant he could only ever engage in ve-sex. Joaquín hated his life. Why hadn't he signed up for a mixed crew?

Nine of the capsules were mangled heaps of machinery. The *lýðirnir* inside were beyond recognition and ruined by the vacuum. Joaquín dispatched spiders to break the spherical cabs into manageable chunks and passing them into quantum-chemical disassemblers. Five were salvageable but without power. It was impossible to see if anyone was alive inside, so he assumed the occupants were dead, hopefully cached, and marked them for the tugs to collect. It would probably take a few days. Joaquín lingered over the remaining transport vehicles. As he watched the constant flow of numbers, he was keenly aware of the vibrant lives hidden inside. There were thirteen human beings, just like the thirteen people he cohabited with, each with his or her aspirations and idiosyncrasies. The undamaged cabs and their perfect passengers waited for Joaquín to command their fate. He knew what he had to do.

Afterwards, Joaquín sat in the kitchen and discussed the operation. Friedrich had been working to secure the Lacuna and stop it flooding with gas and debris from the enclosing megalopolis. He had forged massive bulkheads from decomposed elements of damaged Tion, irrespective of how their previous function.

'You're only worried about your decision for a handful of *fólkið*, Quín. There are eighty K3 tiers where this happened, and the pipe cut up through one-third of them. Do you have any idea how many *sálirnar* inhabited this particular forty SoA?'

'You didn't have to look at each person.'

'Fifty thousand human beings resequenced as an emergency bulkhead. And all of their stuff. So, what did you do with your lot?'

'It's not important. Get Myron and the others.'

The crew sat together to eat and complained about their respective days. They had all signed their lifetime contracts at the end of nonage and could do nothing but grumble, mostly about how they should have explored Tion before settling down. They grudgingly realised their security was almost indefinite. 'Unless the Lacuna bursts and you get recycled for the greater good,' Friedrich reminded them.

After they had rested, the *mennirnir* assembled in a sports vestibule and readied themselves to compete in Fifth Tournament. Millions of people chanted aggressively and opposing groups bayed for supremacy. Sometimes it was sinister or intimidating, but today they heartily joined in. The tournament was as old as Tion and teams had come and gone. Joaquín's crew were now in the safe zone of the second quartile, having worked their way up the lists. None of them had the dedication to go further, so they spent most matches passing the vol to frustrate their opponents. If Joaquín was honest, he was bored. At half-time, they discussed tactics for a few minutes, but their attention wavered, and most of the men teased each other about their various online triumphs.

'Quín has a new regular, someone he hatched with, right? Maybe she's your sister, *ēma?*'

'Fuck off, Nitin,' Joaquín snapped. 'You need to focus on the game.'

'Hey boys, I told you. I bet he's all over her.'

'Looked to me like he was,' Gregory said. 'Pathetic performance, though.' A copy of Joaquín appeared in the vestibule, naked, aroused and writhing. 'Sorry, *náungi*, but you have to see how crappy you are.'

'Not funny,' Joaquín said and attempted to override the visual feed. He had started moving between the simulacrum and his teammates when the entire environment shattered, and he was again in the apartment. The others were still expressionless with online and unaware of his confusion. Joaquín attempted to reconnect, but instead, the FMP directed him into the sterility of an assize sitting. The virtual environment reminded him of his one formal warning, which he received for incurring too much delay, and he felt his pulse quicken. Joaquín found himself in front of a white desk, with three officials presiding. There were multiple views of point-to-point terminals behind them, several of which were damaged.

'Your performance rating for the earlier K3 incident is satisfactory,' one of the assizes eventually said. 'We'd like you to join another, more sensitive investigation.'

'I don't have much recent pe-to-pe experience,' Joaquín said, relaxing a little.

'Which is immaterial. Your tasking and briefing pack are ready.'

The room started to fade, so Joaquín reached out to accept the transfer and gripped the red button with both hands. Although he had passed through a conduit several times in training, he was unprepared for the finality of his situation. If I can't find the return icon, he thought, then this is who I'll be, and no one will be able to help me.

He was a fair bit bulkier, but everything seemed in proportion, although he might be a little taller, he couldn't be sure. There was a slight ringing in his left ear, and his eyes felt full of sand. He was desperately thirsty. Joaquín had heard clients often abused the rented bodies and that no one could be bothered to maintain them properly. The calves ached as he walked, so he requested an analgesic, then temporarily shut the kidneys down and jogged to the pointport.

The assize report stated that thousands of point-to-point cubicles had simultaneously printed incendiaries. Although only impacting a small fraction of the global network, the combined damage rendered the entire system unserviceable. While there was no media coverage, forum postings would soon ensure Sodality was aware, and people would demand answers.

Joaquín occasionally routed point-to-point transfers when none of the other men would trade shifts, but the complex clone-destroy system did not interest him. Its users considered themselves sent from site to site, but the reality was more mundane: the paralysis, analysis, replication, initialisation and recycling of the original subject. The FMP handled the majority of the traffic detail, maintained records for each movement and disallowed multiple copies. The report suggested each pointport had received the exact same device without raising any exceptions. Something was definitely amiss.

When he entered the chamber, several smells assaulted him: the infantile familiarity of a newly hatched *barnið*, failed electronics and sweat. He presented his credentials with a nod to other the technician and set to work. Joaquín had never seen an operational system before but what was left appeared to be in spec. There was no discernible modification to any of the other platforms, and the quantum-keys were all intact. His analysis concluded someone had placed a grenade in the cubicle and detonated it to make it appear that point-to-point was a potential weapon.

He yawned and submitted his return request, but the Pallium was unresponsive.

Joaquín thought he would be more unsettled. He existed in another man's flesh, and it was battered and worn, and he ached all over. His breath rasped from his lungs to his dry, cracked lips because someone had taken too many high gases. There were bruises on his fingers, and several of his nails were blackened, one was missing entirely. He felt like shit.

Somewhere across the arc, his true self lay dormant. The body he had cherished. He wanted to be at home but did not know where that was, or how to get there. For five years he had felt trapped within the suite and spent his life routeing others through Tion. Now he was outside everything. The FMP continued to ignore his request.

Joaquín needed to think and left the chamber. It took a few moments for him to realise he was not receiving targeted advertising or other spam. He reset his connection and prompted the Pallium again.

What is my TUID?

Error.

Was it possible he didn't exist?

Locate Joaquín Ghha-Qui-Baluda-Tlu.
Error.

He attempted to place a call to Jovana, but he couldn't connect. He had no access to staters, and the food dispensers collectively ignored him. Joaquín started to retrace his steps back to the chamber, meaning to ask for help, but instead, he turned and punched one of the vending machines, then smashed his shoulder against it in the hope that it would respond. He was angry and frustrated and started to yell, although he wasn't sure what he was shouting. Two people pushed past him, and he caught a glimpse of the gossamer fibre, which they were using for their private conversation. He tried to rip it from one of them so he could hack into their discussion and make himself heard. The other *sálirnar* began to avoid him as they swarmed past. One woman must have sensed his distress, taking him by the hand back to the machine. She gave him two litres of water before disappearing amongst the crowd. Joaquín drained the bottle and waited for his headache to subside. Her gift was a sign that he had become unjoined.

The late afternoon was fresh, and the alabaster sky complemented Miyu's mood. She had retreated to a virtual beachfront bar to distance herself from her feelings and watched the *eldri-fólkið* gathered around glass tables, talking, playing cards and smoking heady cigarettes. She had curled up on a pale couch over an hour ago and summoned the smiling waiter five times for beer, which he served to her in clearfibre wine glasses. The Pallium, the global processing core, dutifully modified her perceptions to make her feel suitably drunk, so when Jovana arrived, she did not wave her away.

Miyu moved to allow her friend to sit, wishing she had not rushed her drinks and wondering if she should have the FMP delete the last three from her history. She called the waiter over.

'Sometimes it helps to talk about it,' Jovana said kindly.

Miyu felt touched that Jovana had told her about Joaquín; it made her think that it was possible to live with secrets kept from the other women in their elucidarium. She wanted to share all the details about Hyun-jun, why he had left his grass farm, and how she had guided him through the Sixes. 'I have to deal with an unresolved caching for the farm boy I was following.'

Jovana nodded but did not say anything, other than to order a cocktail.

'He was reported missing this morning. Do you remember he broke into a weatherwell? I sort of let him out.' Miyu was aware that Jovana routinely adjusted people's responses to obtain the things she wanted; it was why their home was full of obscure items from across Tion. 'I know it was wrong, and I should have disposed of him overnight and cleared his accounts.'

'So why didn't you?'

'I don't know. Hyun-jun was curious about the FMP and other things. Shouldn't he be able to experience the world?'

'Shouldn't everyone?'

Jovana reached across and took her hands. The two slender women sat for a while, and Miyu gave Jovana access to all of Hyun-jun's records.

'What will you do?'

'He needs some help. There's been an incident. It won't be long until the grass workers report it.'

'Then help him, sweetie. Give him what he wants.'

Sparks landed on the deep carpet and finally, one of them caught. The fire started with a few wisps of smoke, but the flames soon blossomed as the cutting continued. There were fourteen men assigned to the routers' apartment, and all of them were online and unresponsive. The nearest sat just a metre away and oblivious to the danger. The wall reverberated as something pounded from the other side, and the cut-away panel fell to the floor. A burst of white smoke growled from an extinguisher as three people, entirely concealed by their protective *kostymer*, pushed through the gap and inventoried the room.

They silently located all of the inert men and ensured they were connected and not merely asleep. The aether was alive with data as the request to keep them in Sodality were approved. One of the *kostymän* sketched long, rectangular outlines on an empty table. She used a handheld tool to harvest molecules from the air and recombined them to form nanofoam panels, which she rapidly welded together to build packing crates. Her colleagues had grouped the *mennirnir* into one area of the apartment, stripped each man down and checked them for defects, aesthetic composition and flexibility. The bodies were deposited in the coffins as they were completed and stacked vertically into a corner.

The carbon-wright continued to make cases to fit the artefacts collected together while the bids came in. There were no apparent selection criteria, but there was a definite separation between desirable and expendable. In a short time, the *kostymän* had sorted the tenants and their possessions into sets, and the auction commenced. Each lot had been imaged and catalogued, generating reasonable interest, although once the sale was complete, some items, including three of the men, did not meet their reserve and were moved to the discard pile. Within twenty minutes, mechanical deliverers entered through the breach and took the goods away. The *kostymän* turned their attention to the accommodations. They fashioned a temporary door frame from resequenced personal effects and the carbon-wright drew up a door panel. Finally, they collected the last remaining items and sent them for recycling and arranged the new furnishings, leaving a freshly remodelled residence for marketing to potential occupants.

*

After Youssef had eaten and cleaned himself up, he found Rabindra in a reasonably good mood. Youssef convinced him that the proposal, although unorthodox, wasn't entirely inappropriate (providing no one found out) and was practically undetectable anyway (which was not altogether true). It took little under an hour to persuade the foreman to grant him pre-paid Pallial access and more importantly, a quiet room where he could rally his quantum foot soldiers. Youssef was enjoying himself and for a while imagined having some greater *thráfstís* responsibility, a master hacker of Pallial records, and forgot the search for his friend. He hadn't been particularly honest about his ability to erase his virtual fingerprints. In essence, some excited assize would catch him and quite probably quickly, so he had to be efficient and expected to leave the barracks within an hour of finishing.

His directory contained a reference to some old *gocco* and a note from a previous overseer to remind him it wouldn't circumvent his *raja'a*. Youssef considered reading the dossier to recall how he'd tried to use the persona replication code but realised it would only distract him. His dailies were heavy with comments about the purity of purpose, and he was reasonably sure he hadn't written the reports. If he executed the *gocco* bioapp according to its specification, he would be able to duplicate the outline of his psyche, his *sikatā-ātamā*, and use it to find his missing friend.

His first step was to create a false lead, a big, juicy, non-existent issue to mask his more devious activities. With the decoy in place, he started to work on the main event. Someone must have seen Connor and all Youssef had to do was ask around. He started with a generic game template, the sort that average *lýðirnir* liked to play when they needed distracting from their pointless existence by a monotonous and mundane task. Youssef added a little endocrine stimulator, a bit of sexual tension and a pinch of anxiety to keep it edgy; topping it off with ten stupid questions that randomly assigned a characteristic to the user. He put together some marketing crap that suggested people who used it would not only appear cool but would know what sort of genorep animal best represented them. He sent it out into Sodality, with a cut-down Youssef Damaru-Da-Te-Epsilon hitching a ride. The *gocco* process was prolific and liked to make imprints of Youssef and hide them inside real *fólkið*.

Youssef had covered the walls with spurious results and trivialities, and Rabindra occasionally popped in to ask how things were progressing. Once Youssef was certain the app was ready, he used his supervisor as the vector, suggesting he check out this new craze while he waited. Within minutes, most of the workforce had declared themselves to be wolves or starfish or elephants and were unaware of the other personality lurking in the background. They shared the game with old workmates, ex-lovers and distant friends, while Youssef watched the replication count quicken in front of his eyes. He also knew he'd fail to reach everyone, but he'd probably cover enough ground. The app burst out of Eighth into Sixth, then Seventh, Fourth and Fifth. There was a long lag before it reached Third, when it briefly became the most popular download in the Low Numbers, after which it spilt below K8 into the Greater Numbers. It took over an hour to penetrate First, but it hurtled through the entire level in moments.

There was something that caught Youssef's attention, deep in his analysis of the population. The tenor was uneven, and the balance was not right, but he couldn't quite remember why. There were too many individuals tightly bound to the Pallium and involved in activities that could not hold any interest for them. People consigned to performing tasks historically handed off to the global processing core. A chime sounded as the accumulator slowed and Youssef knew it was time.

Across the entire tionsphere, Youssef sat behind the eyes of billions. With a simple wish, he pushed their countless characters aside to dominate their *sikatā-ātamā*. Together they sifted through recent recollections until they found Connor. Those extreme few who knew of him messaged their ultimate grandparent and settled back to wait. All the other imprints let go of their short-lived realities, and for Youssef, the clock started ticking.

Rabindra had the bewildered look of moments forgotten and waited for the next data morsel to spark him into action.

'I've done it,' Youssef supplied. 'I have what I came for, and have made arrangements for you. The only thing left for you to do is supply your shared-secret at the prompt, and the transactions will complete. I strongly recommend that you hold off for a few days, just in case.'

He conjured a small ve-package from nowhere, primed it for Rabindra's passphrase and handed the intangible item across. He watched as the foreman deliberately blinked to ensure the contents persisted beyond normal vision and tested his access.

'Open it when you're ready. You can set it to deliver everything, or choose less-detectable compound growth. To be honest, I'm not really interested.'

The foreman regarded him and the ve-package suspiciously. 'No, I'm good,' he said and watched Youssef leave. Rabindra liked to take risks and always agreed to things that might be to his personal benefit, but he wasn't inclined to accept anything at face value. Rabindra shut down what he could of Youssef's privileged access, even though he had indeed set up his own accounts over the past few hours, and set the ve-package aside so he could focus on a search of his own. Youssef's personnel records were all but missing, and what was available only related to his pay. As usual, whoever had hired him had waved him in the door without verifying his credentials, so he probably wasn't who he claimed to be. It didn't matter. Rabindra could start the process from scratch and pulled all the detail from Pallial Truth.

Youssef Damaru-Da-Te-Epsilon, 32, unskilled worker, [K8 location]. *Appointment: regenerator (temporary). Late-nonage education: standard.*

Rabindra didn't waste time reviewing the dossier as it either concerned the most unremarkable of workers or Youssef had fabricated it. The summary certainly didn't represent the man he had observed that evening. Rabindra submitted a request to match his details with licensed sculptors and known unauthorised re-registrations and asked for a cross-reference with cachier records to see if Youssef had assumed an unused identity. The FMP did not return anything and confirmed he was just a regular, humdrum guy. Rabindra reviewed Youssef's employment records but unusually for someone at the coalface he didn't have a lot of megalopolitan regeneration experience. Most of his roles had been in data presentation, with occasional stints as a sysadmin. Rabindra methodically worked backwards through months of public performance evaluation records, trying hard to focus on each uneventful detail. It was so mundane that he almost didn't realise the man's employment pre-dated the day of his hatching. It appeared that Youssef was always there, indefinitely plodding from one dreary job to another. Rabindra pulled imagery from random assignments and was amazed at his gall: Youssef was hiding in full sight, and no one had found him.

Rabindra knew he would not be able to remain at the coalface if he opened Youssef's ve-package while knowing there was little chance of ascending if he didn't. If he decided to follow Youssef, he would have to be careful, and he was inexperienced in these matters. Did he want to risk being questioned or being caught? Perhaps it was best to go without thinking and hope Youssef had not used him.

CHAPTER THREE
Danesh
বর্তমানে

THE WOMAN OPPOSITE held a paper napkin over her nose and mouth and peered into the pit. One of the rats was climbing the wall closest to her, so she knocked it back using a clearfibre rod. She turned to her group and said something Cristóbal couldn't hear, while one of her friends replayed a video clip that captured the moment. The evening schedule, forced onto the members' eyesight, commenced with three terriers. Two were regular black-and-whites with blotchy brown faces, but the third was almost entirely white with a tan face, like a mask. Cristóbal liked this animal with its overdeveloped ears standing proudly above its head and placed a sizeable bet against a minimum of fifteen kills.

Four minutes remained. The FMP confirmed that the one hundred rats were biological and alive, and provided a recent history for each dog. Cristóbal was pleased with his choice, and sure he would make enough staters to maintain his reputation. The referee appeared to mild applause and introduced each ratter to the crowd. Their enthusiasm grew as the final seconds elapsed before the rat terriers were released. Cristóbal cut the background noise and listened to a vaguely familiar pastorale, while the dogs gripped, tossed and discarded dying rats with practised efficiency. One dog backed its prey into a corner of the pit and silently yelped as it received several sharp bites to the face. With inaudible snarls and growls, it grabbed one of the largest rats and shook it repeatedly, sometimes banging it against the enclosure. Two men were shouting at their animal, but Cristóbal did not hear them. The timer reached zero, and the three dogs froze in their tracks as the Pallium shut them down. Most of the remaining rodents crowded into a corner as a writhing mass of bloodied fur.

With a fantastic eighteen dispatches in just one minute, Lisboa Pit has a new record holder: Tawny Tsutomu III.

Cristóbal did not need to listen to the result or check his earnings: he knew he had done well. The twins came over to congratulate him and invited the others to join them at a table. While the croupiers reset the pit, Tsutomu's owner brought the dog over to them to present the winner. Cristóbal gave him a generous tip and admired the dog. He paid no attention to the gore on its muzzle as he petted it.

'I hoped today might be the day you decided to leave,' he said to Grace as she joined them. 'When we met I thought you wouldn't survive the Fours. I was wrong. You're at home in the pits with all the other bitches.'

She was not flustered. 'Descent is easy to arrange,' she remarked and placed her gin on the table, 'but I doubt I'd be allowed back up because of my association with you.'

Grace was wearing a simple black dress, contrasting with her pale skin. Her arms were bare, and her straight, dark hair fell over her left shoulder. Her status indicated she had not been fortunate with her gambling, but she appeared determined to have a good time. As usual, she invited Cristóbal to spend the night with her, and as ever, he declined.

'You two need to get whatever this is out of your respective systems.' Doha was easily the oldest woman in the venue and had been an affiliate since it opened. Her credentials were indistinct. There was a rumour she was a disenfranchised First who had entered the Lisboa with her last stater and somehow made her fortune. She had provided Cristóbal with financial backing when he arrived in K4, and he dedicated himself to her.

'Now, how shall we help spend his gains?'

'He can pay for us to leave this shitty level,' Bāo said. He and his brother clapped Cristóbal across the shoulders and Liang attempted to use a helper function to syphon off a few of his staters.

'Hey cut that out, you pair of cheats.'

'If anyone's taking from him,' Grace declared, 'it's me. I intend to have it all.'

Cristóbal revoked his public access. 'I might buy myself an attendant to deal with all the crap in my life. Like you lot.'

'He'll invest,' Doha suggested. 'It's his calling. Now, one of you buy this *eldri-kona* some gas so I can pretend to be a much younger woman.'

For a while, they sat quietly, watching the staff restock the pit for the next event. There was a commotion as a dog jumped away from its trainer. A small group of would-be entrepreneurs attempted to rush out of the building with the animal, but the staff expected such behaviour and expelled the men, nulling their takings.

'Excuse me a moment,' Cristóbal said, 'I just need to take a quick call.' He closed his eyes, leant back in his chair and accepted the summons to a potential client's office. When he opened his eyes, he was in a brightly lit room, facing a well-dressed man seated behind a large, empty desk.

'Thank you for sending over,' he said. 'My name is Pazel Sad-Tet-Ain-Resh. I do hope this is a convenient moment.'

Cristóbal studied Pazel carefully, trying to determine if what he was seeing was an accurate portrayal or something created for his benefit. He had never met an outrightsider before.

'Of course. How might I be of assistance?'

'I'm waiting for a new man, a specific *ný-maður*, to be released into your level. He will exit his gestorium in the morning, and I would like to have him diverted from his tedious future into my employ. I presume you can provide a suitable service.'

'Absolutely, including all of the requisite audit alterations.' Cristóbal wondered if the rightsider's mannerisms were a pretence. 'Do you have any particular instructions?'

Pazel indicated a buff box as it appeared on the table. 'All the details concerning the newed are here. Please take it with you.'

Cristóbal picked up the container, and the call ended. The virtual world imploded, and he snapped back to the Lisboa. His hands were empty.

'Something's come up,' he told the women. 'I hope you can enjoy your evening without me.'

'A job?' Grace asked.

'Nothing too challenging,' Cristóbal said and left.

He headed for the transport hub and opened the ve-package as he walked.

Danesh Ne-Baluda-Va-Wa.

There appeared to be nothing unusual about the boy. He was just one in a set of daily talent, one set of many. Cristóbal didn't care because in his view all *fólkið* were the same before they were newed and started their adult lives. What happened in the first few days was the only discriminator, and it entirely depended on what Tion threw at them. He sent data miners into the FMP to seek out information gems, his fifteen-year syllabus, averages and results, relationship networks and chatter pattern matches, submitting a few logistic queries in for good measure. By the time his pod reached the Beurs, the global trading compartment, he had a fair understanding of this Danesh, of his aspirations and desires. He would be easy to motivate, given the right environment.

Cristóbal started to draft his options and inserted his assumptions into a comfortable model he had tucked away for this sort of job, but he discarded his reckoning as he entered the cloister. Things always go better when I improvise, he decided. The Beurs stretched for hundreds of metres in both directions and offered him a physical connection. He pushed through the milling traders, settled against the wall and looked out between two pillars as he prepared to surrender himself. Cristóbal liked to think he was right next to the decision process and that the few microseconds saved would cut him a better deal.

Inside there were people crammed into every conceivable space. Some existed within others, occupying the innards of those not foresighted enough to make themselves virtually whole. A *ný-kona* had impossibly elongated her young body to slide between entangled bidders and pieces of those who chose to fragment surrounded everything. No one was permitted to trade without one hundred per cent representation, but there were no rules about how perfect the individual portrayal. Many were generic, faceless dolls that were indistinguishable from one another, but occasionally a body sported a flash of creativity. Cristóbal regularly used a monochrome epitome.

He posted a request for five men, no one over twenty, each with experience moving goods between levels. He ruled out assizes as an affordability measure, despite their reputation for getting a job done efficiently. Cristóbal still had to review the terms of his contract with Pazel, but his initial assessment was that the client would screw him. He decided to pay the men with narcotics, as while this generally attracted a lower standard of worker, it didn't lock him into a stater price. If he managed things well, he could probably register them for caching and improve his return.

The online crush grew more intense as candidates surged towards him. He reached over with nimble hands and feet, marking most with a thumb or toe, preventing them from applying, and they slowly sunk away. At the same time, he became progressively distracted by the array of targeted advertising. The longer he remained on the floor, the easier it would be for salesmen to defeat his filters and determine his actual vulnerabilities, just as he was doing with his remaining applicants. It was a contest he preferred to win.

Once his five men were finally selected, contracted and en route, he cut his feed and opened his eyes. The press of genuine flesh was more sedate, and he welcomed its relative truth. He felt optimistic, forwarded the signed agreement to a commercial applet and considered his choices. The deal was almost fair, especially if he didn't ask too many questions. Cristóbal absolved his potential guilt with a quick query to Pazel regarding registered human traffickers, just in case. It wouldn't do for his client to look too closely into his background: he did not want a reputation as a supplier for the trenches. Not that he thought this Danesh would be much of a prize, but it wouldn't hurt to be diligent.

Cristóbal paid two-point-one kilostaters to gain access to a Lacuna maintenance walkway. Kathy said the passageway was sometimes used as a *bogdo* by unauthorised up-levellers to move through Tion. He instructed his team to meet him there.

'You really shouldn't be so keen to close,' Kathy reminded him. He had been using her services for a few years after a friend had recommended her for a particularly tedious data theft. 'I might have reduced my fee.'

'Five hundred?'

'I find that unlikely.'

Cristóbal enjoyed working with Kathy and knew he was paying extra for her loyalty.

'So, what's the gig?'

'Pick up some kid, reset his expectations. Nothing special.'

'Who is he?'

'That's the bit that's nothing special. I've given up trying to understand this sort of thing. Too many *sálirnar* in Tion with too many weird ideas.'

He chose an unpublished route to reduce the risk of being tracked and arrived shortly after his crew. None lived up to their profiles, but he didn't think it would matter. He sat them down and passed around an aerocan, noting that two lingered over the gas a little more than was polite.

'Here's the deal. There are six neweds in the tin, and I want one of them. After that, there's one for each of you, do what you want with them. Consider them a bonus if you will. If my boy doesn't make it, none of you gets paid. Once we've cracked them out, you're staying with me. The lovely Aikaterine has supplied tools and code, and here's who does what,' [*data*].

The men spent a few moments assimilating their instructions and rummaging for bits of equipment before they reclaimed their blank expressions. One sat with his face close to the rough walls of the *bogdo* as he muttered to himself. Cristóbal submitted his identification to a discrete service that specialised in protecting its members from undesirables. He received no response. Five desperadoes, he thought: Yash, Saburo, Oriol, Feliu and Yasuo. No sincerity in any of them.

Feliu turned his head from the wall. 'I don't think we should remain here any longer. We've picked up a tag.'

'Says who?' Cristóbal expected an explosion, a rush of masked bandits or at least something to set his heart racing. Instead, three *konurnar* wandered towards them but showed little interest in any kind of situation.

The shortest woman stepped forward and spoke. 'There are two ways we can proceed, but the outcome will be the same. One is more pleasant for everyone concerned.' She inspected each of the men. 'My associates have some fairly sophisticated access, and I have a caching voucher with one open billet. So, which of you is worth the most? A new life within the Pallium would be an improvement for any of you.'

Cristóbal was mildly amused at the assizes' gall and calmly messaged his crew to continue with their work, but Yasuo and Saburo sprang at the women. Their interrupt carried a strong compulsion, *go now*. He turned without thinking and fled into the darkness, allowing the FMP to guide his footsteps. Something nagged at him, the potential for his assailants to use the Pallium to locate him, yet it wasn't enough for him to disconnect. Cristóbal was dimly aware of an unexpected lack of ve-presence for the two men. He didn't think they would have offlined voluntarily; however, they had each acknowledged the possible risks when they agreed to their contracts. Behind him, the three *konurnar* were shouting at each other, so he waited until the women had stalked away. When the remainder of his crew came back, he asked Feliu what had happened.

'Assizes have taken up caching, using tech-ops to hack into our black signals. Some crazy crap that has been going on for a few months. They insert pricey people into an active caching request to syphon off the excess staters, or sometimes use a three-to-one and reverse accruals, and always keep the numbers down to be discrete. Friend of mine sold me some code to sniff them out. Consider it a freebie.'

'Saburo and the other *náungi*?'

'Both gone, but only one fellow will be cached and happy. My guess is they ain't worth shit; hence the ladies were pissed off.'

'Fuck.'

'Which means you probably need more help.'

Cristóbal didn't need to run any sims to figure out that one man per passenger kept the risk low. Unfortunately, a modicum of vigilante spirit amongst the *ný-fólkið* could lead to a chase through the tunnels. The four of them would have to cope. He wanted the other children kept out of the way, so sent a plea to the twins for some additional manpower.

Cristóbal briefed the team as they approached the breach. *Target [TUID] is my responsibility. Six in the pod—seems one has a close social network with my boy [data]. Send some standby messages to the capsule to keep them calm (Yash). All destined for K4 information management posts with unfettered access to local amenities. Probably limited tracking, just Lacuna access, shouldn't be hard to delete the record (Feliu). If you get them out unharmed, they're probably all saleable, might need some processing first. Kathy can give you some contacts if you want. Should have more info when we tap the can. Not long now.*

Bāo and Liang arrived within fifteen minutes of his summons, complaining about the interruption.

Get the spiders programmed up and through the lock (Oriel). Be careful with the gates because there's no fancy failsafe to stop you emptying this whole tunnel into the flight path. There's shit in there pulling eighteen-ex, and we'd probably never know if you screwed it up. Once the drones have them, we'll wait for them to drag the pod to this emergency hatch.

The men busied themselves while Cristóbal sauntered along the passage to the airlock, pulling on data gloves to help retain his identity. The FMP posted the status of the six occupants as soon as the spiders intercepted the transport capsule and blew the expellers. Three girls, three boys, one with his back and left leg broken. All were either in shock or pumped full of adrenaline.

'We'll take the spare boys,' Bāo said. 'I have an up-level client who will add them to her staff, once I've paid to fix up the busted one all pretty. You three can take a girl each. Can't do much better than that, eh?'

Liang pulled pictures of the three new women. '*Kàn!* These *ný-konurnar*, they all look the same, young and silent. We should sell them collectively, you know, like art.'

'You certainly can't let any of them go,' Cristóbal said. 'Their identities are how I'm funding our little expedition. You do want to get paid? *Bueno.*' He turned to look through the wall into the transport duct, relying on the drones' partial interface with the pod to activate his eyesight. His vision juddered and froze while he stared at the boy's face, and he was unable to discern why his client was interested. A collection of disjointed images, he thought, trying to capture a profound moment and each missing the mark. Danesh was saying something to the other children, but Cristóbal could not hear, nor could he interpolate the movements on the boy's lips. Danesh appeared to be frustrated, not panicked. Cristóbal liked that.

'A couple of minutes and they'll be here,' Liang said. 'It'll dock itself and hook up, after which the drone's jamming signal won't be sufficient. It'll take me a few moments to block their access. Probably about as long as it'll take to force the car open.'

Cristóbal was watching from the side of the passageway, allowing his team to prepare, even though he wanted to rip his own way in, grab the boy and finish up. He collated a summary of their agreements, tasking and schedule, and posted it in each of his men's eyesight. Uncharacteristically, he decided to add a stater value as an additional incentive.

'Very important to our client,' he murmured. 'Very important to me. Won't do to be caught. Mustn't leave a trace.'

The sound of the pod hitting the gate rang through the corridor, accompanied by a shrill scraping sound as the drones pushed it into place. It was incapable of mating correctly without internal power, and would stubbornly hold its doors shut while it waited indefinitely for the appropriate protocols. Yash started drilling through the airlock wall while

Oriol prepared the flagellar sealant that would keep the Lacuna safely at bay. There were a pop and a hiss of air rushing into the vacuum, and then silence as the caulk set. Yash dropped the drill and started to work on the doors with a gas cutter. Sparks of molten metal spat out either side of him, punctuated with occasional oaths.

'You have to hurry,' Bāo said, leaning towards him. 'The shitlings will be all over the FMP by now. Work faster.'

Cristóbal wasn't sure how it happened, nor were any of the other men. One moment Bāo was leaning against Yash, hastening him, then he was hurled against the floor with fragments of the door embedded in his scalp. Liang was monitoring the mechanical spiders when it happened and didn't notice his brother was dead. And then, a wail of solitude; he was alone for the first time.

'Not now,' Cristóbal said. 'We have to move. Break their link.'

Feliu and Yash pried the airlock open, and Cristóbal pushed past them into the capsule. He did not try to avoid the broken boy, kicking him squarely in the stomach to confirm he was still alive. There was vomit smeared across the floor, making it slippery underfoot. The children were all frozen with panic, allowing them to identify Danesh quickly. Cristóbal thrust his right hand around the *drengar*'s throat and squeezed harder than he should. I am distracted, he thought.

'Out,' he said. *I have the boy. Shut their cunting access down right now!*

Yash and Oriol were stumbling over themselves in the cramped compartment as they failed to agree which man would take which girl. It was as if they were looking for the best chocolate in the box, Cristóbal thought, idiots. *Where's Liang?* he demanded on the shared broadcast. *Sort these ball-licking* ný-mennirnir *out.*

'What are you doing?' Danesh cried.

Cristóbal tightened his grip. 'Quiet.' He pushed Danesh through the airlock, allowing Feliu to gag and bind the boy, who clutched at his ears now the jamming signal was in place. Twenty metres along the passageway, Liang sat with his head in his hands, rocking gently. Cristóbal assumed he was sobbing.

'What a fucking pain in the arse,' he breathed.

Feliu jumped into the transport to retrieve the last boy, leaving the others lined up in an uncomfortable row.

'Is he worth salvaging?' Yash asked.

'Doesn't look great.'

'Ditch him,' Cristóbal said. 'We've got other problems to solve. Throw everything else into the can, mask the doors and blow it. Should give us enough time to get out before the area vents into the Lacuna. Let's go.'

Oriol marshalled the five children and thrust them along the tunnel. Cristóbal sat beside Liang and placed his gloved hand on his shoulder.

'We can't take Bāo with us. If you want to say goodbye, it has to be now.' Cristóbal watched as an image of the dead man started to form. *Put Bāo in with the busted boy. We can't leave him here to for assizes to find.*

'We have to go. You must come with me.' Cristóbal paid for an override, took over Liang's body and forced him to follow the others. He despised himself and placed a full-service call to Doha.

'There's been an accident. I need you to look after Liang. We've lost Bāo.'

The dusky woman's simulacrum peered along the corridor. 'I can take him from you if you want. Let me know when you're ready to switch him into reality.'

Oriol had disappeared from view, but Cristóbal continued to track him as he trudged forward, dividing his concentration between his footing and Liang's. He had to pay more attention to his movements than he had anticipated because Liang was attempting to reclaim his body. *At least he's not trying to overrule me,* Cristóbal thought. They plodded up a set of stairs but fell further behind. There was an indistinct boom in the distance as the temporary bulkhead protecting them from the Lacuna failed. Cristóbal trusted that Feliu had secured the passageway, but it would only be a few moments before they knew. Liang was quietly groaning and would probably break free before Doha arrived.

Yash and Feliu clattered along, breathless and dragging a few pieces of equipment. Cristóbal was about to admonish them when he realised they were struggling to keep his team safe from the stark vacuum in which the transports operated.

'We need your help,' Yash said.

Cristóbal nodded at Liang. 'I'm busy.'

Feliu did not hesitate; he struck Liang squarely across the head with the butt of his gas cutter, hoisted the crumpled body over his shoulder and marched after the others, dragging the toolbox behind him.

Yash held up his hand. 'We can't convince the Pallium that we're a bona fide maintenance crew. It's not allowing us to close any of the service portals, and we've run out of time to cut panels and weld them across the corridor. You have to contact your *hjörnir* and find someone who can fix this; otherwise, we're dead.'

'You're supposed to be handling this,' Cristóbal said. 'It's what I'm paying you for.'

Yash continued along the access tunnel without reply. It didn't take long for Cristóbal to negotiate with Kathy. She promised to resolve the situation promptly and said they could worry about the price when he finished begging favours. He put it out of his mind and cast his eyesight forward. In ten minutes or so, they would reach the storeroom of the quantum-chemical facility where they would disperse. The newods were in pretty good shape, and while mostly still in shock, they were physically unharmed. Liang was still out cold, but Doha would take care of him. Cristóbal entered the factory to find the men separating tools and clothing for destruction, and readying themselves to part company. Doha was there.

'Liang will be good to leave in a few minutes. We'll take the spare boy with us. If nothing else he can support Liang as we walk out of here. I've still got to wipe him down and apply a lock. I told the others to purge anything that will allow us to be identified and get rid of the three *ný-konurnar*. I think we should atomise the new women, it'll be neater, but it's up to you. Let me know if I can help.'

'Thank you,' Cristóbal said.

He was finally able to inspect Danesh. Blood had dripped from a cut on his forehead onto his white shirt and dried in russet blotches. Cristóbal ripped the tape from his eyes and pulled the porous plug from his mouth. The *drengar* was unremarkable but had a steely look in his eyes.

'My name is Cristóbal, and I'm here to look after you. I'll need to clean you up before we leave and untie your hands. Are you going to be a problem for me today?'

'What about Shu-fen?'

'She's not coming with us. If she is good, they'll let her live. You'll be able to discuss things with her once you're both reintegrated. Dump your clothing with the other crap. We have a lot to do.'

'I heard these men say that someone wants to see me. Who is it? What's this about?'

Cristóbal cut his hands free. 'An investor has selected you, Danesh, don't ask me who. You're going to need to make a choice. Whatever my client wants you for is guaranteed to be better than your legitimate assignment. Personally, I wouldn't fight it.'

Danesh took a cloth and wiped the last of the blood from his face. 'You'd say that just to get me to cooperate.'

'Yes, I would. Hurry up.'

If Danesh had a connection, he would have run some sims to figure out what to do. He tried to let his mind drift and work through the options in his head, closing his eyes to shut out his surroundings, but he was distracted by the sound of his breathing. It was impossible to guess what had happened to Shu-fen, or if the men had already disposed of Haziq. The proscribed life ahead of him wasn't exciting or dynamic, and it would probably be the same day after day. Danesh chose.

He could hear Ahmad shouting at the *mennirnir* and demanding to know where his friend was. A dusky woman was calmly talking to him, saying she wanted to take him to a new life, promising happiness once he was re-trained. Danesh stripped off his clothes and dumped them with the sweat-stained overalls the men had worn. In the pile were the other sets of white trousers and shirts, some ripped and bloodied. Danesh suspected he would never see Shu-fen again, but it did not upset him.

'Cristóbal, I trust you.'

The air was dry and quiet, and Hyun-jun could hear his breath rasping through his body. He felt terrible and remained still in the pale light. His head throbbed, so he sent a request for a pain block and a summary of his medical status. His headache slowly subsided, and apart from an ugly bruise on his forearm, he was otherwise unharmed. He was in a small hut, similar to the ones used by his *fólkið* to tend the elders scheduled for caching or those deemed to be a danger to the grass farm. They must have acquiesced and retrieved him from the passageway.

Where am I?

[*K6 location*].

Other than his position, the Pallium did not respond to his demands. He looked around in the gloom. The pen was a couple of metres in both directions and made out of tightly bound grass timber. Dried grass flowers were scattered on the floor and heaped into the bedding beneath him. It had a musty odour, as if no one had slept there for some time, and his movements stirred up clouds of fine dust.

There were muffled voices, and Hyun-jun could hear people approaching. The furthermost side of the shelter shook slightly as his captors undid the bindings along each edge, and the wall was swung upward and propped open with stout poles. The adolescent man who had struck him waited, probably on guard, peering at him closely.

'We know who you are and where you come from, but we don't know why you are here. We're supposed to help. What do you want?'

'I didn't mean any harm. Please tell me where we are.'

The *ný-maður* motioned for him to get up and follow him. 'It will be fully light soon. I will take you to the others, but I am not your friend.'

They walked through the columns. To Hyun-jun, it was hauntingly familiar, and he remembered the joy of seeing new grasses of his home when he had first started to work. He allowed himself to brush against the glass and tried to gaze at the plants within. There were no young seed heads.

Six adults waited on makeshift stools in a small clearing, while daylight bloomed above them. Some of the *fullorðnir* were wearing blankets across their shoulders or laps and started to fold them away. The young man moved behind a woman who Hyun-jun assumed was their spokesperson. He wasn't sure but thought she had been there when her grass farm opened up to the corridor.

'My name is Noemí. These are my *ljðirnir*. Explain yourself.'

'I'm Hyun-jun, and I live in a farm like yours, close to here. I have a friend there who showed me how to visit you. Her name is Milagrosa. I expect you've met her, but it would have been a long time ago.' Their faces were intent as they evaluated his words. 'Our farm is full, and there isn't enough work for everyone. I want something more.'

His assailant started to speak, but someone cut him off. Hyun-jun assumed it was Noemí.

'You cannot stay here and embed yourself into our *samfélag*.'

Hyun-jun hesitated, searching for the correct response. 'No, your community is like mine, and I wanted to experience something new, but I was unprepared. I have a few provisions but no water. I'd like you to help me.'

He was aware of the hurried exchange of messages between them and could sense their discomfort.

'Where will you go?'

He studied them all. There was grief written on their faces, established and comfortable. They lacked the essential joy that was part of his life, and he didn't want to remain there.

'I will go everywhere and speak about what I see. I will find a way to share with everyone, so all grass workers know what the world is like.'

One of the elders laughed bitterly. 'Go back to your home, *drengar*. You know nothing of the world outside, and no one will listen to you.'

Noemí held up one hand to silence him and looked directly at Hyun-jun. 'The new man to my left is Enzo, and he is just as much a boy as you are, but he was attempting to keep us safe when he prevented your access. He did not seek to hurt you. Afterwards, we received instructions to bring you here. Enzo will give you whatever you need, but first, we have work to do.' She rose with more agility than Hyun-jun thought possible. The farmers scampered and ran and climbed until they had disappeared into the columns.

Enzo remained still with his face frozen and blue eyes unfocused; disengaged from the moment. Hyun-jun had never seen anyone with such fair hair and skin. Surely it couldn't protect him from the intense daylight. He was around the same age but forty centimetres taller and his body, defined through hard work, was covered in cropped hair. To Hyun-jun, he didn't look real; he wondered if Enzo was a thing manufactured by the FMP to protect these *fólkið*.

Enzo blinked, clenched his square jaw and tightened his grip on the *hanbō*. 'I will do as she asks and tomorrow my company and I will expel you.'

Hyun-jun didn't know how to interact with this young man. He was unaccustomed to unprovoked aggression. He asked about the farm and the *hýðirnir* who tended it, but Enzo did not respond quickly, and when he did, his remarks were curt. Their grass farm was failing, the plants were not producing, and there were too many workers. Enzo had stopped harvesting two years ago to protect Noemí even though she protested at every opportunity. He said his life meant nothing and Hyun-jun found he could not understand him.

That evening, after Hyun-jun had negotiated for the items he needed to take with him, Enzo nervously asked if his company could come along. Hyun-jun was wary of the burly *ný-maður*, he felt intimated by Enzo's physical presence and his status in his community. Still, there was also something endearing about his behaviour in the moments they were alone, and despite everything, Hyun-jun found he liked Enzo, so he agreed.

There was a message waiting for Hyun-jun, flashing in his eyesight. When he was sure no one would observe him, he watched it. Her skin was a vibrant colour, and her hair was so black it was almost blue. She didn't identify herself but said she was a friend and wanted to help. She knew how he could move around Tion and would give him the things he needed. She suggested he chose one of these farmers to accompany him, preferably someone he felt he could trust. He thought she had perfect lips.

When Hyun-jun awoke, Noemí was seated on a high stool, surrounded by fifteen young adults. She murmured to them, touched some fondly and kissed others on the forehead. They were all much taller than Hyun-jun, with fair hair and skin, and they all looked very powerful. Hyun-jun felt overawed. Enzo stepped forward.

'Noemí wants us to go with you and told us to protect you as we protect her. We must return with stories of new friends and potentially an opportunity to expand beyond this place, even though the Pallium has denied our disseveration. These are my *ný-mennirnir* and *ný-konurnar*. Guðmundur is my second, and I shall lead.'

'You will do as this outsider says,' Noemí said firmly. 'He has already journeyed beyond his home and therefore has skills you do not. Remember that I will be observing you, Enzo.'

Hyun-jun was genuinely pleased he would not be on his own. He rose and thanked the workers for accepting him into their lives and wished those remaining behind a good harvest. From the columns came several *börnin* and *eldri-fólkið*, who hugged and chatted with the company. Hyun-jun received small gifts from the children and advice from the elders.

They made their preparations for the next few hours. Several of the grass workers noted the farm would benefit from a day without reaping, and some talked about the tionsphere beyond. One of the *eldri-fólkið* said he had lived outside the farm for many years, but the others dismissed it as an old man's fantasy. Finally, they gathered at the portal where Noemí spoke for several minutes about community and truth. Hyun-jun's anticipation of the journey ahead was irrepressible, and he barely heard a word.

'Where will you take us?' Enzo demanded.

Hyun-jun's reverie was interrupted, and he realised he could not answer. What knowledge of anything beyond grass working did he have? He knew he would not survive for long without assistance. He looked to Noemí for guidance, but she did not reciprocate.

Accept ve-package.

In Hyun-jun's experience, the FMP did not initiate dialogue. Its purpose was to respond. The microscopic datrix surging around his body shuffled his neurones to replicate the information structure, and he knew what to say.

'Far above us are the two mighty empyrealodes. They gather brilliance from the sunstar and send life to our farms. We will visit the megametre bands and the factories hidden in Ones to ensure they are stable for generations to come.'

There were mutterings of approval from the gathered crowd and Hyun-jun prepared to elaborate, but the new men and women surged around him and raised his exposed body towards the skyplate, chanting his name. He was high above them with his hands held aloft, basking in the tumescent warmth. It was a moment he would always be able to return to, and it would buoy his mood when all else was gone. Noemí requested the lowering of the portal, and they stepped outside.

Most of the new men and women from Enzo's grass farm had never imagined they would leave their home and milled about, consumed by their Sodality feeds. Hyun-jun glanced around, unsurprised that Enzo had also retreated online to avoid the choices ahead. He considered contacting the *kona* from his private message, but it was obvious what they needed to do. Hyun-jun held up his hands and cleared his throat, hoping it would be enough to gain their attention. Enzo was the first to acknowledge him, but Hyun-jun realised he wasn't going to follow as he gathered the others around him. Enzo started to march the group along the corridor, abandoning the earlier joy. Hyun-jun couldn't determine if they headed back towards his home, so he stepped away and tried to remember which way he had come. The Pallium and the woman from the message were silent. He had no choice but to go with them.

Everyone carried culms filled with water and various foodstuffs. The narrow straps dug painfully into Hyun-jun's shoulders. With shorter strides, he trailed behind the party and all of his earlier excitement was lost. Enzo eventually called a halt, and they settled to rest. The white, curved walls offered little comfort, and the previously pleasant air chilled Hyun-jun's core. He sat alone, watching the company. Their bodies were huddled against each other as they passed a flask of *awamori* between them, yet they did not welcome him in. He sent a brief message to Enzo, asking for his support, but the blond man laughed and gathered his followers around him. Hyun-jun shut his eyes and sat upright with his chin resting on his bare knees. He listened as the chatter petered out and quiet, intimate noises grew. He was cold and tired and felt terribly alone, while the others worshipped their mutual heat.

When he woke, his eyes struggled to open in the brilliant light. The sprawl of people was motionless, and the corridor was silent. Someone had pissed near his feet. Hyun-jun wrinkled his nose at the lingering odour of the company's celebration and closed his eyes. As he did so, he noticed the strangest thing. The signature of the man closest to him was indistinguishable from the decking. Hyun-jun crawled over to him and lay his hand on his face. The body was cold. The woman next to him, her arm resting on his heavy thigh, was the same. Hyun-jun slid his way over the bodies, looking for Enzo's distinctive features. He was there in the middle of their flesh and clearly breathing with a slight grimace on his warm face. The rest of Enzo's company was dead.

Hyun-jun carefully distanced himself from their bodies, intending to flee, but a wave of exhaustion dragged him back to oblivion.

Freja and Caitlyn continued to argue, even though Jovana and the other girls were resting. They could not agree on the course of action the team should take, assuming an undetectable cohort was subverting the FMP. Freja remained convinced the Pallium had contracted them directly and was looking for a way to protect itself; her peers retorted that this was nonsense because a system could not have a consciousness and certainly could not be alive.

If there were people who planned to destroy the FMP and sever a vast population from its means of support, then they had to be somewhere. The women had scoured every second of arc of every habitable level of Tion, a minuscule but daunting fraction of which they had to do manually. There was no one to overthrow the non-existent authority. Caitlyn maintained that this was an evaluation of sorts and someone was evaluating their discretion.

Freja based her assertion on the amount of processing that appeared to be handled by human teams. She argued that a polymeric computational system that enveloped an entire planet should be able to determine the aesthetic value of purloined pieces of jewellery. It wouldn't need people to make those decisions. Caitlyn agreed: if it was capable of measuring, storing and processing all of the particles in a point-to-point transfer, it should be able to match one trinket to another. Ergo, there wasn't enough Pallium to go around.

Caitlyn wanted the team to drop the contract, fearing no good would come of it. Once word got out they would not be taken seriously by any prospective clients, their rating would plummet, and they would receive little additional tasking. Now that Jovana had deferred to her, she felt she had the right to make decisions for them all, and it was time to be sensible. Freja displayed the terms of their contract in front of them both.

'Remember, if we're successful,' she said, 'we will have the right to anything we want. Nothing could be better than that.'

I trust you.

Danesh was used to being in control of his surroundings. He could predict the behaviour of the *ýðirnir* he knew and understood how the FMP managed the environment. He used this to his advantage and had never resorted to trusting anyone. It worried him that he had consented, almost without hesitation. He could not interpret this man or predict his behaviours and was unable to see inside him.

He had been taken to a well-furnished room and told to rest. There was a platter of food, but unusually, he wasn't hungry. Beyond a partition was a recess in the floor full of warm water. He sat and looked at it for some time until he decided it was intended for him and slipped in. He had never been immersed in water before, but the bath was not deep, and he felt safe. There were several small bottles, filled with thick, scented liquids, and he scrubbed himself clean.

Danesh picked at the food before flopping onto the bed and falling into a restless sleep. He was troubled by images of Shu-fen and Haziq, naked and coupled, with broken limbs attaining preposterous positions, grinding to the sound of grating joints. He tried to stop them, but they wouldn't listen. Haziq rotated his head a half-turn towards him and laughed through his orgasm. Danesh knew it wasn't real and asked his oneironaut to redirect his dream, yet the auditor allowed Haziq to mock him every way he faced.

He felt nonetheless refreshed when he woke and was delighted he had full Sodality access. Shu-fen was not registering at all, and he knew it would be futile to try to locate her. He had attempted to trace Cristóbal but had insufficient information to find him. Danesh left the bed and surveyed the room. Something had cleared the food away, deleted the bath and provided a selection of clothing. He dressed and sat down in a wide armchair, closed his eyes and left the room.

There was something peculiar about online, something more expansive about his virtual experience. It took him a while to understand what it was. There was a richness to Sodality he was unaccustomed to, and more depth to the data. The universe had switched from an intricate picture to an infinite fractal. The Pallium opened to him with a dreamlike quality, and he glimpsed its vastness, which left him yearning to explore further. Danesh realised he could quickly lose himself and would never need to return. Occasionally, something tempted him to follow, or he tasted a refrain that drew him in. He knew he was being enticed and submitted willingly. There was a certain familiarity, which he assumed Cristóbal had created. Once again, Danesh trusted.

Sat in a neat row were endless young women. They were all Humaira. Plain but beautiful, bursting with innocence. Each one was slightly different from her sisters, her hair or breasts or aura. They all gazed at him with accusing eyes: he had abandoned them. Even so, Danesh proceeded to pleasure them, one by one, each according to her desires. They all asked him to select from a convoluted set of options, every climax requiring multiple choices. The monotony caused him to despair until his body refused to come, and it was over.

The *ný-konurnar* melted away, and he was alone.

'I want to show you a future,' said the void.

'Is it mine?' Danesh asked.

'It's hard to be sure. There are many futures, but you have already declared your preferences. Perhaps this is yours; perhaps it is what you've chosen to forgo.'

'But I wasn't certain,' he protested.

'That doesn't matter now.'

A man walked towards him, dressed in a white, fitted suit. He was much taller than Danesh, with lighter skin and broad shoulders. He saw him saying something, but despite there being no sound, his wasn't the voice Danesh had heard. A younger man approached and showed the *maður* a stream of empty faces. They often stopped to consider one; sometimes they matched a pair. There was obviously a bond between them, but the taller man did not hesitate to leave and instructed the other to manage his affairs. The void became a crush of people, an emptiness in Bodem's solitude, a swarm of potential workers, a manicured expanse of gardens, and a tangle of opportunities. The variety was overwhelming, and Danesh wanted it all.

'What do I have to do?' Danesh asked.

'To become this *persónan*?'

'If you allow me to.'

For the second time, his surroundings faded away. Danesh waited, but nothing changed, and finally, he left Sodality and rose from the chair. There was a small, insulated flask on a table in front of him, so he took it to the window and sipped the hot tea. He was high up and looked out over an empty, silver-blue plain. More water, Danesh thought, what an incredible waste.

A chime sounded, and a door appeared. It opened slowly, outward from the room, exposing a glimpse of the brightly lit building beyond. Danesh was starting to walk towards it when a woman appeared in silhouette, giving him a glimpse of the *kona* Shu-fen might now become; however, this woman was not at all demure. He allowed his weight to shift back to his heels and disconnected his feeds. He wanted to focus on whatever she had to say.

She did not close the door behind her, and it was apparent they were going to leave. Danesh had no possessions, and there was nothing left in the room to eat. 'Don't worry,' he said, 'I know this is temporary, and I intend to go wherever you want, but I'm also hungry.'

She laughed deeply. It was a harsh, throaty sound. 'My name is Victoria, and I'm here to take you to my boss. He's a decent *maður*, and I intend to keep him happy. Be gracious to him, and if he likes you, then we'll possibly work together. If not, I might bring you back here, although eventually, you would have to fend for yourself. We're currently in K3 and somewhat beyond your station. I think it's a bland level and the *fólkið* here are decorous, for the most part. We're going to descend, and you need to stay close to me. If we get separated, you'll never find your way back. Let's go.'

'I'll probably need to buy some food.'

'We'll find something, but you'd do well to get used to hunger. It can be a strong ally. There will be times when it's the only comfortable thing you can depend on.' She motioned to the doorway. 'For now, don't worry, *drengar*. We'll grab something to eat.'

Outside the room was a balcony overlooking a wide arboretum far below, filled with tall plants, ponds and green spaces. Victoria pressed a small device into Danesh's hand and led him to a break in the balustrade. He followed her instructions to activate the kernel and refused to panic as she pushed him over the edge. He tried to mask his relief as a globoid of translucent clearfibre enveloped him. Victoria floated towards the ground in her own bubble, but while she made tiny movements to hold herself with poise, Danesh struggled to remain upright. Their descent slowed as they approached the lawns, and the pearls evaporated as they made contact.

'Not as much fun as getting back up,' Victoria said blandly. 'Okay, there's no easy way to move between non-adjacent levels without a permit, which helps stop the flow of *sálirnar*. Even in an emergency, there are only a handful of escape routes, and we certainly wouldn't qualify. It's not until you get to be sub-Eight that it all changes. Something to do with the water mining, back when Tion was Formed.'

An automated deliverer approached them directly with two foil-wrapped parcels, each one the size of two fists held together. Victoria took one and indicated he should do the same. The bundle was warm and pliant.

'Burrito. It's better than the crap you're used to.'

Danesh pulled at the insulating wrapper. The pale bread stuck slightly and steamed as it broke, and the aroma excited him in a way he could not have anticipated. Saliva flooded into his mouth as he tore back the packaging and brought the contents to his lips. Some of the filling fell away, and he managed to arch his back to avoid it spoiling his clothes. It exploded on his tongue in a diversity of texture and flavour and warmth and hotness, for which he was entirely unprepared.

'You tell me to be hungry and happy, and then give me this?'

'Don't get used to it. The quality of food deteriorates as you descend.'

He watched Victoria as she expertly ate her food. She turned the tortilla as she took careful bites, and nothing was lost, and no juices escaped. She finished less than half before tossing it onto the groundplate. It dissolved into the grass seconds after it landed and Danesh realised his whole world had started to melt away. All he threw to the ground was the foil, and it too seeped into the parkland.

'We have four transitions to make, and we won't use a direct route. It's not supposed to be possible to move without permits and an audit trail because post-Forming citizens are meant to stay put. That premise was flawed, Danesh. Do you know why?' He stared at her blankly as they walked, hoping there would be somewhere he could clean his hands and chin. She did not seem to notice. 'Who provides the food for the privileged First? Who bears their precious children and processes their waste? No one wants to see those things. So passageways were built into the very world itself, with the Pallium standing guard. They are a complicated puzzle that no human could unravel or learn to navigate themselves. Still, there are those of us who can convince the FMP that an unauthorised and unrecorded transition is desirable, and can make the transition possible.'

Danesh hadn't expected a thrilling journey, and he was far more interested in who he might meet when he arrived. As they settled into a private transport capsule, he was sure the day's excitement was probably behind him. They both sat in silence in the bland vehicle, and Victoria appeared to be asleep. Danesh remained at the brink of online and stared across a multitude of information pathways, but couldn't decide which to peruse. For the first time in his life, he was indifferent. I wonder if this is what Shu-fen experiences every day, he thought.

The capsule deposited them in a station identical to the one they had left. It had the same eateries and commodity stores, and the advertising was still exquisitely tailored to Danesh's new adult persona and his unspent bursary. He looked around with all of his senses, hoping he would identify their destination in a flash of inspiration. Victoria practically ignored him, although she occasionally polled his status to ensure he kept up.

There were a great number of doors against the edges of the broad central court situated within a squat, grey building. They were all indistinguishable from each other in a relentless surge of glistening, brilliant chrome. Victoria purposefully walked towards one and issued a complex series of codes over the Smiž information network. Messages flew back and forth across the aether, and Danesh was almost able to keep up. He was aware that Victoria's heart rate had increased and her breathing had quickened. Clearly, this was not a simple negotiation. It ceased abruptly, a chime echoed across the atrium, and the substance of the door faded away. Inside was a young girl, around five years old and dressed in a simple blue smock, who stared intently at them both.

'I'm supposed to show you the way,' the *stúlka* said.

'Well, it's nice to see you again, too,' Victoria replied, and the little girl smiled. 'Here, I brought you a gift.'

Victoria pulled a small, flat package from her waistband and handed it across as the girl wandered past them. Inside the chamber were a few pieces of furniture and an alternate processor. Danesh knew information subsets could be stored away from the FMP and had heard the devices were commonplace before the Forming, but he never thought he would see an actual unit. He could not understand why anyone would want to maintain a stand-alone computer because data was only meaningful when it had access to other data. Victoria shooed him away from it and pushed him towards a curtained doorway at the back of the room. He stumbled as he stepped through the clearfibre boundary, failing to anticipate the fullerene staircase that spiralled down into the floor.

'Keep moving,' Victoria said.

As far as Danesh could guess, the steps continued indefinitely. There was no illumination, so they had to rely on a composite from background IR and acoustic returns.

'They're called *bogdos*. Some say the *forfeður* didn't know their global construction was flawed, that the controls built into the world to separate people were undermined right at the moment of Forming. I believe the ancestors were aware and wanted a way to move through Tion's levels without record. This particular passageway used to be part of a water mine. The water gushed up from K16, almost as deep as Tion goes, where the weight of construction forced it out. I don't know what the water was for or where it went. The boss says it was full of precious molecules that the *forfeður* used to build the world's concentric spheres, but I don't think that could be true: you couldn't build a world out of unwanted water.'

Danesh didn't know how to respond, so he just plodded after her, trying to make sense of the data the Pallium was throwing at his perceptions. He felt vaguely nauseous and hoped the burrito would not have its revenge.

'All that remains of this shaft is a two hundred metre drop from Third into Fourth. It's the only one for many degrees of arc. It won't take us long. After that, it will take the rest of the day to reach K7.'

Their transition to Fifth was via a freight elevator, and they crossed to Sixth on foot through an abandoned service corridor. Danesh wondered if he was close to his origins, or if he was half a world from home. He supposed it didn't matter. They took a regular transit to Seventh, which included an irregular detour through a private tollway. Victoria refused to tell him what the fees were.

Danesh mentioned he was hungry again, and Victoria laughed. When they left the pod, he was dismayed by the closeness of the corridor. The ceiling was almost within reach, and it produced a dull blue light that permeated everything. The hot air tugged at his body as they walked away from the station, stealing the moisture from his mouth. He was hemmed in by *lýðirnir*; it seemed there were people everywhere.

'Who are all these *sálirnar*? What is this building's purpose? Do *fólkið* live within it?' Danesh asked. The dry wind rushed around him and threatened to knock him off his feet. 'Will we go outside to eat?'

'This is it, kid,' Victoria said. 'We are outside. Jump up and kiss the sky if you want. For most people, there's nothing else. Just a compact living cube with at least three friends. Very cosy.'

'I don't understand,' he said.

'Why would you? It's not a life aspiration for most neweds. It's much worse for billions of others.'

They stopped in front of a dispenser, and Victoria bought food for Danesh to try. He turned the small bundle over in his hands as he searched for the edge of the protective wrapper. He dug his fingernails into it, and it gave way, like soft putty. Victoria paid no attention and continued to walk. He pulled his finger out and sniffed it. There were some residual globs on his fingertips, and he tentatively popped them into his mouth. It was definitely food, and it was definitely repugnant. He threw the mass to the floor, and it came apart with a slop. There was no process to clean it away.

'Hurry up, Danesh. I have a rig scheduled.'

The rig was not much of a vehicle. Inside it had a single seat with an elaborate harness, which Victoria did not hesitate to occupy, leaving Danesh to crouch on the floor. He was aware of the rapid acceleration as he jostled from side to side, but before long they settled into a constant speed.

'This is going to take about twenty minutes,' Victoria said. 'We have some way to go. The rig has decent food and almost reasonable amenities.' She pointed towards the back of the cab. 'Sort yourself out. I have some things I need to deal with.'

Danesh was used to *sálirnar* offlining, but Victoria ceased to exist. Her body was of course there, yet it was almost dead, instantly pallid. He leant over to touch her face, which was cold and inert. He brushed his fingers over her vacant lips and thought about kissing her. Would she know? He felt aroused and ashamed and slumped back onto the floor.

When he opened his eyes, she was there, sat watching him, with a steaming cup in her hand. She knew.

They came to a halt, and the hatch opened. Victoria set her coffee aside and climbed down to the ground. Danesh followed her and blinked in the iodine light. The moment his hand left the ladder, the rig closed itself up and hurried away. They were in front of a long building clad in a corrugated alloy, and they entered through its wide, open doorway. Victoria strode confidently into the facility, helpfully tagging various points of interest in Danesh's eyesight. He followed along and pretended to be impressed to mask his nervousness. There was something final about this place, nestled above Bodem in the heart of the tionsphere. Whatever happened inside would determine his future.

The interior was dark and functional. Victoria and Danesh walked on a fullerene web, and its delicate fibres provided solid support despite its insubstantial appearance. He could see floor after floor of similar walkways below him, and he thought the factory might spill into the kay below, although he couldn't guess how many kilometres might be accessible. There were ducts and pipes all around him, some vibrating slightly and others hot against his skin. Thick, black dust covered everything, staining his hands and clothing. Victoria appeared to be oblivious to the unpleasantness. As she led him up a series of staircases, his anxiety grew. He kept feeling phantom alerts caused by his unease. It was a nonage phenomenon which he thought he had outgrown.

'I suspect we won't meet Pazel in person today,' Victoria said. 'There might be a sending, or he could use a rehosting into a rented body, although that's not very likely. Probably just a call, I would think.'

'Then why did we come all this way?'

'Beats me.'

Victoria showed him into a small meeting room and indicated he should avoid sitting to keep the seats clean. Danesh whimpered as the door shut and he lost his Sodality access. He felt incredibly vulnerable; it reminded him of the information void in the Lacuna. Victoria touched him on the shoulder as they waited, but it did nothing to calm him.

Danesh was unprepared for anyone else to enter the room. Pazel was an elderly, squat man and was wearing a one-piece that was tight across his round belly. Danesh thought he was the ugliest *persónan* he had ever seen.

'I don't need to be connected to be able to read your status,' he said. 'Do bear that in mind in the future. Victoria, please leave us. Thank you.'

'Looks good on you,' she said and left.

Danesh tried not to observe the man too carefully. 'She tried to be nice to me,' he said and regretted his inference.

There was no response. Danesh remembered Haziq lying twisted on the floor, and he felt uneasy and remote. The past two days had left him numb, but he was not worried about his safety or fate. He wanted to sit quietly and avoid thinking.

'I'm pleased you made it here safely. I'm sure you have questions, which I shall answer in good time. I asked Victoria to bring you here because I think you'll work well in my organisation. Or you have the potential to, at least. And I usually look a little better than this.'

The plaza undulated with wave after wave of indifferent people, flowing after one another without any cognisance of their surroundings. *Fólkið* habitually distracted themselves from reality and were thoroughly dependent on the soothing embrace of online. Most could not even see the stricken man's erratic behaviour, and those that did glance his way hastily absolved themselves of any responsibility.

Joaquín had spent several hours wandering through the arcades trying to establish a connection with the Pallium. How could he be prepared for this situation? He had lived his entire life in just two places with all of his needs met. Initially, he had struggled with the realisation that he was physically outside and not operating within a simulation. The nagging hunger and desire to rest had become familiar and were now part of him. He was amazed at how quickly the flesh became his but knew it would not last long.

Busy people crowded the K4 public spaces, hurrying from place to place with precious burdens. Joaquín had nothing and no way to return home. He did not recognise himself and the FMP refused to acknowledge his former existence, just as it refused to identify the person he had become. Joaquín did not have anything to bargain with and realised his survival depended on what he could take from others until, without connection, he finally lost his ability to exist in the *māsadā-sarīra*. He wondered if he should despise himself for thinking that way.

Joaquín spotted a likely mark and followed her across the plaza. He wasn't sure what it was about her that caught his attention. She did not seem particularly affluent and was unremarkable to look at, but that was probably the attraction as maybe no one would miss her. He knew his intentions were wrong, but he attempted to assuage his guilt by speculating about his fate. There were rumours of unauthorised trade, and someone might have reassigned his body by now. The same might even be the case for his co-workers, his friends. Perhaps they had all been recycled. He would never find them among the endless people within Tion.

The woman was entirely unaware of anything except her basic environment and did not realise Joaquín was following her. He craved bland food, and his body hurt, yet he still wasn't sure what he planned to do as he copied her pre-programmed steps. Joaquín knew he needed to take things from this *persónan*, yet he didn't intend to hurt her, though she would never help him voluntarily. He wondered if this was who he would have been if he had chosen another life.

There were many opportunities for him as they progressed through the streets: covered walkways, unbolted doors and private spaces. He could reach out with his rough hand to grab her, put his arm around her throat and drag her into a quiet corner. He imagined how that would feel and how he would react to taking something from a stranger. It excited him, but he put it down to a desperate need for water and a lack of staters. He was sure she would struggle, but she would eventually yield. He could force her to take him to her accommodation, where he could clean himself up and order a fresh shirt on her account. If she fought him, he would overpower her and push his larger frame against her to take what he needed. His pulse quickened, and sweat chilled his body. She would taste sweet. He wanted her.

She entered a building through an open doorway. Joaquín checked that no one was paying attention to them and followed her in, hoping for his chance. He had anticipated her being within his grasp; however, she wasn't where he guessed she would be. Joaquín turned his head slightly to find her standing calmly with a weapon aimed at his face.

'Not too clever, unjoined.'

Shit, shit, shit, he thought and froze.

She indicated he should continue into the building and sent him curt Smiž messages to provide directions. He could not understand how she had obtained the body's TUID so she could address him. Each time he slowed his steps, she silently jabbed him in the back with the gun, and he felt his earlier excitement dissolve into a certainty that he would soon die.

They reached a small precinct in a residential complex. The *kona* pushed Joaquín to the groundplate and all but ignored him while she made some calls. He watched as she unconsciously mouthed her inaudible questions and tried to decipher what she was saying. He became calm and stopped worrying about his future. His day wasn't going to get much worse.

'I don't know who you are, but you're using one of our rentals, and you're not authorised. It means you're a crook or an idiot.'

Joaquín didn't reply. He felt like an idiot.

'You have no idea why you're here.' Again, he did not reply. 'This is what we're going to do. You're going to tell me who you are and I'm going to give you access, funds and some decent clothes. In a few days, when you're in better shape, we'll get you working for us. You're wearing a valuable asset, and if we don't get a return on this particular investment, then you've got nowhere to stay. Your turn.'

This time he didn't hesitate. He spoke about his profession, his workmates and the circumstances that brought him here. He asked her to check on his friends, and she said she couldn't find them. They speculated about the point-to-point sabotage and what it might mean. He said his name was Joaquín, but he didn't know who that was any more. She said it didn't matter, re-registered his name against a bogus identification and topped up his credit.

As soon as he was alone, he onlined and made his way to the nearest concourse. He rented a room and ordered food and new clothes. He took two cycles in a cleantube and studied his unfamiliar body in a wrap-around ve-mirror. This *einstaklingur* has been through a lot, he thought. There were bruises and scars, patches of hair missing and pits in his flesh left by cheap surgical procedures. He did not like the look of this man.

Joaquín ate again, dressed and combed his dark, wavy hair into place. He finally felt okay.

CHAPTER FOUR
Nikora
বর্তমানে

SHU-FEN HAD struggled to keep up with the man who bound and dragged them through the tunnels. Afterwards, she was grateful to ditch her bloodied clothes and huddled with the other children, holding Danesh tightly. The lead man asked Danesh to choose between them, and she cried out in anguish as she realised he had discarded her. She had always expected him to leave her, but nothing as ghastly as this. She loved him, and he walked away with their abuser.

For a moment, she hated him.

Then she rationalised that he had not abandoned her but made a choice that would protect them both in some way. He was diffusing the situation and would find a way back to her. Or maybe he was ensuring their captors got what they wanted to appease them. His actions were born out of devotion. Shu-fen relaxed a little.

Ahmad, Humaira and Zara were withdrawn and entirely compliant. She did not care and felt no responsibility for them, but she knew she could shield herself with them and hide behind their docility. Shu-fen did not resist when the old, black woman pulled Ahmad away, but clung to the other girls and shivered with them. The man called Feliu said they would be kept together for a quick sale before inserting a compeller into her *sikatā-ātamā*. As it drifted down on her mind, she wondered if she should be concerned. And then she could not remember why she was anxious and followed along with the other new women.

It seemed Pazel Sad-Tet-Ain-Resh wore his name with the same indifference he showed for his *māsadā-sarīra*. Danesh couldn't understand why anyone would contrive an outrightsider TUID and concluded he had disguised himself ironically. Despite his gruff countenance, he appeared to be genuinely interested in the journey between levels and asked for detailed descriptions of specific steps along the way. Although Danesh didn't warm to him, he felt almost safe, and his earlier apprehension waned.

They remained in the same room, far from the welcome glow of Sodality. Pazel explained he was easily distracted by online and asked Danesh to prepare for a new experience. He apologised for dragging him through the kays and suggested there was a more elegant way to move around Tion.

'I'm going to open up a socket for a particular protocol,' he said. 'Please don't waste any time trying to hack through it. You'll have plenty of opportunity for that later.'

Danesh was aware when Pallial access became possible and resisted the urge to exploit his slight knowledge of informatics. A fist-sized red button appeared in his eyesight, with an orbiting ve-label tempting him to *Press Here*. He looked at Pazel, who nodded. Danesh put his hand on the icon and was amazed at how real it felt. It functioned with an audible click and started to suck at his fingers. Pazel was calmly watching, so Danesh didn't resist. He felt the virtual maw syphon his arm and felt his body begin to stretch and melt. His breathing stopped, and he knew his heart was no longer pumping, and then somehow, his head had also squeezed through the small aperture. Just as he began to relish the void, he was pushed through another conduit, stepping away from the exit.

Danesh almost tripped over because his centre of gravity was too high. He thrust his hands out to break his fall and was shocked by their pinkness. He sprawled on the floor.

'Relax,' an unfamiliar voice said. 'We're here. Pick yourself up and follow me.'

'Where are we?' Danesh's low voice sounded strange.

'The Interdiction. The FMP. Amid the second kilometre into the tionsphere. It's a space that can't possibly exist because it's supposed to be one continuous machine.' The man talking to him was of indeterminate race, more mature than Danesh but not old. 'This isn't a simulation. We really are here, in this flesh. We've borrowed them for the afternoon. I'm still Pazel, and you're still Danesh. No one can enter or leave this level,' he laughed. 'It doesn't exist, so how could we? I wanted to show you something you'll never forget to help you understand what is at stake.'

Danesh found he was already used to his new senses. They were both dressed in snug-fitting tunics and calico shorts. Pazel pointed to the door and motioned Danesh to leave. The view beyond the small room was breathtaking and surpassed anything he could have imagined. The world was an expansive and lush place, filled with flawless, beautiful people, but its quantum quietness was shocking. 'There is no Sodality here. How can I know them? How can they live?'

They settled on a bench overlooking a pond where some children played. 'These *lýðirnir* are Tion's destiny, Danesh. One day they will rebuild the world and create a future in their own image. I have so much I want to share with you, but there are some things I should attend to while we're here. I'll return soon. Please ensure I don't have to track you down.'

Danesh didn't look over his shoulder to watch Pazel depart. The only proof he had of this person's identity was his say-so, plus the possibility that he, himself, was loitering in someone else's body. The more he considered what was supposedly happening, the less likely it seemed. Danesh was not ready to trust Pazel and picked up a sharp stone from the path. It hurt when he ripped it over the pale palm of his hand and blood dripped onto the yellow tunic. He hastily unbuttoned it and tore off a strip to bind the wound, feeling somewhat uneasy about his situation.

Danesh glanced at the children on the grass. They all looked perfectly happy and alive. He sat back to study them and tucked his overlong legs beneath the bench. His hand throbbed, and he felt foolish and tried to cover his body. One of the children loitered nearby, staring at him. Danesh was unable to infer what she was thinking or what her emotional state was. He felt incredibly alone amongst all this exuberant life. She walked towards him solemnly and clasped his hand, turning it over, examining his rough bandage.

'Why did you do that?' she asked.

'I don't know,' he said simply. 'I wanted to be sure I was real.'

She continued to gaze at him, smiled, then turned abruptly and ran back to her friends.

There were no data services to help him draw conclusions. Danesh had nothing to bargain with and could see no way to profiteer from the things around him. Once he had determined he was entirely dependent on Pazel, he was content just being. It was warm, so he removed the torn shirt and rolled it into a ball, lay across the bench and pushed it under his head. He stayed as still as he could, with his fingertips resting on his chest and held his breath, surprised at how long he could last. He could feel his heart beating slower and slower, and he drifted into a light sleep.

When Pazel woke him, he didn't comment on the cut on Danesh's hand, he just pushed his legs aside and sat down. Danesh felt refreshed and inspected his wound. The bleeding had stopped, and it looked like it would heal in a few days. He showed it to Pazel.

'We can't stay much longer,' he said. 'I've only arranged for one hundred minutes each. I must say I'm interested to see how you used the majority of yours. No matter. Poor Tion is about to face a crisis, one that anyone could have predicted. At the post-Forming zenith, growth was the only manifesto. The *forfeður* commissioned an enormous world, which was crying out for *sálirnar* to occupy it. So, they generated a population, most en masse, a privileged few in utero, and they all became reliable consumers, and so on. They begat a bold solution, yet once Tion was full, it reinvigorated the original problem the Forming was designed to resolve, identical in every way except for its enormous scale.'

Danesh looked at him without comprehension.

'These *sálirnar* living here will be the population of a new world. Not you or I, well, not yet. We can't remain in these rented skins because our data degrades without a Pallial connection to maintain it. The future of Tion will be orderly, organised and well-maintained. When we're ready, there will be millions of people hidden within the Pallium itself, ready to start anew. We have to keep them safe because there are countless others outside who will do almost anything to join them.' Pazel reached for an icon that only existed in his eyesight, and his essence faded from the borrowed *māsadā-sarīra*.

Danesh tried to remember the specific details of everything he could see. Three soft chimes rang in his ears, and he was reasonably sure it was a genuine sound and not an artefact. There was a short gap before a fourth, longer chime, which ripped him from this body and crammed him back into his weaker self. He wondered how anyone could be blasé about shifting between flesh. Danesh wanted to flop into one of the chairs around the edge of the meeting room but remembered what Victoria had said about keeping his dirt-stained clothes off the furniture. He looked at his hand, which was small, filthy but unharmed, and took a breath that was too deep for him. He spluttered unexpectedly.

'You'll get used to switching *māsadā-sarīra* soon enough,' the pot-bellied man laughed. 'Get yourself cleaned up and I'll send someone when I'm ready for you.'

'Who actually are you?' Danesh asked awkwardly. 'This isn't you.'

The dwarf grinned. 'I can't say that I can rightly remember, I've swapped out so much. The real me probably doesn't exist any more. Not to worry, eh?'

The door opened, and Sodality blossomed back into the room. Danesh's instructions appeared in the form of bouncy, friendly graphics showing him which way to leave, so he complied. Danesh hoped he would be able to bathe again, but the small chamber he was guided to only had a simple cleantube and recycling bin, so he disposed of his clothes and made use of the facilities. Afterwards, he waited in the warm air, enjoying the magnitude of online and burrowing into areas he had never even imagined. He was startled when Victoria arrived and presented him with a clean jumpsuit.

'Impressive, isn't it? You'd hardly expect it to be true.'

'Perhaps it's not,' Danesh countered.

'I can see why Pazel might like you.'

Once he had dressed, he meekly followed Victoria to another meeting room. He was passingly familiar with open spaces in the Sixes but began to feel that outside was a concept that didn't apply to him. Danesh wasn't sure what to make of his short episode in Second, or whether it should even be trusted. He thought about the things that had happened and about the contrast with his life before. Could all of his memories be artificial?

'Are you rested?' Victoria asked.

He nodded, and she indicated he should make himself comfortable.

'Pazel wants me to bring you up to speed with his operation. You should feel privileged, as most of us can only piece together the things we can access. It's going to be a bit strange. Once the procedure is complete, you'll have subsumed a lot of his experiences. It will be part of who you are, and you'll probably struggle to remember who you were before. If you would join me in the vestibule, we can make a start.'

Hyun-jun opened his eyes. Enzo's angular jaw was centimetres from his face. He had an uncertain look about him, but he drew his half-staff and pushed it into the smaller man's cheek.

'Where are they?' he demanded. 'Did you see them leave?'

'No,' Hyun-jun said truthfully. 'Perhaps Noemí sent for them.' He looked up and down the corridor, but there was no sign of the company, their possessions or disappearance. The floor was clean and, apart from Enzo's food sack, offered no clues. 'Perhaps,' Hyun-jun repeated. 'I think we should move out.'

The TUID attached to the fresh *māsadā-sarīra* had access to a reasonable expense account. Even though it was a different body, the alien *sikatā-ātamā* now nestling within Rabindra could still feel the dirt that had seeped into the skin and a cleantube would not suffice. He walked away from the coalface and through the barracks, into the arcade. There were three water shops in the directory, so he requested details of their clientele to determine where the affluent spent their staters. The receptionist in the most sophisticated store chattered at him and continually pointed at the rows of glass sarcophaguses; however, Rabindra brushed her aside and directed his enquiry at the manager app. The software negotiated with him for a short time before posting directions in his eyesight. The upper rooms of a single-sex bordello offered him the exact service he required.

Rabindra relinquished his clothes in the lobby and padded up the narrow staircase. He had never cared what people called him; each body came with its own name, which he always assumed because every TUID was as irrelevant as the last. He was indifferent to the people he had deposed; each discarded *sikatā-ātamā* was immaterial. Fatigue nagged at his borrowed bones, yet while he did not feel robust, he was the master of his purloined flesh. It did not argue with him any more than it complained, and he was whole again. The bedroom was surprisingly clean, compact and unoccupied, and at the foot of the bed was a small bath. He shrugged the bordello's overpriced menu aside and set the temperature to forty-six degrees. The water surged up while remaining entirely still, waiting to receive him. Rabindra tucked his limbs into its warmth, his head, his back, his shins pressed against the bath's smooth sides. He lay on his side with his elbows resting on his thighs and his hands supporting his jaw, and let the water ease the past away. It was a ritual of sorts, a preparation for whatever was to come, a bonding with his new self. Rabindra soaked in silence and eventually slept without using an oneironaut to navigate him through his restless dreams.

When he woke, Rabindra had been lifted onto the bed and wrapped in scented, white sheets. He held a brown hand in front of his face and studied his fingers, watching the way the unfamiliar joints moved. His Pallial connection was robust, and the rehosting was explicit, they belonged to him, but it was only ever a partial ghosting, and he knew his true self raged somewhere beyond the coalface. He did not care to look because it angered him to see what he had become. Perhaps he had loved her after all and had made the right choice, even if the consequences were more than he could bear. The familiar taste of suppressed fury flooded up his throat, and he had to divert it away, his punishment was not her fault.

He opened his assumed TUID's inbox. It contained a series of messages: one included a passphrase reminder and a link to an unopened ve-package, so he contracted a *thráfstis* to prowl around Rabindra's private files and recent searches. Youssef Damaru-Da-Te-Epsilon would be the focus of his attention.

The man was squatting with his arms wrapped around his legs and his chin on his knees. He looked like he was trying to contain himself, so Nikora knew it had to be his first rehosting. She couldn't remember the first time she had melted into a new body, and now every *māsadā-sarīra* felt the same, even her own. He stared through her as if submerged in Sodality, but the tightness around his eyes betrayed his offline status. He evidentially did not know how to put himself on hold. Nikora had not long retrieved the occupied *māsadā-sarīra* when Pazel's flunky requested a meeting. It still wasn't apparent if the body's user might offer her a decent replacement point-to-point technician.

Nikora was content to be distracted because she despised talking to Pazel's staff. Their proximity to her long-standing friend provided them with a false intimacy, of which she did not approve. He delighted in their fawning and referred to them all as his adherents, and this made them even more presumptuous.

She placed a return call to Victoria. *What do you want? I'm in the middle of something.*

Shall I send through to your location, Nikora?

No, I don't think that will be necessary. It was essential to maintain an appearance of authority, but Nikora had to be careful not to offend Pazel. In her opinion, he was overly sensitive when it came to his employees.

He wants to know what you're planning to do with the pointports. It's been hours since you screwed up and he's not pleased at all.

Nikora clenched her jaws and took a deep breath. Nothing registered in the call for a few seconds. *Tell him it was a small, isolated issue, and I instigated the broader damage to protect his investment.*

What guarantee can you give?

Why don't you put me through to him?

Nikora finished tracing the *maður*'s rehosting. The ghost originated from a routeing elucidarium in the Fives and carried the appropriate authorisations. He had spent a few hours in one of the damaged pointports, before submitting an evaluation to an assize. She released a data miner to obtain a copy of the report discretely and waited for Pazel to connect.

Victoria tells me there's no need to worry. Take all the time you need. Did she sort out your little problem? Why don't you pop over so we can chat?

An access icon appeared, and she accepted his summons. Pazel was working in his favourite office in the Sevens. Nikora didn't care for the damp chill and switched off her simulacrum's sensations, watching him tend to one of the air plants growing from the chamber walls.

'I do enjoy seeing you,' he said. 'We really should try to spend some physical time together.'

Nikora studied the epiphyte in his hands. She thought the plant was probably dead. 'Everyone's so busy. It's probably a function of the population. There are so many more *sálirnar* to stay in touch with these days. Everyone has so much they need to do.'

'Yes, yes.' He slowly stripped the knife-like leaves away with his fingers. 'Mehdi tells me there's a *forfeður* process that some of those busy people covet. Once activated, it restores the user's physiological systems to a preselected state, prevents ageing and repairs injuries. That sort of thing. He said you'd discussed it.'

'You mean the *raja'a*? I'm aware of the process.'

Pazel set the plant back into the wall. 'He mentioned a man called Youssef Damaru-Da-Te-Epsilon. He's been prolific in his recent online interactions and raised a few flags. It turns out that Youssef is almost as old as you, my dear. What surprises me is that you're already trying to locate him. I have to say that Mehdi was somewhat disappointed you didn't ask him to join the search. I hope you're not working independently of me, Nikora.'

'Mehdi has enough to worry about as curator of your flesh.' An incoming call blinked in her eyesight. 'Even if this *maður* is a lifer there's no indication he's using specialist tech we do not already possess. How many times have we had this conversation, Pazel? Mehdi asked me to look into it, and I'll let him know what I find.'

Pazel wiped his hands on the front of his suit. 'Will you tell the Curator you placed a contract to acquire this Youssef, or shall I?' He indicated one of the benches flowing out of the wall and surrounded by luxuriant ferns. 'Please, sit with me. It makes me feel better, even though you're not physically here.' She allowed him to take her simulated hand to lead her to the seat. 'There's a lovely independent taverna in the Fours. We could meet tonight for supper. It has a sea view.'

Nikora laughed despite herself. 'Maybe on another evening. I promise you to notify you if I make any progress with Youssef. It will be hard to persuade him to share the bioapp with me.'

Pazel cut a red flower from a large bromeliad at his side and offered it to her. 'Why don't you stay with me, instead of hiding amongst work crews with those terrible *fólkið*?'

'I can't take it with me, Pazel. You should have let it flourish. I'll message you.' She saw the flower fall to the floor as she ended the call.

The ghosted *māsadā-sarīra* continued to stare at her, and she pointed at it to warn the user to be patient. She realised Pazel would not rest until he had the *raja'a*. Although the bioapp might release him from endless genomods, he desired it only because it existed. His aspiration for longevity was somewhat exotic and not particularly aligned with Nikora's way of thinking. For her, it was less complex. She wanted a guarantee beyond the Pallium.

She ran a trace on the missed call. It originated in Eighth, and she waited for the TUID to be unsuppressed. Pazel had not told her how he planned to implement the disunion and claim Tion for his people, but she knew he did not anticipate opposition from K1 and the levels below. Without referring to her logs, she could not recall when he first discussed the finality of his intentions, and in truth, she did not care. By unspoken agreement, she would join his adherents, but she did not want to be dependent on him in any way, which is what had sparked her interest in the *raja'a*. Nikora anticipated a future where her unallocated staters had no meaning, and the costs of survival would be more personal. In her darker moments, she was scared of what that might mean and wondered if the bioapp represented a sentence, not salvation. Nikora would not wait for two decades until Pazel was ready. When she eventually located the solution, she would incorporate it swiftly and without hesitation. She had already made her choice. The trace returned and confirmed that she had gained Youssef's attention. Nikora tongued through tiresome Sodality pages until he called.

You're not where you're supposed to be [*K3 location*], Youssef said. *There are some questions I would like to ask, and it will be better in person.*

My name is Nikora, and I don't know where your friend is. Instead, I have a question for you about your designation. She thought he would drop, but the messaging service confirmed that he was still present. *Does it pre-date the Forming, Youssef?*

Why should I confide in you?

Because we have much in common: I no longer have any interest in the forfeður, *but I am interested in their methods. You must want something in return. I have a few things to attend to, but please join me in my hotel in an hour* [K4 location]. She did not let him respond.

Joaquín Ghha-Qui-Baluda-Tlu had compiled the point-to-point evaluation, and his TUID subsequently registered as absconded-on-assignment. A note on the assize report said a compulsory caching voucher was an option for the rest of his work crew. Nikora thought this would help keep things contained, and hacked into the file with an approval. She hadn't decided what to do with him when he completes his work.

Once Youssef gave the *raja'a* to her, she would have to decide about Pazel. They had been acquaintances since the early days of the Forming. If she failed to disclose the bioapp, he would see it as a betrayal, but if he had access to it, he would be reckless with its use and her advantage would be lost. She considered her future without him and was unalarmed by how little he mattered. *Sálirnar* routinely left her world and were readily replaced by others. Long life was a commodity just like any other.

Nikora stepped towards Joaquín and pulled him to his feet. He appeared calm, and she worried that he might be plotting his escape, so she used the gun to punctuate her words until his former nervousness returned. She threatened him and offered him hope, and he repaid her with everything he knew about the pointport damage. When he asked about his friends, she was non-committal, but she gave him a fresh TUID and some staters and said she'd be in touch.

There had been almost two hundred leads to follow up, scattered across seven degrees, but even so, it appeared Connor had not managed to leave the level. If there had been one or two, Youssef might have attended to them in person, but there wasn't sufficient time, so he sauntered back to the barracks to work via his quantum progeny. A high proportion had been straightforward sightings. Connor had been clumsily wearing someone else's identity but made no other attempt to hide as he walked away from the coalface. The witnesses re-ran their experiences and augmented them with archived records from their surroundings, which were conveniently accessible through Youssef's recently acquired credentials. A small number of people retraced their steps to see if they had missed anything.

Eleven *sálirnar* had sat with him in a capsule as it drifted through the Lacuna with subsonic lethargy. Youssef had not imagined his search to utilise more than a fraction of the population but was surprised that all-bar-two passengers hosted his outline *sikatā-ātamā*. He hadn't expected to intersect with Connor and decided the remaining individual, a perfectly slender *kona* with dark hair that tumbled across her pale shoulders, was either his accomplice or his captor. Most of the passengers had been distracted, and Youssef was unable to discern if they had any relationship.

When the bus docked, the two *lýðirnir* were the last to disembark, and none of his imprints saw them together again. There was nothing for a further quarter of an hour, after which all subsequent contacts were data-rich. A woman who served him hoofoo. The owner of a karaoke studio, offering to help select the ideal song. A personal trainer who pumped him full of performance drugs. A dozen perfect interactions throughout the day, all of them full-sensory with lots of correlating factors in the Pallial Truth. It set Youssef's teeth on edge because they were too contrived and too uniformly spaced; it appeared someone intended him to follow the trail.

He decided to let his copies do their work without his oversight and disconnected. Some people enjoyed solitude, but it left Youssef feeling edgy and exposed. It is the nature of *fólkið* to root things out, and it is the chase that excites them, he thought. It triggers endorphins, and they become addicted to the data. He tried stretching out and snoozing, but the noises surrounding him—usually lulled away by better distractions—drove him out of the dormitory in search of a diversion. He made his way to a playpen at the back of the workers' quarters, reviewed the day's agenda and chose an imagery session. Leaving his workwear in the waste bin at the door, he entered the warm chamber and received a Sodality access code. There were two *konurnar* entwined on a podium, and some of the surrounding workers were staring at them intently as they constructed images. The women stayed locked in their embrace for several minutes before slipping into a new pose. The rest of the men were unashamedly enjoying the spectacle. Youssef sat and attempted to immerse himself in the scene. The *konurnar* were young but experienced, and although their flesh was as real as his, it failed to stir any emotion in him. He told himself he wasn't already sexually over-stimulated by online encounters, and that it didn't matter. Youssef concentrated on them until he ultimately succumbed.

After the session, the women chatted idly with the men, studying the photos and admonishing those who hadn't cared about composing their shots. Some of the workers stayed behind to relax, but Youssef was no longer interested, and besides, it had been over an hour since he had commenced his hunt for Connor. He cleaned himself up and took some sealed workwear in case he needed to leave the barracks. When he onlined, the sale price for the discarded data from his search greeted him. He was pleased that Rabindra had not opened the ve-package, and diverted sufficient funds for the foreman to think that Youssef had amended his balance through a sophisticated hacker's trick. The remaining staters would suffice for the coming days.

None of the surviving outline *sikatā-ātamā* had arrived at a useful conclusion before folding, and for a time Youssef did not know what his next move would be. There had been no new interactions, and he did not have time to start hunting from scratch, so he settled in to review each contact in turn. There was no recurrent thread, no mutual companion-in-common, and no linked activity or suspicious pattern. All he could fathom was that Connor welcomed observation.

Or he was being displayed.

Lýðirnir are not always what they appear, he pondered. Connor is not an *einstaklingur* undercover; instead, he is transparent about his experiences and aspirations, and I can read him. He has either left of his own accord or accompanied someone under duress. If it is the former, then he won't want to see me; if it is the latter, then he needs me more than ever.

'You're a difficult man to locate.' Rabindra, smug with his cleverness, was dressed for an expedition beyond the coalface and its surrounds. He lowered a bag from his shoulder and clasped his hands behind his back. 'Get yourself ready,' he said. 'Assizes are coming for us, and I want to spend the staters you've promised me. There's more to you than I thought and my prospects are probably better with you around. Come on, let's go.'

The situation was not working out the way Youssef planned. He certainly wasn't accustomed to a travelling companion and didn't know how to respond. He posted some data on the wall as evidence they both had a better chance alone, but Rabindra had made his decision and would not back down. There was an assuredness about the foreman that Youssef was positive wasn't usual, so he rummaged through his dailies to try to make sense of things. As he suspected, his references to his boss were a catalogue of expletives: there was nothing with which to compare this *maður*. Youssef did not know where they were going, but it probably didn't matter. He would start with Connor's last sighting, a mid-life woman half a minute of arc away, and work backwards. Hopefully, the supervisor would lose interest when he realised there was nothing to gain from accompanying him.

It was going to take about fifteen minutes to reach the *miðaldra-kona*, irrespective of how they travelled. Youssef elected to walk and offered Rabindra a private line so they could talk. His datrix, the artificial microbes installed at conception, located the fibre as soon as it broke his skin and their myriad interconnections delved into his nervous system. He waited for Rabindra's thoughts to reach him, but he was silent, and for a while, he tagged along at the end of the invisible tether. When Rabindra finally did pose an unspoken question, it cut to the nub of the matter.

How old are you?

Thirty-two, he replied truthfully.

Rabindra considered that. *How long have you been in your thirties?*

Youssef smiled and broke the delicate data fibre, admitting the truth by forgoing an answer.

'I've arranged to meet someone who may know what happened to Connor. You might as well find somewhere to wait.'

Youssef started sorting through his messages. There was a warning from his overseer that the cybercytes that maintained his physique were overdue an audit and had probably drifted, and a request to review investment proposals within his portfolio. The remainder was junk, and Youssef could not be bothered to delete it. He knew he should sign up for a service to manage the trivialities of his life, but it was best to restrict his interactions to his overseer, even if it meant things were untidy. He purchased two K3 identities so they could freely up-level, and was delighted that he could claim a forty per cent rebate if he relinquished them once they had arrived at their destination. If used correctly, the purloined TUIDs would not arouse suspicion.

Nikora Vayanna-Yayanna-Vayanna-Cheh was not at her published location, so Youssef called her. Their brief conversation left him feeling annoyed: the *kona* had faked her participation in his search in an attempt to acquire the *raja'a*. It came as no surprise that she had identified him, but he told Rabindra the woman had given him some new information. The foreman regarded him suspiciously but did not comment. Youssef straightened his workwear and said they would visit a tailor once they arrived in Third. He noted Rabindra's expression and advised him to relax while creating an automated task to pull background information on him. Rabindra requested a pod without comment, and their pre-paid journey was unhurried and uneventful. A five-level ascent was unusual, but there were a few professions that required inter-level transit, and they were both credible reconstruction workers. Youssef had no intention of stopping off to meet with Nikora. He rented a suite in a busy district and told Rabindra he was expecting a guest to up-level for the evening.

Youssef was troubled by this unexpected companion who had no interest in Connor's disappearance and a consuming indifference to their destination. Was it possible that this individual, with his standard schooling and mediocre leadership training, a decade's experience as an Eighth foreman and little-demonstrated ambition for progression, would whimsically decide to partake of such a gamble? None of the character projections Youssef ran supported this supposition, and his gut concurred. *Sálirnar* subscribe to whatever they place in their profile, he reminded himself, it keeps them in check and maintains their relationships and status, while the Pallium monitors any deviations and corrects noteworthy errors. Was

Rabindra's unexpected departure from his usual patterns significant? Was he resisting intervention, or was there something more unlikely? He was sat motionless in the adjacent room, happily absorbed in Sodality, and even this was atypical for the ill-tempered man.

Youssef closed his eyes and scrutinised his gathered data morsels. Two men, Connor and Rabindra, both were exhibiting anomalous behaviours, forcing him from his quiet, necessary routine. Imposed choices that exposed his true self for anyone with the desire to chase him down. A disproportionate number of people slaved to the FMP to sift through binary dross, *mennirnir* and *konurnar* indefinitely bound to each other. Contrived sightings of his good friend, possibly designed to lure him out, unless he truly was a simple bystander.

He tongued through his dailies and lingered on an unjoined from the *valse huis*. The man had no connection and was presumably sidelined by others who had fled, left behind to flounder in a barrage of extracted metals. He was a casualty of the regenerators' inevitable progress, and if he had made his home in some other degree, progress might have spared him. His life wasn't regulated or monitored, so he was free to follow his desires, but it hadn't saved him. Youssef replayed the *eldri-maður*'s last moments and marvelled at the difference between him being conscious and consigned to oblivion. There would be no clue to his humanity in the Pallial Truth and nothing that would be traceable. This lost man was an unfortunate spectator too.

'I like this arc's fashion. I think these clothes will look good on me.'

Rabindra appeared rested, but it was the entire lack of self-congratulatory bravado that struck Youssef. He was sure the man he had worked for was gone, as if he had drifted away during their journey.

'You should open the ve-package.' Youssef didn't think he was likely to leave.

Rabindra's stance was different, with a readiness in his musculature: he clearly anticipated his next opportunity. Was his body composition different? It was hard to say. Youssef routinely discarded any imagery he acquired, so there was nothing with which to compare, and he wondered when the change of *sikatā-ātamā* might have occurred.

Rabindra smoothed the front of his shirt. 'There was once a man called Kamsa who convinced himself an unborn *maður* would be the one to cache him. Even the notion of his potential caching infuriated him. Kamsa had a cruel nature, and eventually, all of his associates broke their connections with him. He spent years amassing staters to buy processing time with which to run an insane search routine and finally narrowed his prospective nemesis down to just one of eight future *börnin*. Shortly after each one's conception, he broke into the gestorium and smashed the *ungbarn*'s shell with his bare hands; however, the Pallium predicted his actions and assigned an assize called Vasudeva to identify the eighth child before he hatched. Vasudeva forced her way into the facility and stole the boy away, substituting a *stúlka* in his place. When Kamsa realised he became enraged, but he disappeared into the Pretermissions to avoid detection. The girl grew into a beautiful *ný-kona* and hunted Kamsa into the Sixteens. When she found him, she revealed her brother, Krishna, was alive and had become a talented cachier. Kamsa offlined and fled, planning to live without the Pallium, but his data dependency overwhelmed him and as he connected his caching took place.'

Youssef regarded him cautiously. 'I have heard this tale before; none of us can avoid the inevitable. Yet while I don't care what you've done with Rabindra, I care what happens to me. You haven't been honest, and I don't trust you.'

'I intend to be nondescript and inconspicuous, and I refuse to share in Kamsa's fate. Thank you, but I won't be opening Rabindra's ve-package if you don't mind. I already have a few resources at my disposal, and I would like to go shopping.'

Youssef laughed heartily and held out his hand by way of introduction.

The man clasped it in both hands and smiled back. '*Baṛhiyā*,' he said.

In the gaps, in the places of clarity where he knew who he was and what he represented, Connor forced himself to reflect on his change of circumstances. He was sure she was doing this. She was there when Connor had woken up, a good half hour before any of the other men, and sat watching him. She used a soft finger to silence his flustered questions and smoothed him until he was alert. It only took her three words to tempt him to follow, and he hoped for the fourth time in his life that he might find release. In one rushed heartbeat, he obediently agreed to do everything she said.

Their exchange was a cordial, polite discussion between strangers. She didn't try to get to know him and thwarted his attempts to discover who she was. The anxiety of his uncertainty welled up when they reached the transit, and Connor realised her motives were not the same as his. He had already missed the start of his shift, and even if he arrived late, Rabindra would dock his pay. So Connor had decided to board the busy pod and sat offline opposite her. She asked how he had ended up in the Eights, if that was the life he had aspired to and he admonished her, hoping a degree of forcefulness would encourage her to explain her intent. Their conversation subsequently waned.

As they arrived, she explained she was in some difficulty and had enlisted him to help her slip away. She had chosen Connor because he seemed trustworthy and was an early riser. Hadn't he seen her watching him? She wanted Connor to wear an identity-repeater and be conspicuous. In return, she would pay for his time and offered a price that would keep him out of the barracks for a year or more. Connor said he didn't understand how she could reassign her TUID, but if it were possible, he would do his best. Her name was Grace Mu-Tlo-Ue-Jhan.

Connor found his first few assignments exciting. It had been a long time since he had eaten anything that delighted him, and he asked his waitress if she would trace the individual that made his hoofoo meal. Her response was a blank stare, but Connor didn't mind. Next Grace sent him to a speakeasy, and he spent fifteen minutes in unfamiliar luxury. He moved from place to place: a brief journey and a handful of minutes to indulge. Whatever Grace had done must have been reasonably bad to justify the expense of his day's entertainments.

She sent Connor to a high shop where he received a pre-paid course of gases. It left him feeling nauseous and uncertain, and he sent Grace a message asking for her to moderate his tasks. He became concerned it was a test to see what she could make him do. For the first time, he panicked. What if there was no threat to her existence or if she was using him for her own amusements? She sent Connor to a depot to hand-deliver a package. She said its contents weren't relevant and he shouldn't concern himself with its recipient. When Connor told her he wouldn't carry something if he didn't know what it was, he felt her push him aside and take over his body as if it had always been hers to use. He was distraught and impotent and couldn't understand why he had agreed to accompany her. He could sense her intent. Grace would ultimately kill him.

He relied on the gaps. Occasionally, after Grace had enacted a deed, there was time during which nothing happened. He pounced on those opportunities for self-awareness, but he didn't rebel. Connor studied her intentions, looked for patterns and tried to understand this *einstaklingur* who had seized control, the way he might inspect someone's work at the coalface. He was compliant, and each activity demanded less of her attention. His eventual defiance rewarded him with two faces stolen from her *sikatā-ātamā*, a woman and a man, before she clamped down on his free will. The woman was just another unknown, but the other was his good buddy Youssef.

Connor was comfortable with oblivion. As a man who felt awkward in Sodality, it was a familiar place. He was rarely entirely disconnected but he also rarely looked. When he closed his eyes, before sleep, he would float in vacuity, so when Grace displaced him, it did not take long to find himself again. The experience reminded Connor of being aware of a dream as it was unfolding: a conscious unconsciousness. Tion exists for countless *sálirnar*, Connor thought, so if my captor was concerned with Youssef, then I must be her lure. Grace was illicitly rehosting him.

Connor wondered how she had persuaded the Pallium to handle the transfer. The ghosting wasn't complete, and he decided she must be using unauthorised software. Even so, Connor couldn't fathom how Grace had so easily displaced him and felt he had no control over his own self. He could no more stop her than he could tell his body to stop being alive, although he suspected the FMP would readily send that instruction when Grace obtained a caching voucher. Connor had not faced his mortality before and tried not to imagine a nonexistence where he couldn't find himself. Connor did not want to let her do this, to cast his sentience aside and deny him his right to being. He searched for a hook into reality and something to cling to in the gaps because he could not wait for Grace to let him go. Connor had taken a silver ring because its pale blue stone was enchanting. Where had he left the things that defined him? He needed to reassert his dominance over his flesh so he could warn

Youssef of the danger, whatever it was. He had no idea what else Grace might want from him.

Who was Youssef? Connor tried to remember his friend. He was nothing special, an absent-minded but decent man working in reconstruction, yet he afforded Connor a sense of normality. Why was he important to Grace? He doubted it was a lovers' quarrel. Who then? If Grace had no interest, she had to be working for someone else. Connor had no way to determine who this might be. Youssef rarely spoke of his time before the coalface, and even if Connor had a connection, he did not know how to generate the appropriate query. All he had was a vague unease and a feeling of inadequacy. There had to be a way to contact Youssef.

Connor had to prepare for Grace to return. She might stop pushing his *sikatā-ātamā* aside if she felt she could once again trust him. He had to make her see he could behave, so she would send him out for Youssef to find. He constructed the notion in the most precise way he could, as an awareness of her desire to acquire Youssef. He refined his visualisation and moulded it to what he hoped would entice her ego and possessed the thought in sharp focus. She had to notice it next time she slipped into him. He held the notion very still. When it tried to evolve, he forced it back to his design. Sometimes his task was impossible. When it tried to escape, he corralled it and constrained it to its optimal shape. It was like attempting to silence an unwelcome melody that monotonously prevented sleep, but Connor persevered, and in good fortune, Grace arrived to discover its stable presentation. She instantly knew what it meant.

'You cannot deceive me, Connor. I won't allow you to disappear into the Dens.'

He felt the shackles ease from his personality, and he had one opportunity. *There is a better way to acquire Youssef. Accompany me, as you did before: he'll come.* The blackness hurtled towards him and engulfed Connor's awareness. He assumed it was death and welcomed its caress.

There was a message in Nikora's hotel room from Youssef: she could up-level and join him in person, or he'd happily take a call. Nikora requested three times her bodily water content for her ablutions, which she estimated would give her almost ten minutes to think. She had no interest in going out and arranged for the room's communications sentinel to accept his simulacrum. The water was approved, and she shed her clothes and kicked them into the waste, before standing motionless in the shower. Warm vapour enveloped her as she thought about what she would say to him, and for a time, she enjoyed the sensation. All too soon the FMP warned her that her purchase was almost complete, so she requested an additional body's worth, not caring about the disruption to her schedule.

The room did not contain a stocked wardrobe, but there was an extensive complimentary catalogue. Nikora draped a large towel over her shoulders, threw the clothing directory on the wall and went to greet Youssef. He had been waiting for several minutes but did not seem at all perturbed. He wore his black hair closely cropped, and he appeared to be in his early thirties. He was dressed warmly in thick, dark trousers and a grey jacket, but his white shirt was open at the throat. There were deep blue, purple and red patterns swirling on his exposed, raw skin. He was aware she was watching the motion intently.

'I recently had them done to see if I liked them. Perhaps the e-ink is a bit pretentious. What do you think? Maybe something a little more pre-Forming would be better. It is of no matter because the *raja'a* will erase the tattoos next time it claims me. I can't resist trying things before permanence occurs. Do you know there is a way to revoke the *raja'a*? A safeguard to ensure no one could abuse the bioapp. Or steal it.' He was openly admiring her body. 'You don't have all the data, Nikora.'

She settled into a couch and wrapped the towels around her. It wasn't clear that she was listening. Instead, she flicked between outfits, presented on models ideally suited to her physique, occasionally selecting items that might complement each other. Youssef was patient, and he did not seem to covet her attention either. She assumed his reality was one of constant opportunity.

'I would like you, and maybe a few others, to join me in a venture. It's a lifelong commitment, so your comments pertain.'

'We're similar, Nikora, in many respects. Endless existence, whatever the process, is arduous, but I do not know what motivates you, nor you me. That might be where our similarities end. How far do you go back? I have a terrible memory. To before the Forming possibly? Did you experience our history? I think it started at seven billion—one-third of the world's *þjóðirnir* already connected through portable devices. By eight billion, it was anyone old enough to hold a tool. A global population, the entire *fólksfjöldi*, connected but disconnected from their actuality. No wonder no one protested the Forming. They were too preoccupied in their own quantum microcosms. People obsessed with communication but communicating nothing. Expansion was inevitable, and the plans were bold and unlikely to impact the discrete individual. Countless blank faces crammed into Tion.'

Nikora sat quietly, selecting items of clothing as if she were choosing exquisite morsels, a bite to experience one taste, a crumb for another. She breezed with indifference and did not respond.

'They accepted everything because a ridiculous economic model ruled their lives. If every *maður*, *kona* and *börnin* contributes to society, each additional billion must surely contribute more. These policies begat an enormous human resource, barely utilised other than generating theoretical revenue. I can't believe anyone thought we'd survive through to stasis. Our civilisation couldn't possibly have any kind of legacy.'

His presumption irritated her, and she almost closed the call. Deliverers would bring the clothing within a few minutes, and she did not want to prolong the conversation. 'Will you share the bioapp?'

'The *raja'a* will strip away your ambition, and you will require an overseer to chart your progress. Your past will dissolve, and your desires will become immutable. I hope your purpose is strong because nothing else will matter. What are your aspirations, Nikora?'

She had no intention of answering him. 'You have my offer. Please don't take too long. If you'll excuse me, I need to dress. My time is limited.' His slight smile betrayed his divided attention, and she started to worry she had said too much. Nikora saw their failed discussion reflect Tion's ultimate doom and tried to steel herself for what was to come. Youssef's simulacrum faded, and she knew he would only yield if she forced him.

Grace, it's Nikora. Your approach isn't going to work. Threaten the co-worker.

Danesh stood under the shower and enjoyed the play of water across his face. He was no longer a *ný-maður*, a new man. Despite his physical appearance, which he might alter as it pleased him, he had lived for decade upon decade and had been old and young and male and female and countless states in between, and given himself as a template to a hundred protégés. The depth of his personal calm seemed endless, and its simplicity was a joy. He was also still himself.

Nevertheless, Danesh was appalled by Pazel's desire for a surface-only world, and he rejected the destruction of everything that remained below. He understood the needs of a future population, and without unfettered diversity, it was unsustainable. Pazel's elite community couldn't wipe their collective arses, let alone discard almost all of *mannkyniŏ*. Even an extraordinarily small group of dissidents would overwhelm them, given enough time. Eventually, Danesh would have to kill Pazel.

CHAPTER FIVE
Connor
বর্তমানে

TWO TUBULAR RAILS ran along the left-hand side of the corridor, one just below the knee and the other above the hip. Neither was of use to the two *ný-mennirnir* as they silently walked among the shadows cast by the evenly-spaced lights. The interminable passageway had no end, and they might easily circumnavigate the grass farm. Enzo was furious that he had allowed this stranger to manipulate things to his advantage. Yet Noemí had sanctioned it, so he had tried to commit to that single fact to help steady his emotions. He realised she had betrayed him, and now he was exiled with this stunted, feeble dark-skin. The boy would be easy to dominate, but Enzo did not know where they would go or how they would survive. His company had abandoned him, people he loved and trusted, and he was seething. As he followed behind Hyun-jun, he forcibly banged the *hanbō* on the decking so that the thud of his half-staff accompanied each step. He had to stoop with every stride, but he hoped the sound intimidated Hyun-jun.

Enzo was puzzled by his connection to Sodality. It was unfamiliar, as if even the Pallium was unfaithful. He thought about the despairing *eldri-fólkið* from his farm, left amongst the grasses by their friends. Was it also his time to die now that he was alone? The outsider was presumably too scared to start a conversation but occasionally broadcasted friend requests. Enzo ignored him and loudly double-tapped each footstep.

He knew he would eventually have to concede because, without Hyun-jun, he had nothing. This boy-man had knowledge that was otherwise unattainable and left Enzo dependent on him. He wanted to strike Hyun-jun fiercely across the back of his head, beat him to the ground and take his life away, but he could not. How did Hyun-jun know which way to go? Who was helping him? Enzo felt terribly alone: he loved Noemí unconditionally and longed to be back in his grass farm. He wanted to see her again, so he would have to survive this humiliation.

'May I carry your water for you?' Enzo eventually asked.

Hyun-jun barely slowed his comfortable pace. 'So you can drink it all and leave me to die of thirst?'

Enzo would have to entice him and earn his trust. 'Forgive me. I'm not used to this. I had to protect my *sálirnar*. We got on well before.'

'You should have helped me last night.'

'It was wrong of me. I made a mistake.'

The two new men continued in silence for a kilometre, but their separation reduced until they were walking side-by-side. Enzo reached for Hyun-jun's hand, and their simple physical connection seemed to diffuse the situation. Slowly, they started to open up and spoke about their homes. Enzo's description of Noemí inspired Hyun-jun to quip that she might be from the same fertilisation as Milagrosa, and they clung to one another as they laughed.

It's about time.

Enzo was startled by the voice in his mind.

My name is Miyu, and before I tell Hyun-jun that I'm sharing his secret with you, I need some assurance that nothing is going to happen to him.

Please protect him. He's very special to me.

Enzo agreed to Miyu's terms, and she was gone. The corridor retained its blank countenance and gave no clues to their destination. Its continuous archway tracked on a barely perceptible curve to the right and offered no branches or visible doorways. He knew they were circling his home, and there would be a decision point ahead of them, it was just a matter of reaching it.

'Do you know how much further we have to go?'

Hyun-jun stopped and looked at his companion. 'You know I only left my farm two days ago, Enzo. We can stop here if you're tired.'

Enzo strode out in front of him in mock defiance. He was amazed at how quickly he had come to trust this *ný-maður* and realised he had stopped worrying about his lost company. He reassured himself that they would be back in his farm by now, and they would remind each other that Enzo would be fine without them. As soon as he spotted the woman's silhouette, he tightened his grip on the *hanbō* and allowed Hyun-jun to rush past. He wanted to maintain his distance to give them a feeling of privacy, but he jogged forward when the FMP denied his request to spy ahead. As they approached, they saw it was a simulacrum, but were both thrilled by Miyu's ve-presence nonetheless.

Miyu was six or seven years newed, and her skin was nearly the same tone as Hyun-jun's, but while he looked sallow, she exuded a radiance as if flowers blossomed within her. Enzo was brazenly attracted to her even though she was a sending, and Hyun-jun laughed at his embellishment, telling him to be more respectful. Miyu ignored their banter and said she was authorised to help with their journey and would arrange for someone to meet them before up-levelling.

After the call, they followed the narrow passageway and

talked about their encounter. Hyun-jun was in high spirits and said he knew something remarkable was going to happen to him, and Enzo poked him between the ribs and told him that no one so scrawny ever amounted to much. They had several kilometres to walk until they reached the service hatch and their route out of Sixth. Before meeting Miyu, it seemed perfectly natural that everyone lived in communities working together to produce grain, meat and other foodstuffs. Yet she had enticed them with the diversity of the world beyond. They were astounded that the Sixes also grew people in vast numbers and prepared them for discrete, separate lives, scattered across within the world.

'If gestorium technicians had propagated me,' Hyun-jun asked, 'what level would they have assigned me to?'

Enzo tried to keep a straight face. 'The Greater Numbers, everywhere from the Tens to Fifteens, require manly *mennirnir*, Hyun-jun, ones who have a bit of strength in them.' He demonstrated his entitlement by flexing various muscles. 'Sixth is just a nursery for organic things so you couldn't stay there, and First is for the beautiful *fjöirnir*. All the Fives are locked into their cerebral prisons so it'd have to be K4 or K3 for you. Unless we sent you to the Depths with the unjoined.'

'Anything above the Nines is too good for you.' They arrived at the service hatch, and Hyun-jun dropped his culm to the floor. 'You'd end up right down in Mariana with the dregs of *mannkynið*.'

'Fuck you. They're real men in K18 and nothing like you. You know nothing about humanity.' Enzo unfolded his arms and rapped his fist on the nondescript portal while Hyun-jun studied its ve-panel. Miyu had not provided them with access codes, so they silently waited to be collected.

Connor decided that death was overrated. To start with, he hadn't expected to endure it. Caching was supposed to be an end to suffering and welcome respite, while death was an absence of everything, but Connor had a surprising sense of self that jarred with his expectations. He was unmistakably deprived of sensation and felt nothing quantum and nothing real. He was also incredibly aware, and this disturbed him. Some of the workers in the barracks shared stories of cachers who stayed in contact with their loved ones. *Lýðirnir* said Sodality was awash with cached personae who were going about their business as if nothing in their lives had changed. Connor had thought it nonsense although now he was not quite so sure. No one believed in abeyance, so without caching, there was no existence after death. He focussed on himself as much as he could and was sure he lacked appendages. He couldn't hear anything, and there was no taste or warmth or any other indicators of his status.

He couldn't judge the passage of time. Was it an hour since Grace had killed him? Ten minutes? He couldn't decide. It might have been much longer and only now had he come to his senses. Connor wanted to laugh. Had another minute passed? There was no way to tell, so he settled into himself and thought of Erica and the other women he had known, but it did not arouse any feeling in him, and he eventually let the thought go. What use was death if there was nothing to feel?

He started counting to mark the time and contemplated various sequences: powers, primes and perfect numbers; however, without a Pallial connection, the solutions began to elude him as they developed in complexity. He tried to imagine digits spiralling out from within his centre, but it gave him a headache. It was a curious feeling, a familiar pain, but disassociated from his reality. The more he thought about it, the more it grew, and the less convinced he was about his existential status.

A *maður* generally needed a head to have a headache.

He began to suspect he was right where he was supposed to be and a familiar *kona* was smothering him. Connor's revelation left him feeling cheated because he wasn't ready for another battle with Grace, and if he had a measure of strength, he was sure it would swiftly ebb away. He needed to connect with his life.

He would use the numbers to drive Grace out. One, one, two, three, five, eight. He would focus his awareness entirely on arithmetic until she was unable to hear anything but endless digits. Thirteen, twenty-one, thirty-four. She would see the numbers whirling outward and be powerless to stop them. Fifty-five, eighty-nine. Now the answers came effortlessly to him, one hundred and forty-four, so he immersed himself in their simplicity and waited for his headache to return.

Connor imagined he was counting individuals, the *afkomendur* of those who had conceived Tion, the decedents of the *forfeður*, and his total quickly exceeded pre-Forming population. The world had changed in a simple step between seven billion and twelve-and-a-half. He wondered if the *forfeður* had envisioned his current predicament in their strategy. As he concentrated on the numbers, enjoying their progression, he sought to block Grace out. He marvelled at how easily the sequence would exceed Tion's capacity and wondered if one more generation would be enough. He marshalled his headache and concentrated on the series to avoid thinking about the densely populated Eights. He reduced his world to an endless torrent of values and despised everything else. His head throbbed, and he was sure that Grace could feel it too.

Enough.

He had caught her attention and pushed the progression harder. The pain grew dramatically.

I said that's enough. This isn't going to work; we can try it your way.

Connor stopped counting and waited for her to continue. The universe slowly welcomed him back as his awareness grew sense by sense. He was in a small enclosure; her simulacrum sat in a chair beside him. He was hungry and overly warm, and his muscles ached. Bile rose from his stomach, and he collapsed to the floor.

'The identity repeater was a ruse,' Connor groaned. 'You didn't find Youssef.'

She watched him closely, studying his face. 'That's none of your concern. Will you go out again, or do I have to displace you entirely?'

'He won't come if you hold me in here. It's too risky,' he said.

'I disagree, but I'm running out of time.'

'Then we share. Divide ourselves between our two *māsadā-sarīra* so that neither of us can betray the other. I presume that's within your capability.'

It was a peculiar feeling, akin to indecision. Connor could not quite identify with his own being, or with hers. The Pallium did not split them as he had intended but maintained their complex duality between their two bodies. Connor found himself in both *māsadā-sarīra* at once, so that he was man and woman, saw with multiple eyes and moved in two directions. He carefully studied every perception, determined what belonged to who and tried not to be overwhelmed by the entanglement of their being. While Grace struggled to keep her identity separate, Connor had nothing to hide, and he adapted, recognising this as his opportunity to prevail.

She took his shared body down to a sensation warehouse where Eighth workers enacted fantasies for affluent clients and packaged their experiences for incorporation. Many of these were degrading, even abusive or physically damaging, although there were also occasional requests to enjoy solidarity, friendship or love. Connor found he didn't care what he was required to do and made no comment to Grace.

We only need to be signed in for fifteen minutes. We'll probably avoid any sophisticated clients. Just long enough for you to register and Youssef to spot you. She told him to manage the transactions with the front desk before they entered an experience booth and sat on the clearfibre bunk. Nothing happened for the full quarter of an hour, and as Grace took them offline, he asked why.

Something is wrong. Her words sounded remote inside his skull. *I assumed we'd not have to interact, but surely it's unusual for no one to show interest? There are billions of* sálirnar *out there after all. What did you do?*

Connor could feel the hatred raging beneath her calm veneer. He allowed her to fill his frame with her presence and enticed her to take control while trying to sink into her delicate flesh.

Did you mask us from Youssef? She marched them out of the booth to the reception desk and barked instructions at the terminal. When they returned to the bunk, it was only a few moments before she had negotiated a private session. Fortunately, there was little instruction from their audience. He knew it was two people, collocated, but couldn't obtain any more detail about them, so Connor tried to withdraw to the safely of her distant flesh. Grace seemed entirely unaware of the malice in the room and did not notice his retreat as she stepped him out of his workwear and loosened the integral belt from its rough fabric. Connor could sense the tension growing between the absent woman and the voyeurs, and realised they had purchased an end-of-life experience.

Grace, you have to stop! Do not do this!

She took the belt and looped it around his neck, winding it around once, twice, and attached it to a hook. Her excitement escalated as she found his erotic triggers and Connor tried to flee. He poured as much of himself into Grace's faraway *māsadā-*

sarīra as he could, and in turn, allowed her to fill the space he left behind. Connor could sense her rushing into the ecstasy she had created as she generated a premium experience for his customer. He knew she would not stop and demanded the FMP store his entire essence within her body. Connor had unwittingly encouraged her to become him. She only realised in her last moment and desperately tried to cling to him as he departed. The Pallium showed him Connor's body as it crumpled to the floor, confirming the delivery of a copy of the experience to all available parties.

Connor accepted the ve-package without question, even though he wasn't sure who he was representing. It was discretely wrapped in virtual brown paper and bore no markings indicating what it contained. He had no interest in watching his own death, and he found it hard to accept that whatever happened in the future, he would not be himself again. It was not a liberating experience, but it did not depress him either. The man Connor used to be was a cold, greying corpse with bluish lips, a fitting vessel for the woman who had killed him. Perhaps she too had found a way to jump from his body; perhaps her claim to it was too binding. Connor wanted to believe that Grace was gone.

Several degrees across Tion, Grace Mu-Tlo-Ue-Jhan's *māsadā-sarīra* reclined in a large padded chair that enveloped her in its embrace. Her breathing was shallow but regular, and her closed eyes were motionless. The technician glanced at the air display above her head and rolled back the trace. There were three notable events: the latest joining, the foreign persona becoming dominant, and finally the moment it pushed her out. His client had said this might happen, and she had warned him to prevent it. He switched off the display and instructed the Pallium to stop monitoring. Hopefully, she would stay asleep until he could send her to some out-of-the-way, distant arc. He wasn't willing to switch her off because there was someone in there. He hated his job.

An automated deliverer arrived and scooped Grace up in one of its pairs of arms. The technician threw a sheet over her, in no way hiding the body it carried. He added some iconography so bystanders could tell that it was alive, and also a description of a fictitious communicable-and-expensive-to-eradicate disease. He administered another sedative as an afterthought. The *vélmenni* adjusted its balance, grew an extra pair of legs and hastened into the Eights to hide her away. When Grace came round, she wouldn't know who she was or where she had been.

The deliverer hurried along the glaring thoroughfares. The K8 streets were simple passageways running between the bunk rooms and facilities densely packed into the Depths. People marched purposefully along with them, calmly ignoring the sleepers that lined the corridors and pretending to have somewhere better to be. They regarded the covered body warily and gave its bearer a wide berth, but showed little other interest. No one cared if there was someone in a worse situation than themselves, and they wouldn't risk contamination. An awareness rushed before the deliverer so that it no longer needed to pick a path through the *ljóirnir*. The deliverer's instructions were in terms of its cargo. It should remain mid-level while clearing as many degrees as possible, and deposit the *māsadā-sarīra* as soon as the chemical coma began to pass. The Pallium would purge the record of its tasking and performance.

Connor kept his eyes shut: he wasn't asleep but did not want to see. He vaguely recalled being left on the ground, and he knew nothing good was about to happen. A woman who he had only recently met had brutally and efficiently killed him, and now he was probably trapped within her. He wasn't sure if it was a ghosting, and he did not want to find out the truth. If he opened his eyes and they turned out to be hers, then he would be forever wedded to the FMP less his essence drift away, but he had no staters to pay for an endless connection. He was in trouble. He considered trying to contact Youssef, but Connor knew his friend would not respond to Grace's request. He had to find a way to separate himself from the woman but if he had become her—

What is my TUID?

Grace Mu-Tlo-Ue-Jhan.

Display my profile overview.

The contents of the woman's life danced in front of his closed eyes. Finances, contacts, employment networks, biographical logs, preferences ranging from pharmaceuticals to food groups. Everything he needed because the Pallium assumed he was her. Grace's most closely guarded secrets concerned one man, Cristóbal Hie-Ngo-Sharp-Damaru, and his litany of misdemeanours: nothing that would incriminate him, but data he would surely prefer to keep hidden away. Connor read that Grace loved this man and that Cristóbal had no reciprocal interest in her. The FMP presented all of her details for him to exploit, and it was clearly labelled and ready to wield. He prepared a summary for Youssef and submitted it to his public queue, even though it would probably remain unopened. He did not have the skills to spoof the message header and didn't want to trust someone to handle it for him. Other than that, he had no plan. He hoped Youssef would sort through his junk mail.

Caitlyn had received an enquiry from an unidentifiable prospective client a couple of years after starting her job. She knew the other *konurnar* accepted private work which didn't contribute to the group. They had spoken about it early on, agreeing it would be fine if it didn't damage their reputation or interfere with their productivity rating. The women rarely spoke about their various independent workload before they accepted the contract from the Pallium. Caitlyn knew they all had discrete agreements in place, which they neglected to mention. It was part of the natural order now they had been operating together for several years. Their close community relied on the support they gave each other when they weren't busy, and it was a precious thing. Even so, she hoped their newfound openness did not encourage routine sharing.

Caitlyn's position in the elucidarium allowed her to schedule her work without anyone asking what she was doing: it was the same privilege that Jovana had used to keep her K5 boyfriend from them. Caitlyn simply wanted to understand what Youssef was doing. It had taken almost a year to sort out the terms and conditions of her oversight agreement, and three years later, despite never actually ve-meeting Youssef, she wanted more from him. Sometimes Caitlyn observed him sleeping in the humid barracks and longed to descend and be with him, but also recognised that fantasy for what it was. She would not survive in the Eights and would be passed from *maður* to *maður* until she begged to go to a cacherie. Caitlyn wished Youssef had stayed put.

Her induction stated that Youssef required a friend: it was an essential part of his integration. Connor gave him someone to worry about and therefore, a connection to the world around him. Youssef maintained a life as long as his meant people and events could happily race by without any assistance. He would survive them all because his purpose was to keep a record of what had been. She knew it was not his true vocation. No one could remember the pre-Forming as he could, although she countered that without her help Youssef could not remember yesterday. They had laughed at the notion, and Caitlyn agreed to observe him and ensure someone could account for his contribution. She had tried to call him when he had set off with his supervisor. She was sick of telling Youssef that Rabindra was not to be trusted, but he clearly wasn't reading his dailies.

Miyu and Jovana were both ghosted out of the chamber and to Caitlyn they looked dead. Their pursuit of answers through Hyun-jun and Enzo was an unlikely approach. It occurred to Caitlyn that she could rent a body and be with Youssef, finally caressing his close-cropped hair and resting her head on his firm chest. Surprisingly, Freja and Kavya were doing the work they were assigned, each staring into the middle distance and responding to information that only they could see. Caitlyn kicked herself into action and requested the surveillance data from Rabindra's office. Youssef had been in there for hours, clearly writing code. Caitlyn couldn't tap into any of the data and was baffled by his actions. All of his skills were pre-Forming, and it was unlikely he would be able to produce anything that she, with access to almost a millennium of algorithmic advancement, wouldn't understand. She wound back the feed, and the supervisor came in. Caitlyn had muted the video, but the FMP belligerently synthesised his words, so she switched that service off too. She wanted to think. Youssef had supplied Rabindra with a ve-package, and as soon as he had accepted it, he had passed out. Ninety minutes later, Youssef had helped him to his feet, and they had gone their separate ways. He had seemed enormously pleased with himself.

Caitlyn spent the rest of her afternoon trawling through archived data exchanges, but it was difficult to focus on those that centred around Youssef. He had readily hidden his intentions, and whatever audit trail there was, its significance eluded her. Kavya had previously suggested they reduce the Pallial backups to a few minutes, which would free up extraordinary capacity but only impact its resilience by one or two per cent. Caitlyn was glad she had overruled her colleague. There had been a peak in processing requests while Rabindra was out of action, and this surely wasn't a coincidence. She pondered what she had been working on at the time, and there it was, the interruption by Freja, a simple little feel-good game and an invitation against her address book. She traced all of the requests back via their parent processes, and they all led to Rabindra Schwa-Rha-Ta-Te. It wasn't his code; he was the vector. Now she had to pull it apart and figure out what Youssef had done.

The quiz code was mundane, poorly constructed and created with little thought. After a bit of digging, Caitlyn tracked it back to a *drengar* in the Sixes who was approaching his mid-nonage. Youssef had grafted some potentially damaging endorphin triggers onto the applet and added a replication facility, but there had to be something else hidden underneath. All the usual markers were missing, and there were no references to anything readable. At the end of her decompile, Caitlyn could tell Youssef was searching for something, utilising everyone who ran the code to do so, but there was no clue as to what he was seeking. It took her almost no time at all to map every instance of the applet and identify the few processes that were still running. Youssef had been looking for his friend, and a handful of *lýðirnir* had seen him. When Caitlyn located Connor, Youssef would be close by, and she could tell him about the Pallial Decline. She would then have her own *maður* on the outside.

She made some tea and tried not to think about it too much. She summoned her favourite picture of Youssef, lying on his side and propped up on one elbow. Caitlyn had stored the image during a discussion they were having about associations, and she had admonished him when he said he only had room for one friend in his life. She asked if it could be her and he gazed at her and pulled a forlorn face, saying that Connor was his only friend. Caitlyn closed the photo, sent a few complex queries into the

Pallium and waited for it to complete. She decided Youssef was easily her peer and imagined they would be extraordinarily successful if they ever had the opportunity to work together. Kavya came over and picked up her empty cup. 'How's it going?' she asked.

Caitlyn rubbed her eyes and smiled. 'Nothing much to report. I've been chasing down some anomalies but nothing spectacular.'

'Seems like a fairly complex search routine to me.'

Caitlyn decided to leave her displays active as there was no point in trying to hide. 'One of my clients has gone missing. I think he'd be useful to help us understand what's happening to the FMP, so I'm trying to find him. I'm pretty sure he'll be trying to locate this man.'

She pulled a surveillance feed from a recycling facility: an inert, bloated body, with bluish skin and ugly red marks around its throat. Apart from some tiny insects buzzing about, there was no movement at all.

'What are you waiting for?' Kavya asked.

'His name's Connor. Someone will eventually be along to dispose of him in a desequencer. He's definitely dead, but that's not the interesting part. As far as I can make out, he affected a swap with another *sikatā-ātamā* moments before he died. Who would want to ghost into a man that was about to be killed? It doesn't make sense to me.'

'Thrill-seeking that went wrong?'

'I don't think so because several hundreds of people have purchased the experience already. It appears he's now resident in this *kona*, or at least as long as the rehosting holds.'

Kavya smiled. 'So you've found what you're looking for.'

'Unfortunately not. Youssef won't go anywhere near her. I don't know if my client has enough time to figure out what happened. He's not answering my calls.'

'We're more than co-workers, you can tell me what's going on.'

'I'm not ready yet.' Caitlyn shrugged and nodded towards the kitchen, so Kavya made more tea, and the two women sat together and talked. They shared some favourite media reports, replaying clips that either one found interesting or amusing, and relaxed. Eventually, Caitlyn went to bed, turned her dreamer up to its highest setting and accepted the oneironaut's fee, hoping her subconscious would provide an answer. She was a *stúlka* again, just six years old, dashing around as the other children chased her. One of the caregivers called them together to play a game and arranged them in a circle, boy, girl, boy. They held hands and rotated to the left, chanting words that Caitlyn couldn't remember, although they came to her as she joined in. She felt someone pushing at her *sikatā-ātamā*, making her uncomfortable. It had to be the boy holding her right hand. Caitlyn saw her opportunity and jumped into a boy opposite, allowing her assailant to fill her vacated body. She carried on chanting, this time with her boy's voice and leapt again when the moment came. She began to enjoy herself, moving from host to host, until the caregiver commanded them to stop. Caitlyn was firmly residing in one of the youngest children and couldn't help giggling because there weren't enough bodies to go around. One of the *börnin* was lost. The adults encouraged them to keep moving, and Caitlyn saw him quietly kill one of her young companions. The *fullorðnir* removed child after child until there were two bodies left and three poor minds hopping between them. She started to panic when she realised she might lose. Their urgency grew, and the words came quicker and quicker until Caitlyn was sure she would fail. She didn't know if she would end up male, female or lost. It will be what Connor experiences forever, she fretted and woke up.

She didn't want Connor to depend to the Pallium, to be yoked to its processes to ensure he stayed anchored to Grace's body. She needed a way to allow him to remain there freely, if he chose to do so, without having to be permanently online. It was similar to the problem Youssef faced, except the *raja'a* also prevented him from remembering without some support. She considered giving the *raja'a* to Connor; however, she would only replace one dependency with another. There had to be a way to solve the bioapp's underlying technical constraints, without creating a process that would be abused by the burgeoning population.

As far as Caitlyn could determine, Youssef was the only person who had access to the restorative technology, although there had to be other users. If she could modify the *raja'a* to permit contiguous experiences, there would be no end to the *sálirnar* who would demand her secret. Caitlyn could be financially independent and not have to worry about their contract. She could leave the other women behind, join Youssef and live forever with him, and be his faithful friend. Even though Caitlyn recognised the idiocy of her desire, it left her optimistic and determined to make it work. She would name the new process the *tabi'a*, a continuance. She estimated it would take eleven months to update, protect, properly debug and market the bioapp, assuming the simulations went smoothly, so she filed a discrete prospectus for any existing users who might require an upgrade.

Tion was slipping away from Youssef, and its comfortable dependencies were in question as he tried to determine who Rabindra was. Youssef found himself caught in his wake, a convenience to this man who inhabited the foreman's flesh, while its previous occupant was discarded somewhere in Eighth and unrecoverable. Different luck for different *lýðirnir*, Youssef thought. However, their relationship had started to develop beyond dependency, and he was pleased, knowing he needed to nurture his network of allies now he was back in the game. While trust was elusive, Youssef was optimistic about the future and took control of the situation by granting Rabindra reasonable access to his personal profile, delighting in its reciprocation despite the lack of identity. When Rabindra took a knife from his jacket pocket, Youssef wasn't concerned and didn't question how he had come by it in a stylish clothing store. He was, however, startled when Rabindra pushed the blade carefully into the suite's floor, cutting through the carpet to reveal an armaments locker, and his former confidence slipped away. Youssef had started this journey as the spearhead, but this man was calmly and totally in control of their destiny.

Rabindra posted a plan of the hotel in front of Youssef. Several people were homing in on their location. He tossed Youssef an automatic firearm, saying he had been unable to foil the software agent, selected two guns for himself and kicked the compartment shut. Youssef checked the weapon over and requested the appropriate ve-package for its use, which he combined with his own pre-Forming experience. Even so, as they left the room, he was uneasy about what was to come.

He wondered if he would see his friend while his future was so uncertain, but he still hoped that Connor would flourish. Then he sublimated his will into Rabindra's, and they ran as one. A battalion of armed *sálirnar* met them and did not hesitate to open fire. The two-in-one had the advantage through pervasive code that monitored each firing decision, sometimes predicting the bullet's path, sometimes overruling the gunner's aim and clearing their way through the crowd.

Bulkheads exploded around them, glass shattered, and lumps of sundered fittings hurtled through the air. The percussive noise was deafening. Youssef could sense the frustration of the assizes as they failed to hit their mark and watched their internal battle for control. There were thousands of bullets per minute, and Rabindra interrupted each one's trajectory with practised ease. Youssef felt a rush of relief as he realised they might break away, and then a searing tear to his left shoulder as the first bullet struck.

The silence was unbearable, so Jovana interrupted Miyu for the third time with the same pretence she had used earlier that morning. She claimed Caitlyn had assigned her an impossible task and all she could do was guess the result and see if it solved the problem at hand. It didn't matter how hard she looked, no solution was likely to be better than any other, so how she structured her search was irrelevant, but she was struggling to derive a sufficient number of possible answers. It was where she claimed Miyu could help. In truth, both women knew Jovana wanted something to eat and someone to chat to about the boys.

Jovana thought they were both beautiful, in their different ways. She described Enzo as vigorous and virile but vacuous, which made Miyu giggle. She persisted: he was nice to look at and would be able to protect Hyun-jun if the need arose. The other *ný-maður* intrigued her. He was supple and smart, agile and astute, and despite his modest physique, just as stimulating. She hoped they would be late subscribers to the fashions of their ascent.

Miyu wove a representation of a thick ve-book in her hands and made a big show of closing it and putting it on the table. She ensured the numerical mapping app she was running was able to look after itself and sat back for what was becoming a regular discussion.

'We need to tell the others about them in case it gets out of control. We're taking a terrible risk in our approach, Miyu, even with all the security measures.'

'I disagree. If we even knew of a way to provide Hyun-jun and Enzo with the permission to move around Tion, we couldn't give them enough staters without arousing suspicion, assuming we even had them. Someone would notice. If we bring them to the world's attention, people will want them to succeed. It's a perfect solution.'

'We have to be careful,' Jovana noted. 'What if the boys mention you? There are going to be a huge number of *lýðirnir* observing them. It won't just be the media feeds that we'll need to monitor. Each time they interact with someone, they'll be recognised.'

Miyu pursed her lips. 'There has to be a way to restrict how unlicensed contributors portrayed them. We have access to unlimited FMP resources so we should be able to maintain control. I've spent more time studying it than the rest of you, well maybe not Kavya. We can override anyone they have contact with, I can put together an app for that, so we only need to worry about the offliners. Still, I suppose they're not interested in video entertainment.'

'I don't understand why you told Hyun-jun about the empyrealodes.'

'It was something that Kavya was talking about before we took this contract,' Miyu said. 'She was working on the external skyplate problem, and new issues were surfacing so rapidly she suspected someone was sabotaging the project. I think I can use the boys to find out what's going on. I'm convinced it will help explain the Pallial Decline.'

'Then you have to tell Caitlyn,' Jovana suggested. 'She'll be irritated if you don't.'

'I'm not worried about her knowing yet. I think she'll be pleased because this gives us a physical presence outside, although I'm ready to go full-sensory with someone yet, and I definitely don't want to be Enzo. He's too big and awkward.

I can't tell the others how I became involved with Hyun-jun in the first place. I wasn't doing my job.'

Jovana sighed. 'Is that all, sweetie? I don't think anyone is going to care about you shirking off. Have you planned where to send the boys?'

'I'm going to up-level them,' Miyu declared. 'I've been cycling a clip of Hyun-jun's stable generation speech across all the farm communities. His popularity is enormous despite a farm's inherently insular nature. The simple fact that two men from separate, struggling *samfélögin* have overcome their differences for a common goal is marvellous. People are asking questions and want to help. I've set him up as a recognised entity and applied for him to access parts of Fifth. It's unprecedented because there are almost no commissioned programmes below First that use physical people. Hyun-jun's an explorer, and I'm his guide, and *lýðirnir* everywhere will want him to experience all of Tion, and even visit closed accommodations.'

'They absolutely cannot come into our home.'

Miyu smoothed the front of her shirt. 'I need the *sálirnar* from the Fives to fund their up-level and so on. By the time they reach Third, I'll probably need up to a stater per resident to make a valid case for them to reach K1, and to do that, everyone needs to be engaged.'

'It's going to take an awfully long time and a lot of effort unless we automate.'

'You're right,' Miyu agreed. 'I'll get the others. Will you tell them, please?'

Only Freja was unsettled. She was reportedly too busy to have noticed the quality of the other girls' work. Even so, she thought the idea was sound and providing the right measures were in place would assist with their objective. 'Remember we are on the hook to deliver something,' she scolded, 'not to be media magnates. Is there anything else you have neglected to share with the team?'

Jovana held everyone's gaze, and Miyu knew she wouldn't mention Joaquín.

Some passengers could only find space to stand, and swayed as they hung from the straps in the carriage ceiling in a pre-programmed response. Other people lay at their feet. It was overly warm, but the ammonia coming from the propulsion system masked the animal odour of the masses. The passengers undulated together with the train's motion while their combined mental essence hid in Sodality. Wasters tended the remarkably clean compartment, scavenging between the occupants. Sometimes they pulled at loose hair and clothing as they hunted for scraps to take to the desequencers. The majority of the bodies had been picked clean as they slept, and occasionally the machines repaired faults in their skin, healed wounds and erased scars. Two of the small devices scurried over Grace's inert body and tried to comprehend the extent of the damage. They came to a halt on her face and rested on her cheekbones. Tendrils exuded from their polymer bodies and probed her mouth and nose, and pushed through the delicate membranes seeking prominent arteries. The fault was potentially within. She stirred and unconsciously tried to brush the things from her mouth, but they moved away from her hands and continued to delve inside her, signalling to the FMP for additional support. As suddenly as they had arrived, they pulled away, leaving faint lines of blood on her chin. Their work was done or rendered unnecessary.

The carriage came to a halt and docked. Its doors joined with the tunnel's and opened harmoniously to allow the swell of *lýðirnir* to board. Few disembarked, as most of the occupants had paid to reach Eighth topsky, where they might find a way to ascend. A few of the hangers lost their grip during the surge and stumbled to wakefulness, muttering at their loss of personal space. Some simply leant against other passengers, held onto them discretely and disappeared into online. As the doors closed, the woman's body floundered under the *sálirnar* who towered over her, but the passengers paid her no attention. Most of them had never seen a *vélmenni* before, and none noticed it enter the carriage at the top of the closing door. The robot slid across the ceiling, skirting air ducts and the wire mesh over the lights, securing itself tightly, with its conical shell pointing directly at the woman. Threadlike elements span from its tip, floating between the hanging *fólkið* and descending towards the body on the floor, each tendril almost invisible but full of purpose. The *vélmenni* continued to spin, and her skin rapidly lost all colour under its translucent shroud. A tiny deliverer abseiled down, landed on her belly and made a delicate cut in the cocoon, then through the skin beneath. She did not move as it pushed its way inside her. Several minutes later it emerged and climbed back to the robot, its payload spent. The wound bled slightly until a group of wasters arrived, removed the webbing and tidied the cut away. The woman rubbed her eyes and tried to sit.

She pulled herself upright using the various legs surrounding her, indifferent to who she touched, or what. She wormed her way between the tightly packed men and women, resting her head against thighs and buttocks and worse.

Connor lay suppressed within her, and no one would ever read his message. When he was offered the ticket in exchange for her body, he initially baulked, but he had no other ideas and needed to keep moving. Connor found it easy, natural even, and welcomed the experience. Now he had slept he felt alive and thought he might be able to formulate a plan.

Connor, get off the train.
Who are you?
I'm a friend of Youssef's.

Where is he?

I don't know. I have to find him. Please disembark at the next station.

Connor forced himself upright and pushed the comatose out of his way. He didn't recognise the voice and suspected it was just his mind personifying a message he had received. Connor worked his way near to the door and waited for the vehicle to stop. Once he had alighted, he found a seat on the crowded platform, expecting another message. He avoided online, not trusting the Pallium to understand who he, or she, actually was, so he wasn't sure if the *kona* who approached him was really there.

'Hello, Connor. My name is Caitlyn, and I've been working alongside Youssef for a few years. You've been through a terrible experience, and I almost lost you when you entered the Lacuna. Thankfully you didn't make it out of K8.'

Connor touched his face, Grace's face, to show Caitlyn how much has changed.

Caitlyn took hold of Connor's hand to prove she was physically present. 'I haven't got a lot of time, so please let me explain. Your colleague Youssef is a lifer. My guess is he's probably older than the tionsphere. He's been waiting in the Eights for a long time, but I don't know why. He needs my help to stay focused, but he hasn't been in contact for several days, and I'm worried.'

None of this makes sense, Connor thought. Youssef is just the same as the other *mennirnir* at the coalface.

'I believe someone tried to use you to expose him, and that has cost you dearly. Your physical body is lost, but I have some influence over the FMP and helped ghost you into this body.'

Nothing Caitlyn said seemed to be about him.

'Grace's *sikatā-ātamā* didn't survive, so I guess it's yours now, providing you maintain your connection.'

Then I'm screwed, he thought. I have no way to pay for Pallial access.

'You have an alternative, though. I've installed a bioapp which is capable of restoring your physical state after almost any amount of damage. It's how Youssef has survived so long. It relies on a small vesicle which will contain cybercytes coded with your DNA, which the *forfeður* referred to as the *raja'a*. I suspect it's a borrowed process from the genorepositories, but it's hard to be certain. It will remain inactive until I can install the cybercytes.'

He didn't know why she was offering to help. 'What do you want me to do?'

'I would like you to help me find Youssef. I think he'll do anything to prevent this technology from being exploited by others. Now I acknowledge this makes me the same as Grace, of course, using you, but I have also given you an incredible gift if you want to accept it.'

'I suppose there's a catch,' Connor said.

'You'll be dependent on me, or someone like me, to explain who you become, day after day, otherwise you'll return to who you are now. We can't automate because it would generate an audit trail. There are also some barriers embedded in the bioapp preventing unauthorised tampering. There may be a way to make the process more flexible in the future, but for the time being, it's nothing more than an inconvenience. You need to do this, and you have to be her. I will tell Youssef how to find you.'

'Who was Grace working for?'

'I'm not sure. Grace is part of a group of traffickers from Fourth, although she was originally from K3. They are very good at hiding their transactions. I expect they rely on word of mouth. Someone wants to find Youssef, and you were the bait. If you help me, you'll still be the lure, but no one else could possibly know who you are. You'll be safe, and Youssef will come to find you. I promise.'

'What if I don't agree, Caitlyn?'

'You'll survive. I can give you staters to maintain your connection and help you get back to Fourth, where she belongs. I have to go. Promise me you'll think about it.'

He nodded, and Caitlyn disappeared amongst the crowd. He looked down at Grace's delicate hands and clasped them in her lap, between her legs. Her feet were splayed outward in an ugly fashion, and he realised it was time to discover what kind of woman he was supposed to be.

For a long time, Grace did nothing. Eventually, she purchased some beers, sought temporary accommodation and settled back to skim through her past. She was amazed at how much information was maintained online, and by how freely the Pallium shared it with her. Grace decided it was self-voyeuristic, a past-tense, intellectual onanism that one could only do in private, pawing through excruciating volumes of trivia that documented every moment of her life. Somewhere back in her early-nonage, Grace had installed every journalling tool she could find, and that data continued to mount up. She was surprised the FMP was able to store it all, especially if billions of other subscribers were doing the same. She thought about requesting an overnight install, but it was endless, and Grace was unwilling to consume it all.

She considered Caitlyn's offer. If she activated the technology, Youssef would surely seek her out, but how could she make the subsequent days count? She would have to document everything, continuing the same foolish practice, but this time with the burden of necessity. How could she aspire if tomorrow was a duplicate of today, and how could she better the life left behind? Connor had wanted to improve but had been consigned to the Depths, barely surviving in the Eights, and now he was her, he could be much more, providing Caitlyn was there to maintain his record. She struggled to think, so returned to her log. There were endless references to Cristóbal, who was a co-worker of sorts. He was an olive-skinned rogue, and she thought he was a reasonably refined version of Youssef. Grace's documentary burgeoned with bogus liaisons in a partnership never lived, because the man she loved didn't want her. She decided she no longer liked him and would give him the distance he desired.

Cristóbal was devoted to an *eldri-kona* named Doha; however, Grace secretly detested her. They were bound together in a personal way that Grace didn't understand, as while it wasn't sexual, it abounded with love. The old woman held him in thrall. Cristóbal used to rely on two men, but one had been lost and left the other debilitated. Grace thought Liang was borderline unserviceable and Cristóbal should ask Kathy to arrange for his caching. Kathy was a problem. It was difficult to determine who she was, and Grace worried she was an observer, similar to Caitlyn. Kathy was a threat.

Connor had been an unassuming man. He was compliant and hard-working and had made a decent life for himself. Grace could easily be that *einstaklingur*, that *persónan*, rejoining the workforce to enjoy her privileges the way Erica had. It was a disappointing ambition but a step up from Connor's lot.

It wasn't what she wanted, so she sent her affirmation to Caitlyn.

Grace wondered how long it would be until the alteration occurred. Could it have already happened? What would she take into tomorrow? She resolved to avoid Cristóbal and his crew and hoped he was sufficiently indifferent to let her go. She had an opportunity to become something unimaginable. Two pasts overwhelmed her, the tangible nonage which was familiar and fleeting, and a detailed other childhood that didn't seem to be hers. Youthful decisions that Connor and Grace had made shaped them as *ný-fólkið* and led them to the terrible consequences of their final meeting. Too many experiences crammed into one person. Now there was a possibility of a fresh start, a life where she could welcome his wisdom and leave the hurt behind. She wouldn't take the *kona* with her and wanted to leave the *maður* behind. She requested a simplified map of her fragmented *sikatā-ātamā* and discarded as much as she dared, chancing her *raja'a* had not commenced. She wanted renewal as a serene, empty place that would not be threatened by conflicting personalities.

Her tiny room contained a slumber sling, secured to the floor and ceiling at a sharp angle. She climbed into it, tucked the straps under her arms and buttocks and fell into a deep, almost-vertical sleep. The room switched off the illumination and lowered the air temperature and pressure to conserve energy, causing her heart rate to plummet for the fifteen-hour isolation she had requested. Grace did not react when the surgical *vél* attended her, or later as the door was forced open. When the sling was cut away from its fastenings and fell to the floor, nothing registered. The bundle was heavy, so it was carelessly dragged from the room and heaved onto a trolley.

When she woke, she still wasn't sure if Caitlyn had administered the *raja'a*. She couldn't remember where she was or how she ended up in the large, comfortable chair, but she felt rested and safe. People surrounded her, lounging together in agreeable groups, chatting idly about various nothings. The woman in the chair next to her regarded her intently, waiting for her to speak.

'I'm sorry,' Grace confessed. 'I forget myself sometimes.'

The woman laughed and pushed her blond hair away from her eyes. 'Of course. You've had a busy day. You said you were interested in donating.'

Grace did not know how to respond and tried to hail Caitlyn for assistance. Her connection was weak, and she didn't get an answer, but she wasn't particularly disturbed. Grace couldn't recall the woman and wondered if the *raja'a* had reset her right in the middle of their conversation.

'So, are you happy about the procedure taking place? It's not like we could make this work without your consent. The benefits to both you and our organisation are considerable.'

'Yes, I believe so, but I would like to run the details past my counsel. I'm just having a slight problem raising her.'

The woman looked momentarily unsettled but responded quickly. 'We're all struggling these days. Everything is so slow, it's outrageous, given the subscription fees. I, for one, think the FMP needs a damn good overhaul. What if there was an outage? How would people survive?' She leant closer, obviously sharing a confidence. 'It has to be now, Grace. I have a valuable client who is impatient for the procedure, and there are only a few viable suppliers. Hence the generous compensation. I suppose a less scrupulous *einstaklingur* might find a way to reprogram the cybercytes before extraction and disable the host-specific suicide routine. I think that would be disastrous for you.' She smiled an arid smile that evidently had no emotion behind it at all. 'It's time to sign the contract.'

Grace felt the rush of information services as the woman plucked a ve-package from the aether. Had she been suppressing the Pallial connection all along? Grace hadn't thought that was possible but was less confident than ever. She made a show of reaching out for it and inspecting its contents while desperately hailing Caitlyn. Grace received a *do not disturb* notice, and her anxiety grew. The woman wanted the *raja'a*, and she would take it if Grace did not cooperate. Caitlyn must have activated the bioapp, but she couldn't understand how, unless Youssef had visited in person. Yet if Caitlyn had virtually transferred the *raja'a*, then there was no need for it to be obtained as the woman implied. Grace intended to make the best use of her slight advantage.

'I'm happy to share the *raja'a* with you, but I need to make sure you're only going to use the technology for its intended purposes and that I'm not the cause of some awful pandemic. If you could provide me with your identification and let me validate your credentials, we can carry out the procedure this afternoon.'

'My client relies on absolute discretion, so there will be no disclosure. You're welcome to run whatever checks you deem necessary on my details: I have nothing to hide. I will return in an hour.' She patted Grace on the knee and left without further comment. Grace closed her eyes to inspect the package details better and then sent the whole thing off to Caitlyn, marked for immediate attention. She requested a forty-minute sleep, but it never came. The other *hðirnir* in the lounge continued to chatter on, and Grace was acutely aware of the images, sounds, video and animations crammed into the room, plus adverts for services and products attempting to win her attention. These were things familiar throughout her life and seemed to be her only constant. She pushed her shoulders back into the couch and thought about the *persónan* she used to be. The changes had been sudden and unexpected, but she could easily see how one choice had led her to the next. She realised she didn't miss Connor and decided to relish each experience as it presented.

Grace, it's Caitlyn. This woman is a registered proxy for private transactions. Her published name is Nikora, and she's up-levelled you to K7. Her rating is a little above average, so I have no reason to believe she's a danger to you. I can't trace her client. You mustn't agree to her proposal.

Did Youssef visit me?

No. Part of my contract is to maintain a bio-backup of the raja'a *technology. I tailored it for you and used a* vélmenni *to install the cybercytes. It's fully integrated with your systems. You genuinely are Grace now, not ghosted in temporarily. There's no going back. Youssef isn't aware yet.*

How will you tell him? Will he come for me?

Not if he thinks you're safe.

Do you think that Nikora will hurt me if she doesn't get what she wants?

I doubt it. Nikora wants the raja'a *and won't care if it comes from Youssef or you.*

Why couldn't I contact you earlier?

Nikora was using a jammer to keep you offline. Please install this acoustic receiver applet. It's a bit annoying, like the sound of the reconstruction engines from Eighth, but she's unlikely to notice. If you lose your connection, I'll be able to guide you.

Is she not entirely proper then?

No, but please don't worry. You need Nikora to give Youssef reason to help you. You're still his friend, no matter what.

Grace kept her eyes shut and regretted her lack of rest. She was uncertain about Nikora and was worried about what she might do. Connor hadn't experienced the range of emotions and autonomic responses that were familiar to Grace and found it unsettling. Men and women are not the same, she thought. At the end of the hour, Grace opened her eyes and hoped that Nikora had not returned, but she was watching from the entrance to the lounge, dressed in a dark jumpsuit. She pointed to identical clothing folded on top of the small table next to Grace's armchair. Grace sighed, slipped the one-piece on and walked towards the arch.

'I assumed you wouldn't agree,' Nikora said.

'No, I can't. Why should I come with you?'

'Because Connor Va-Six-J-Jhan is very much alive.'

Grace found she couldn't breathe as Nikora showed her the video feed. She felt her heart race and slow and threaten to stop—she wasn't able to think. Caitlyn said I am committed to this flesh, that the bioapp would bind me tightly in this body. She wanted to be herself again, wanted to be the *miðaldra-maður* who worked in the Eights and continue to be a quiet, mid-life man protecting the unjoined from being recycled.

'The woman whose body you took very much wants it back, especially now that you've safeguarded its future. She won't care what happens to you. I will ensure that you survive if you give me what I want.'

Grace is alive, his mind raced. I'm Grace now. She looks like me, like him. I'm trapped. I cannot.

Nikora took Grace by the hand and led her from the lounge. Dressed the same, the two women looked reasonably similar despite the decade between them. As they left, Nikora gathered Grace's hair tightly behind her head and fixed it in place with a clip. They walked amiably along the promenade with the air of old friends, but Grace's thoughts continued to reel, yet she made no effort to protect herself. They entered a high-end surgical shop, and Nikora confirmed her booking. She told the receptionist they had requested some routine modifications, and she very much hoped the technician was skilled enough to make them indistinguishable. They identified on-demand, were escorted to adjacent bays and told to undress.

No one suggested a sculptor would be more appropriate for their adjustments, but Grace knew why. Nikora wanted the cybercyte vesicle hidden in Grace's abdomen. Without the *raja'a*, Grace would be unable to protect her claim to this body, and its rightful owner would be able to return. Somewhere in Tion, Connor would be left vacant, no longer dead and sold as an affordable rental for *fólkið* to ghost into the Depths. Grace felt her despair grow and called out to Caitlyn for help. As before there was no response, but she listened intently while the technician meticulously scanned her body.

He's seen you. Hold on.

She relaxed, allowed the preparations to continue, wincing as the sculptor pushed a sedative through the smooth skin of her belly. Her friend was coming to her aid, and he would make sure she was safe. He was forceful and dependable and would keep Nikora away. She looked at the other woman who lay calmly in the next bay. Her only interest was the bioapp, and she wouldn't protect Grace from Connor after the procedure. Nikora would tell her anything to satisfy her desires. Obviously, there was no client. She was going to rip the cybercyte vesicle from Grace's body and have it for herself. Youssef would not get there in time.

Grace lay quietly and felt defeated. She knew she needed to be powerful, but she was Connor, and he was timid and vulnerable. Cristóbal would have taken her if only she had been demure. How confusing to be powerful one day and weak the next. If she could be herself, she would easily fight for her survival and wouldn't have to submit. Nikora was watching again, but this time her face shone with sharp triumph. She had already won, and she knew she had beaten Grace and Connor before her.

I am still that *kona*, Grace mused. She gingerly pushed herself up from the bed. Her lower torso was numb with anaesthetic, but her legs were still strong, and she would be able to stand. The orderly tried to push her back down, but he did not persist, so Grace was able to stagger to the tray of medical equipment and grab a scalpel. The colour ran from Nikora's face as Grace pushed the instrument against her numb middle, and a line of crimson life oozed from the superficial wound.

'I will cut it out and swallow it,' Grace panted, 'so by the time you can reach inside me, my stomach will have ruined the bioapp. Then you'll have to go to him, but he'll refuse you what you want. I am not the pathetic *stúlka* you want me to be. I will not give in to you.'

'Then I shall help Connor find you and take what I want after he has gone. Or stay here while you feast on your entrails. Either way, you die.'

The technician whimpered and tried to take the blade. Grace knocked him out of the way and stepped closer to the other bed. In one swift movement, she jammed the knife into Nikora's throat. Cradling her bleeding belly, Grace stumbled out of the surgical shop. Pain blossomed and then subsided with each step, and she could feel the blood running freely from her body, yet the throbbing seemed to belong to her other self. She looked down at the blood, staggered forward a few steps before looking again. The flow had lessoned; perhaps the *raja'a* did belong to her and would preserve her, allow her body to fix itself.

Grace hid in a crowd of *hðirnir* and brushed the dried blood from her skin. She was grateful so many citizens were not wearing clothes, and no one paid her any attention. If Connor were alive, he would come for her and would not relent until he had what was his. Her confusion faded, and she headed for the nearest beltgate, cradling her sore belly. She would meet him head-on.

Caitlyn, I need you, Grace called.

I'm here.

I think I killed her. And Connor is coming for me.

Connor? His caching is a matter of record.

I saw him, Caitlyn, and he wants Grace back. Is it possible?

There might be a way. Are you hurt?

Nikora tried to take the raja'a *from me. I stopped her.*

There's a record of an assault near your location, but I can't determine who filed it. There were no fatalities.

I need to go somewhere familiar, a place like the coalface where I worked. Can you find me something close to here?

I'll do my best. I'll send you routeing as you go. Be careful on the beltway. You'll be an easy target.

Grace untied her hair and let it fall over her small breasts, noticing them for the first time. She didn't want to be lost, but she didn't want to be Connor again. Grace tried to keep her distance from the people around her and avoided the fastest moving part of the belt. She started to receive routeing information and wasn't sure if it came directly from Caitlyn or a third party, but it didn't matter.

Her journey was brief, and as she stepped onto the pier and climbed up the ramp, she didn't care if she stepped on the unjoined that lined the walkway. These *sálirnar* were there through a series of choices, and their actions had determined their fate. She was determined to survive.

The air was thick with the smell of organic decay. It made Grace gag; the olfactory tolerance she had previously built up was a distant memory. Two oversized cats picked their way through the squalor as if they were immune to it. There were piles of rubbish everywhere, which residents had fashioned into improvised shelters. Grace occasionally spotted a hand or a leg or a face buried in the debris. This was home to these people. Connor wasn't Connor at all, and this place would be unfamiliar to him. He was the stranger here.

Grace eventually found what she was looking for, a set of sturdy compartments desperate *þjóðirnir* had been living in. She cleared a path over them, pulling some clearfibre panels together between the rows to create a flimsy walkway above the groundplate. Grace scouted about for some rags to cover her pale body, found a child's smock and ripped its seams apart to wear it like a jerkin, and rubbed grime into her exposed arms and legs. She continued searching until she found a strip of perforated steel, about the length of her arm and a good few centimetres wide. Grace took the metal and climbed up amongst the junk just beyond her trap to wait.

She knew she would kill him as soon as he picked his way through the filth. Just as Grace had struggled to realise she wasn't the woman had become, she hoped Connor wouldn't be a man from this environment. He would be cautious, tentative and loathe to touch anything, and he would expect Grace to be the same. She hoped she could rely on his naïveté. There was something damp underneath her legs, but it wasn't cold, so she ignored it. Off to her right, she could hear two *sálirnar* whispering to each other and far behind her were the rhythmic rustlings of people passing the time. One of the cats sauntered past with something ominously unidentifiable in its mouth. Grace had no desire to investigate. Something brushed across her feet, but she refused to move. When the message from Caitlyn arrived, she almost ignored it too.

Connor carried himself with more confidence than she had expected, and she recognised it as the same purpose that drove her, the need to survive. The bruising around his neck was horrible, and his face swollen. He held a weapon of some sort in his hand. Grace wasn't sure what it was, but it wasn't long until he aimed it at her covered body.

'Come out,' Connor ordered.

She shook her head and cowered. He was uncertain of his footing, carefully edging towards her even as she tightened her grip on the metal, holding it just beneath the dirty clearfibre sheeting. The structure gave way as Connor stepped forward, falling just over a metre onto the groundplate. Grace gripped her makeshift stake tightly as she leapt into the gap in the rubbish and, before he could aim his gun, thrust the metal bar into his chest. She stared at the dead body and decided that it had never belonged to her.

Chapter Six
Enzo
বর্তমানে

AS FAR AS Enzo could tell the portal had never opened and wasn't about to do so. He decided the maintenance crews Hyun-jun spoke of must laze around while they waited for things to happen. He did not comprehend that their transit was challenging to arrange, or that the way things worked outside his grass farm would be at all different. They had been sent a procedure for incorporating ve-packages, but while Hyun-jun was absorbing the techniques, Enzo filed it away for later, and promptly forgot its importance. Success was a product of main strength and did not require him to be able to construct a better set of queries. He would leave that to others.

Miyu had explained there were no large communities in K5 and that things would be different and potentially confusing for the two young farmers. She advised the pair to maintain an active link and apologised for not being able to remain with them at all times. She gave them two interrupts for their safety. One was hers, and the other was a closed group, but she didn't mention who might be there to help. As with the informatics, Enzo tucked these contacts away out of reach. He was confident he would not require them since the *lýðirnir* of this sphere were pathetically bound together in restrictive cells and couldn't harm either of them.

Enzo was beginning to see Hyun-jun differently. In some way, he was reminded of Noemí, because they shared an optimism and confidence that Enzo could never understand. It didn't arise from their flesh; instead, there was something that urged him to follow their lead, and it inspired him. Enzo knew in that moment of realisation he had lost his supremacy and his importance. He was a mute observer, and it was Hyun-jun who would talk to the masses. Once again, he assumed the role of protector and vowed to demonstrate his worth, and he hoped Hyun-jun would honour their friendship.

Enzo hadn't expected there to be anyone to escort them when the portal opened. The *eldri-kona* looked worn. It appeared she had not taken care of her body, and it no longer respected her either. She was possibly the oldest woman he had ever seen, but Hyun-jun welcomed her with a jubilant hug as if she was young on the inside.

'This is Jovana. She works with Miyu, and she's going to up-level us.' Hyun-jun almost burst with his new-found secret. *She's not really here!* he messaged. *She's borrowed this body in exchange for staters.*

Ridiculous, Enzo replied, *only children would believe such things.*

'We have to leave now,' the woman said. 'We only have a minute or so to access the tunnel.'

There was an intense glare behind the door, and Enzo wondered if it was as bright as the daylight Hyun-jun described above his farm. As his eyes adjusted, he saw three horizontal, incandescent flares flowing without any conduit. They formed a triangle about four metres across and suspended within them was a transparent capsule. It had milky arms that stretched towards each streamer and ended in a solid hoop that circled the light.

'Why should we trust you?' Enzo demanded.

She just looked at him, raised an eyebrow and the most searing pain he had ever known ripped across his naked skin. Just as quickly, it was gone.

I own you Enzo Gim-Six-Be-Upsilon, and you will do as I say.

If Hyun-jun was aware of their exchange, he showed no sign. Everything he saw captivated him, and he motioned for them to enter the gig. The woman took control of Enzo as readily as she had hurt him, and soon they were all leaning against the glass walls of the enclosure.

'The Pallium controls the plasma streams,' she said, 'which burn at around a million Kelvin, making it impossible for anyone to divert them. Minute changes in the magnetic fields between the three streams force the payload along with almost no loss of energy.'

As she spoke about mechanics and physics and the like, Enzo stared at the dazzling spectacle surrounding them. He thought he could see the wave in the light that silently propelled them, and watched as debris from the chamber floor rushed up and over the capsule and hurled into the fire behind them. His grass farm had not prepared him for the world outside, and he loathed his weakness.

There was nothing to indicate their transition between kays other than the woman welcoming them to her level. She said the network was dependent on the two empyrealodes, but it only moved maintenance workers and equipment between facilities on K5 and K6. The tightly controlled Lacuna dispersed commodities from the farms, factories and gestoria, and gave the freest access across the tionsphere. There would be plenty of time to experience it in the days ahead.

Hyun-jun was struggling with the slow pace of their ascent. 'I made a promise to protect the sunstar collectors, Jovana, not to spend days hiding in endless tunnels. When do we reach the surface?'

'Sweetie, you can't just stroll unannounced to the top of the world and ask for a tour of the technology that sustains it. You need support, a reason to be there, permission and sponsorship. Everything you do is going to be critiqued by the masses: if you entertain, we will find our answers. If not, I might be able to get you home.'

Enzo was comfortable with this exchange. Endure or decay was an imperative he understood, but he was unable to contribute and found himself feeling increasingly isolated.

My lovely boy, Jovana said to Enzo privately, *Hyun-jun will secure the intellectuals, but the asinine* ný-fólkið *and apathetic* eldri-fólkið *will want something handsome to watch. He can't do this without you. Of course, it's still your choice.*

Hyun-jun was visibly concerned. 'I don't know how to win them over,' he whispered.

'Soon, *lýðirnir* everywhere will be following you.' She looked pointedly at Enzo. 'Be yourselves, but please remember that someone's always watching. Whenever there is a choice, think carefully about everything that could happen. I'll be documenting things as we start. Once you reach accessible areas, we'll use footage from a variety of collectors, including everyone you interact with, and later, what they post to Sodality. We'll try to control that as much as we can.'

With a fraction over a trillion hits, the first instalment of Odyssée became Fifth's most-watched video. Its reign was brief, but over twelve hours it was consumed by two in seven residents. Later, while documentary makers interviewed Enzo in K4, he professed to have no understanding of the impact his experiences had on people in the Fours and Fives and certainly didn't know what he and Hyun-jun could have possibly done to inspire the population.

Even before the show published their genomes, most *fólkið* assumed Inès Psi-Two-Zeta-Dha shared Enzo's genetic heritage. There was speculation about the pair as soon as she became an Odyssée candidate: the genorepositories must have made Inès and Enzo for each other. The viewers generally agreed that the disclosure of their chromosomes had swayed the final vote. Some said that the producers had released the data in a move to boost the programme's ratings.

Although the team behind Odyssée might not have anticipated such a broad following, they had seized the opportunity to increase their potential advertising revenue. Within hours of the first video's release, an unprecedented number of people self-nominated for a chance to take part by submitting short clips of their own for consideration by the masses. The voting was rapid, and despite many repeated applications, the producers quickly selected five finalists. With elaborate ceremony, the hopefuls were extracted from their elucidaria, leaving their shocked colleagues bereft as a member of their team walked away. None of the five ever asked what happened to those they had left behind.

No other programme surpassed the second episode's viewing figures. The number of simultaneous subscriptions to the feed caused interruptions to processing services across each of Tion's levels. The Odyssée project was not shut down at that point because the extraordinary demand was not forecast for future programmes, even if the contestants managed to progress through the Fours and Threes. The undisclosed production team became improbably rich, and there were calls for the publication of their identities.

The Five from Five were brought to a refurbished routers' elucidarium, cleared of its previous occupants specifically for the show. The level's entire population watched as the candidates were encouraged to make their most favourable impressions in the hope of selection. Of course, no one could predict how they would react after breaking their lifelong contracts. Some *sálirnar* thought the psychological stress would cause them to lash out at each other and suggested Odyssée was nothing more sophisticated than a baiting pit for young professionals. Just as viewers were beginning to lose interest, Enzo and Hyun-jun were brought into the spacious apartment and left to make their acquaintances. By the time Hyun-jun had earnestly spoken to all five candidates, Enzo had slept with each *konurnar* and one of the *mennirnir*.

When the programme concluded, and Enzo and Hyun-jun had left, the producers gave Sodality full access to the competitors. Debate raged for three hours until Inès was selected to join Odyssée. The online consensus suggested the producers should have kept the outcome from subscribers and announced it during the next instalment. Though less than ten billion people viewed the third episode, in the weeks that followed the content was replayed, transcribed, examined and picked apart, and theories abounded.

INÈS: I had to apply for Odyssée because I couldn't bear to watch you fail.

HYUN-JUN: There are countless *lýðirnir* who fail every day.

INÈS: Yes, but your success will give them hope.

ENZO: By granting disseveration to grass workers?

HYUN-JUN: Potentially, but we have to protect all production and distribution from the Sixes. Tion's future is entirely dependent on the empyrealodes.

INÈS: I disagree. The future is supposed to be the same as the present. The Pallium guarantees it.

HYUN-JUN: But the empyrealodes aren't self-regulating. Their degradation is a symptom of a systemic issue.

Inès: Which has nothing to do with Odyssée.

Enzo: Sodality chose us to make *mannkynið* aware. Someone told Noemí to help Hyun-jun.

Hyun-jun: We shouldn't speculate. What if it led to an uprising? The FMP will document everything we do, and others will interpret it. You know that.

Enzo: Popularity is empowering, Hyun-jun. Sodality will give us everything we require to reach our goals.

Hyun-jun: We have to be wary, Enzo. What if we lose their support?

Inès: There's no need to be anxious. Don't forget Sodality selected me. It's why I'm here with you.

The show was allegedly unmoderated and its subjects undirected, which was part of its appeal. Critics found examples of millennium-old video that followed a similar format, yet the language and behaviours were incomprehensible, and with no discernible goal other than survival, it was nonsensical. Odyssée's reimagined version was demonstrably using the same presentation techniques, particularly the selection and preparation of footage to support the documentarists' supposition, so no one could understand why Hyun-jun's carefully guarded words weren't expunged from the record.

'But it's not what I wanted from this contract,' Freja complained. 'We've committed too many resources to Miyu's entertainment, and someone is going to find us.'

'I agree,' Kavya said. 'The Five from Five left us with unexpected cachings for their abandoned co-workers. We should have found a better solution, and there's still the issue of the remaining four candidates. We're only getting away with it because of the advertising revenue. It's not justifiable.'

'At least Caitlyn was able to obtain caching vouchers for them. If it makes you happy, we can invest their fees in helping the unjoined or some other noble cause. We certainly don't need the staters.' Freja groaned. 'Now I sound like them.' She settled back in her chair and closed her eyes. 'I'll deal with the remaining contestants, if you can status our work schedule to check how far behind we are.'

Freja summoned the four dossiers and tiled them on one side. She presented the licence code that Jovana had discretely obtained and made a requisition to route a maintenance team up from the Sevens to wait outside the apartment's recently installed door.

Two men and two women had taken an enormous risk for the chance of a transformed life, and they sat silently in the closed room, disconnected from their constant technological companion for the first time. They did not know how to support each other in their information isolation and were probably too disconsolate to function together as a new unit.

Such little lives, really. With her extended access, Kavya had idly checked what happened when one segment of an operational team was no longer functional. She had complained bitterly to the others that labouring crew from the Sevens could recruit a replacement, while the Pallium dissolved groups from K5 and made the remaining individuals inoperative, clearing them away.

The maintainers were wearing *kostymer* and awaiting permission to move in, while their clients remained inert and unsuspecting. Freja lingered over her view of the black-clad people. What possible threat could *sálirnar* in the Fives be? she thought. Why do these workers feel compelled to protect themselves so fully? The FMP confirmed it was her responsibility to administer the caching, and yet she remained frozen while she considered the data.

What if she left them in their quarters, reconnected them to Sodality and subcontracted tasks to them? They would be grateful for the reprieve and welcome the opportunity. Freja thought it was better than disposing of them out of convenience. She could responsibly make this decision, just as Miyu had made hers. The additional staff would reduce the workload pressure, and allow Miyu and Jovana to concentrate on getting the boys into Second to inspect the projected processor damage themselves. It was a good plan, so Freja requested a remote simulacrum from the FMP.

She arranged to enter the room in full sight, with a slow fade into their reality to limit the shock of another *einstaklingur* joining them. As she expected, there wasn't much reaction, given that their vapid personalities were tenuous at best. She moved from *persónan* to *persónan*, but without any substance, the only way to connect with them was to give them a reason to listen. She hinted she could provide them with access to reality again.

Freja spoke earnestly about their project, withholding nothing and explained their importance to the tionsphere's future. She allowed them to join her team and explained that their destiny was uncertain without her. She told them their colleagues had already been legitimately cached. The first to affirm was the nineteen-year-old man who had not been intimate with Enzo. Freja privately informed him his abstention had secured him second place because the viewers were hoping their union would be the topic of a later instalment. The remaining three followed in quick succession, so she created a secure compartment for them to work in and sent the waiting *kostymän* back to the Depths.

When the women met for their evening meal, Caitlyn and Kavya were furious. The FMP had revoked the vouchers and Caitlyn received a fine for non-use. Freja argued for over an hour about their backlog and the motivation the new team had to be successful. Caitlyn threw everything back at her, screaming that no one cared about the real issue and none of them was likely to wake up in the morning. Jovana and Miyu were somewhat understanding but also expressed their concerns.

'We have to make this work,' Miyu said. 'I've found a way to get Hyun-jun into the FMP. He's the best tool we have to discover what's happening, but we shouldn't trust these other *lýðirnir.*'

Caitlyn listened patiently to their rationalisations and waited for them to reach an accord. She unwrapped a fresh pack of vouchers and instructed the Pallium to stop the four remaining participants' hearts.

Jovana met Hyun-jun, Inès and Enzo before their transition to K4. Enzo had an uneasy feeling about the coming days, and when he discovered the woman was not accompanying them, he became visibly agitated. He adamantly maintained that ghosting was not possible, and when Jovana inferred she was not permitted to take the rental body out of Fifth, he assumed she was abandoning them.

'The Sixes and Fives are practically the same article,' she explained. 'There is no free movement of *sálirnar* beyond either level, except support staff from the Depths. Occasionally, there is a need for specialists from higher up, but they rarely attend themselves for fear of not being able to re-ascend. Most of the time, people purchase a simulacrum, but if they need to interact with the environment, they ghost into it. The owner of the *másadá-saríra* is ghosted elsewhere, usually into a cheaper rental or, if he has an enormous sum of disposable staters, might be buffered by the Pallium.'

'What if the client doesn't want to release the body?' Inès asked.

'The owner can request a forcible offline if the user breaks the contract. Remember that ghosting isn't permanent. The FMP has to refresh the memory traces every eighty hours or so, otherwise, they degrade. Sometimes the original personality reasserts itself, but not always. Ultimately we're stuck with the flesh we're conceived into.'

Her reasoning made sense to Enzo, but still, it was an implausible claim. He could no more occupy Hyun-jun than he could behave like him. He was who he was, and so was Jovana. Enzo realised he would have to anticipate sedition in the *ljðirnir* he met if he was going to keep his party safe.

'Odyssée has amassed sufficient funds for you to transfer to K4,' Jovana said, 'but the advertising revenue can only generate a fraction of what you're going to need to ascend further. Miyu thinks we can rely on Fourth's numerous citizens to sponsor you. They're sophisticated and understand Tion, so you will have to entertain them. Remember everything we've spoken about and trust each other. There are always choices. I'll see you on the other side.'

'How will we know it's you?' Hyun-jun asked. A small cube materialised in the air before him, and Inès leant forward to take it. Hyun-jun was adept at creating images but had never seen anything so intricate. It was hard to focus on its surfaces as they rippled in minute detail.

'It's a representation of a quantum key,' Inès said. 'Jovana has the other one. They're virtually impossible to fake. If she can't produce hers when I ask for it, then it's not Jovana.'

Enzo thought about questioning her authenticity as an attempt to assert his authority over Inès. She was by far the most knowledgeable member of their group, and he would ultimately have to defer to her. Hyun-jun was also subservient and was continually divulging his most secret thoughts to her. Enzo sighed and readied himself for the journey through the Lacuna. Jovana left in the first transport and said they had to get used to being self-sufficient, and moments later they departed. Miyu had chosen a destination one hundred and sixty degrees away in the hope that an extended journey to the Fours would give sufficient time for the viewers to widely anticipate their arrival.

There were crowds of *fólkið* when they disembarked, but none of them was interested in migrants from below. Hyun-jun was profoundly concerned and placed a call to Miyu; however, Enzo didn't care. He was excited by the array of promotional stimulants that bombarded his senses: his heroism was recognised; he was sexually magnificent and his intellectual agility valued; several items of clothing could increase his appeal; some useful apps that would better manage the sudden influx of data and a variety of surgical enhancements that were frankly mandatory. One sophisticated advert offered to collate his future finances and allocate them across a multitude of services, promising to manage all the details once he agreed to an unbreakable contract. If Inès hadn't intervened, he would have committed his staters, and they would have lost him.

Hyun-jun addressed them authoritatively. 'Miyu provided an orientation ve-package that you need to install. I've rented a room and arranged an initial interview.'

Enzo barely slept over the next ten days and quickly had to prioritise requests for his attention. He was distantly aware that Inès and Hyun-jun were busy in their own ways, but when the notification came that their application to K3 was accepted and payment taken, he knew his contribution was the greatest.

A younger Jovana met them at the crossing into Third. She said she had ghosted in at significant cost on the other side and merely ridden down an unmanned escalator between levels. She did not have any paperwork to return the *māsadā-sarīra* but had a contact who would take it off her hands, so to speak. 'Hyun-jun is going to leave Odyssée at the border, and we've ensured there will be no record of him entering K3.' She looked directly at Enzo. 'Turn the e-ink off. Coloured teeth are not in fashion in the Threes. Or here. You two will continue the programme, but we're recasting you as gestorium engineers, which should boost our ratings. Please incorporate the ve-package as soon as you're able. We're hoping to get you to First inside a week using exploitative imagery of children. That should give Hyun-jun enough time.'

Jovana took Hyun-jun away before they could ask questions or say their goodbyes. Enzo and Inès waited hand-in-hand at the checkpoint while the demarcators scrutinised their TUIDs. At the next kiosk, the assizes confiscated their few possessions and scanned their bodies for hidden contraband. They were held for forty-five minutes and endured extensive searches, and two of the demarcators discretely asked how Odyssée had changed their lives. When the inter-level assizes finally allowed them to leave, they were offered an elevator to themselves, and Inès and Enzo walked naked into the Threes.

It was a long wait until the others went to bed, hours until it was possible to submit to Sodality, all the time knowing the exact sex service she needed, selected from an appropriate forum. To be someone different, reckless, young enough to make mistakes and old enough to understand the consequences, and without the other *konurnar* knowing where she was. The service assigned each participant with the previous customer's physical identity, and Freja had chosen a provider with a mandatory duration and breathtaking fee so that each client was unlikely to abandon an undesired persona and every persona was desirable. When the transfer was complete, she remained with her eyes closed until she received notification that her own identity had been utilised, and then offered her new self to herself. When Freja returned home, she felt a little more in control of her emotions.

Objectively, she understood Caitlyn had needed to tidy away Odyssée's loose ends, to cache the four remaining applicants and ensure the programme had a future. Yet Freja's passion, filled with resentment and bound tightly with pride, had left her resentful. She had been embarrassed by her previous decision to utilise the remaining finalists, and now she was ashamed of her online exploits. Freja set about purging all record of her activities associated with recent transgressions and spent the majority of the night attempting to clear her backlog. By the time Miyu woke, she had all but convinced herself that no harm had occurred.

'Any better?' Miyu asked.

Freja wasn't entirely sure what her question meant. 'You remember the population estimates you were working on?' Miyu nodded. 'I was studying the figures and depending on how you think about it; there's more we should take into account. It's a bit hard to prove, but there were active cultivators,' she threw some metrics on the wall, 'but their progeny never identified with the FMP. Millions of *tánin-fólkið* who've never connected. Miyu, these young people aren't even in the catalogue, unless they're utilising bogus TUIDs.'

'What about the closed communities, places like Vínculo? We have to be able to conduct experiments on actual people, for the good of *mannkynið*.'

Freja shook her head.

Miyu looked away from the numbers. 'Why are you doing this? Nobody cares how many *sálirnar* there are, as long as they all generate staters.'

'I know it's not a huge proportion but even the worst of the unjoined turn up eventually, either by forcing a connection or by being observed among the populace. Where would you hide that many people? At first, I thought the Pallium was failing to register them, but there's something more complex going on. Miyu, it's deliberate. My mistake now seems insignificant.'

Miyu poured some coffee and settled back to listen.

'I'm supposed to solve problems,' Freja said. 'I used to be good at it, but I can't design anything that would account for this delta. And it's well hidden, as though someone is managing it. I found something fairly odd last night, and I could use some help in making connections. It involves a Lacuna capsule forced from its routeing. Someone took the six *ný-fólkið* it was carrying to Fourth. It's not noteworthy, you know it happens all the time, and there is a healthy trade in bonded people. I tracked five of them down, but the last one, Danesh Ne-Baluda-Va-Wa, is elusive. The data suggests he has passed up and down through several levels and then made an unauthorised ghosting out of K7. I can't find where he went, which means I can't determine if he's returned. The signal didn't go anywhere, it just disappeared at the Pallium, and it will have been purged by now. Also, there's no evidence of the vacant *māsadā-sarīra*'s reuse, but there's no disposal transaction either.'

'What do you think it means?'

'Danesh is not living virtually in the FMP, Miyu. He'd have to be cached first.'

'Some *táningar* is missing. So what? New people go missing all the time, and we make adjustments. Fake a caching record and move on.'

Freja changed the presentation to show two complex decision trees, one starting with the missing adolescent and the other with the ailing processing level. There was no connection between them, and most of the branches ended without association, but there were two credible correlations between the structures, each tagged with a TUID.

'What can you tell me about them?' Miyu asked.

'Nothing much about the *ný-maður*. All that's unusual about Danesh is his trafficking didn't end up with him in a recognisable service. He was flitting about Tion like he had unlimited staters until I lost him. The other man, the *eldri*, is worth a whole lot more but he's trading fraudulently under an assumed TUID. His ghosting failed at the same time, but his transactions resume around an hour and a half later. I still have a lot of questions.'

'Have you submitted them?'

'Not to the Pallium. It can barely cope with the endless requests from Tion's population and all the pointless information the global *fólksfjöldi* generates. Have you noticed how slow it has become?'

'But if it is related, as you suspect, then the solution will be in there. You think the FMP tasked us. If that's true, then it will help you find an answer.'

Freja cleared the displays and began to extrapolate her new premise. They started to associate disparate observations and ideas and made tentative conclusions and tenable theories, which gave them more ideas to test. One by one, the other women joined them and debated their inferences. Kavya said their representation resembled a living system which evolved and changed as they worked, adapting to its environment.

'It's still a big jump to conclude the FMP is sentient,' Caitlyn said. 'The idea that it's behaving in a way to defend itself is improbable, no matter how much we want it to be true. Why would anyone want to cripple it?'

'Especially a fifteen-year-old man.'

'The trafficker is a bad lead,' Jovana declared and offered a ve-package. 'He delivered the *ný-maður* to order. We could spend hours digging up records that would tell us what we already know. He must be working for Pazel, and we should focus our efforts there, assuming the associations between your inferences are sound. That's a big leap too. I am concerned that this is just another distraction and we're already dividing our time unnecessarily.'

Caitlyn nodded. 'We know what we've committed to, but there's nothing much we can use. Maybe Hyun-jun will give us some answers. Maybe Pazel will lead us to some resolution. Maybe it will all come to nothing. We need to do something to move forward, and we will eventually have to take action.'

Freja was struggling to pay attention to the debate. She had chanced upon Pazel Sad-Tet-Ain-Resh and assigning him any blame for the Pallial Decline was naïve; even so, she could not abandon the idea. Nothing she discovered about the outrightsider made sense, her knowledge was a few scattered pieces of an immense puzzle, and she couldn't even calculate its extent. Freja opened a circular ve-pad and sketched the outline for a new search routine, something she could submit and then ignore. She might arrive at a better conclusion through metaheuristics, rather than her methodical approach thus far. Pazel had purchased the boy and, if he still lived, he wouldn't abandon him. She would locate Danesh again and find a way to gain his trust.

Freja wasn't sure what else the other women wanted her to do.

Danesh completed his review of several *bogdos* that Victoria recommended as well-protected with a high success rate. She said he was employed to move people discretely through Tion and should learn everything he could. Danesh had expected every transition between levels to be as smooth as his own had been, but Victoria soon realigned his expectations. There was a long list of things that might cause her to abort, notwithstanding a lack of hard staters. She suggested he'd pick it up as he went along and promised not to expect him to cope with anything too unpredictable.

He was struggling to separate Pazel's experiences from his own. It was easy to rationalise: Danesh's life comprised an unremarkable nonage in Sixth, an uneventful journey through Tion and an unexpected job. His head was full of people, places and peculiarities that clearly were not his, even though they felt as real as his time spent with Shu-fen. He also recognised there were gaps in the narrative where Pazel had not shared. Danesh did not question why because he was engrossed in the motivations of the *sálirnar* around him.

Victoria preferred to use certified routes between spheres for her clients and frowned on spontaneity. She claimed it increased the likelihood of failure. Of her two favoured options, Victoria recommended he focus on the quiet diversion of scheduled transports, either through clever code inserted into the FMP or via a third party. She assured him there were always decent, honest *hÿðirnir* who would do almost anything for a discrete bribe. Most of the fixed corridors were manned, like the one they had used to leave K3. Victoria warned him not to underestimate the attendants and said the little girl could bring the might of the Depths to bear if she chose to. He thought better of asking if she was actually a child.

Within a few days, Danesh was managing clients through low-risk movements between Seventh and Eighth. Some of them were so trivial that he protested any involvement, reminding Victoria that anyone could walk down into the Eights. She said he was right, but pointed out that certain *fólkið* wanted to do so without an audit trail and that was where Pazel liked to help. Throughout his training, he worked alongside Victoria and met with the majority of his clients. Danesh appreciated the simple human contact with them. They handled most of their negotiations in person, and he found his need to be continuously engrossed in Sodality had waned. His short time with Pazel had already made him doubt its truth. Unfortunately, he had no interaction with other workers and started to think that life in a K4 district may have given him more freedom or at least some form of payment.

'This need for compensation comes from him,' Victoria said. 'He's driven by it, and you've inherited that desire. Do a good job, Danesh, and Pazel will reward you.'

'Did the same happen to you?' he asked.

'I'm just a regular employee, charged with showing you around and helping you understand the way things work. He's usually got a few *sálirnar* learning from him, and I think he considers it a kind of insurance. I have a lot of respect for Pazel. He has some bold ideas about the future, and I'm sure he'll make them happen. That's his talent.'

'You agree with him.'

'The world is a complicated place, and you've experienced only a minuscule part of it. You're a child in almost every way, Danesh. Your entire adulthood comprises what Pazel gave you. You should be grateful you didn't have to figure it out for yourself.'

'Like you did, Victoria?'

'Hey. I'm on your side. You want something to eat?'

Danesh sifted through everything that Pazel knew about Victoria. He remembered her as a *ný-kona*, warm against his skin and keen to learn about the world. She had chosen him, and he had allowed her to stay and taught her to be of value to him. He had made her responsible for his new adherents, which left Danesh conflicted because he felt he had tasked her to look after his induction, and it was very confusing. He also saw the résumés of other young people making a line of *ný-fólkið* preparing for whatever came, and he was the least experienced. He stared at his competition and understood his place in Pazel's contest. Victoria was dedicated to Pazel and served him without question. It did not matter that she was an employee; she was not concerned with his schemes and did not care if they were just. She feigned hiding her love for this man, but Pazel knew she was his. Danesh found he felt nothing for her.

Somewhere a young girl cowered, inert and oblivious. She cried herself silent because the only *maður* she had ever loved had abandoned her. Shu-fen trusted him, and he had let her down and bequeathed his loyalty to a stranger. Danesh tried to imagine what she felt while she waited, but he was empty. He wasn't even concerned that he couldn't envisage Shu-fen's face. She was simply an amorphous abstraction of an individual and an idea poorly formed in his boyhood mind. He attempted to picture her as he had done so many times since mid-nonage, but she wouldn't come, no matter how much he willed it. How many other *lýðirnir* had lost each other, he wondered, missing in the complexities of semi-forgotten? Danesh did not want that for himself. He wanted to be counted and to have an impact. The future that Pazel had cast for him was not one he would have chosen, despite the choice he made before Cristóbal. Tion's vast population would cry out in anguish at Pazel's plan. It was a drastic reduction where no one would know anyone who survived. Danesh tried to list his nonage friends and managed to recall a hundred, but if he could reach them all and each could do the same with theirs, he could probably reach Tion's entire *fólksfjöldi* with a few messages. He realised the odds of anyone he had known making it through were depressingly small.

Danesh knew he deserved something better. They all did.

As he walked alongside Victoria towards the plaza, he became increasingly distracted by the barrage of commercial interrupts. Pazel had divorced him from his identity on their return from Second: Danesh Ne-Baluda-Va-Wa no longer existed and he was grateful. He was a little uncertain about who he had become, but one small benefit was that the marketing apps couldn't target their wares. The software made assumptions about his desires from his physical appearance and concluded he was important enough to have an identity-suppressor installed. It was easy to ignore things that held little interest for him, but there seemed to be an algorithmic breakthrough occurring all around him. There were identical girls dressed in white with various morsels to delight him, rugged men with the latest tools, ready to rescue him, and paternal figures promising to make everything better. He tried to block the messages, but it was evident that something had found him.

Every plaza was built to the same design and sized to suit the local workforce. Danesh admired the ease of it. He knew wherever they went his choice would hold and the quality of one offering would be as any other, but the food was awful, and it tasted like re-processed shit, which Victoria assured him it was. He had asked her why people were so accepting, and she said they were conditioned to by the infomercials. The advertising became more personal until a woman finally approached him.

'You must try this,' the image said, 'you'll like it… Danesh.'

Victoria was entirely ignorant of the exchange because, for her, the advert did not exist.

All around him, epitomes generated by the Pallium were speaking his name, and he felt the grey mush rise from his stomach as panic set in. He looked around the narrow passageway. There were vendors crushed along one side, benches for eating on the other and thousands of people surrounding him. He was sure that one of them would spot his discomfort, or recognise him as the advertisements started collaborating to win market share. He held his hand to his mouth and willed his stomach to desist because he did not want to draw attention to himself.

'Danesh,' crooned a sales agent. 'Come with me. I need to show you something. You'll like this, Danesh. You mustn't ignore me. Shit fuck cunt. This is all that you need to feel incredible.' The image beckoned to him and tried to lure him away from his associate.

'I'll catch up with you in a bit,' Danesh said. 'I just need to hang out.'

Victoria mumbled something through her food and waved him away. *Ten minutes*, she messaged.

Danesh thought about all of the adverts he had seen and everything that had been ignored by Pazel. Except for specialised services, the commercials he had seen were uniformly polite. There was an *alþýða* behind this epitome, an actual person, he was sure of it, and although he was supposed to stay in the shadows, he wanted to know who it was.

The advert didn't take him very far, and they stopped just out of Victoria's view. He settled on a bench between two women who stared into the infinite while they ate. He ignored them as their elbows dug into him and grey drips of food fell to their feet. Neither of them acknowledged him in return. The epitome didn't hesitate to play him its sales material, which was a repetitive set of animations showing Danesh with increased physical prowess, accompanied by her soothing voice, explaining how he could have statuesque beauty for minimal cost and zero effort. As he listened, there were occasional words that didn't belong: help, save, connect; words out of context and expletives forced into the patter, hoping to reach him.

He wanted to help the messenger and touched *More* at every opportunity, hastening the pitch to its natural conclusion. Eventually, it asked him to confirm his identity.

Danesh Ne-Baluda-Va-Wa.

Gotcha.

He waited to see what she would do, but when the commercial ended, the figure faded away. Danesh was already a few minutes late, but Victoria did not comment as they returned to their work. He followed her instructions quietly, and when she asked why he seemed subdued, Danesh blamed the food.

Throughout his life and Pazel's, Danesh had wanted something else. It didn't matter if Shu-fen was the most attractive girl or if Victoria could teach him new skills, whatever he had right now was not enough. This *alþýða* who had found him had something he needed, and he couldn't anticipate what it was. Danesh felt the excitement of it welling up inside of him until it was ready to erupt from his being. He thought of nothing else while he feigned interest in his clients, a pathetic trio from K7 who wanted to disappear into the Greater Numbers. For the second time, he faced a choice. This one was no less uncertain than the last, but he felt its poignant difference. It was a goal he would have to pursue, not select when if the opportunity arose. He felt empowered and secure in the knowledge that he was in control, not Pazel.

No more targeted media attempted to tempt him with hidden messages or unexpected profanities. For a while, Danesh thought he had lost his unspoken struggle, and so he was not ready to decide when it was finally time.

He was astonished by her brashness. Victoria introduced him to a new client who wanted someone to accompany her on multiple transfers between adjacent spheres. She said Freja was hand-carrying certain legitimate information which her patron did not wish to be uploaded. If the relationship went well, Freja might also hire someone to up-level her, and she hoped they would be willing to help. When he shook her hand, she smiled and turned to Victoria. 'It's so nice to meet him. I vetted him a while back, over lunch. I think you were there. I do believe he's the right *maður* for the job.'

Victoria simpered through the polite conversation while she battered Danesh on a private channel. He told her he didn't realise what had occurred and that he felt violated. Secretly he was delighted to meet this woman and couldn't wait to be alone with her. They made the round-trip three times before he had an opportunity.

'Why are you here, Freja?' he asked.

'I need your help, Danesh, but I don't trust you. I think you have a problem with maintaining your allegiance. I'm part of a team supporting an influential client, and I suspect you're working for someone who is causing significant harm. I can't prove any of it. So, I want you to.'

'If I help you?'

'And Pazel finds out?' She looked at him coldly, daring him to refute her assertion. 'Have no doubt. He'll kill you. There will be no caching.'

'Not really what I need.'

'Help me make the connection, Danesh, and I can deal with the rest. There's minimal risk to you if we're careful.'

'And what do I get?'

'Assistance. I can acquire priority processing and access to a significant amount of information.'

'Do you know what he's planning?' Danesh asked.

'He's not who he appears to be, and he has a lot of influence across Tion. We're struggling to determine his net worth due to complications with identities. His behaviours have recently changed, and I suspect he is preparing to execute his plan. Do you know what it is?' Freja took him by the hands and studied his face.

'Yes. You won't survive it. None of us will.'

They stood silently at the bottom of the escalator as torrents of people flowed past them, trying to push them towards a better life. The walls swept up above the staircase in a great circle with metal panels welded together, each one the width of Danesh's outstretched arms. 'I think we need each other,' he said. 'If I'm going to stop him, I might need some help.'

She laughed but not in spite of him. 'You will have to tell me.'

He tugged her onto the moving stairway and pointed into their immediate future. 'Eventually, when I understand it all. If you tell me what he's doing, I can probably tell you why.'

'Where did he take you, Danesh? Before you disappeared.'

'He called it the Interdiction, by which he meant a forbidden place,' [*data*]. 'It's somewhere that's not supposed to exist.'

They reached the top and entered the narrow queuing lanes for their access to K7. Danesh leant his head on one wall with his fingertips brushing the wall opposite and allowed Freja to press against him. They settled into the familiar crush and edged towards the demarcators' desks, sidestep by sidestep. There was no Sodality for them to languish in; not even a clock to show the passing of the slow minutes. It left the people around him unsettled due to their lack of connection to the FMP. It amazed him that there wasn't an overwhelming cacophony of voices as people so used to constant communications searched for some kind of intimacy.

Freja was watching him. 'I suppose the silence helps to unnerve people,' she said. 'It doesn't upset you, though, and I wonder why that is. You don't strike me as an isolationist.'

He tried to cherish the solitude, but his face quickly broke into a broad smile. 'I have a lot to consider at the moment, so I enjoy the peace. It's been quite a surprise. You think that Pazel has a vision, but it's much more simple than that.' The smile faded. 'He has a survival instinct raging deeply within him, so much so that I can taste it. It is bitter and sharp and makes me want to escape from him and run to him. It smells of fresh opportunity and the decay of the Depths, and it's ugly and noisy and jagged. Pazel's shown it to me, and it's not something I could forget. It's a beast of a thing, and he will use it to keep us at bay while he creates a new world. Everything else is irrelevant, and he'll leave it behind, cut-off and rotting.'

'What is he surviving?'

They edged along the glass corridor, not caring who overheard them. 'I think Pazel doesn't understand the world. With care, there could be a balance if we want it, or even a managed reduction. What he wants is a dramatic conclusion. He's impatient for it. He'd cut off my arm rather than wait to see if my hand healed.' He looked at his unblemished palm.

'You speak like an *eldri-maður*, not a young man who has recently newed. What happened, Danesh?'

'Pazel shared his aspirations with me and expects them to be mine. He wanted to tempt me with a view of the future that I should have anticipated, in a place that can't exist.'

'Second? Is that why the Pallium is failing? Is it that simple?'

Danesh was silent as they crept towards the desk. The throughway was still busy but not overcrowded and had a sterile peacefulness that he quite liked. He composed himself, and she didn't interrupt him as he dressed in his character. By the time they reached the demarcator and identified, he was a licensed escort charged with taking his distinguished guest out of the mire. They passed through without question and collected her meagre belongings before requesting transport to the accommodation Victoria had arranged.

Once he had washed and shaved, Danesh felt a lot less enigmatic. He was disappointed that he had danced around the choice. Now his indecision was forcibly leading him back towards the security of what was known. Freja had told him about her contract and the other women working with her to understand the Decline. If parasites were eating through the FMP, surviving in hollowed out spaces within its quantum innards, then there was no mystery after all. Danesh declared her team would fail because Pazel had more ambition. His plans thrived on the wreckage of the Forming and the despair of abandoned multitudes. He would build his world on the husk of the old. Pazel willed it and would bring that death closer in every way he could. Danesh told her he was terrified, even though it wasn't the case. Secretly he yearned for confrontation because surviving Pazel meant outwitting Pazel, and the anticipation was overwhelming.

Freja had told Danesh she could show him how to hide his thoughts from his employer, if he chose to help, and how to be an independent *maður*. He would be safe, she said, and he would be able to save countless others. There might be a way to transfer Pazel's assets to the man that defeated him. Freja didn't know how much time they had but mentioned she was sending someone into the Pallium to find the truth and thanked him for his cooperation thus far.

Danesh suspected his future depended on preserving the processing level. He thought about the densely-packed, awesome quantum machinery that encircled Tion. It seemed impossible to him that such a small number of people could cause so much havoc and could destroy its capability so readily. Surely, if he lost such a small proportion of his brain, he would adapt? Freja said this was correct; however, he was using so very little of his brain. It was remarkable that the FMP could accept every request from the proliferating population, and its ability to comprehend that information and respond appropriately was miraculous. She assured him the Pallium fully utilised every component within its vast structure.

Danesh intended to supplant Pazel, assume all that was his and reach stasis. Yes, he wanted to profit from it, but he had no interest in destroying the world to attain his goals. It required a certain subtlety, patience and hushed determination, and he was far from ready. He hoped Pazel would continue on his cautious path, but in the meantime, he was hungry and sent a request to Freja for some decent food.

His nonage cuisine had been a thick sludge that came in a variety of colours, two temperatures and one taste. It was an addictive mix of sweet and salty and umami, full of protein and fats and essentials for growth. Food was freely available wherever he wanted, and there were no set times for its consumption. It contained molecular machines to regulate hormones and thus the FMP controlled hunger, thirst, development and body composition. The gestoria manufactured little children, governing every stage of their development from conception through a process that lasted fifteen years, guaranteeing a full complement of adult characteristics. Now the Pallium's distant and ever-present service was slowly eroding, and billions of children would perish within days of its demise. Danesh could prevent that after he had eaten.

Freja promised to take him somewhere where the food was incredible. Home-cooking, she said, was the answer he sought. They were en route to a water crew's quarters, a few degrees away and high up in Seventh. The team were often absent, and their sysadmin had built a quiet reputation for her hospitality, providing you knew who to ask. Freja had arranged to eat with her and promised Danesh it would be worth his while.

Tingting Kaf-Ayin-Beh-Keheh was a fair bit shorter than Danesh. He wondered if her nonage food had contained algorithmic errors because she looked much older than the average person. Her black hair was angrily pulled away from her face and accented her already narrowed eyes. She spoke swiftly and misformed some of her words, as if she was unable to comprehend their importance. He assumed there was something wrong with her.

'Call me Tabitha,' she barked as they entered the workroom, 'I cook for you, you enjoy.' And that was that. The chamber was easily large enough for a dozen *lýðirnir* to live in without feeling that they crowded each other. Nothing was out of place; the simple furnishings were genial and the ambience considered.

She's an outrightsider, Danesh exclaimed. *Like Pazel.*

Four right-to-left mojis doesn't make either one of them stupid, Freja said. *Be careful you don't attract a bias tariff.*

But something is wrong with her.

She's forsaken. She's never connected.

Like the fólkið *I saw in Second?*

Possibly.

So how did you find her?

Her crew are her advocates. 'She looks after them,' Freja said aloud. 'Don't worry because she's not paying us any attention. She doesn't interact the way we do, and it's difficult for her to understand. Tabitha's crew reward her for her loyalty, and when they are absent, she takes on occasional jobs. The cost is breathtaking, but you certainly won't beat this.'

She guided him towards the low table, and they sat cross-legged on the floor. There was room for at least twenty *sálirnar* to eat, and Danesh wasn't surprised when, in twos and threes, more people arrived. They seated themselves comfortably and chatted in quiet voices with their neighbours as if this was a commonplace activity. There seemed to be very little in the way of quantum exchange. Gradually the guests, mostly mid-life, excused themselves to use one of the two cleantubes and returned to the table looking relaxed and happy. An ebullient palette of flesh tones surrounded Danesh, and his golden skin was nestled warmly among them.

Tabitha brought a jug to the table. One of the *miðaldra-mennirnir* went from *einstaklingur* to *einstaklingur* and leant across them as he poured the pale wine into their beakers. The man pressed his hand against Danesh's shoulder as he served. 'You will prevail,' he said before moving behind Freja and offering her other words. Danesh sipped from the cup and waited as the liquor attacked his tongue. He felt alive.

They took it in turns to serve the food that Tabitha brought to the table. When it was Danesh's turn, he almost shrivelled from view, but Freja reminded the guests he had only just newed, and his every experience was fresh. He found the courage to mutter a few words to each diner and gained confidence as he went. Each dish was small, just a mouthful to savour, but it seemed as endless as the wine, and Danesh felt sated. As the meal continued, they shared their stories, some of which were fantastical and others heart-warmingly simple.

'I've not much to tell,' Danesh apologised as they urged him to speak. 'You genuinely are the first *lýðirnir* I've met, other than clients.' Some of the women nodded their encouragement and waited for him to continue. 'Nothing happened to me when a little *drengar*, but some of the other *börnin* were important to me. One of them. I'm not sure what happened to her because some *útlendingar* took her and I won't see her again. I don't know what happened to the strangers.' He had retained nothing of her at all. 'Now, I help people realise their ambitions, and that's how I met Freja. We're accompanying each other for now. It's exciting, but we'll leave each other eventually because that's what happens. There must be a reason. I can't make a difference if I can't understand.'

One of the *konurnar* waved him back into his seat. 'There are too many *fólkið*,' the woman whispered. 'It's impossible to tell a story from a lone vantage.'

'Do you think the growth will stop?'

'Some say that equilibrium occurred decades ago, long before any of our conceptions. Cultivators are very few and provide only to Third and First, and they represent a tiny fraction of the population. The gestoria manufactures everyone else because the FMP wills it in response to cachings or the occasional loss.'

'You speak like it's alive,' the naked man next to her said.

'It's certainly not dead, Oliver,' she retorted, patting his penis condescendingly. 'What could a carbon-wright know of such things?'

'But what if it's dying?' Freja asked. 'If it were, we should surely save it.'

Let me try, Danesh messaged her.

'We need to pool our knowledge,' he said. 'Our future is threatened by certain *sálirnar* who have attained great persuasive power. We don't matter in their future, not you or I as individuals, but everyone, in every level. There is evidence of destruction, arc by arc, with no hope of repair. Parts have infestations, and the rot is spreading. We need to do something.'

Ridiculous.

Liar.

Outrage.

'We already know.'

Tabitha approached the table, empty-handed and expectant. She had silenced the discussion with her words and pointed at Danesh.

'New man speak truly but need assist. Many group suspect, he prove. Future rest in one *mannvera* grasp, obliged aid that one human being. Finish food, talk, love. Decide help.' She brought warmed fruit and overly-sweet sauces for pouring. Danesh was no longer hungry and toyed with his serving. The murmured conversation was now between individuals, and he was aware of his exclusion, but it didn't concern him. These *fullorðnir* might decide to accept him and his unsettling thesis, or they could reject him as a child, despite his sanctioned status. If Pazel were an actual threat, someone would respond, and these people might choose him to represent them. He doubted Pazel would reserve a place for him in the new world.

As the guests finished eating the conversation became more light-hearted and focused on the moment. One of the younger *konurnar* sang a complexity of alien lyrics that both puzzled and delighted Danesh. She meandered through endless pre-Forming languages, selecting each word for its sound, the shape of her lips, the tone of its release, not caring that her lyric was incomprehensible. As she became more absorbed, she circled the table, and he wondered if he could ever become immersed in such music. She brushed against him, and her fingers traced over his chest and neck, then moved from man to woman and sang her strange song. One of the *mennirnir* kissed her throat, and his glistening arousal pierced the ambience, others helped him, drew Danesh in and gained his support. There were mouths and hands, lips tasting of the ripeness of youth, expert touches from years of experience, nipples alive and invitations made, and a slick shared heat that brought them together. Hope and challenge, commitment and optimism charged the aether, it was inside Danesh, and he was also inside, and the caresses never ended. These people needed to survive. It was his assumed responsibility, and he did not want to lose the moment.

'I can't stay with you,' Freja breathed. 'This body isn't mine, Danesh, and all we've shared is a borrowed experience. It's probably true for all of Tabitha's guests. You may have been the only genuine *alþýða* here tonight. I have more work to do, and I can't risk a recognised association with you. It would make us both vulnerable. You need to find allies of your own and create opportunities, not wait for them. We think there are many years left before action is required, and you will have time to make a difference.'

Danesh slept soundly after Freja left. When he woke, the table was gone, and there was no sign of the diners. His clothes were fresh and folded neatly, so he tubed before slipping them on. He rummaged hungrily through the kitchen area, looking for something to eat. There was nothing that he could associate with food, except for a large device which the FMP informed him would quietly weave free molecules from the air into a variety of edibles. He set the sequencer running, but all it produced was a sweet, sticky foam, and he could not see how to reprogram it. He decided not to interrupt his host's rest and switched the food printer off.

As it had been previously, his transition to Eighth was uneventful. Other than a brief validation of his assumed TUID, the demarcators showed little interest. They did not care about a *ný-maður* who chose to leave the more prosperous third of Tion behind. Victoria was waiting for him at the company office and demanded to know why he was almost a full day behind schedule. He still did not know if she was his ally or even his friend.

'It was different without you,' he ventured. 'When we were alone, Freja said she wanted to spend time with me. I didn't know what to do.'

'I doubt that. Did she have you?'

'Of course. Why wouldn't she?'

'That doesn't account for the rest of your time. Pazel's been asking questions. Quite rightly, I believe.'

They were in a tiny room, furnished with an oversized round table and two chairs. Danesh felt they were crammed into the space, the unwanted furniture pushing them together and separating them at the same time.

'What else happened?' she demanded.

'Nothing.' The pause was uncomfortable, and he felt compelled to add, 'nothing untoward.'

The cubicle rapidly darkened until Danesh could barely see Victoria. He became aware of the fresh smell of heat and intimacy, and he tasted his sweat on his lips. Voices moaned his name. He heard himself cry for more, and groans filled his head.

Danesh, Danesh. There were hands on his body, and he felt damp secrets at his fingertips. People held each other in the shadows. He saw his own face, and it was numb with elation.

'Well?' Victoria stared at him with ice in her eyes.

His mouth was dry, and he could not speak. Everything around him stopped.

'Well?' she repeated. Her slap was sharp across his face; it stung deeply but did nothing to suppress his hardness. 'You little fuck. Didn't you know I would be watching you? Three hours I listened to your bullshit and watched your pathetic attempts to satisfy those arseholes. What's wrong with you, Danesh? Why would you do this to me?'

His arousal faded, and tears welled up in his eyes. He was not used to these emotions, but he let them wash over him because they might be useful and enable him to reclaim his stake. How much had Victoria understood? She would have killed him if she thought he had betrayed Pazel. Victoria would invoke the caching voucher he was sure she held for him, but he knew she would want to hurt him first and make him pay for his betrayal. He was determined not to incriminate himself.

'I didn't think you wanted me like that,' he said. 'You should have told me. My experiences before now were all childish, and it was inevitable that this would happen. I wish it had been with you and not with them.' She stared at him, coldly. He did not know if this was sufficient and if he had found the source of her anger.

'You're all I have, Victoria.' He hardly dared to assume she was so foolish as to believe him.

'I listened to you speak to them. It's not your place to share Pazel's dreams with anyone. How dare you!' She raised her hand again, and he leant towards her to welcome her intention. The blow did not reach him in the way of its predecessor; instead, it brought him to life again. He would have her, now. He got up and slipped his clothes from his lean body, sprang with anticipation, and devoured her. At his moment of victory, he pictured himself standing over Pazel, shooting death into him, and she saw.

Victoria clamped down on him with her legs around his buttocks and hands around his throat. In his cresting incapacity, for all of his vitality and youth, he could not fend her off, and he felt himself slip from consciousness. Danesh was dimly aware as she bit down hard on his lower lip, and then he was lost.

Chapter Seven
Freja
বর্তমান

HE CAME ROUND with a start, as though the Pallium had switched him on. Immediately he knew he wasn't entirely Danesh and that she had cut parts of him out, but still, her work wasn't complete. He could not feel himself. She had taken him from reality and was hacking away to find the truth. Danesh did not expect to survive.

His world was without any sensation at all, nor was there any connection. He was aware something had splayed out his *sikatā-ātamā*, the way a killer might display the intimate secrets of her victim, heart and lungs to the left, liver and kidneys to the right, intestines tumbling below. Victoria was examining him: each of his experiences separated from his hopes; his past from his fantasies and his loyalties from his deceits. His essence had been pared back to its progenitor, the psychological root of his very nature, tailored at conception by the Pallium according to its unfathomable strategy and now the subject of fierce scrutiny. There was a pervasive sense of disappointment, tinged with frustration, as if some other hunter had previously removed more precious organs and the real trophies were already gone.

Nevertheless, he was also sure he was still himself. He remembered everything that was his and the borrowed vignettes that belonged to Pazel, but when he tried to focus the detail eluded him. Danesh felt something pull at a memory, but its elasticity failed, and it broke, disappearing from his life. Disparate memories evaded her examination altogether, until out of desperation, she sliced again and again until they were lost. He couldn't mourn them because they meant nothing to him now. *Sálirnar* he had once loved surrounded him, and they were slowly becoming strangers.

Everything was black, and Youssef found it intolerable. Fire had always been his salvation, and he needed its searing sterility to keep the night at bay. Youssef would purify everything and use the flames to reveal the features surrounding him. It was the only weapon he possessed, even if he could not summon its legions at will. Simply imagining its fury did not cause it to exist. He needed a catalyst to create the spark, but from then, he was the master. Youssef respected fire because it was hard to acquire and often impossible to subdue. It was his ally, and he relied on its burning support to remain conscious and find himself again.

He searched in his private gloom, and sorted through the details, cataloguing the inconsistencies. There was pain, not caused by his internal blaze, but from the tears in his flesh. The first bullet had knocked him onto the groundplate, but he had caught only one other, which had shattered his left knee. The rip in his shoulder was deep but confined to muscle tissue and would be easy to repair. Youssef visualised the regiment of tiny *vélarnar* deep inside him, cellular machines sheltered in the cybercyte vesicle. He called them to arms and demanded they attack the damage and disassemble the two bullets and broken bone fragments. Pour these atoms into my bloodstream, Youssef commanded, and put them to good use. He did nothing about the pain. His microscopic, manufactured foot soldiers left their slumber behind, furiously multiplied until they were an overwhelming force and started to make him whole again.

He usually kept the *raja'a* at bay while he was awake, despite the protestations of his overseer. Overnight, he trusted it with routine aftercare and always woke up the man he was on that first day. Sometimes he would use drugs to remain awake and stubbornly deny their purging, but ultimately, his cybercytes always won. Often as he drifted into sleep, Youssef thought about the man he could have become if he had been able to evolve, but that stranger faded in the morning.

Youssef permitted his mind to drift, but when there was so much damage, he worried that, without supervision, the molecular machines might misbehave and utilise his precious stem cells to form unwanted limbs or other protrudents. He endured in his usual, stoic fashion to keep their exuberance in check. Youssef was not sure he had chosen wisely, even after all this time. The cybercytes did not let him mature or adapt, and he was in every way the same man who had signed the covenant in his optimistic youth. Youssef could not control their relentless determination, only influence the eagerness with which they operated. As the years rapidly slipped by, he imagined he became more aware of the price he had paid.

The *raja'a* ensured Youssef always woke refreshed, but with no recollection of the previous day's experiences. If he had remembered to offline his short-term memory, he could access its content, but it did not feel real. Youssef used to read his dailies to interpret who he was, but the reports had become increasingly unfamiliar. He was a *útlendingur* to himself, other than the bright recollection of everything before he received the cybercyte vesicle. He had tried different technologies to remember from one day to the next, but after he slept, they were always gone. His internal machines spent each night comparing every aspect of his *māsadā-sarīra* with his baseline and diligently resolved any discrepancies, biological or otherwise. He had relinquished his ability to die, becoming a stranger to himself, but at the cost of recall when the busy cybercytes repaired him. It was altogether possible he would endure forever.

The pain reduced, and Youssef took this as a sign his cybercytes had started to repair his injuries. In particular, his knee charted circuits between numbness and oblivion, each one less protracted than its predecessor. In a short time, he would be able to walk again. He tried to lift his arm and push himself up from the bloody pool, but the limb did not yet belong to him. The busy *vélarnar* would find it again and reconnect its nerves, restoring him to his optimal pattern. He wondered if he should have recast before they gave him the cybercyte vesicle and the cellular machines synched with his genome. In his haste to escape the pre-Forming, he had not realised how imperfect his physique was. The current pain continued to subside.

He focused his eyes to look for Rabindra, but his head would not move, so all he could see was the devastated wall and the too-close skyplate. The smell of bloodshed was overwhelming. There were wet sounds near him as slippery things moved over each other without any volition. Youssef was sure he didn't want to see and was suddenly grateful that he never remembered.

Youssef's Pallial connection brightened, and he glanced at his backlog of dailies. The master record detailed his overseer and general status. Caitlyn had left him an endless repetition of his life, and it disinterested him. It was unlikely to be more than a list of *sálirnar* to avoid and things he should do, and Youssef reasoned he wouldn't have made it this far if he had been compliant. At least she had kept on top of his public queue. There were a handful of messages from *lýðirnir* he didn't know. Youssef emptied his ve-box.

Give us this day our daily reset. Youssef did not resent the *raja'a* because it was as much a part of him as anything else, and it was who he was. Each time he slept, the bioapp ensured the details of the weeks leading up to the surgery were fresh in his memory. They would always be his vivid reality, and Youssef could never forget why he had agreed. He was unaware of how many decades had eluded him because they were never his in the first place. Youssef checked his records. He was nine hundred and forty-nine years old.

For most of that time, he had never been able to love. Every woman he embraced was a stranger in the morning, and he found self-voyeurism repugnant. He could not form deep connections with anyone following the surgery and everyone he remembered from before was gone. Youssef had understood this fate when he signed up, although he had not contemplated its true meaning. There were two relationships he tried to maintain, but he would have to let them go too, just as he did their predecessors. He kept detailed logs on his interactions with them both. Connor was an easy-going regenerator. There was nothing special about him, except he did not complain about Youssef's forgetfulness. Caitlyn was Youssef's overseer and the current owner of his contract. He had not met her in the three forgettable years they had worked together, but he had researched her well and trusted his selection. Her only job was to keep him discretely hidden away until he was finally required to carry out his *konservator* designation, bestowed on him by the *fullorðnir*. Once he had achieved their goal, he would be free to pursue his own life again. Youssef was pleased that Tion had not changed in all of his time.

When the cybercytes returned his right arm, he breathed deeply and pushed himself into a sitting position. The pain had regressed, and his knee looked whole. He steadied himself until he was standing in the crimson gore and started pushing at the corpses with his toe. Unless he was mistaken, none of these men was Rabindra. He made a note in his log that expressed his extreme dismay at being left behind for dead. Having unlimited time meant a man could plan to catch up with people, but not knowing from day to day lessened the incentive. Rabindra had disappointed him, and he was determined to make his feelings known.

Youssef felt strong again and strode away from the carnage. He stripped the torn and bloodied workwear away as he walked and commanded the cybercytes to slough his cropped hair and outer layer of skin. He was a perfect, flawless, brown man who couldn't possibly have survived the onslaught.

Danesh was lying in the dark, cold and naked, with his knees tucked to his chest, and he remembered everything. He knew without touching that he was inside a small crate, scarcely larger than his young body. She had put him in there, without water or concern for his hygiene. He was vaguely aware that the box was moving, probably in the mechanical arms of a deliverer. He didn't remember why she had done this to him or why he deserved such punishment. Maybe he wasn't sure who he was.

He was dimly aware of open sockets around him, but as he groped towards them, he failed to understand their protocols. He was alone with thoughts that made little sense. As Danesh sifted through, there was a mouth-wateringly familiar aroma that reminded him of contentment, so he followed it as it led to memory after memory, until he eventually understood who he was. Buried in these scraps were the rules of his *sikatā-ātamā* that made him Danesh, and they were ready for him to claim. There was someone else hidden too, an old man, an *eldri-maður*, who had once been part of him, and was now an illustrated explanation of the other personality.

Now he was apart, Danesh found he missed Pazel desperately. He was appalled at their separation and wanted to be made whole again, but was terrified of the consequences. Was

Pazel the best hope for the future and a guarantee that at least something remained? Or was he deluded, doomed to force an unnecessary apocalypse? Was Pazel the cause of destruction or the saviour from it? Icy dampness seeped beneath Danesh's buttocks, and he recoiled because of the chill it brought. He was too confused to feel degraded.

Why was he being kept alive? If they were taking him to Pazel, what would he say? Had Victoria sold him into service or Freja rescued him? He wasn't sure what he would tell any of them or who he would prefer to see. Danesh shivered as he dozed and in his waking moments, thought about his various futures and the possibilities they carried. There was no one left to teach him so he would have to decide on his own, even though he had done so several times before. He would wait until his captors released him and he hoped that would be enough.

The motion of the crate became impossible to anticipate, and he repeatedly hit his head and arms against its sides. He held out his hands to protect his skinned elbows, and they smashed into the wall until his fingers became numb. A wave of nausea bore down on him as the movement stopped, but his relief was overwhelmed by panic as the lid opened. Rough hands pulled him up by the armpits, a familiar smell of sweat assaulted his nostrils, and the omniscient silence scared him.

Danesh wanted to focus on his surroundings, but his eyes refused to stay open in the bright light. The cut on his lip throbbed, and he tried not to pull at the broken skin with his teeth. He listened intently. There were two, or maybe three people pushing him roughly forward and he slowly became more certain on his feet. Muted aches called to embryonic pains and his head began to pound.

'That's it, boy.' An *eldri-kona*'s voice. She was carelessly pulling him along, and he could hear her laboured breathing as she ran.

'The next time I come for this little fucker, it'll be to kill him.' Cristóbal.

Danesh's heart sank with realisation. He had promised allegiance to this man, but he had reneged and failed to respect another bargain. He had meant what he had said to Cristóbal, but it had lost its relevancy in the deluge of unspoken details. The decking under his feet was uneven and hurt his bare feet. He was aware of the cold sheen of his sweat, as if he had a fever or worse. When he looked down at his body, he was shocked at the thinness of his legs, his ribs alarmingly visible and his penis shrivelled beyond recognition. He was caked with blood and worse, and his hair was matted and stank. What had she done to him?

Cristóbal was somewhere behind him. Both the woman and man were familiar, and as he searched for their names, he couldn't help but wonder what they had done with Shu-fen and the others. Danesh wanted them to be safe and hoped they were faring better than he was.

The *bogdo* ended in a dark bulkhead, and the *maður* ran his hands over it until he found a way to remove one of the panels, squeezed in and reached back to grab Danesh's hand.

Danesh didn't want to go through the hole because it felt like being returned to the enclosure, but he complied, almost willingly. What else could he do? No one paid attention to them as they climbed out of the head-height vent and dropped one by one to the ground. He assumed these things were commonplace. They were in an open thoroughfare packed with *fólkið* going about their business. The mass of pedestrians allowed them space to stand unnoticed and contemplate their next steps.

Cristóbal grabbed him by the back of his neck and propelled him forward while the others melted into the crowd. He pushed Danesh into a public cleantube and paid for a wash cycle. 'You have two broken ribs,' he said. 'Not my problem, but there's some bruising I want you to cover up.' He dragged Danesh into a small workwear store and told him to pull on some acrylic overalls.

'Where are we going?' Danesh asked.

'I'm taking you back to where you're supposed to be, and then we're going to have a little talk.'

The cell contained a small bunk with storage below and space for little else. The wall's default configuration gave the appearance of a sizeable room with an assortment of furniture and decorative items, but the illusion did not make him feel at home. Cristóbal fell onto the cot and stretched himself out, which left little space for Danesh to sit.

'I don't bear grudges, *ný-maður*. I've had two contracts to find you, but another won't look good on my profile. You're lucky, though, two different clients. No one's reported you missing, so you're back to work today. If I were you, I'd buy some musculature before I returned, because you look like shit. As far as Pazel is concerned, you're still in training, so he's not paying much attention. Victoria's another matter. She's majorly pissed with you. Don't know how you're going to get out of that one.'

'Who hired you?'

'I didn't ask, and the job came from a third party. Told me to give you a message. They've installed a process that will keep you safe from any pervasive overlays, other people's experiences, thoughts, that sort of thing. My guess is it saved you from a difficult situation. You need to stay close to Pazel and don't give him a reason to think you're not fully engaged. You need to deal with anything that makes him suspicious, particularly the *kona*.'

'Will you help me, Cristóbal?'

Can you pay?

No.

'You're on your own, but I'll make sure you can contact me if your circumstances change.'

Danesh only gave himself a few minutes to reflect after Cristóbal left. He felt weak, so he ate some grey and decided not to waste time with a sculptor. He ordered a tight-fitting shirt to try to hold his ribs in place, and some loose clothes to pull over the top. Victoria was surprisingly easy to find. Her status said she needed a high and her diffused locator put her a few minutes of arc away. He identified a couple of places she was likely to be and applied for routeing. Whoever had hired Cristóbal would be monitoring him, so he set his status to *difficult job complete*, cheated his physical and mental health indices and mentioned he might opt for uninterruptible sleep until his shift.

He had started to appreciate the subtle differences between the two levels. Of course, there were fewer people, but the arcades had more height, and to Danesh, they were just as busy. The *bjðirnir* in K7 appeared no more affluent than their counterparts in the Eights, but they were more assorted. There was variety in apparel and body art, and most *sálirnar* had some augmentation or other. He was astounded by the variety of sexualities in this arc and at the range of body hair. One woman had a champagne mane that flowed from every part of her body to her ankles. Diphallic men abounded, and several were selling their services to a group of *ný-konurnar* who flocked around each other, their coloured feathers flashing in the white light. The majority of *fólkið* were indifferent to their surroundings, uniformly absorbed in online and unconsciously shuffling past him. In that respect, they behaved identically, and he realised there was no way for them to differentiate themselves from their cousins below, other than changing what was on the outside. While Danesh was indifferent to his own body, he might consider revising his *māsadā-sarīra* in the future, but first, he needed the high shop.

Inside, one of the walls was playing ancient footage of substance use. It was dirty and hidden away, laced with danger. The opposite wall showed the luxurious highchairs used in the store, with beautiful customers tended by a beautiful team. Danesh attracted a lot of attention from the staff because he had not registered or made an appointment. He explained he was looking for a friend and the receptionist unequivocally told him to leave. After a fumbled apology and a promise to buy a starter course, he was allowed to stay. An attendant said that even if his friend was a client, she might not agree to see him when her session ended. One of the staff came over and led him to a chair. Danesh tried to tell her he wasn't ready and that he still had to decide what to try first, but she brushed aside his protestations with a shrug: it didn't matter what he wanted, he had paid for a starter pack, and that was what he was going to receive. He would be back soon enough to work his way through the menu. He started to struggle and tried to pull away when he saw Victoria as she came out of a cubicle.

'You! How?' she started to say.

Is she actually your friend? the attendant asked.

Yes, she is, Danesh replied.

I need something better than your word. I'm not going to get into trouble. [*Data*].

Do you want to go up together?

Please, he said.

They were bundled into a tiny room and fell in an embrace on the clearfibre-covered bed. The server naturally assumed they were intimates, called up their respective profiles and deftly administered their progression. For Danesh, his first recreational drug beyond school lent him a clarity he could not have imagined, and he was thankful. Victoria slumped beneath him and was shivering but otherwise inert. The door closed on them.

Victoria knew he wasn't trustworthy, but she had been unable to prove it. She had not recognised the meaning of the conversation with the diners, misinterpreting his words as the protection of Pazel's optimism. Victoria had not understood what was in his heart, but she knew there was more and would not stop until she found it. When she did, she would expose him, ruining him. Victoria's face was pallid, but she was still beautiful, and she had been kind to him. So it was with some tenderness that his thumbs sought her carotid arteries. Danesh held her for almost fifteen minutes until he was sure she had left. Afterwards, she would be recoverable for several hours, so he waited beside her and tried to remember who he was.

Two measured chimes indicated their session was over. *Are you done in there?* The server waited a respectable time for Danesh's response. He struggled to think. He had killed a *persónan*, and the Pallium would call him to account. *I'll give you five minutes more.* He did not have enough staters for Cristóbal's services. Should he put a call to Freja? She could help him by faking a caching record. He would have to tell her what he had done, but she wouldn't understand. *Time's up.* The door opened, and the woman who had scored them popped her head around, wrinkling her nose.

'Aw hell,' she said. 'What'd you do to her?'

'I don't know,' he said. *Can you help me?*

'Hey it's not my fault, I follow process.' The woman looked panicked. 'I'll have to get my manager.' She glazed over for a few seconds, clearly making a call. 'Alright,' she said. 'My name's Wyatt, arc supervisor. What seems to be the problem?'

Danesh looked out blankly from the bed.

'Your woman fold on you, son?' Wyatt asked. Danesh just nodded. 'Happens sometimes. She must've done something she didn't disclose, Marwa here tells me that everything is in order. You want her stuff?' Danesh shook his head. 'Says here she's the property of some big corporation. I don't necessarily need to register her today because of the current processing lag, and it'd be easier for me if you weren't here.' Danesh nodded again and rose from the bed. 'Now get out.'

'My supervisor says I'm to purge your account,' Marwa said as she helped him to his feet. 'He's not listening now. You'll be fine. Did you love her?'

Danesh thanked Marwa for her assistance and used the last of his staters to give her a reasonable tip. Either Pazel would give him more funds, or he'd have to work something else out. Victoria had been there for him; she had made sure he survived, and now she was gone. Days ago, he had vowed to kill Pazel, and already he was practising his art. Danesh marvelled at how fragile life was and hoped she had definitely left. He was supposed to feel remorse, to feel something, but he was indifferent. Would there be no victory when he deposed Pazel?

He ambled to the Eighth transition without paying attention to his surroundings and identified at the booth. Descent permits were freely available, so he was concerned by the unexplained refusal of his down-levelling. When Danesh queried the Pallium, he was dismayed to find his own TUID was null, and when he cycled through the others he had been using, they were all rejected. He hated being a non-person.

The demarcator showed little interest in helping an offliner, but Danesh offered him seventy-five per cent of his personal happiness for thirty staters and purchased an innominate connection. Danesh figured the high shop had already registered Victoria, but her profile was still active, although he could no longer access much of her detail. It had been almost two hours since she last checked in and he presumed this had caused the deletion of his identities. He found somewhere to sit amongst the countless others who were waiting for opportunities and, feeling somewhat dejected, placed repeated calls to Freja. When she finally accepted, she couldn't understand what had happened to his sanctioned status.

'The man I paid to collect you said you were fine,' she said. 'You were going back to work, and everything was in place. What have you been doing? I'm struggling to trace your movements because someone's tried to erase several transactions. It's an awfully shoddy job. What's going on, Danesh?'

'Cristóbal said I had to be careful because some *lýðirnir* didn't have my best interests at heart. I trusted him.' He couldn't bring himself to tell Freja what had happened, so he copied the memory, edited out his emotional response and sent it to her. Moments later, she dropped the call.

He slept where he sat and woke with a full bladder. There was nowhere to go, so he got up, relieved himself and started to walk. No one paid him any attention. He missed the feeling of power he had found in the high shop but could not return there. He had nothing and was nobody. Pazel wouldn't come looking for him, and he wouldn't survive.

He peered inwardly and examined the part of him that was Pazel's legacy. Freja had been wise to separate the two personae, and he was pleased the knowledge was still there. It would enable him to be decisive and use these past experiences to guide him, no matter who's memories they were. Danesh was determined to endure, he had endured, and this other life was all he could trade. His body was sore, he had scraped his fingers badly, and he was hungry and sick to the stomach. Yet he was a survivor. He had killed one friend and been discarded by his only other. He would have to find one of Tabitha's diners amongst the people packed into K7. Danesh couldn't predict his future, and he didn't have a plan, and though there were tears in his eyes and devastation deep within him, he wasn't afraid. There was a trace of bitterness, but he knew it would become sweet with patience.

For the first time, Danesh was truly alone. He understood why Shu-fen had loved him. It was because she needed someone to give her life colour. He had loved her in his own way too, and while they might have been content together, it could never be enough. He had abandoned her without a second thought. He had loved Victoria, yet that was insufficient, so he had held her warm, inert body against his as he chose against her. Somewhere deep inside, he might find remorse. He had loved Pazel, that special part of him that had shown him how to be strong, but Danesh could not endorse his other self's fatal vision. There would have to be a resolution. And he had loved Freja, if only for one brief moment. She had to know that if she didn't help him, he would have to destroy her too.

Kavya cradled Freja's head in her lap and allowed the tears to flow. They had talked for several hours, but Freja remained distraught, blaming her failure on a desire to impress her closest friends. She said the humiliation of the remaining Odyssée four was nothing compared with what she had done to Danesh. Instead of preparing him to prevent a massacre, one in which they would lose everything, she had protected his *sikatā-ātamā* and nurtured his natural destructive tendencies. Jovana told her that in the fight to save the Pallium, they would need strong *hjðirnir* capable of terrible deeds, but the others had told her she was wrong. They would win through logic and righteousness.

'What if he was our best hope,' Freja said, 'and I have tainted his ability to choose? He is a killer, and I set him loose. He'll come for me unless I help him remove Pazel.'

The other women sat together and tried to comfort her. Privately they all agreed with her.

*

At first, the compeller was Shu-fen's only way to maintain her ability to reason. Its algorithms were there to explain the day's occurrences, and she relied on its rationale at every seduction. An assault meant she would eat, while another provided a safe place to sleep. It was often Feliu who supervised their engagements, and he offered encouragement to the three new women and reminded them of their responsibilities. Apprehension became a tool she used to judge the forthcoming awfulness, and she wielded it against the *fólkið* who pawed at her body. Slowly she understood the compeller and learnt to overcome its influence.

Humaira and Zara rarely spoke and spent their resting moments clinging to each other in their shared bed. The compeller was all they could comprehend, and each time they were taken from their room, washed and prepared, they responded with attempts at online immersion. None of the *nýkonurnar* had any access rights, and Shu-fen assumed Humaira and Zara were seeking switch-off, but she wasn't going to follow them because she was waiting for Danesh to return. She had asked Feliu about him, and he answered with a stinging slap across her face.

Kathy came to prepare them for their next appointment. She lined the young women up in the centre of the viewing hall and used an adjuster to sculpt their bodies until they were aesthetically identical. Kathy said the afternoon's fee required nothing less. When Shu-fen looked at Zara, she could find nothing of her own features in the silent face and was glad she could not glimpse herself. Kathy whispered to her, saying she was the prettiest, but Shu-fen knew she meant she was the one who was most aware. They were going to exist for a *miðaldrakona* who had paid to co-habit all three and direct their intercourse. Unusually, no record of their activity was requested, and Kathy warned her that only the client would asses their performance. Shu-fen didn't care. Unlike the others, she preferred to be aware while she was occupied. She was not only cooperative; she sometimes presented options for their congress, drawing on her recent experiences. She took no comfort, but it helped her to maintain some measure of control, and so she became stronger as each experience washed Humaira and Zara away. Danesh would release her, and she would find a way to punish her captors.

When they were ready, Kathy asked them to sit on the wide bed, keyed into their compellers and invited the client to the session. For almost an hour, they caressed one another and explored familiar bodies with soft kisses. Shu-fen was an expert in her craft and watched herself and herself and herself as she unfolded into gentle orgasm, and as she mastered all three *māsadā-sarīra*, she ensured one of the *ný-konurnar* was always at apogee. While they progressed, she lost track of which body was hers, became overwhelmed by the experience and wanted to flee, but the compeller demanded her contribution. Each wave pushed her rapture towards torment, and she wondered how much longer she could survive.

Afterwards, Shu-fen was raw and withdrawn. She yearned for Sodality, but any connection promised pain. Humaira and Zara stared at her with empty eyes, and she wondered why there were no tears. She stumbled into the cleantube and scrubbed at her burning skin in the hope it would restore her life, and when she had finished, she cleaned the others. They showed no interest in themselves, but as they waited for sleep, Shu-fen thought she heard them murmuring.

Shu-fen awoke alone and cold.

Humaira and Zara had taken the lacing from their undergarments, looped each one around the other's neck and back to their own. They had set a sturdy chair between them to use their slight body weight to maintain the tension in the cords and reclined into death. Shu-fen returned to the bed and waited for Feliu. There was nothing similar about them, after all.

'Why didn't you prevent them?' he asked.

Shu-fen did not feel responsible for anything but for her sanity. 'I was asleep. They didn't tell me they had found a way out.'

Feliu looked defeated. 'Uniformity was your merit. Singly you could not generate the staters to justify the overhead.' He turned away, and she felt the compeller consume her.

An *eldri-kona* watched her as she tried to focus. The woman's once midnight skin was a chalky brown and her face lined with age. Shu-fen recognised this *einstaklingur*. She had been there when Danesh chose. They were in a dimly lit communal area, probably where people gathered to eat. The compeller was gone, and an array of sockets offered her Sodality, but the promise of escape could not tempt her.

'Doha,' she said, 'I don't know why I'm here.'

The old woman smiled, her teeth a brilliant white. 'You are a gift from Feliu. He said you were worthless to him. I yearn for feminine conversation, and in return, I will give you some freedoms. In time you may crave independence, and I will show you how to provide for yourself.'

Shu-fen looked across the room and recognised Cristóbal, leant over a railing surrounding an open pit. He was earnestly talking to the empty air, and she assumed he was in a call. 'What did he do with Danesh? Can I see him?'

'No dear. Your friend has gone to a new life, and you shouldn't pry. The Pallium will deter attempts to locate him. You belong with me.'

Shu-fen could easily discern Doha's meaning. She continued to be a possession and didn't care that one type of companionship had been replaced with another because the subjugation continued. Shu-fen made a decision: her future would be free of any individual's constraint, which included Danesh. She took her hope, wrapped it in layers of self-love and hid it deep within her being. She would nurture it every day until it finally blossomed into the strength she needed to break free, not only from these *sálirnar* but from the technology that tied her to them. Her independence relied solely on herself.

There wasn't a roster or any other system the women used to maintain their apartment. They had a variety of devices that kept the broad, beige circle of their lives free from the filth they witnessed in the Depths and Greater Numbers. Minuscule electronic mice scurried around at night to keep things clean, but the machines couldn't distinguish the items the five *konurnar* cherished from those they might discard. Freja's disarray slowly began to impact her friends. Pieces of clothing, scraps of unwanted food and stacks of clearfibre printouts littered her bed. It was unruly, and lately, it had become unpleasant. Her bunk was nestled between Miyu's and Kavya's, and as yet neither had complained, but it wouldn't be long. Freja sat squashed into the corner of her bed, eyes unfocused and part-dressed. Two days ago, Kavya had offered to tidy her things away and brush her hair, but she gave no response. The women suspected she hadn't slept since Danesh had shared with her, and in hushed voices, they discussed having the Pallium sedate her.

'Caitlyn, you have to help her,' Kavya said. 'Freja's getting worse. She hasn't tubed for almost a week, she smells bad, and she isn't eating either. She's hiding what we give her in her sheets. It's revolting, and it has to stop.'

Jovana and Miyu had taken to ghosting away as much as possible, excusing themselves to help Hyun-jun, Enzo and Inès.

Their *māsadā-sarīra* looked slightly neglected too, as if neither woman had selected the appropriate upkeep while they were absent. Caitlyn suspected they were enjoying their freedom and that Kavya would eventually join them. It was likely they would break their set of contracts, including the agreement with the FMP, assuming it really was their client. It didn't matter to any of them now that Odyssée had made them rich, and Caitlyn thought they would be better if they divided their staters and disbanded the elucidarium. If Freja blamed herself for what had happened, she probably wouldn't survive on her own. Caitlyn didn't know how to deal with the situation.

Kavya regarded her coldly. 'She's convinced herself that Danesh will find a way to destroy Pazel and that the loss of his life will be her fault. I don't think that's true—he made those choices on his own. I know what she's searching for: she wants to warn Pazel, even though he is presumably aware of what might happen. I think the only way she'll come out of this is with his support.'

'That's dangerous, Kavya. He mustn't suspect what we're doing. Pazel is a reasonably powerful man.'

'Then cast her out or request a caching voucher. She can't remain here in this condition.'

'You want me to get rid of her because it's inconvenient.'

'She's offlining, Caitlyn, and there's a place for people like her. If you can't help her find herself, then she forfeits her right to be here, and to the staters.'

Caitlyn couldn't find a reason to disagree. It was a difficult choice between her friend and her apparent obsolescence. Kavya was right: enough time had passed. She could either use the Pallium to edit out Freja's recent experiences or emotionally manipulate her. She politely pushed Kavya to one side, reached into the bunk and grabbed Freja by her matted hair, held her head still and slapped her smartly.

Stop, she commanded and hit her again. *Pay attention.* Caitlyn held Freja's head in both hands and peered into her eyes. *We're your friends, and we love you.* There was no reply, so she continued to provoke a response using messages, images, sounds and sensations. She tried to entice her and draw her out with calm promises, but when that failed, she resorted to cruelty. Freja had submitted herself to Sodality's caress and discarded her reality. Caitlyn could not tell if Freja's instability came from her apparent focus or if she had forgotten herself entirely. *Please listen to me,* she finally pleaded and slumped onto the filthy bed.

Caitlyn lay there in a daze not knowing what to do. Freja wormed back into the corner, picked up a handful of indestructible documents and started pawing through them. Kavya is right, Caitlyn thought, the bedding is repugnant. She called up the caching voucher and read through its terms, trying to stall her action as long as possible. Kavya was out of sight: probably the last person still working on their actual job. She broadcast a forlorn message in the hope of support. Kavya brought her a mug of green tea, which Caitlyn sipped gratefully.

'There is another way,' Kavya said. 'You feel okay?'

Caitlyn nodded, and Kavya closed her eyes.

Freja, Kavya coaxed, *I've found him: Pazel is coming. He wants to thank you for warning him.*

To begin with, Freja did not respond, so Kavya continued to message her with details of Pazel's imminent arrival. The dishevelled *kona* looked up from her stack of quantum papers but did not make any other acknowledgement, giving Kavya time to create the simulacrum. Eventually, Freja put down her documents and swung her legs over the edge of the bed. She patted Caitlyn on the thigh and tried to smooth her unpleasant hair into place.

Kavya leant forward to help her. *It's not him,* she told Caitlyn. *It's the best I could do with the time available.* The man coalesced before them, slowly walking towards them as he formed.

'Thank you,' he said. 'I've lost Victoria because of Danesh, and now this *ný-maður* wants to take me too. You have saved me from him, Freja, and I am grateful.'

The simulacrum remained motionless, waiting for a response. Freja started to reach towards him but recognised the futility of it as her sentience returned.

'Is this a trick?' she asked. 'Did Caitlyn do this? She tried to hurt me.'

'No one can enter your chambers, Freja. You've helped me, and now the debt is paid. You should return to your work because there are *hjðirnir* who depend on you.'

Kavya allowed the image to fade and Freja blinked deliberately as if finally opening her eyes to the things around her. She tried to organise the documents into a pile, but they had become sticky and repellent, so she dumped them on the floor and headed to the cleantube.

Kavya, it can't be that simple. Does Pazel know about Victoria? Caitlyn asked.

Shit. I don't know. Probably. Depends on how good Pazel's data miners are.

Will Freja contact him?

We'll keep an eye on her and sort something out.

Caitlyn swung down from the bed and walked over to the kitchen. *I thought you made quite a good man.*

Reassignment is all the rage at the moment, Kavya said and shook her sleek hair.

Caitlyn purchased an interrupt and Jovana and Miyu stirred from their couches, joining the other women. They chatted idly about their workload without referring to the impact their extracurricular activities were having on the schedule and returned to their decision to split Hyun-jun and Enzo up. Miyu reminded them that no one would be interested in the intellectual, wiry farm boy, while Inès and Enzo could quickly become a celebrity couple, stressing intelligent management of the media stream was vital. Freja returned and appeared relaxed and in control. 'Have they gained a following yet?'

'Not yet, but it is early,' Caitlyn said. 'How are you?'

'Fine. Great actually. I was feeling a bit low before, but not now.' She poured tea for all of them. 'I think it's about time we talked about our outstanding tasks.' Freja did not acknowledge the unspoken dialogue between the other women. 'We had more than enough to do before Odyssée, but we should be able to cope if we put in extra time. I was stupid to think we should contract some of that work out. Enzo and Inès will raise the staters we need to progress, and they're not much overhead. I suppose if we needed more finance, we could appeal to the FMP directly. If we can get Hyun-jun into Second, then we should make some progress. I'm curious about it, aren't you? I've correlated everything we have and recommend we try here,' [*K2 location*]. 'The only other thing I think is important is making sure Danesh doesn't hurt Pazel.'

She's worried that Danesh will hurt her, Jovana remarked to the others. 'Why is that, sweetie?'

'Pazel is a prominent figure, and we're not sure how influential he is, although maybe he isn't powerful at all. If he has a wide network, then potentially he's aware of the Pallial Decline. He probably has a huge processing requirement. It would be in his interest to help us. He'll say he doesn't need us, but he'll appreciate what we're trying to do.'

'That's true,' Kavya said carefully, 'but remember he's aware that you befriended Danesh, and even though that's over now, Pazel might not completely trust you.' Freja started to protest, but Kavya cut her off. 'I think we get someone he sees as neutral to handle the communications with him, maybe Jovana. Would you be happy to do that?'

'Of course,' Jovana said.

'Then that's what we'll do. We mustn't scare Pazel off or cause him to ask any questions he's not already thought of.'

Freja looked from woman to woman with slight confusion on her face. 'Do you think that's the best approach?'

'Yes. We should focus on the FMP issue, and Jovana and Miyu can manage the other projects. Right now, we all need to turn off our interrupts, have an hour of cardio and get a decent night's sleep. We can set to work in the morning.'

They exercised in silence, each tuned into whatever distractions suited them the best. Caitlyn monitored Freja, but she hadn't subscribed to any published feeds. Perhaps she was quietly running with her thoughts. It did not fill Caitlyn with confidence.

Lines of *ný-fólkið* queued patiently at the start of their adult lives, ignorant of the beautifully imagined balcony above them. Kathy was pleased Cristóbal had agreed to take her full-service call at such short notice. The *stochastís* set her perceptions to fully-opaque and gently squeezed his hand. She relished being integrated into any ve-environment and habitually gave the FMP carte blanch to smooth away anything that might be incongruous. The new people below had no inkling Kathy was appraising them, nor did they realise their assessment was for potential redeployment. When Cristóbal had referred to them as an untapped resource, Kathy suggested a megagestorium might be an engaging backdrop for their next catch up. She glanced at the call's diagnostics and was disappointed to read Cristóbal's low presence score.

'I can't see any reason for you to include a *stochastís* in your crew. It's rare for your heists to require any trade in data,

Cristóbal, let alone require manipulation of the Pallial Truth. I'm not going to condemn one of my well-trained *sálirnar* to the Lisboa Pit in the hope of a challenging assignment. If you want my help, you can pay by the hour.'

Cristóbal was watching the *táningur* prepare to board their assigned Lacuna cars. 'What if I need someone I can count on to be discrete? I might not want my data capitalist sharing certain details with his employer.'

Kathy deleted her laughter from the call. 'If there were something I wanted to know about you, I would already be appraised. You can't keep your secrets from me.'

He shrugged and continued to study the young men and women.

'You're in love with Doha, yet you won't admit it to yourself.'

'You think that's why I won't fuck Grace.'

For a moment, Kathy wondered if he was genuinely open to deepening their business relationship. His hand was hot in hers, so she queried the Pallium for his heart rate. 'She's not busy working on a job; instead, she's down-levelled out of the Fours to be with a *maður*,' [TUID]. 'Grace has finally replaced you. They've spent most of the day together. The rest of the time she's been piggybacked onto his *sikatá-átamá*. It's all very intimate.'

'Well, good for her.'

There was a commotion as one of the *ný-konurnar* refused to leave the gestorium, while one of the new men tugged at her arm.

'That boy should focus on his own troubles,' Cristóbal said. 'His life's about to take a turn for the worse.'

'His most interesting experiences are almost certainly behind him,' [data]. Kathy enjoyed spending time with recently newed *lýðirnir*, but as they matured her fascination for them waned. 'It's a wonder any of them last into mid-life.'

'You place too much faith in divining secrets from deep within the FMP. You ought to trust your gut.' He plucked a blue ve-pen out of the air and took the virtual cap off with his teeth, spitting it over the railing. 'Who shall we consider?' he asked.

Kathy took the pen and one by one crossed out the faces of the queuing adolescents until only a handful remained. 'You should choose,' she said, changing the pen to a luscious red.

Leaning over the handrail, he drew a broad circle around one of the *ný-mennirnir* and watched as it settled into place.

'His name's Budi Phar-Tet-Che-Thorn,' Kathy revealed. 'That's all you get. Tell me who he's going to be.'

Cristóbal lifted a copy of the new man onto the balcony, turning him around a few times and checking his white, pristine clothing for clues. 'We might as well cache him now and save him from condemnation. Twenty staters say your Budi trained as an oneironaut. Please don't make this poor boy spend his life appraising dreams and billing clients for their content. I refuse to have anything to do with them, and so should you.'

The Pallium confirmed the Lisboa, Cristóbal's regular gambling club, had already accepted the wager and placed their staters in escrow. It didn't matter. Kathy had carefully selected this batch of *ný-fólkið* and had primed Cristóbal with hundreds of references to dream auditors throughout the morning. All of his targeted advertising, everyone who served him and all of his favourite Sodality groups all mentioned oneironauts. He had seen Budi's face a thousand times already and couldn't have chosen otherwise.

'How about higher stakes?' she tempted. 'If you're right, I'm prepared to buy into your outfit and give you the staters you need to expand. If Budi trained in some other profession, I would appreciate your services at a significantly reduced rate… indefinitely.'

Kathy watched as he considered her proposition. Cristóbal suspected she was playing him yet would not pass up an opportunity for investment. Kathy had offered him exactly what he needed while sparing him the indignity of asking for her help. She edited her broad smile out of the call when he accepted. Below them, Budi approached the Lacuna lock and looked up at her before he left, sending a shiver down her spine. He could not have known she was there. It was probably just the FMP ensuring her full integration. Kathy miniaturised the copy of the *ný-maður* and held him up for them both to inspect. Budi's complete dossier unfurled across their eyesight, and Cristóbal squeezed her hand, even though it was Kathy who had what she wanted.

Over the past weeks, Caitlyn had reviewed a variety of leadership theses, but there were no useful examples for her to refer to, particularly concerning the pre-Forming period. How any group of people could have created the world without strict organisational doctrine was beyond her, so she assumed assizes struck it from the official record. This revelation left Caitlyn feeling the onset of the Pallial Decline was the latest in a long saga of information devastation. Privately, she continued to struggle with her role and was dismayed at how hard it was for her colleagues to accept her authority. Caitlyn held up a finger to indicate they should stop speaking and waited for quiet.

And the Smiž back-chatter, ladies.

She longed for it to be over so she could descend and be with Youssef in a place far from assessment and interaction and governance. Mostly she was tired of living with these *sálirnar*. It shocked her and left her feeling she had let each of her friends down in some way, yet she was sure they all harboured things from one another. It was the secrets, the little surreptitious conversations and tiny lies, that had forced them apart. She wondered whether if left unchecked, they would become a cancer that destroyed them. They needed to talk.

'Thank you,' Caitlyn murmured. 'It's hard to find the time when we're so busy. There are several things to discuss, and I'm certain you'll see the benefit of taking stock. We need to consider our contract with the FMP, where we are with Odyssée, and we should discuss Pazel.'

'Pazel is not an issue,' Freja said. 'Once Jovana speaks with him, he'll understand how we can help. It's been ages since you asked for an appointment.'

'Yes, sweetie,' Jovana said without making eye contact.

'I can help him find Danesh in my off time. We should all be worried about what he might do. That should be acceptable, Caitlyn.'

'Let's talk about everything we need to do first and then make plans. I suspect none of us will have much free time over the next few weeks. We need to focus on the Pallial Decline now Hyun-jun has reached Second. Odyssée has served its purpose well and has generated a sizeable income. Miyu, you've been spending a lot of time on the production.'

It was clear that Jovana and Miyu were passing messages between themselves. 'It's too soon to close it down,' Miyu ventured. 'Enzo wouldn't survive without our guidance, and Inès will eventually go her own way, and anything could happen to Hyun-jun if we don't constantly monitor him. He's breaking into Second, Caitlyn, into the FMP. Do you realise how dangerous that is? He's going to be able to see what's happening for himself and share his experiences with us. Aren't you interested in what he might find? It's worth my attention if we want to keep him safe. And Jovana's too.'

'That doesn't help with our real work, Miyu.'

'You have to see why it's important, Caitlyn.'

'She does,' Kavya said. 'We all do. What we need is balance and to make sure we keep things in perspective. Hyun-jun's not going to crawl through every metre of the Pallium and Inès is smart enough to keep Enzo out of danger. My guess is you enjoy being outside and there's nothing wrong with that. When this is all over, none of us will have to stay here. That's why we took the contract in the first place. Have you considered the consequences of non-delivery?'

'Have you thought about what Pazel might do if he's displeased?'

Kavya tried to remain composed. 'Pazel isn't interested in us, Freja. He said he was grateful. There isn't anything else to do.'

'I have to see him. After that, I'll knuckle down and sift through the backlog. It's not like you keep the others locked up in here.'

'Ghosting is nothing like making a call,' Jovana said.

'I know what I'm doing,' Freja countered.

'It can be emotionally draining. Are you sure it's not too soon after—'

'I'm fine,' Freja said. 'I just got myself into a tight spot, but it wasn't that serious. You're all treating me like I'm unserviceable.'

'We care about you, sweetie, and we want to make sure you're okay. We were worried.'

'Please let me speak to Pazel. I need to be sure he understands I didn't think Victoria would die. She was important to him, and I made a mistake. How many *hjörnir* have to pay for my poor judgement?'

'Let her go, Jovana. It's what she wants, and we can't stop her.' Caitlyn looked deflated, as if she had already lost her prominence. 'We all have different things we wish to achieve and the things we believe in, even though we took a lifetime contract together. Normally if a team were to disband, they would have little to fall back on, but that's not an issue for us.

When we separate, our staters will buy a lot of opportunities. Jovana can spend her time collecting relics from before the Forming and Kavya can retire to the Ones, whatever we want really, but we have to outlast the present, defend our investment and not give up on one another.' She regarded them with wide eyes. 'We have to believe in ourselves and remember how to trust.'

'You lied to me,' Freja accused.

'Yes.' None of the women dared to speak, and they sat quietly for a long time. Caitlyn was grateful that Freja didn't question her again. *I'm sorry, Freja. Please stay until we have finished.* She became aware of Miyu and Jovana's private discussion, presumably details about Odyssée or how to gain the group's approval to be absent more often. In the silence, she wondered what she would finally do when it was over. She had spent all of her adult life solving problems and questioning until she could appreciate all the associated issues. Why did she find it so difficult to do the same with these *konurnar*? They had lived together for half a decade, and until recently the closest any of them had come to leaving was a full-service call with an old friend, or new. She wanted to understand what had changed, and when they had become so fixated on dispersing. Even she yearned for it, and once confidence in the *tabi'a* grew, she could leave her imprisonment and join Youssef.

Odyssée had made her regard her home as a cage, showing them the reality of outside, even if it was through naïve eyes. Maybe she had stumbled upon the truth. Maybe she was just jealous of Hyun-jun's abounding joy or Enzo's discoveries. Through their work, the women assumed they knew all about the world, but these two *ný-mennirnir* had shown them all that they were wrong. Her own immaturity struck her soundly and vibrated through her bones, but oddly it also made her feel content. Jovana and Miyu would only be happy managing

Odyssée and Freja was no use to them. 'Kavya, what do you want to do? The others have already decided, so it's up to us. If we want we can break our contracts now and go our separate ways.'

Caitlyn, I don't know. I can't concentrate.

'We don't have to decide yet. We have other things that require our attention. What else needs to happen?'

Jovana smiled at them; it blossomed from her heart and was not the faux smile she reserved for cajoling. 'The *forfeður* conceived the FMP as an integral part of the tionsphere. The proliferation of processing devices before the Forming became the most significant threat to humanity because resources were scarce, and individuals were hoarding under-utilised potential. The three major conglomerates offered centralised services and at least one intended to host these in orbital platforms, but the orbital debris from the lunar dismantling and the water mining prevented off-world expansion. When construction started, it made sense to locate the Pallium below Tion's new surface, and the *forfeður* chose Second to reinforce the separation of the elite from the majority. The *forfeður* must have calculated the ultimate demand and planned capacity accordingly, using teams of specialist *visionäre* to specify its subsystems. The current population is almost optimal, so the gradual failure of the FMP is unanticipated at best. Maybe demand is far beyond expectations, or perhaps there is an end-of-life issue, although I think it is degrading for some other reason; maybe a design flaw or a systemic problem, but why now, after a thousand years of stability? Other than something disastrous, which would be obvious to everyone, the main contender is sabotage. Two kinds make sense: terrorism and altruism, and both are misguided.'

'So, what are our options?'

'If the problem is obsolescence or design inadequacy, then there's nothing we can do.' Jovana looked from woman to woman. 'If a body of *fólkið* is actively damaging the Pallium, we should be able to find some proof, either via surveillance or through Hyun-jun.'

'Or ghosting,' Kavya said. 'I think you're right and I want to see it for myself. I need to be outside. We should go with Miyu and Jovana, so we can all protect Hyun-jun together. He doesn't need to do this on his own. If your hunch is wrong, then all we've lost is time.'

Caitlyn motioned them to be cautious. 'There are no legitimate organisations that would benefit from destroying the FMP. It would mean the forfeit of every measure and control, including financial services. Even the extremist groups routinely use global processing to handle their transitions, and I've never noticed one with offline in its manifesto. We know the Definitive Sitting has software designed to seek such factions out and disband them, which might cause dissidents to rebel, but it's unlikely. We're absolutely dependent, and without it, bad water would poison everyone and so forth. Anthrocide can only be the product of a deranged mind because no one would profit from the loss of all human life.'

'What about caching parties? The beach ones are incredibly popular.'

Caitlyn shook her head slightly. 'There are no documented cases of mass cachings beyond a few hundred thousand citizens. The tight control of information flow between levels limits hysteria. It is one of Tion's safeguards.'

'There are ways though,' Jovana said. 'We managed it with Odyssée.'

'A passing obsession with other people's lives is very different from persuading billions of *sálirnar* to archive themselves. The Pallial Decline must be wilful destruction and is most likely attributable to a private *einstaklingur*. The number of potential candidates is overwhelming.'

Jovana made a tutting noise under her breath. 'But where would they go to be spared, Caitlyn?'

'I don't know.' None of the other women commented.

'You think it's him,' Freja said.

'No one said that, sweetie.'

Caitlyn reached for Freja's hand. 'That would be a wild supposition. The only way we could have made that connection is if someone had guided us.'

'Or something. What if it is conscious? What if it has finally become self-aware and psychotic all at once. Jovana's options are terribly narrow, Caitlyn.'

'What do you suggest?' Caitlyn snapped.

Freja was resolute. 'We walk away now.'

'The Decline is progressive, and if it's not resolved, the suffering will be universal.'

'You have no proof it is escalating, just a supposition based on recent observation. What if the change is nearly over? Maybe it will repair itself. We can't tell, and all the work we've done might be worthless.' Miyu's eyes glazed over as she hooked into the Pallium to submit a request.

'Except unprecedented access to compute resources, which you are revelling in,' Kavya said.

Jovana banged the table with her hand. 'That's unfair. We worked hard to be successful. It doesn't just happen. And we all benefit from it.'

'What about all of your time spent in full-service calls?' Kavya asked.

'Oh, Miyu,' Jovana breathed.

'When you were apparently working.' Kavya looked away, her face flushed.

'Who with?' demanded Caitlyn. 'What did you do?'

'Nothing. Just a *maður* I used to know. We've spent some time together. Miyu promised not to mention it to anyone.'

'I want to talk to him. Call him up now.'

'I can't. Joaquín is missing, and his TUID is invalid.'

Caitlyn looked at Kavya, and they both started reviewing the daily logs. 'When did this happen?'

'Just after we took the FMP contract.'

'Coincidence?' Kavya asked.

'Unlikely,' Caitlyn suggested. 'Try to find out what happened to him.'

The room darkened slightly, and the walls came alive with text and graphs. 'Not good news,' Miyu said as she returned. 'If we renege on the contract we could face anything from confinement to compulsory caching with truncated personae. It's still better than failing to meet our targets, which would crash our rating and might forfeit our right to work in the Fives. Much as it pains me, we have to meet the agreed terms, however inconvenient.'

'I'm sure that life in Seven or Eight would be fine if you had enough staters,' Freja said. 'That's where Pazel spends a lot of his time, and where he's agreed to meet me.'

Miyu glanced at Jovana. 'I've also rerun our initial Decline analysis. The performance degradation has slowed, but the projection shows it's not going to stop before there is a catastrophic system failure. Once that happens, there are no staters.'

'Anything else?'

'Jovana's correct,' Miyu informed the group. 'I'm sorry, but Joaquín never existed, nor did the thirteen other *mennirnir* in his apartment. Or the apartment itself. It's odd because I distinctly remember reviewing their records when I first heard about him. I think it's the most sophisticated deletion I've come across. It's unprecedented.'

'Miyu, wait. Someone has taken Inès and Enzo. A *maður* met them at the K3 entry point. That wasn't supposed to happen.

What if they're in danger?'

'Slow down, Jovana. Where are they now?'

'I can't locate them. Hyun-jun's okay, he's sleeping, but the others—'

Caitlyn put her head in her hands. 'I can't do this. Too much is out of control.'

Chapter Eight
Mehdi
বর্তমানে

IT WAS NOT uncommon for others to fake his identity, but Pazel knew how to spot its unauthorised use. He dealt with the fraudsters swiftly and without a trace. When a *kona* from the Fives impersonated him in front of her associates, he sent a familiar caching voucher, thinking nothing of it, until seconds later the Pallium returned it unapproved. He was somewhat surprised. The only other time this had occurred was when he accidentally tried to cache one of his adherents, and his safeguards had kicked in, but this was a flat refusal from the FMP to kill off a stranger who had irritated him. Pazel added it to his growing list of Pallial wrongs and set a reminder to deal with this woman next time he was close to her arc.

He habitually used a complex array of alarms and other interrupts to manage his precious waking moments. Pazel had long ago realised that his success came from initiating action, not completing activities, and was accustomed to distributing the actual work to the people who surrounded him. His life was all about gathering data and making long-term plans, and he continued to thrive. He had chosen his TUID on a whim and marvelled at how often people referenced it. He was not an important *alþýða* in any kay, or a media darling or socialite, he was an efficient businessman who was quietly successful and absolutely focused on his goals. Sometimes his vision was clear, and he delighted in sharing it with a few essential *sálirnar*, but often he struggled to express himself and became irritated with his confidants, even though he cherished them. His desires were pure, if not dignified, and now his plan for Tion was all that mattered.

Zero will not be another Eleven-Two, he told himself. I will not allow anyone to interfere with my world. Not again. They will all love me because I already love all of them. I created their dreams and their wishes and will make sure they are happy. They need me, and they are not like the people who stole Eleven-Two from me. I will protect them as they ascend from the Interdiction and take their place on the surface of Tion. My *ljðirnir* carry editions of my *sikatá-átamá*, and they will ensure success and Zero will triumph. There are just a few more things to do.

He considered a multi-dimensional representation of Kavya Ngo-Dza-Ta-Thorn. She was twenty years old and assigned to her elucidarium at the end of her late-nonage. Her skin was a golden brown, her lustrous hair a deep black. He thought she looked very close to the baseline standard, except for her green eyes. The other women in the workgroup were equally unremarkable. Pazel could not comprehend why the Pallium had denied his request.

Pazel floated without essence in the emptiness. It failed to register on the senses so profoundly that some might assume it was death. The lack of sight was not just an absence of brilliance, but it was also an absence of darkness. It did not manifest, in the same way he could perceive nothing beyond his field of view, not even blackness. There was no sound but no silence either. The suppression of all of his inputs meant his untroubled mind responded only to his limited subscriptions. He attributed his personal well-being to his ability to focus on the single, most vital thing without a distraction of any kind.

These *konurnar* were a reprehensible interruption.

The women were cautious. He had to bring some of his most precious routines into play to access their logs. This was software that he did not care to use lest it becomes easily recognised by the FMP. Their sockets were closed or otherwise well-protected, and their grasp on Pallial systems was impressive, but he knew how to bleed their secrets from them and with little effort tapped into their data share. Every system is only as intelligent as those that created it, he mused. Secure is an organic place, and even that can be compromised. He examined their complement from the regular listing and pulled all of their journals. Each was a featureless account of daily activities and lacked the usual ramblings of a bored *kona*. They had expertly disguised the erasure markers, so he primed agents to reconstruct the deletions. Kavya had used his TUID to cajole her colleague, and the Pallium had denied her caching without an audit trail. Pazel would look into that peculiarity later.

Pazel knew his visits to Second were detectable as failed ghostings. He was surprised that Freja had connected his absence to Danesh's, realised the boy had been diverted from his K4 destiny and gripped those connections with such fervour that she had contacted the new man. She had cleverly concealed her rehostings to the Sevens and Eights from her cohort, but the telltales were there. Pazel analysed the series of events and forwarded a summary to Mehdi. Freja had corrupted Danesh, and he had killed Victoria, and now she sought redemption from the consequences of her meddling. He couldn't determine if she was a danger or an asset, but he knew she would continue to pry into his activities until she exposed him in some way. Mehdi suspected Freja had attempted a splice on Danesh's *sikatā-ātamā*, updating his psyche and leaving him less susceptible to Pazel's influence. If he couldn't remove her from play, then he would adapt her to suit his needs, and if his future ultimately required her sacrifice, he would find a way.

He reached for his design. It murmured in his non-vision and shimmered inaudibly. It was a fine thing and reminded him of the moment when Nikora had given him the notion, and he finally abandoned the water. The habitat was a limited thing which was physically confined and hidden away. This template was a sweeping vastness, and open to a new sky, held in only by its weight. He would delve beneath the surface and extract whatever he needed because the resources below were inexhaustible. The model unfolded at the touch of his qu-key and changed in response to his varying focus. It asked him to approve shallow seas, filled with orbital water, and to divide the open land between small groups of people. He had already placed a tenth of the adherents, name by name, into suitable settings and watched as their lives played out in rapid simulation before him. Pazel dedicated himself to them, not out of benevolence, but out of power. He needed them to recognise that their survival was according to his wishes and that they lived because he had granted them the opportunity. He expected them to be grateful. Pazel ran his simulations and updated his suppositions until they became the assertion of his authority.

With a contented sigh, Pazel closed the emptiness down and returned to the mundane, scrutinising himself. He wondered what had happened to his body, although he didn't care to remember what was indeed his. Perhaps these were his original limbs and appendages, his sex and torso. He gazed at the mirrored window and studied his face carefully, decided that it probably was his after all, and left his small office. Years before, he had used a variety of support staff to take care of the trivialities in his working life, but in the end, he had tired of their interference. They had insisted his approach was inefficient, and his methods were outdated and said he did not understand his stakeholder complexity. Pazel had not hesitated in issuing caching vouchers for them all, and now he took care of himself and felt all the better for it. He had only retained Mehdi Gim-Het-Fa-Feh, whom he referred to as the Curator of the Flesh, and maintained that he was not a valet but a biotechnician. His task was to guarantee that Pazel always had a reasonable selection of bodies to slip into, should the need arise. Mehdi mostly relied on third-party suppliers, and in truth, his role was primarily administrative. He could set the Curator aside when circumstances demanded it, although he had become an occasional confident and Pazel liked having him around.

The depository was one of several in the Sevens. There were standby facilities in all other levels, except the Greater Numbers, all unmanned. Mehdi tried to be near Pazel at all times and ghosted between sites at will, but he rarely travelled in person due to the menace other *fólkið* posed to his own delicate flesh. He did not intend for anyone else to make unscheduled repairs to his body, because any updates that required were always administered by his own, ghosted hands. Unlike other technicians, he spent most of his time with his product and lavished care and attention on each one. There was no need for him to wallow in opulent offices and waste his time in Sodality. If that was his life's desire, he could hide away in the Fives. He took pride in his work and treated each *māsadā-sarīra* as if he or she were a precious friend.

Mehdi had collected Victoria's remains from the high shop long after Danesh had fled. Wyatt, one of the brand's arc supervisors, had failed to register her death within two hours and when his staff finally filed the ticket, she was irretrievable. Mehdi could tell that Pazel was irritated by her loss and offered to see what he could do. Her body was bloated and bruised in a few places, particularly her throat, and the rest of her skin was a blotchy grey. She was already losing the firmness of life, and it would continue until she finally melted away, but Mehdi wouldn't allow that to happen. He reverently hooked her up to his machines and flushed out her stagnant blood with fresh plasma, reseeding it with artificial white cells to reverse the necrosis, and red ones to deliver life to her systems until her marrow was operational. He sent nano-machines into Victoria's arteries to repair structural damage and install a few specialities from his repertoire. The body waited on the clearfibre table, inching towards independent function and slowly becoming the physical beauty before the drugs, deception and despair. The cost was ridiculous, yet Pazel would be happy to pay.

Pazel had asked to be present for Victoria's reinitialisation, claiming it as a turning point in her existence. Mehdi worried Pazel thought Victoria would be restored to life but listened while he said she was obviously gone yet she would remain nonetheless. Privately, Mehdi thought Pazel coveted her body and wanted to satisfy his desire.

When Pazel arrived, he stood silently alongside his curator and waited for him to speak first.

'I've done what I can. You must recognise this isn't Victoria, just what she left behind.'

I do.

'And can you confirm there are no backups hidden away that I could use to bring her back?'

I can.

'Do you promise to look after this one properly, Pazel?'

I promise.

'Very well. All that's left to do is spark her up, and she's all yours. For the record, I think this is a bad idea. You've fixated on her since Danesh absconded, it seems she's worth more to you now than before. Do you have any regrets?'

No, Pazel said. 'She was a good employee, and I didn't protect her from harm. I don't want to forget her sacrifice, so I will celebrate her memory for as long as I can. It sets a good example for the rest of the team and helps them recognise their value.' *Is she ready?*

Mehdi had removed all of the equipment and dressed Victoria's body in a translucent, white robe. Her pale features did not look real to Pazel, and the stillness was disconcerting. Inside her, tiny machines were shunting fluids around to regulate vital systems, but technically she was still dead. He gently placed his hand on her chest, directly over her heart, as if he had the power to breathe life into her. All he could do was make the request and allow another to give her that gift. One slight beat, almost imperceptible. Then another, until it became commonplace. Finally a breath, but not gasping in desperation, more a gentle recommencing of the natural state of things.

'What do they think when they're empty?' Pazel asked.

'There is no consciousness and no desire other than self-preservation. Sometimes, if they are left alone long enough, they will clump together, seemingly holding one another, but it is without volition. Occasionally, there are reports of sex between *māsadā-sarīra*, but I've never known it. There's no such thing as animal lust; even the animals had emotive drives. They're empty containers, Pazel, just biological systems that process air, water and nutrients and leave a whole lot of mess for me to clear up. They're reactive though.' He picked up a needle and turning over her hand, jabbed it into her palm. 'See how she responds. You'd think Victoria was in there somewhere, but it's an autonomic response, a preservation of the body. It's not real. I have prepared her for you. Everything's ready.'

Pazel summoned the button and slipped through its maw in a transition that had become so familiar to him it was as if he'd stepped from one room to another. He could feel the sting of the needle in his hand and remembered Danesh's self-harm in the Interdiction. He lay on the cold gurney, not wanting to move and savoured the sensations that consumed him. He was dimly aware that Mehdi had left the workshop, but instead of rushing to experience the fullness of her *māsadā-sarīra*, he waited quietly, knowing there would be plenty of time for that in the future. Hers would be the body he ascended in, and he wanted to relish each discovery between now and then. He had plenty of time yet. After he returned, he asked his curator to join him.

'How was it?' Mehdi asked. 'Everything you anticipated?'

Pazel didn't want to discuss his feelings. 'This is the facility where you keep my body, isn't it? Show me.'

'That's not permitted, boss. We've been through this before, and you've always been very clear on this matter. You said that if I retrieved it, you would want to try it on, for old times' sake. You wouldn't want to let go, and if it were damaged, you wouldn't forgive yourself. I take care of it, and that's all that matters.'

'I'm not an it, I'm a he, and he's my flesh, and I demand that you allow me to inspect my investment.'

'It's only a bio-machine Pazel, waiting to be filled with whoever the I tell the FMP to put into it. This *māsadā-sarīra* is not you: you are, whether you're in your current body, Victoria's or some other vessel.'

'I want to see him.'

'No.' Mehdi smiled at the brewing tantrum and summoned a selection of footage from similar discussions.

Pazel stamped his foot in a show of exasperation and placed his hand on Victoria's warm shoulder. 'Have you solved either problem?'

'The *raja'a* is still your best bet for the persistence issue, but don't get excited because there are significant downsides. There's a rumour of a new version, but I can't locate a purveyor who might confirm. As to the duality, I still think you're crazy. An entire life, a person's *viakatī-pūrā*, can only be a unique symbiosis between a single *sikatā-ātamā* and a single *māsadā-sarīra*. No one could exist in plurality; the Pallium won't permit it.'

Pazel surrounded himself with his adherents; each representation faithfully recreating the emotions played out on his face.

Mehdi snorted his disdain. 'Where would it stop? One replica? One thousand? Ghosting isn't a transference of your *sikatā-ātamā*, it's a shitty imitation that feels real. The Pallial connection tidies away all the contradictions and idiosyncrasies and who knows what else that might screw up. The source persona never leaves its original flesh. It is deeply repressed to the point of non-existence until its rightful owner returns.'

'You're saying the man in the freezer really is me and I'm a facsimile?'

'Isn't it what you feel that's important, not the underlying actuality? It doesn't matter.'

Pazel didn't argue the inconsistency. He knew there wasn't enough capacity to represent the intricacies of the populace, their personal data and everything that it took to keep Tion operational. No matter what its theoretical capacity was, its efficiency was nowhere close to its biological counterpart. Mere engineers could not rival the phenomenal results of aeons of evolution. He reluctantly saw the truth in Mehdi's words.

'If we remove the safeguards, Pazel, what would stop citizens copying themselves into every piece of flesh they could afford? Once that process is available, however covertly, there will be no going back. I won't do it.'

'You've helped me be a part of thousands of *ný-fólkið*. Surely it's no different.'

Mehdi started to prepare Victoria to be returned to storage. 'I've distributed aspects of your experiences, thought processes and mannerisms between your adherents, although each one has little more than a summary. It's not the same thing at all, although I could reconstruct you should the need arise, assuming I could get hold of a representative set of contributors, and I guarantee you wouldn't know the difference. How do you even know I've not done that already? But tasking the FMP to ghost sovereign instances of you into two *māsadā-sarīra* at the same time is dangerous and irresponsible.'

'The proposed dream tariffs will require a huge number of oneironauts. There are rumours the FMP is copying the best ones into the unwanted bodies of the recently cached.'

'They're using registered multitenancies, some fancy *gocco* and a single *sikatā-ātamā*. There's no independence to each imprint, so it's not the same either.'

'I want it once and for a short time only. When I have finished, you can finally dispose of the real Pazel. I will have no further use for him.'

'I assume you feel the same way about me.' Mehdi didn't expect a response and continued clearing things away. As soon as he had finished, he brought his palms together with his fingertips to his chin, inclining his head in Pazel's direction.

After he had gone, Pazel deleted his comments and skimmed briefly through the facility logs. Mehdi had not moved the body since his last visit, and he considered having a quick look, but the Curator was right, it wasn't the real Pazel at all, and its importance had waned for the moment. He knew where it was when the time came.

Freja had left several messages and offered to ghost down from the Fives to meet with him. He was unsurprised that she wanted to find him, even though her associate had warned against it. Pazel was sure she would be trouble and hoped his silence would deter her. He studied the words that Kavya used while imitating him. She had made him appear ethereal and benevolent, which amused him greatly but had not made any real connection. Pazel decided a coercive approach would be best—he was a master of pre-emptive subjugation. He was glad he did not have to seek approval for his behaviour and that no one was there to judge him, not even Nikora. Pazel had fostered the people for ascent, chosen his own ultimate image and guaranteed his line. No one else was capable of achieving such things, and he would not allow an isolated woman from the Fives to intervene, no matter what they had seemingly shared. He could taste his ambition every way he turned.

Danesh was lurking a few degrees away, no doubt suffering from a clash of personalities. Pazel understood the boy's choices because he would have done the same thing himself. He would have to forgive the *ný-maður* as he was only enacting the impulses that Pazel had instilled in him. Danesh had destroyed Victoria because, in that situation, Pazel would have destroyed Victoria. It left him with a stark, uncomfortable feeling of self-loathing. He knew he condoned the young man's actions, and he might need to put him to good use in the future. Danesh was still trying to operate as a non-person and was not being very successful. If he survived the next few days, Pazel would visit him and allow him to absolve himself.

Did the *drengar* actually intend him harm? Tidy resolution rested in his caching. It prevented awkward interactions and unexpected repercussions. Its neatness outweighed any consideration of propriety, and it was a familiar and comfortable course of action. There were always plenty of *ný-fólkið* in the pipeline. Danesh had scored very highly in the areas in which Pazel was weak, and they complemented each other well, but this was not a discriminator either because Tion was full of compatible *sálirnar*. This new man was agile and creative, manipulative and driven, and Pazel enjoyed those characteristics. When he sifted through the evidential data, he conceded that Danesh was straightforwardly the better man. It seemed a shame to destroy him for a minor indiscretion, no matter how lovely Victoria may have been, but the fact remained that his protégé, if that's what he truly was, constituted a threat.

Pazel built a robust simulation, and Danesh killed him at the end of every iteration. He added a significant amount of complexity, but the result remained the same. He tried inserting other characters with random aspirations and beliefs, and yet Danesh still triumphed. The only way to beat him was to alter one of the principal variables within the model: Pazel. He pondered the outcome for several hours, and it was clear that unless he changed his own behaviours through ruthless splicing, Danesh would succeed him. Pazel had never known defeat before a confrontation, and his emotions were uncertain. He did not like the feeling, so he called up his *sikatā-ātamā* profile and looked for a solution by brute-forcing the parameters. Once the Pallium had come up with a best-fit, he loaded the revised profile and administered the patch, hating himself for his weakness. Moments later, the feeling of uncertainty ebbed away, and he reran the simulation. He could let Danesh live, and the odds were he'd stay away.

She was called Nikora, and she was beautiful. Joaquín had never met a woman like her, and he thought about her constantly. Gregory had been right to taunt him about his ve-dates with Jovana. She was an unremarkable *kona*, and he was a pathetic *drengur*, but this new *māsadā-sarīra* had made him into a man. He had rested and exercised for two weeks and was surprised by his vitality. His reflexes were sharp and his self-control absolute. Nikora occasionally stopped by to encourage his recuperation, while he became increasingly excited by his capacity for desire. She had laughed when he mentioned his untested urges and patiently explained that sooner or later, he would have to fend for himself.

He was half-way through an early morning workout when he spotted her across the crowded gym, running on a treadmill. Nikora was obviously elsewhere, and the equipment was regulating her movements. He gave himself to the rowing machine and sent an invite, which she declined with an alternative appointment. When he arrived, she was shopping in the clutch of a pale-cream epicentre of endless clothing. Her virtual undress was the only thing that stopped him from leaving.

'I heard that being absent makes this about as useless as sleepercise, in which case I should head back to the gym.'

'Unsubstantiated crap. I don't have the time for one thing at once, Quín.' She looked at him with enigmatic eyes, and he wanted her even more. 'Your Jovana has been busy, and I have to say I'm impressed. She is a co-producer of a multi-level media product that is doing rather well. The show has captivated the residents of Fifth and Fourth. Now her team are bringing their epic to K3, where I have some interests. I'd like you to ghost up, meet the two Odyssée *ný-fólkið* and make sure they are safe. You have about an hour. I suppose you plan to leave the *māsadā-sarīra* in the gym while you're gone. Hand it over to a personal trainer; otherwise, you might do yourself harm. Maybe you can ve-meet with Jovana afterwards.'

Joaquín wanted to finish his session, tube and have a decent breakfast, but Nikora expected him to work for his flesh and he had nothing else to return to. As soon as they had met, she had identified the unknown facet missing from his life, and she wielded it against him. Her authority came from outright manipulation and the knowledge that should he test her, she would destroy him. There was much yet for Joaquín to learn. He was nervous about slipping into another rental while he left his new body behind, even though Nikora was unlikely to take it from him. The ve-package contained instructions to intercept Inès and Enzo before they embraced their new identities as gestorium engineers, and hold them securely until they were required.

His hired *māsadā-sarīra* was of significantly higher quality than the one in the level below, and he assumed Nikora was taunting him, but its youth and lean stature left him wanting to return home and be himself again. Nikora is making sure I know where I belong, he supposed.

Joaquín arrived at the checkpoint in good time and told the bored demarcators he came to meet with some up-levellers. No one thought to check his TUID. The FMP informed him that Odyssée was not available in Third, but the inter-level assizes said they'd intercepted a lot of gossipy traffic from people passing through and were hopeful that the programme would come to the Threes. One of the *konurnar* said she'd reviewed some footage and she would be extremely interested to see how Enzo coped after Inès tired of him. When Joaquín said he needed to collect them, she promised to handle their transit herself.

The assize was despondent when she returned. 'They're already being processed. I was hoping to descend and speed them through, but there's a lot of interest in their departure. Someone must think they represent a loss to the Fours and is insisting on a thorough inspection. I have suggested they have a private elevator, as befits their status.'

'Which is meaningless here,' Joaquín reminded her.

'Only until Odyssée's full launch.'

Joaquín was startled by how compatible Inès and Enzo looked as they strode into the Threes. It wasn't because they appeared similar, energetic and excited; it seemed to him they must have been designed to be together. The demarcator fussed around them until Joaquín poked her with a blunt reminder and she released them into his custody.

'Jovana sent me,' he lied. 'You're supposed to come with me until she's ready. Hold out your wrists.' He jabbed inhibitors into their left arms. Neither Inès or Enzo questioned his authority, and they followed him meekly through the quiet plaza. Joaquín assumed they were disappointed to have left all of the attention behind.

'Do you know how Hyun-jun is?' Enzo finally asked.

'Jovana didn't say,' Joaquín said. 'I'm sure everything's fine. Do you have something you'd like me to relay?'

'No,' Inès muttered and continued to walk behind him without further comment. Neither of them expressed any interest in replacing their confiscated possessions and seemed content to be deposited in whatever accommodation Joaquín deemed appropriate. He selected a modest apartment with a secure concierge to guarantee their safety and ensure no one entered or left without permission. Enzo appeared to trust his judgement and bade him a pleasant evening. It took Joaquín twenty minutes to return the rental and shrug his own *māsadā-sarīra* back in place. Nikora had left a message for him to call her about point-to-point.

'Were you responsible for the damage to the network?' he asked. Nikora held his silence comfortably, so he continued. 'I assumed as much. You sought me out after I submitted my report and blocked my return request. What did you do with my body, Nikora? And Myron and Nitin and my other friends? You've taken everything from me.'

'And given you much more in return. I relocated each of your colleagues, and this is your *māsadā-sarīra* now. I know you prefer it, so you should be grateful.'

'When can I see Jovana?'

'Soon. My previous tech-specialist wasn't able to make the changes I required. The damage she caused was quite specific, which left me exposed, so I had explosives placed into a few thousand pointport cubicles and trusted that a generic assessment would occur. I ensured their engineer used my rental, but I didn't specifically select you, Joaquín. Nevertheless, I do expect you to succeed where my last technician failed.'

'What did you do with her?'

'She didn't make it.' A fresh ve-package appeared next to him. 'Her notes are in there. I would read them very carefully before you decide how to proceed. You will remove four pointports from the network and configure them for independent operation with units located in the Twos. I have to be able to send certain items into the Pallial infrastructure. You will need to contact this *maður*,' [*TUID*], 'to arrange support. The receiving pe-to-pe cubicles are almost ready. You have thirty-six hours.'

Her request seemed simple enough for Joaquín to action but left him puzzled as to why his predecessor had been unsuccessful. Although there were some test scenarios she probably ran, none of them should have led to catastrophic failures, and he was unable to determine what had actually gone awry. Joaquín estimated it would take eight or nine hours to make the updates and the same to ensure the process was safe. He would have to coordinate with the receiving party, which might take a while to set up, but he probably had half a day to spare. Joaquín decided to forego sleep, just in case he was equally unsuccessful and summoned his ranked list of local bars. He had no confidence in re-qualification when Nikora had finished using him.

*

Pazel didn't want to be interrupted. 'What is it, Mehdi?'

'I thought I should call. You've been tinkering with your persona again. I received a couple of warnings.'

'Nothing that concerns you. Enhancements mostly.'

'That's not how I read it. You've pushed yourself beyond the tolerances we agreed. Technically you're not yourself any more.'

'Who am I then?'

'Beats me. Just want to check you're okay.'

'All good.'

'Then I should flow the updates down to your editions.'

'Sure. I'd hate to failover into someone who isn't me.'

Pazel was having unpleasant fantasies about not fitting in with people. He did not look like himself and did not feel like himself, nor did he act like himself. In truth, he did not know who he was or remember who he had been. It didn't feel important, but he was desperate to know his legacy remained intact. The recent damages reported by his Curator of the Flesh were unremarkable in all records bar one. There were a few routine deaths, thankfully no one in the Interdiction, and a smattering of injuries that didn't require caching, but one of the *konurnar* was registered as having ghosted into a dead man. Pazel summoned her record and let it hang in the air before him. She was typical in her cultivation but had not stayed in the Threes once she newed. Her genetic expression was pleasing but did not explain why she had decided to descend a level because she certainly wasn't disposed to lowering her expectations. He wondered what might have been more compelling. Pazel pulled her financial transactions and was dismayed at the time spent in high shops. He didn't disapprove, that would be ignoble, but he did not care for persistence. Pazel assumed she had fled her body to break the dependency and botched the transfer. It didn't matter because there was enough slack in his estimates to ensure his personnel quota sufficed, so he didn't concern himself and sent a note to Mehdi to collect the *māsadā-sarīra* for his personal use.

'I can't bring the body in, Pazel. It's occupied.'

'Rented?'

'It doesn't look like it. Grace Mu-Tlo-Ue-Jhan is going about her normal business without raising any flags. But it's not our Grace. I'm certain she's gone, although it's difficult to prove. Do you still want me to collect her?'

'No, but keep a watch on her. Let me know if anything untoward occurs.'

Unusually, the Lacuna was empty, but still, the traffic was sluggish. When Pazel boarded the four-person capsule by himself, the two women in the queue behind him started to complain, but he silenced them with an aggressive look and a raised hand. *Lýðirnir* were basically the same, he thought, universally scared. The two seats faced each other and were almost too close. He imagined that if passengers occupied all four chairs, his knees would touch the *alþýða* opposite, which might have excited him in his distant youth. The surveillance equipment was visible and protected, and he was sure that somewhere in an elucidarium, a worker would be tutting as he stretched his legs out luxuriantly on the seat in front of him. There would undoubtedly be a fine of sorts, although it would never reach his consciousness. His transition into the Sevens required several documents and fees, but they were dealt with remotely while Pazel let his mind reel. He would find Danesh and watch him from close quarters. It was unlikely he would be recognised.

Beyond the Lacuna, the crush of people was extreme and far surpassed the K7 average. The grey street had a polished concrete floor with specks that glistened, but it was puckered with overuse and marked with blackened gum and other debris. There were two columns of *sálirnar* shuffling in opposite directions in the warm, enclosed corridor, three abreast and listless, some carrying boxes or bags and others with no burdens whatsoever. A strong wind rushed hotly through the passageway, and a few pieces of litter danced above them. The *fólkið* were universally absorbed with somewhere else, and there was no focus on their circumstances, they shackled themselves with music, chat shows, social mutterings, anything to distract them from their weary march. Pazel found the whole thing infuriatingly mundane and desperately slow and was content that this would one day pass. He felt a sweaty hand on his back, attempting to push him forward in the humid air. Though he spent much of his time in the Sevens, he was rarely abroad with the proletariat, and he absolutely despised them. Pazel could not turn to see who pressed against him, so he called up local surveillance and studied the dirty, oversized man. Obesity was a possession that no one could steal. Pazel obtained the *maður*'s details and requested immediate caching, and tried hard to break free before he became caught in the hiatus. He experienced no emotional response at all, not even relief because the pawing had stopped.

Danesh moved amongst the swirl of people wandering from dormitory to canteen to workplace and back. He had nowhere to go but acknowledged the need to keep moving to avoid being a target for default caching. He had to look like he was full of purpose, that his TUID was expensively suppressed and not missing, and mostly that he belonged in this place. Initially, the boy had been challenging to track down, but Pazel had interrogated the Pallium for potential unqualifieds across this arc and visually inspected each match. The *ný-maður* was grimy but easily recognisable. Danesh's enforced disconnection would mean that he was gambling on his physical senses, and he would be watching his environment closely. Danesh was aware that Pazel preferred to switch *māsadā-sarīra* regularly and was unlikely to be noticed. Still, the new man could also predict Pazel's innate responses, so when they met, he might be discovered, unless the recent modifications had thrown him beyond his acceptable behavioural pattern. However, Pazel was not satisfied that someone could intuitively make such elaborate connections without the Pallial Truth to support their assertions.

He spotted the boy sat between two *lýðirnir* in a food hall. Danesh had engaged the *eldri-maður* to his right in conversation and nonchalantly turned down an offer to share his meal. There was no acknowledgement even as Pazel arrived, squeezed himself between them and feigned interest in the general chatter. When the old man left, Pazel took a filament, jabbed it into Danesh's side and declared his presence.

What do you want? the boy asked.

To know you're all right.

Why should I trust you?

Because I would have done the same to Victoria. In the end.

But you've taken everything away to punish me.

Not true. I can offer you prosperity for a promise of allegiance and identity to shield you from danger.

If you give me these things, I will use them to destroy you, Pazel.

You'd be destroying yourself.

Not true. Your vision is flawed, and I reject it. You must desist.

'You speak like a man,' Pazel said, discarding the wire, 'but I see you. Return when you are ready.' He got up abruptly and pushed into the crowd. He had a sudden, desperate need to escape this reality and shoved people out of his way as he hurried to the transit hub. He wanted to shower and let the water cleanse away the depressing filth, and forget about this new man who carried his past. He may have given away too much, but felt that Danesh had taken more.

He settled into an empty pod and started to tongue through his ve-box. There was a package that tasted familiar: Freja had left another message. For a moment, he considered swallowing it, but it might contain information he could use to reorientate Danesh's expectations. It shimmered as Pazel opened it and she coalesced on the seat opposite. The image did not speak or move but sat motionless and expectant, and he assumed it was attempting to connect back to its sender. Pazel waited patiently for the call to proceed and thought about the offer he had made. Had he forgiven Danesh and absolved him of his misdemeanour? Pazel wasn't even sure if there was a wrongdoing at all because Victoria had taken insufficient care of herself and enticed ruination through her lack of constraint. The call remained frozen for several minutes, and Pazel's diagnostics showed there was not an issue with bandwidth or connection. His best guess was Freja was unavailable, so he submitted a high-cost request to delete the image, but it persisted.

When he left the pod, the thing followed him. It was not configured to deal with its environment and didn't walk alongside him; instead, it floated in Pazel's eyesight and clipped through *fólkið* and fixtures. It unnerved him. He didn't like it at all and worried that it was a test. Freja, or her entire elucidarium, would be observing him through its interfaces. Pazel submitted caching vouchers for all five of them, even though he knew it was futile. He ambled around the extensive arcade and looked for something to eat, moving from vendor to store to emporium without knowing what would do. The press of people was immense, and the heady aroma of cheap fatty meals, coffee and highs masked the pervasive stench of human animal. It was searing and damp in the food court, and the *sálirnar* were just existing through it and basking in their ignorance. These *lýðirnir* did not deserve to live like this, and Pazel was glad he had pledged himself to end their misery.

Moist, warm bodies slithered past him and their hot flesh stung with each touch, thighs, shoulders and hand after hand after hand. He could not decide what he wanted to eat and failed to choose between sickly rich or insipid stodge until finally, Pazel ended up where he had started and queued for the disappointingly familiar. He was the same as the very people he loathed, going about his business, day after day, repeating the same dreary cycle.

How could Danesh not see that Tion was tainted? Each individual had no significant contribution to make to the world, and nothing to leave behind except an exhausting audit of images, sounds and words, the almost infinite Pallial Truth squandered on banality with no measure of control. He had been right: better to destroy it all rather than waiting for it to fail. Danesh did not contemplate his reality; he avoided it and ignored the gift he had received. Pazel could not abandon his course. It was time to cut the boy loose.

The simulacrum turned to face him. Pazel was not sure how long it had been studying him.

'It's the only thing you could do,' Freja suggested. 'You trusted Danesh and gave him every opportunity to work with you. Now it's time for you to share your ambition with me. The Pallium is sufficiently complex to protect itself but cannot discard the very data that is poisoning it. I suspect you've also been damaging it in some way, and with so much disregard that it can't be part of your intended future.' She paused, but the simulacrum's gaze was not at him. 'I helped shaped Danesh into a killer, and I'm appalled. I know that Kavya faked a sending, but it showed me that I should contact you. Let me help you, Pazel. All I ask is that you include me in your plans.'

He did not have to check his records to know she did not meet his requirements, but she could be useful, assuming she could protect him from her peers. 'Can this call be tracked? The FMP will retain a record of our conversation, no matter how you try to encrypt it.'

'It will, but there is no cause for concern. I've specified the storage nodes that are handling the call, which is an unusual but unremarkable request. They are adjacent to a disused refuse bore which runs between First and Third. I expect there will soon be an attempt at sabotage, and the record of our transaction will be lost before the system can replicate it.'

'What of unintended consequences? Other information lodged in the nodes?'

'I don't believe you care. I want to help you because of unintended consequences.'

'I'll think on it.'

Pazel bought a flatbread, as he usually did, and did not taste it while he ate. Eventually, he returned to his K7 apartment where Mehdi was waiting for him. The Curator looked drawn, as if years had passed in the few hours they had been apart. 'A depository in the Threes was wrecked during the last FMP outage. Several *māsadā-sarīra* are unserviceable due to an overload.' He looked at Pazel critically. 'What have you done? Something is definitely missing.'

'Don't worry about the bodies. There was nothing I could do. Was Victoria one of them?'

'No, she's right where she's supposed to be. All of the important *māsadā-sarīra* are. Hold still. I want to run a quick checksum.' Mehdi waved his arms around to gather his thoughts and assemble his algorithm.

Pazel was accustomed to his manner and tried to let his *sikatā-ātamā* drift so he could expedite the diagnosis. His quarters were clean and his possessions neatly arranged, but tonight everything seemed overly tidy, his personal effects might have been inspected for secrets and put back according to a set of undisclosed rules. He suppressed the urge to mess things up a bit.

'It seems you're definitely not who you're supposed to be. I can trace back all the original parts to your progenitor, well what's left of them, and it's relatively easy to see where you've administered psychological self-abuse. I was about to recommend a cutover to this morning's baseline when I detected this.' Pazel glanced at the tiny coloured spheres surrounding him, interconnected with gently curved pipes, almost impossible to unravel. Mehdi understood his confusion—the nodes sprouted text labels and arrows adorned the connectors, and the whole thing rotated around him. 'It's here,' he said, 'look.' The lustre faded from the network, except for a few nodes stranded on one side. A few of them began to swell and shine and dance before him.

'Oh. Those ones. You should have said.'

The image rushed towards him as the orphaned nexuses became his focal point. 'Look at this, Pazel. There's a whole piece of you that someone has removed, very precisely. It has been replaced with a very sophisticated set of triggers, tied quite closely to your autonomics. It's alien connectivity that is particularly resistant to any kind of tampering. I don't think I could realign you without significant damage.'

'Then get another *māsadā-sarīra* and splice together a new mediary from my editions. Start the ghosting again. I don't care what you do with this version of me. It's been a crappy day after all. There's nothing worth hanging on to.'

'Whoever did this was smart and knew an awful lot about your configuration. There's a tap into your tally routine that contains some cascade code. It will take me a day or two to unpick it, but my guess is it'll catch every one of your editions. We can't do this.'

The display faded. 'How long did it take to install this code?'

'Easily under a minute if there was a direct hook-up.'

'Fuck. Danesh.'

'The cascade gives us another problem. I can't automate a comparison to determine what Danesh took. You might be able to tell if you searched through your journals. You certainly won't feel like anything is missing. Do you feel like yourself?'

'I feel intact if that's what you mean.'

'If you can work out what's gone, I might be able to reinsert it from the archive, although I never intended it for a partial restore.'

'What else did Danesh leave behind?'

'Again, no idea, other than the snuff stack. I only spotted that because it's artificial and blatantly out of place. What will you do?'

Pazel took off his jacket and stretched. 'Turn off my newsfeed and sleep,' he said. 'It will be better in the morning.' He lay disconnected in the dark for several hours and considered his day. It was impossible to tell what was real and what was an artefact, so he assumed his life was unmistakably one of perfect probity. There was no way to remember the things that were lost or comprehend their demise, and he did not dare to delve into the Pallial Truth for fear of what he might regret. Pazel knew any stolen part of him was somewhere within Danesh himself, and without the boy, he would never be who he was. He wasn't sure it mattered and reinstated the *drengar*'s TUID and staters.

When Pazel woke, nothing had changed. Whatever Danesh had taken remained unfathomable, and he realised his reality remained unbroken. He was Pazel Sad-Tet-Ain-Resh, and whoever that was, he would be content. Pazel asked Nikora to ghost over for breakfast and sent her the location of the small taverna hidden among endless rows of commonplace eateries.

The proprietor had lowered the ceiling with densely woven vines which blocked out the light from the skyplate. There were wooden pillars every few metres, cut from manufactured timber and distressed, as was the fashion for the arc. Although the establishment was entirely synthetic, it still charmed him, especially the contrived view over golden sand and endless ocean. Pazel had to admit it was a job well done. The neuro-suggestion blended the dynamic vista and Pallial projection splendidly. The notion of expansive empty sands occasionally tempted the patrons, and they would lean towards it as if they expected to run along the surf. The view did not leave Pazel thinking the pre-Forming world was any more desirable. It was a distant fantasy, which it had always been for the majority of the population anyway. The rustle of the leaves in the warm breeze pleased him, as did the organic reality of the canopy. The waiter arrived with his order and left him to his thoughts.

Nikora arrived, ordered a bottle of champagne and chose an adjacent table. She ignored the ocean and drank quickly. The third time she glanced at him, Pazel smiled and beckoned to her. She maintained her focus on the bottle, so he hauled himself to his feet and sat opposite her. She did not acknowledge him, not even to check his identity.

'What's wrong?' he asked.

She put her tumbler on the table and studied his face. When she requested his TUID, she frowned and looked away. 'I don't believe you,' she said.

'What do you perceive, Nikora?'

'Something I don't recognise. It doesn't make sense because I've seen you in dozens of *māsadā-sarīra* and you were plainly yourself. Tell me who did this and how. I need to be able to trust you.'

He sipped at his coffee and attempted to wrangle his thoughts. 'It's hard to explain,' he said, 'because I can't honestly see it myself.'

*

Things were undoubtedly more straightforward when they worked on separate contracts, yet Caitlyn didn't know if she should feel better or feel defeated. Jovana had been incredibly supportive during the hours after their discussion, helping her to her bunk and bringing hot, sugary drinks. Caitlyn was overwhelmed and blamed herself for the team's disarray. She maintained they only had a few simple tasks to complete, but as long as they didn't focus obsessively on any of them, nothing would change. The wild look faded from her eyes as she sat in the familiar pile of soft cushions. Eventually, Caitlyn couldn't quite remember why she had felt so anxious.

'None of us is truly in control, sweetie. When you looked to me for guidance, I frequently didn't know what to do. You all assumed I was doing what was best for the group, but sometimes it was just the only thing that came to mind. You know as well as I do that nothing is binary, despite expectations. You're in charge,' Jovana coaxed, 'because you're the best suited to the tasks at hand.'

Caitlyn frowned doubtfully.

Jovana pressed on. 'You're not interested in flitting off around the spheres or enacting some crusade. You want us to meet our commitments, and you approach them methodically. I certainly couldn't face what you have to deal with each day. None of us could. We need you to make sure we know what needs to be done and make sure we do it. I know you can find a way to balance everything.'

'I feel so stupid, Jovana. It's like I'm no longer able to hold everything in my head and I'm too scared to entrust the FMP with the detail in case it gets lost. Can you spend more time here to help me? The others trust you and prefer working for you. I'm just our problem-solver.'

'So, solve the problem. It's not beyond you, and there aren't that many things to take into consideration. Only a battle to save Tion's citizens, repair a quasi-sentient machine and look good in the eyes of Sodality. Everything else, just details.'

Caitlyn smiled thinly. 'Even Pazel?'

'Maybe not Pazel. Whatever his involvement, he complicates matters.'

'You think he's responsible somehow.'

'It's doubtful Freja could have stumbled across him. If she did, the Pallium must have shown her how to make the connections, and that would imply that it is guiding us.'

Caitlyn considered her words. 'I cannot conceive of an artificial system, whatever its size or complexity, being akin to you or me. The inherently poor human recall process forces us to fill in the gaps, to synthesise new possibilities and invent stories to explain things. If you know everything you don't have to think or feel, you can just look shit up. It's our inattention that separates us from technology. Being stupid has made us smart.'

'Indeed,' Jovana agreed, 'but given access to everyone's data and sufficient time, even a *vél* could reach its own conclusions.'

'I don't see how it could organise itself sufficiently well. It's too distributed. It cannot mimic the chordate brain's connectivity and ability to be non-binary. The Pallium is a thing to which we try to attach biological attributes, but really it's just a lot of interconnected independent, non-uniform processing nodes.'

'So why is it dying?'

'Malfunctioning.'

'That's what we're supposed to be finding out. Come on. You're ready now.'

Jovana led her to the kitchen, and they set about preparing their evening meal. While they worked, they started to chat about unimportant matters and finally, their laughter drew the other women in with offers of help. For a short time, they forgot their differences and enjoyed the simple task of making supper and supporting one another.

As they were seating themselves around the low table, Freja motioned restraint and held her arms wide as if to embrace them. 'We've come a long way together and while our futures may be apart, that time has not yet come. Our opinions conflict but that does not need to drive separation and bitterness. Instead, it should be something that gives us the strength to surpass our limitations and achieve great things.'

'Nicely put,' Caitlyn said.

'Are you okay?' Miyu asked.

'I'm good, now I've had time to think. If the Pallial Decline concludes, we're all dead, so we need to work to understand it. If Pazel is its architect we're probably too weak to stop him anyway, but we might be able to work with him. The simplest explanation is he's a regular businessman without sinister connotations, in which case he'll be happy to have us support him, for the right price.'

This doesn't sound like Freja, Kavya commented to the others.

'That's a fair assessment,' Caitlyn said. 'We focus on the FMP but don't neglect our other obligations. Have we located Enzo and Inès?'

'Not yet. There are a lot of FMP outages at the moment. I want to put in a demand for more compute.'

'It's probably wise, or at least increased priority for our requests. We're entitled to that in our contract, assuming we apply appropriately. It's a fairly obscure protocol.'

'I'll handle it,' Jovana promised.

Kavya and Freja set out utensils while Caitlyn filled their wine glasses. There was a renewed optimism in the air, so Jovana selected a music service to complement the mood.

Miyu added a freeform fractal algorithm to paint the air displays in time with the music. The feeling was reminiscent of their first months together, and they tried to forget their differences. The patterns swirled across the walls with deep blues and violets chasing the blackness away, reds and amber bleeding into green as the image endlessly zoomed in on detail after detail. The design wandered freely around the room, not settling on any particular surface and sometimes clipping onto the ceiling, furniture or floors within the broad, beige circle of their lives. One patch stubbornly refused to bloom, no matter how the algorithm developed, but only Miyu noticed. It upset her mathematical order, and although she tried to ignore it, she became distracted from the conversation until she was left behind. At first, she could not fathom it, so watched closely. There was a break in the pattern, but she was unable to see the familiar wall behind. Eventually, Miyu concluded it was a glitch in her routine and did not pay further attention, so it was Kavya who jumped up as she saw the newly formed door open.

Miyu ended the decorative routine, but the doorway remained. She raised the lighting and saw the twinkling signs of a carbon-wright's craft. An *alþýða* could not have worked in their apartment without them knowing, and she was at a loss. The other *konurnar* were also on their feet and huddled together: someone was standing in the new doorway. It was a neutral figure, average and without discernible gender.

Freja was the first to move as the door opened fully. 'It's real,' she said, reaching towards the interloper. She did not flinch when its hand grasped hers. 'It's not a simulacrum. It's an actual *mannvera*. It's not the same at all.' She guided the newcomer into the room and beckoned to the others. 'You're a human being. You're Pazel, aren't you.'

'No,' it said in a voice that sounded much like Freja's, but the way she would sound if she were a young man. 'I am not the same.'

'Let go of it, sweetie,' Jovana said. 'Come and sit with us.' She moved towards the outsider, squaring up. 'What do you want?'

'Answers. Something you are failing to provide.'

Jovana spoke carefully. 'We weren't expecting anyone to join us, not a physical human being. We're a little surprised, anxious even. We want to know that we're not in any danger.' She did not receive any response. 'Tion unique identifier,' she said.

'Moshe Nnna-Schwa-Sharp-Pha.'

'How old are you, Moshe?'

'Fifteen.'

'Are you recently newed?'

'I am. Today.'

Caitlyn raised her hand to interrupt. 'What is your assignment, Moshe?'

He grinned. 'I am assigned to myself, just as you are.'

'Are we in danger?'

'Definitely.' Moshe turned away from the women and circled the room, much as Jovana had done countless times before, and sealed the door. Caitlyn casually reached across the low table, opened the small drawer underneath and rummaged through its eclectic contents. Once she had found the paper envelopes containing new fibres, she dealt them out. Each *kona* jabbed one end into their own exposed flesh for their datrix to discover, and the other into her neighbour, connecting them in a circle.

He might not be able to intercept if we avoid Smiž.

Who is he?

What is it!

There's no way for anyone to get in here.

It's a thing, a creation.

Of course there is. How do you think Jovana smuggles her trophies in here?

Some of your trophies are pretty big.

The TUID came online moments before he appeared.

Yes. It was the next on the stack.

Ný-maður *or a* vélmenni?

It's not a new man, so it must be a machine—definitely a thing.

How do you know?

Caitlyn cleared her throat. 'Moshe, how many years did your maturation take?'

'All in, nine hundred and twenty-eight.'

We're screwed. It's the Pallium.

It could be lying.

I'm sure it can hear us.

'Yes, I can hear you, Jovana Omega-Beta-Zha-Ge.'

'Then explain the danger.'

'It's time to review your results. If they are not ready, I may process the caching vouchers queued against your identities.'

'Who's the originator?' Miyu asked.

'Pazel Sad-Tet-Ain-Resh.'

It's a trick, Freja said.

No conclusions yet, there's still time.

Caitlyn pulled the fibres and discarded them on the table. She calmly crossed to the kitchen, arranged six bowls on the counter and patiently distributed sweet-greens between them. Occasionally, Caitlyn shed leaves that did not meet her unvoiced criteria. When she had finished, she requested some fibrous protein from the dispenser, broke it up in her hands and arranged chunks in each dish. Finally, Caitlyn dressed the salad with a tart oil that Jovana had obtained from a K1 redesign but typically refused to share, emptying the dark bottle. Without speaking, she served each of the women and placed the remaining two dishes on the table. She sat down and took her bowl. 'Moshe, come and eat.'

His responses were entirely routine. He slouched as he sat, and picked through his food with his fork as if it were another boring meal. He made little unintentional noises as he chewed his food. Moshe didn't focus on one thing at a time, nor did he dart between everything presented to him. Caitlyn could only think of one word to describe him: normal. She conceived explanation after explanation for his presence, knowing from her own experience how simple it was to ghost between *māsadā-sarīra*. Nothing pointed to Pallial intervention, other than in the usual sense of facilitating a transfer. How the *māsadā-sarīra* entered their apartment was more challenging, although he might have suspended them to permit his arrival. There was no way to know for sure. Perhaps it was Pazel after all, bringing retribution.

'Thank you,' he said as his fork clattered in the empty dish. He did not sound as if he had particularly enjoyed the food. 'Something to drink, and then we should discuss the future. Whenever you're ready.'

Caitlyn regularly interacted with characters in sims and they were easily as sophisticated as Moshe. It was not beyond the FMP's capability to create such a complex personality. We are all algorithms, she thought. It would be impossible to tell what he was through questions and answers. Artificial people were the basis of the entertainment industry on every level except First. It didn't matter. She needed to decide what he wanted, not what he was, and if they would be able to satisfy that need.

'Will you stay here with us?' she asked.

'I need a base for my operations,' he said smugly. 'I may pop out from time to time. I'm ready for your presentation now, ladies.'

CHAPTER NINE
Hyun-jun
বর্তমানে

THE SEETHING MASSES of people going about their seemingly essential business almost obscured the filth of the Sevens. Their sustained absorption into online rendered them indifferent to the general stickiness of the groundplate, the mephitic haze lingering in the narrow space above their heads and the constant white-noise drone that caused everything to vibrate. Sodality afforded delightful inconspicuousness while providing virtual exposure to desperately-needed followers.

Danesh ran his fingers over his chest and stomach. His ribs were tender, and he wondered if his internal pain was due to something he had damaged, or a response to the things he had decided would have to be food. There was little for him in Seventh other than discomfort and disappointment, and he resolved to leave it behind. He had become a fragmented *nýmaður*. The piece of him that was still Danesh, recently newed and far from his assignment in the Fours, was smothered by the others, and he needed it to survive. Even so, the part that Freja had separated would always remain and Danesh had to learn from it. If she had failed to intervene, his submission to enforced surrogacy would have been inevitable. He was disgusted by Pazel's desires, but his skills eclipsed everything else, and

Danesh would be foolish to ignore his advice. The other *sikatā-ātamā*, the stolen psyche, frightened him. Pazel had contained numerous people, and Danesh had captured one of them. He heard a chime as the Pallium confirmed his TUID and credit. Danesh did not want to survive on Pazel's largesse, but it would definitely give him options. He would use the staters to restore his health, and offline the troublesome personality fragment. He sent a message to Cristóbal asking for help his with ascent.

Danesh switched tagging on and walked through the dirty, enclosed streets until he reached a coextension store. The attendant welcomed him and suggested he relaxed in the small reception until they were ready to work on his psyche. Danesh didn't want to perform his own disassociation as he would surely suppress himself during the process. The splicer returned with a circular ve-pad and asked if this was his first time.

'Everyone makes changes when they have self-access,' Danesh said. 'I think I've made a bit of a mess of things.' He approved the attendant's request to display his *sikatā-ātamā* on the wall. 'This is me, and these are some experiences I've purchased that I prefer to keep. This last part is something I've been working on, but I've allowed it to get out of hand. I'd like it placed in encrypted storage until I have the time to finish. Would you purge this transaction, please? I don't want to change my mind, although I have left myself a note.'

'You don't have to tell me why, *náungi*, you just have to tell me what, and sign.'

It is another ending, Danesh thought. All I have done is let *lýðirnir* go, and I will continue to do so until I am all that I have left. The bitterness that stung in his belly was the consequence of his actions, and he needed to find another path. He wondered where Shu-fen was, and his awareness ended.

Afterwards, as Danesh walked away, he opened Cristóbal's reply. *Don't be in a hurry if you want to go unnoticed.* He checked into an overnight capsule and tried to rest, but thoughts of leaving the Sevens taunted him. Although Victoria had shown him how to move between the spheres, he had insufficient knowledge to plan his route. He did not want to wait to qualify for up-levelling. *Cristóbal, can you give me a job?* He requested a recast consultation to freshen his genome and asked Sodality to help him sleep.

The coalface hadn't moved in over a month, and the rumours suggested it was due to some Pallial complication or other. Some of the *mennirnir* said the Firsts had become so wealthy they were buying all of the FMP's capacity, leaving nothing for the Depths. Tāne told them it was a load of *komurumurua* and it was unlikely to be stater-related. There had been cutbacks in the workforce, and he couldn't remember the last time a fresh *maður* had started, but it did mean less competition for assignments. Even so, Tāne was pissed off that Rabindra's replacement had been a transfer from a distant arc. The new supervisor had reduced them to working every other day. He said it was better than six days on, six days off, which was what the cuts had meant in his old position.

Tāne had deleted his sleepercise app and signed up for extreme isometrics during his downtime, but he didn't feel fulfilled. Invariably he ended his day with a canister pressed to his mouth, which left him washed out for the next day's shift. The other workers didn't comment, and he was content to take odious assignments if they left him alone, so when the next body showed up, they called him over. Tāne wasn't concerned. It was rare for the Pallium to confirm a TUID from visuals, so he took a sample for identification. Connor hadn't spoken about his experiences and Tāne assumed it was normal to encase the *māsadā-sarīra* in clearfibre for deferred processing. A week later, they came across another packaged body, and he realised the resequencing of the Eights had stopped, and they were clearly killing time.

Hey chāy*, get your fat arse up here. There's a woman who needs some help.*

Walloppong was alone in a narrow corridor that someone had meticulously picked clean. The surfaces glistened in his torchlight, and there was nothing to see. 'She's round that corner,' he whispered. 'There's a *maður* as well, but there's something not right about him. They look like a couple of unjoined. She says he's messing up her space.'

'I'll tell them both to leave. They shouldn't be here.' Tāne took the torch and strode along the passage. The *miðaldra-kona* was waiting for him with her hands clenched on her hips. She was well-dressed and appeared sure of herself. Tāne assumed she was from the Low Numbers, probably Third or Fourth, and had needed to descend. He was about to speak when she stepped aside to reveal a shabby *eldri-maður*, bound to a chair.

'I know I'm not supposed to be here, and I'll go when the time comes.' She reached down to untie one of the man's legs, and he immediately tried to kick her. 'It's not his fault. He can't stop it. I think he's defective in some way. He said he misplaced part of his *sikatā-ātamā* and demanded I retrieve it. I don't know what else to do, other than taking him to a cacherie.' She calmly loosened the other straps, and he fell to the floor, squirming and tugging at his unkempt, grey-white beard. 'I have one sedative, but I had to wait for someone to help me move him.' She did her best to avoid his flailing limbs and stuck the patch on his neck. Within a few minutes, he was almost still.

'This is nothing to do with me,' Tāne said. 'I haven't got staters to waste on a *útlendingur*.'

She shook her head. 'This stranger is unjoined, so there won't be a cost. I can't carry him on my own. I'll find a way to repay you.'

Tāne queried the Pallium, and it confirmed her request could be considered part of his duties. He grabbed the struggling man, hoisted him over his shoulder and headed towards the arcade outside the barracks.

There was a small cacherie tucked in the rear of a bustling water shop. Tāne pushed passed rows of translucent sarcophaguses, moulded to the user's physique to minimise the amount of liquid required for immersion, and dumped the unjoined man in the cachier's couch. A *nȳ-maður* waved them away, but the woman remained calm. She checked the sedative patch and motioned the cachier to attend to her. 'You'll need to online him to obtain a TUID. We'll match assets for the caching.'

The cachier was obviously unhappy about the woman's request for probable default caching and did not move from his desk. 'I'm not interested if there's nothing in it for me,' he said. 'Abandon him beyond the barracks.'

Tāne shook his head slowly. 'Do as the lady says.' He wondered how recently the cachier had newed and watched as he weighed his options. Finally, he got up, took a fibre out of a cabinet and inserted it into his client. 'Good *tamaiti*,' Tāne muttered. 'Now tell us who he is.'

What if he's worth something? Walloppong said privately to Tāne. *I haven't got staters to waste on him. Can we just leave?*

He won't be, but if he does have a balance, it's her problem.

And if she can't pay?

The cachier continued with his preparations, although none of the *eldri-maður's* details appeared on the air display. He took a scalpel a made a small, superficial cut in the old man's arm to collect a spot of blood. As he submitted the sample for identification, a warning flashed across their eyesight instructing them to remain in the cacherie. A shrill alarm sounded, and the cachier ripped out the line. 'You fucking tell me who he is!

There's no TUID, and this place is crawling with his datrix. The FMP says he's corrupted and someone's coming to collect him. They've revoked my warrant.' The *ný-maður* picked up his jacket and stormed past them. The woman held up her hands in protest.

'He's your problem now,' Tāne said and grabbed Walloppong by the arm. One of the water attendants was walking purposely towards them, and Tāne readied himself to push past her, but as she locked eyes with him, he felt the FMP take control. He was unable to move as Walloppong and the woman marched out of the shop.

Evidently, someone was using the water attendant to make a call. 'My TUID is Xin-yi Nn-Fi-Omicron-Psi. I was requested because the attempted caching of this man is not appropriate.' She placed a hand on her sternum. 'I've commandeered this *māsadā-sarīra* without the owner's agreement, so I need to be brief. I have severed your contract, and you are now working for me,' [*data*]. Tāne was unable to resist as the Pallium forced him to hold the twitching man still until his breathing stopped. 'After our conversation, you will down-level with the body and find somewhere to dispose of it.'

A deliverer scuttled into the shop and presented Xin-yi with a small canister. She popped it open, removed the syringe and used it to take a blood sample from the *eldri-maður*.

What about his sikatā-ātamā?

'He will have ensured it survived. He probably ghosted out, although there are no records. Has anyone gone missing recently?'

Tāne watched as the life drifted away from the man. *No one I can think of,* he said. There was no need for her to know about Connor or the others.

'I'll give you your next assignment when you've finished,' Xin-yi said and left the water attendant. The FMP released Tāne, so he opened the ve-package. She had settled his severance fee, and he had received a substantial advance, but there were no details about the transaction or the identity of his new employer. Tāne didn't care. He smiled, paid for high-grade access and picked up the old man's corpse.

There were hundreds of *lýðirnir* loitering in the arcade. The reduction in work at the coalface had given them surplus time and insufficient staters, and if not resolved, at least half of them would end up unjoined. They regarded Tāne suspiciously. He was an outsider, and anyone not contracted to the coalface did not belong in the barracks. The online consensus determined he was a demarcator, and his burden was in the wrong level.

Tāne headed towards the barracks to find an empty bunk for the *māsadā-sarīra* until he decided what to do. There were a few things to collect, although nothing of value, and he wanted to talk to Walloppong. His co-worker's location was stale, his presence inactive and he wasn't answering his calls, so Tāne paid for public surveillance footage from the arcade. It took him a few minutes to shuttle back through the video, but he soon found Walloppong and the *kona* walking from the water store. They had entered a busy café and joined by the *ný-maður* from the cacherie. A waitress chatted to them as she took their order, but when she returned with their drinks, she found all three slumped on the table. Tāne assumed Xin-yi had requested their caching, but he had no intention of waiting for Walloppong's ve-persona to become available. Whatever had happened didn't concern him.

It was time to leave the coalface for good.

Tāne considered walking out of the barracks and leaving the body behind, but he knew Xin-yi would be watching. He sighed and returned to the bunk. The two assizes were expecting him.

'Tāne Six-Kha-Omicron-V. You were with this *persónan* in the arcade cacherie twenty-five minutes ago. Did you kill him? Reparation is required.'

'No, it was a three-to-one caching.'

'It seems your associates have subsequently cached themselves. Unusual situation. You agreed to match his assets?'

'Yes.'

The assize nudged the old man's body. 'And you're certain you didn't kill him?'

Tāne felt his irritation grow. 'It was just a caching. There was something wrong with him. He was unjoined and worthless.'

The assize was absent for a moment. 'All updated.' He turned to his colleague as they left. 'You notice how long even a simple request takes recently?'

There was nothing left for Tāne at the coalface. Perhaps something similar had happened to Youssef after Connor disappeared and he had no reason to stay. He decided to look Youssef up and maybe stay with him until Xin-yi required his services. Before he could finish building his query, he received an alarm from the FMP.

Warning. Nil stater balance. Further transactions and services denied.

Tāne's world dissolved into things he could see or hear or touch. Everything else was gone. Three days later he was hiding from the workers in the confined corridors of the abandoned Eights.

Pazel lingered over the last details of the sale and did not care if the decision to release ownership of the genomic-prosumer process was in his best interest. Others might benefit from his choice or discover the worthlessness of their purchase. It was of no immediate consequence and neither would it matter following the eventual disunion. There was an overwhelming number of issues that required his attention during the remaining two decades, but now his prioritisation stack presented him with the one task he was nervous of addressing: Eleven-Two.

He had not looked for Nikora after they had walked arm-in-arm in the habitat's warm confines. She had been unable to leave until it had docked, so if she had wanted to be with him, she would have sought him out. Instead, she had mingled with the other delegates, celebrated the success of his triumph and attributed kudos to a faceless conglomerate. At the time he had decided that no one would hide in Eleven-Two again, however for a variety of reasons he had found more pressing things to attend to and the years passed.

Pazel requisitioned a pod and advised the routeing agent he would be driving himself today. The *eldri-kona* grumpily reminded him that Lacuna accidents were up thirteen per cent, which correlated with the increased number of people who were refusing routeing. Pazel told her to fuck off and do something productive with her life. He returned the first pod she sent and demanded a replacement printed within the last seven days. When it arrived, the newer vehicle exuded an unpleasant aroma, and its seats were stained. He thought about issuing his edicts directly from his spartan K7 home, but he wanted to experience Eleven-Two once more.

His journey through the Lacuna was uneventful, and he arrived in good time. He was amazed his access to the cistern was approved, he expected to be locked out and have to hack into the airlock's systems, but things responded as they should, and he smiled at the whirr of the winch systems that would bring Eleven-Two to him. He was pleased the habitat's infrastructure would survive decommissioning even though it would never be watertight again. Of course, others could rebuild it, lavish it with attention and make it viable once more, but he doubted those idealists would want to part with their staters.

The pronoas gurgled as it opened and water splashed onto Pazel's shins. Poor maintenance was a clear indicator that Eleven-Two's days had come to an end, and he felt content in his resolve. He ran his fingers over his carefully constructed instructions and opened his palms to release the routines. The door had closed smoothly after he embarked, but the habitat juddered as it moved through an unfamiliar progression to approach its final resting place. He had not designed the cabling to transfer Eleven-Two to the bottom of the cistern, so it had to be released. The habitat plummeted silently through the still water while Pazel counted the seconds. An alarm sounded as it struck the cistern's floor, and he knew the seals between the various units had failed. He considered halting his code and allowing some other edition of himself to be the one that survived to the surface, but he had made his decision. Pazel ignited the devices.

A single instruction dumped a teralitre of water into Fourth and caused significantly more damage than the previous disaster. Pazel thought he might drown in the outpouring or that the swirling current would tear the habitat apart, but his preparations were sound. A battered Eleven-Two protected him so he would not have to ghost out and give up his current mediary. The Pallial analysis of the situation was immediate, and it condemned the reservoir, but before it tagged the cistern for forming it was purchased by Pazel's conglomerate, negating any application for repurposing.

Caitlyn was undeniably pissed off. Her carefully prepared prospectus was vague at best and contained nothing that linked it to the *raja'a*, while still having enough implied content to entice the existing users scattered throughout Tion. She had been confident that enquiries would be discrete and that she would have time to attend to each one personally. The first Sodality post occurred while she was tending to Moshe, and by the time she was alone, several million requests were in her queue. She sighed and sifted through the messages, discarding those that originated below First alongside anything that looked remotely like spam. She was confident her actions could arouse too much attention and created several new groups to debunk the bioapp. Within an hour, most of the requests were withdrawn by their originators, leaving a manageable number of people who might have the *raja'a* installed. She then stripped out anything that could have come from Pazel, or potentially Moshe. She responded to the remaining messages, thanked enquirers for their interest and asked for confirmation of their current status. The price Caitlyn set to upgrade was beyond ambitious, but she felt the risk warranted it. Even so, one non-user persisted and was demanding a meeting: Nikora Vayanna-Yayanna-Vayanna-Cheh.

She had searched unsuccessfully for Nikora after the attack in the surgical bay. There was so little other information about the woman that Caitlyn assumed her credentials were dubious at the very least. Nikora had determined that Caitlyn controlled the restorative bioapp and knew Grace carried its secret. Caitlyn was unsurprised by Nikora's enquiry but hoped that if the *miðaldra-kona* found another way to sustain herself, she would discard Youssef as an exploitable resource. What was puzzling was why Nikora might choose to endure the constant reset of the *raja'a* over conventional restorative methods. Surely she wasn't planning to offline.

Their discussion did not sate Moshe, but he faded into Sodality nonetheless. Despite his complex questions about their work, assumptions and findings, the women were unable to determine what the artificial man was. He had no knowledge that a skilled analyst could not acquire from the FMP, so if Moshe were machine-incarnate, then he would have access to the answers already. Caitlyn wondered if Freja was correct: Pazel had sent Moshe.

Freja had ghosted out of the apartment shortly after Moshe arrived. Jovana had ensured she rented a high-end *māsadā-sarīra* and offered to supervise her transition. Caitlyn had no idea where she had gone to, and none of the others was confident that Freja even knew herself. Jovana and Miyu had left moments later, citing pressing matters requiring their attention, while Kavya was engaged in a full-service call from her alcove. Caitlyn regarded their abandoned bodies, and said aloud, 'These four women might as well be dead, they are no use to me now.' Caitlyn requested a caching voucher and wondered if she would feel anything should she invoke it for all four. She felt so very lonely. Her only real friends had outgrown her, and now Caitlyn was solely responsible for the contract to understand the Pallial Decline, but it no longer held her attention either. Perhaps she, like Nikora, could be set free of its administrations. Caitlyn was in the kitchen and picked up a sharp knife without thinking. She crossed to Moshe and clasped his inert, perfect hand. I want him to be gone to simplify our situation, but he isn't our greatest threat. She turned, and using the knife, moved the loose fabric of Freja's shirt until the skin above her heart was exposed. Caitlyn could free her from her madness with a single stroke. It would be clean and efficient, and without fuss. She could readily dispose of the body in the waste desequencer and modify its log to show a penalty for recycling unwanted food. She would then request a maintenance crew to unseal Moshe's door and calmly walk into the future. The other *konurnar* would not know she had killed her friend. A drop of blood welled up at the knife's point.

'Caitlyn, what are you doing?'

She hadn't seen Kavya leave her bed. 'I don't know,' she confessed, 'looking for an answer.'

'You won't do it.'

'No.' She returned the knife to the kitchen to be cleaned and fetched some healer to erase the small cut. Kavya watched her without comment. 'I need to leave this place,' Caitlyn said. 'We all do, but we also have to finish what we started. The FMP, Odyssée, Pazel.' And Youssef. 'I have a feeling that abandoning even one thread could cause us real harm. I'm not prepared to take the risk.'

'So why remove Freja?'

'She's a danger to us. Maybe we'll be safe if I prevent her from returning.'

'She'll still pose a threat to us and potentially one that we couldn't anticipate. If you want her gone, request a caching voucher and the Pallium will purge her ghost. You need to hurt her.'

'No, Kavya, that's not it. Look at their empty bodies. Do you think this is natural? No one should be able to jump between different people. What the Pallium is doing is grotesque. I don't like it.'

'Have you ever been outside?'

'That's not the point. The knife should have woken her. It's not right.'

'It was only a scratch and wouldn't register. When she's ghosted out, it's a thing, not an *alþýða*.' Kavya slapped Freja fiercely across her face, and her *māsadā-sarīra* tucked its knees into her chest in an attempt to protect its head. 'How is this any different to the other services the FMP provides? Look at Moshe, lost in Sodality. It's been the way of things for a millennium. It's our reality. I think you wanted to alter our group by killing her and forcing us all to adapt.'

'Will you tell them?'

'Who would that benefit?' Kavya poured tea for them both, and they perched on stools, facing one another. 'Is that better?'

'Yes. Thank you. Please help me find Freja so that I can decide.'

It seemed like a trivial matter. The ghosting transaction report showed the agency Jovana had recommended and the particulars of the *māsadā-sarīra*, including costs. Freja had been allocated a high-end female body of similar specifications to her own, which Jovana condescendingly suggested would be easier for her to use. The Pallium had authorised the ghosting and provided Caitlyn with options to trace Freja via allocated host or her transferred TUID. They were able to review footage as Freja moved through K7 and arrived at Pazel's offices. She had quietly waited in the public lounge for over an hour before she entered a meeting room, at which point she vanished from the Pallial Truth. As far as they could ascertain, she remained hidden in the facility.

'She will have to interface with the FMP if she's going to maintain the ghosting. If you invoke the caching, nothing will happen until she does. There's no way to tell what she might do in the intervening time. My guess is either they've discretely escorted her out of the premises, or she's dead already. We have no way to know unless she onlines. Perhaps she's achieved her objective and wants to come home.'

Caitlyn shuffled uncomfortably. 'Freja reminded me there are always other options, and she was right, but I can't see any. She shouldn't trust me because I could have killed her. I want to run, Kavya, but I feel obligated to stay. I'm scared of Pazel and what he represents, and I can't help think he is responsible somehow. If Pazel finds out, he will destroy us. I'm sure of that. I have no idea what to do about Moshe. What if he's an ally? I certainly think Freja has it in her to betray us while believing she's doing the right thing. We can't take the risk, can we? We have to protect ourselves from her.'

Kavya remained silent as Caitlyn summoned the caching voucher. Neither woman examined its details, they quietly sat with Freja, and each took a hand. Two simple questions appeared before Caitlyn, *yes*, *no*, and Freja stopped breathing. The FMP told them to remove her clothing and bind the body in clearfibre film from the dispenser, which they did without speaking.

'What are you doing to her?' Moshe asked from behind them. 'Oh. I see you've shut her down. That was a mistake, and it's undoubtedly going to irritate someone. Maybe a few someones. I think I'll sit with her until she's collected.' He leant against her body, and the wrap rustled slightly. He held Caitlyn's gaze and frowned. 'What will happen to your workgroup rating now there are only four of you? Do you think Jovana and Miyu will approve?'

'It doesn't matter now. Will you be coming back to us?'

'I am undecided,' he said and returned to online.

'You should have pushed that knife into his chest,' Kavya said.

'Caching and killing someone are two different things.'

'Dead is dead, Caitlyn. We have no idea where Freja is, so the Pallium can't incorporate her *sikatā-ātamā*.'

Caitlyn bit her lip but did not respond.

'What better choice could you have made?' Kavya ventured. 'You had to act. I think Moshe's a threat too.'

All Caitlyn could see was Youssef, waiting for her with his arms open. She could heal him with the reimagined *raja'a*, and he could dare to remember. He could help her implant a cybercyte vesicle into her belly and fill her with his opportunity, and in return, she could ensure he remembered everything. He would thank her with endless kisses as they ascended to a remote place to enjoy one another. She didn't want to care about the others or the vast masses that depended upon the global processing core. It was time to cast aside her responsibilities, although just as she had picked the FMP over Freja, she suspected she would select the Pallium over Youssef. The realisation was final and overwhelming, and her heart was ready to break. Caitlyn hoped she didn't have to choose Moshe in the end.

Caitlyn was dimly aware that Kavya was sitting beside her, but her familiar smell and softly spoken words held no meaning. She desperately wanted to let go of her, despite the lure of their growing friendship. Eventually, she submitted to Sodality because she could not think what else to do. Caitlyn wandered between rooms and idly chatted with strangers about things that didn't interest her. She observed online reactions and hoped to maintain her balance, but the world seemed small and dull, and the *Jýðirnir* were an infestation that she needed to remove. She struggled with her cold, dark thoughts, so she sent out a summons to the other *konurnar*, asking them to meet with her in their calm, bluish vestibule.

They arrived in different formats: a faithful representation, a fantastical creature and a poorly imagined caricature. Caitlyn knew the others were self-absorbed and indifferent to how she represented herself and selected an old two-dimensional image from her time as a *ný-kona*. She thought those were happier days, although now she shunned the sterility of the ve-space. On the few occasions they had worked together, their collaboration in the quiet, distraction-free absolute had produced their best work. Lately, they lacked the motivation to sign into its coolness, preferring to work in an undisciplined, unfocused and undedicated manner.

'The *alþýða* who intercepted Inès and Enzo as they entered K3 was an unqualified. We've not been able to identify him at all, despite inspecting a huge amount of surveillance footage. The *maður* spoke briefly with them, and they accompanied him into the general tumult. Their TUIDs fritzed out shortly after, and something has obscured every captured image of them. It's a sophisticated piece of work, beyond anything even you could do, Kavya. We would have to physically inspect everyone in Third if we wanted to find them. My guess is they're gone already. We're not exactly on-plan.'

Caitlyn studied Miyu's Sodality representation. 'Would you mind toning down your epitome?'

'So I can be more like you? I don't think so.'

'What have you learnt about Moshe?'

'Nothing, except he intends to leave us.'

'That's not a surprise. Moshe doesn't belong here anyway.'

'He'll take Freja with him,' Kavya said. 'It's for the best. He used a cutter tool to find his way in so he can probably leave whenever he wants.'

'Did he ask if anyone else wanted to go?' Miyu asked.

You have to tell them and soon. 'It was very quick, so there wasn't a lot of time for discussion. Where is Hyun-jun?'

'He spent two more days in Third before he managed to reach us. We disabled the monitoring where a spoke intersects,' [*K2 location*]. 'This spot may once have been an entrance to the FMP, probably during the Forming. Freja suggested it, probably by analysing historic shipments from the Threes to K1. Occasionally, deliveries of basic foodstuffs, manufacturing tools and other things not normally required by First citizens went astray. She found a handful of places where this has occurred. One of them was active until just a few months ago, so we ghosted in and waited for Hyun-jun to arrive.'

'What was it like?'

'Overlooked. We ran several passes through the Pallial Truth, and according to its physical model, it leads to a space that doesn't exist.' Miyu wove complex equations in the air, which none of the women followed. 'I can't tell if it's by design or if someone, a *thráfstis* perhaps, deliberately corrupted it. It happened a long time ago, and now it's part of our common understanding. Simply put, there are slivers of Tion running all the way up from the Pretermissions to K1 topsky that have escaped the Pallium's representation of Tion. In every case, they align perfectly with Lacuna services running towards the surface. There could be errors in the global model, and the Lacuna spokes intentionally align with them. It makes sense as there would soon be limited impact on operations, but it is also a weakness that anyone could have exploited.'

'Access to K2 which the FMP cannot comprehend and therefore monitor?'

'Yes, it would be perfect. In theory, there are thousands of places where this is possible. It wouldn't take much to adjust the system's concept of reality if we wanted.'

'Not advisable,' Caitlyn said.

'What about services, heat and light?'

'Although the Lacuna is a vacuum, there are parallel service tunnels, even running through the Twos. If just one intersected a non-space sliver, there would be all kinds of opportunity, irrespective of level.'

'Hyun-jun is a very capable *ný-maður*,' Jovana said. 'When he arrived, his pack was filled with things he thought he might need to survive in the FMP. He was dressed in adaptive clothing and said he'd be good across a wide range of temperature, humidity and air pressure. When I asked why he told me he needed to be prepared and reminded me that a place where *fólkið* aren't supposed to be doesn't come with much in the way of utility. He didn't hesitate to enter Second when we hacked the entrance open.'

'Did you accompany him?'

'We walked with him for almost thirty hours but had to leave so we could return the *māsadā-sarīra* before our ghostings failed.

Thankfully, Miyu requested bodies hardened against disconnection sickness: in all, we were offline for sixty-three hours. It's definitely the longest I've been away.'

'And me, obviously,' Miyu said. 'It's not an experience I want to repeat. We don't know where Hyun-jun is now because unless he finds a way to connect, it's impossible to track him. He is much more resilient than any of us. He's coping with his isolation but said he would find a way to contact us as soon as he could. I'm positive he'll be successful. I'd like you to wait here until he does.'

'What about Moshe?'

Miyu rustled her scales. 'He'll find us if he needs us. I've set an alert. If he wants to expose us, it doesn't matter where we hide.'

Caitlyn felt uneasy. She frequently disengaged her clock while working to allow the disparate moments to merge into one, but now she found she needed to delay what was to come, despite prolonging her trepidation. The other epitomes were frozen and greyed out, spurning interruption, and for Jovana, Miyu and Kavya, Hyun-jun had already appeared. Caitlyn hoped he would and that her wait was not eternal. At least their biological systems were suspended while their artificial mitochondria fuelled their cells through induction, not respiration, and held their motionless bodies in perfect balance while they paused. When the Pallium failed, this too would be lost. One day an implementation would be devised that did not require the subject to be frozen, and her solution for the *raja'a* would be a curiosity, nothing more.

Throughout the levels, there were unknown numbers of *konservatorer*, and each of Tion's protectors had their own way of ignoring the passage of time. Caitlyn was sure that the *raja'a* was not unique to Youssef and worried that one day she would be reprimanded for selling the bioapp. What if a *konservator* was assigned to prevent the distribution of the process? She searched for Youssef because she wanted him to say he would wait for her once he had served his purpose, but he was ignoring her hails, and she could not locate his TUID. She cautiously pinged Grace, but she was asleep in a rented compartment. Caitlyn should have mediated Connor's dispute with Grace. Each could have returned to his or her *māsadā-sarīra*, and they would have been happy. They both had something the other coveted and could have compromised, could have allowed the FMP to undo their various exchanges. Now it seemed likely that Youssef would select his newly formed friend as his partner. This fluidity was too complicated for Caitlyn, and she decided it was an abuse of the ghosting technology. The processing restrictions her team recommended would, by necessity, limit its use, and Tion would be better without it.

In quick succession, the four epitomes unfroze and continued their discussion in ignorance of the missing hours. 'We have him,' Jovana said plainly and opened a panoramic representation. It didn't matter if Caitlyn closed her eyes, he permeated her senses nonetheless. Hyun-jun was alongside her and fully aware that she was watching. She heard his breath, smelt his exertions and touched what he touched, while the other *konurnar* faded from her existence.

'The Pallium is a labyrinth of crawlspaces. Hyun-jun thinks they are remnants of its construction. He estimates that no more than twelve per cent of K2 is processing component, much less than we thought, which means we've based most of our calculations on a bad assumption.'

'This one fact has justified all of the risk, Jovana.'

'How are we observing him?'

'He rigged a follow'long which is tapping directly into the FMP, leaving a web of fibres behind. The Pallium has no way to recognise the exotic data source and therefore assumes it is the product of an internal process. It doesn't matter. There's just enough bandwidth for us to speak to him and see what he sees, but little more. He knows we're with him but has asked that we don't distract him unnecessarily.'

'How long can Hyun-jun survive in there, Miyu?'

'Indefinitely. He's able to generate food and water, it's warm enough, and in a few days, he will have mostly acclimatised to the low air pressure. The biggest risk is major trauma because we have no way to help him if something catastrophic happens. My guess is Hyun-jun will stay until he's learnt all he feels he can learn.'

'That could take a lifetime,' Caitlyn said. 'What about his priorities, the grass farms and the empyrealodes?'

'He appreciates the dependencies and interactions, and can see why this is important.'

Hyun-jun's workwear was close-fitting and made from a grey fabric. There were narrow bags attached to his slim chest, back, hips and thighs, and occasionally one of the bulging pockets caught on components as he crawled through the unending processor. He swore quietly under his breath as he moved. The follow'long used his reflected body heat to guide him through the absolute darkness, providing a wrap-around immersive view of Second's interior. He traversed this world without colour confidently, never hesitating at intersections and moving steadily towards the centre of the level. The Pallium's composition was not regular, suggesting competing crews hastily built the FMP. In some parts it towered hundreds of metres in the dark and in others it was crammed into tight spaces, yet nothing was out of reach. There were catwalks and poles, and ladders close by, as if the Pallium was once worker-maintained. It implied provision for light and air and heat if only Hyun-jun could interpret forgotten protocols, but the spiders that tended the vast system did not need such things.

The four women watched Hyun-jun progress, indifferent to the passing of time. He frequently removed his mask to sip sequenced water from a fount, or to take bites of engineered food, but he never stopped for long. Caitlyn scrutinised the incidental data from the tapped FMP nodes, but there was little of interest, and she began to doubt that they would find anything valuable. It didn't matter to her that the physical volume of the compute engine was less than they had expected. It probably meant it was denser than they anticipated. She decided there really wasn't anything for him to discover.

'How long is it since he slept?' she asked.

'Almost ninety hours. Hyun-jun's using the routines you provided to keep himself alert, though I'm amazed he's lasted so long,' Kavya said.

'He can probably go another day or so,' Caitlyn said. 'It's time to bring him back.'

Jovana was unable to hide her frustration. 'Let him continue while he's awake. If nothing happens, he can rest and journey back refreshed.'

'Okay. You and Miyu keep observing him. Kavya and I can return to the vestibule if anything new happens. There's a lot of other stuff that requires our attention.'

Caitlyn stretched up her arms and tilted her head from side to side, smiling as Kavya made tea. To be truthful, she was not motivated to observe Hyun-jun's every action as he wormed his way through endless aisles of compute core, but she wasn't interested in working either. She was happy to relax with a friend and wait to see what might happen. Either the *ný-maður* would find a clue that meant he had to stay, or he would return to one of the spokes to be collected. She had not received a response from Youssef nor any indication that Grace was abroad. She would hold herself in reserve for either of them.

'When might we know more about Freja?' she asked Kavya.

'I have no idea. It depends on when she next onlines, assuming the caching request is approved.'

'They've taken her *māsadā-sarīra*,' Caitlyn said. 'I hate the thought that someone has been in our apartment while we were unaware.'

'I'm sure it happens all the time. You won't need to be concerned about it soon because we won't receive another major contract. Is there any sign of Pazel?'

'Is that who you're constantly searching for?'

'No.'

'Ah. I can't locate him or Freja, so other than her ghosting into his facility I couldn't tell if they've even met. Maybe he'll offer to protect her. He does have a lot of resources at his disposal.'

'Moshe's still here. I wonder why he didn't leave when they took Freja? It would have been a good opportunity, although he must have wanted to be here in the first place. You think he's an embodiment of the Pallium.'

'Not at all. Why would a system that vast constrain itself into a negligible human-esque form? Whatever else he is, he's undeniably a *mannvera*. Maybe you need to ask why a few times.' Caitlyn smiled thinly and prepared their dinner. Afterwards, as they were contemplating sleep, they received an interrupt from the Odyssée feed.

'Look at the spike in the viewing figures,' Kavya said. 'Miyu has patched Hyun-jun's sensations directly into Sodality, although she should have checked with you first. Hold up.' Kavya cleared a space on the wall, not choosing to immerse them both in the experience, and opened a link to the programme. There was a lot of background noise, so she muted the audio channel, and they settled back to watch. The commentary, which Kavya assumed Jovana and Miyu were dictating while Hyun-jun was quiet, was auto-routed to subliminal ticker-tape. Neither one was answering Caitlyn's calls.

The image was overly bright. Hyun-jun was crouching in a cylindrical corridor, or maybe a large pipe, peering through a metre-wide tear in its side. She thought he was lean enough to squeeze through it without hurting himself. The follow'long's composite view was generated behind Hyun-jun, but it was clearly about to float through the gap. While this might cast doubt in the minds of viewers wanting the most authentic representation of the events deep inside the FMP, many would accept the tantalising glimpse of a carefully maintained, ornate garden as sensational.

'The little yellow fucker's found something,' Caitlyn hissed.

They sat in silence, absorbing the ticker. It detailed each of Hyun-jun's discoveries since trespassing into the Pallium, providing stale statistics about the processing systems he had seen. He had climbed slowly towards the middle of Second and not cared which arc he attained. He said the slight movement in the thin air had drawn him to the service pipe; he thought it might be an area of slightly higher pressure, somewhere warm he could rest before abandoning his search. When he found the breach, he asked the Odyssée team to provide a live feed. A transcript of his excited voiceover was freely available for download by anyone in Third through Sixth.

The follow'long floated through the opening in the bulkhead. It was evidently a well-used passageway, its users had carefully folded or smoothed the metal edges to avoid harm, and fused a few small protective plates into place. The view wavered to compensate for the ambient light and, for a moment, the image flared. When it stabilised, Caitlyn held her breath as the scene displayed on the wall panned around. She wished she had returned to the vestibule but did not want to miss anything as she logged in. Without a doubt, there was a permanent community living within the processing core and Sodality was aflame with the news. One-third of the viewers had already decided it was real.

There were concrete steps up to the pipe, which Caitlyn realised was an exit and not an entrance. She could see from the garden that the gap was a few metres up a vertical, pale blue surface, which met with the sky twenty metres above. She couldn't discern the source of the chamber's illumination. Caitlyn wanted to stare endlessly at the rows of manicured box hedges and low shrubs which surrounded the neat lawns and shallow ponds, at the majestic banana trees and rocky boulders which broke up the uniformity, and mostly at the squat brick buildings that should not exist. She could hear her heart beating near her throat and wondered how many *lýðirnir* in their audience felt the same. Moments later, the follow'long spotted something and zipped across the garden, and the eyesight feed blurred.

A small child snapped into focus, five years old and only just a *tánin-kona*. She immediately saw the floating imager and tried to reach up for it. She laughed and jumped a few times, making Caitlyn want to gather her into her arms, but she failed to grab the strange object, and sullenly sat on the lawn with her arms folded and a pout on her lips. The girl cast around as if she needed assistance, before drawing a miniature gun from within her skirts and firing at the follow'long.

Three *ný-mennirnir* came running from beyond the outlying buildings, followed by a steady stream of onlookers. They wore warm robes, some hastily thrown on, a few *fólkið* brandishing weapons. As they swarmed towards the crying girl, another shot rang through the chamber, and the imager fell to the grass. The girl picked it up triumphantly and stared directly into its matrix. Caitlyn knew, without checking the viewing data, that millions of people would be joining the feed each second and hoped for a positive outcome. Most of the *sálirnar* stood apart, but the younger men and women started to examine the foreign technology while the Pallium struggled to maintain a steady video stream. They were muttering to each other under their breath, but Caitlyn could not interpret their words. Like the young girl, they appeared healthy and comfortable in the rarefied atmosphere. She became worried about Hyun-jun, hidden behind his mask and tucked behind the bulkhead, straining to see what had occurred. She tried to message him, to warn him to escape and to hide, but she could not make a connection.

A *ný-maður* had taken the imager, bound it tightly to a pole, brandishing it as a trophy, high above his head. The feed juddered as the FMP started interpolating the swaying input, and then the footage stabilised. Caitlyn estimated that forty *lýðirnir* were moving towards Hyun-jun's hiding place and hoped he had learnt from his experience at Enzo's grass farm. *Stay down. They are not your friends.* Her messages went undelivered. The people continued to whisper back and forth until one of them brought the group to a halt in front of Hyun-jun's hiding place.

'Come out,' he called. 'We have your device.'

Hyun-jun's unruly, black hair was visible at one end of the fissure. Slowly his forehead and then his dark, wide eyes appeared. Caitlyn despaired at how trusting he looked and desperately wanted him to flee. Instead, he pulled himself upright, removed the mask from his nose and mouth, and squeezed through the gap, leaving the rest of his equipment behind.

'Who else is with you?'

'My name is Hyun-jun, and I'm trying to understand. I am alone.' He started down the steps, moving slowly, with his hands in full sight and his attention focused on the lead man.

'What will you do with the images you've gathered?'

Hyun-jun smiled broadly. 'I have good news. There is a lot of interest in my journey through the spheres and much excitement in the levels below. You will all be pleased that I've brought Sodality to you today. There are many *þjóðirnar*, many people who will want to meet you.'

The headman nodded at Hyun-jun before signalling to one of the women from the group. There was a murmur from his community. It appeared their leader had a way to communicate that had nothing to do with the Pallium. The *kona* reached behind her back and calmly raised her gun. For a moment, everything was still, a perfect tableau to explain contrasting views: recluses and explorers; and then another nod instructing her to fire. The bullet ripped through Hyun-jun's face just before the tethered follow'long was brought crashing to the groundplate, and the connection was lost. The FMP neatly closed out the programme, added the appropriate credits and handed off to a barrage of advertisements.

'Oh no,' Kavya wailed and burst into tears.

Caitlyn wanted to wait for the others to return and tried to keep her thoughts from reeling. She knew Hyun-jun was dead and Odyssée would now bring destruction to them. She had allowed billions to access the uncensored footage, and many of them would attempt an ascent into the Pallium. There weren't enough assizes to protect it. Strange and dangerous *lýðirnir* hid deep within. They were a threat to the general population, and she should have kept it a secret. Caitlyn could not imagine what Jovana would say to her when she returned. There were *fólkið* in Tion who had facilitated this secret community, and they would be incensed. Caitlyn would have to pay for what she had done, and she could feel her culpability and the guilt rise within her; she was sure to be punished. The assizes were certain to blame her in the wake of her inability to prevent an uprising. There had to be a way to share the responsibility.

Why did you give him unfettered access to Sodality, Miyu?

Please wait for us to divest, Jovana said bitterly.

Caitlyn was aware the others had returned to their bodies before they opened their eyes. She didn't want a confrontation, but nor did she want to be blamed for what had occurred. They had shared their commitments and were all responsible.

'There's general outcry across Sodality,' Jovana said. 'The consensus is that we had no right to kill Hyun-jun when he had little opportunity for a dignified caching. Some are revelling in his death and demanding more footage, but of course, nothing else exists.'

Moshe's light voice startled her. 'Don't be so sure. Your collective stupidity will have far-reaching consequences. Who's to say that no one else was observing, or if the Twos will swarm down upon us. What will they do with the boy's *māsadā-sarīra* and the equipment he was carrying? Where will they go now you have exposed them? Will they come for you? The Pallium is off-limits for a reason and, despite everything you have tried to understand, you haven't even learnt why. In all of your investigations, you didn't stop to consider the reason you won this contract, and now you've reneged on your promise, and there will be retribution. Once that's over, I will ensure you are aware of my thoughts on the matter. So, bring your work crew up from the Depths, Caitlyn, and have them cut you free from your prison, discard your identity and hide amongst Tion's grotesqueries. Do what you will with the time you have left, because we will reward you for your actions.' Caitlyn breathed in sharply as she started to respond, but Moshe held up his hand to silence her. 'Not now,' he said and onlined.

You should kill him too, Kavya said.

We can't. We have no idea who Moshe is or why he has come amongst us. He may have information that we require, and the risk is considerable. What if he is linked somehow to the processing core? There could be awful consequences. Caitlyn's breathing was rapid, and the others could sense her distress.

Jovana did not look at her and clearly wanted to leave. 'We can't alter what's happened, even if we spend a lifetime revising the Pallial Truth. *Þjóðirnar* will remember, and they will talk about it in Sodality chatrooms. There are *sálirnar* living like parasites within the FMP. Moshe is right: there will be complications. Do you want to run away, Caitlyn? Miyu? Kavya?' All three women slowly shook their heads, but Jovana did not believe them. 'Then we have to prepare for what's coming and support each other.'

'Who do you think Moshe is, Jovana?'

'I think he is here because of Freja. Maybe she persuaded Pazel to send him. What happened to her?'

'We're not sure. Freja was gone when we returned from the vestibule. There's no record of what occurred.' Kavya hoped she was correct. Somewhere beyond the beige walls, muffled machines were hammering and grating as they worked. 'Someone's outside.' They knew what it meant and stopped talking. Jovana tucked a couple of keepsakes into her clothing, and they gathered around Moshe's door. Sparks appeared and danced across the floor, and seconds later, six *kostymän* swarmed into the chamber, one brandishing an extinguisher. Two of the figures went directly to Moshe and carried him out of the apartment, while the others squared up, one-to-one with each of the *konurnar.*

You have broken the terms of your agreement and forfeit your right to work. In addition, I have revoked your media licence and various other privileges. It's all detailed here. A ve-pad appeared before each woman. *You are fortunate that you protected the profits from Odyssée, and consequently, you have a reasonable degree of independence. A new elucidarium will utilise these quarters, and you are required to leave. You are permitted five minutes to attend to your affairs.*

Caitlyn was not sure if she was elated or experiencing anguish. She had longed for autonomy and an opportunity to be alone, but indecision paralysed her. She could see the devastation on Miyu's face too and thought that Jovana was merely hiding her feelings. Their desire for truth had resulted in Hyun-jun's death, and their inability to protect him had ensured Sodality voted with amassed emotions. She hoped that was the case, and that their expulsion was not the direct consequence of an individual's appraisal or that of a covert group. She would not stay with the other women: it was time to be her own *kona*. She did not want to ascend because she knew the solitude would destroy her. She would burrow down into Eighth and wait for Youssef to return.

Now that Miyu finally understood Freja's guilt, she could not stem the tears streaming down her face. It was her fault Hyun-jun was dead, that they had lost their elucidarium, and she would end up alone. She had protected Hyun-jun from his first moment of vulnerability when he climbed from the grass farm, but all she had done was stall his inevitable death. He belonged in the K6, and she had pushed him beyond himself, and he had paid for her error. She had to find Enzo and Inès, lost somewhere in the K3 and readily swayed. They did not belong up-level, and without Odyssée, their sense of preservation would be misguided. The thought that she could be responsible for their destruction too was overwhelming. She had to get them home. The tears continued to flow, and she was terrified.

Kavya watched the emotions play across Caitlyn's face and felt nothing. Caitlyn had failed them, just as she had failed Hyun-jun, and she wanted nothing more to do with it. She dismissed Miyu's tears as a cry for help and a pathetic display for the others' benefit. Ever since the initial possibility of ascent, Kavya vowed to live out her days in First, and she was relieved it was finally time. She refused to worry about the consequences of their actions and, as she followed the *kostyman* carrying Moshe, she started to query the Pallial Truth for an affordable apartment in the Ones. If the assizes stopped her, so be it.

Jovana commenced her last circuit of their chamber, and lightly touched the meaningless things that had surrounded her. The elucidarium had been her home for five years, and she had never actually been outside. Every glance at the door forced into their world reminded her that ghosting was a lie and held no more reality than the simulacrum in a full-service call. The only truth in her life dwelt in the relics she had collected from ancient abandoned places, and now these treasured possessions were worthless. She could read the decisions on her friends' faces. Caitlyn would pursue her other contracts, and Miyu would try to protect Odyssée's legacy. It was hard to decipher the root of Kavya's resolve as she pushed her way out of their lives, but she had always carefully hidden her desires. Jovana's only other friend was Joaquín, yet he and his fraternity were gone. She desperately wanted to forget him, but her memory was his only persistence. Jovana had once asked Joaquín to watch out for her, but she had failed to do the same for him, and she found herself making a new, secret promise.

Blood had ebbed away from Milagrosa's body even as she reminded him that she had encouraged Hyun-jun to leave their farm, no one else, and now her favourite boy was lost. Riley Khar sat quietly with her cold *māsadā-sarīra* cradled in his arms. Each breath was erratic as she wavered between continuance and respite.

When the *táningar* had started to follow Odyssée, Milagrosa and the other *eldri* had shown little interest, but eventually, it captivated the entire community of grass workers. She revelled in her decision to equip Hyun-jun for his journey, flaunting the sky tool as a talisman of opportunity and never letting it out of her grasp. The *samfélag* gathered to watch Hyun-jun's excursion through the Pallium, and their mutual shock briefly bound them together before forcing them apart. When Milagrosa was sure everyone was safe, she had used the sky tool's sharp edges to open her femoral artery.

She had waited until most of the farmers were asleep, scattered across the clearing in ones, twos and threes. The *börnin* were a mass of juvenile bodies, innocently resting and unaware of what had happened in distant Second. Most of the *ný-fólkið* scattered into the grasses to grieve in their own ways, furtively relieved they had not followed their hero's example. Of course, Riley Khar wanted to blame himself for her actions. He had yelled at her when Milagrosa confessed Lior had followed Hyun-jun into the sky and she had done nothing to bring the other boy back. Riley Khar predicted she would be responsible for his death too. She had looked into his eyes with such sadness.

No one had anticipated her action. There were sharp intakes of breath from the community as Hyun-jun died, careful moans and tacit wails, but Milagrosa remained silent at the back of the group. Afterwards, Riley Khar declared they needed to revitalise the grass farm and said he knew Milagrosa would be strong enough for what was ahead, but he found her slumped in her culm chair with the bloodied sky tool in her lap. Bailey reached her first and knocked the implement away as he thrust his hands against her groin. The Pallium had recommended swift caching as the best course of action, but before Bailey could accept its prescription, Riley Khar gathered his friend into his arms and took her amongst the columns. If Milagrosa were to die, he would ensure it was close to the grasses she loved.

Riley Khar rubbed glumes into the wound to stop her bleeding and held a flask of *sato* to her lips, dripping foam into her mouth until she was able to drink. If he could rehydrate her, encourage her to eat and prevent the laceration from further threatening her life, then she would be saved, but the report from the FMP indicated there were problems in her *sikatā-ātamā* and it warned Riley Khar that these were irreparable.

Chapter Ten
Inès
বর্তমানে

ONE SIDE OF the room, which included their large bed, was a featureless, mushroom-brown expanse. Other than the two free-standing lamps and the plush, oval rug, there were no adornments. The facing wall was staggered in three sections, so that the windows, which Enzo had set to a pre-Forming cityscape, broadened the room in stages. An unused comfortable chair and side table waited opposite the bed in the widest section. The floor, panelled in manufactured wood and polished to a mirrored surface, was strewn with their new clothes and felt warm underfoot. Neither had anticipated such luxury.

Inès sat on the bed and studied Enzo while he slept. They were both exhausted when Joaquín collected them and had been content to be left alone. Her dreams were complicated, centred around the grass worker, and when she woke, her sweat had soaked the sheets. Her oneironaut's fee would have been breathtaking, so she was glad of her disconnection. Inès was far too tired to tube, so she wrapped herself in a robe and lay on top of the bedclothes. She was unable to drift off again, but was comfortable nonetheless, and wasn't about to rob Enzo of his opportunity to rest.

Odyssée was precisely what she needed to make her life bearable. She hadn't felt integrated with the others in her elucidarium and, though there were no sustained pairings, she always felt neglected. Jovana and Miyu had provided her with an opportunity to break her contract and do something interesting with her life. Enzo's unsophistication excited her, and she liked that Hyun-jun had helped her to see Tion differently. She admitted to Enzo she enjoyed the sudden celebrity and was looking forward to being introduced to the Threes. Miyu had all but promised they would soon ascend to First topsky.

Enzo's breathing was slow, and his chest was barely moving. She touched his warm neck lightly to check his pulse, and he flinched from her in his sleep. Inès knew he was suffering from data withdrawal. She watched while he started to shudder, and his hands became caught up in the bedding as he cowered. Small noises eased from between his dry lips, and she realised he was trying to speak, but all she heard was a frightened whimpering. She breathed his name, not daring to touch him again and hoped he would wake at the sound of her voice, but he continued to moan as though pursued by something unspeakable. The inhibitors were still active, and the FMP refused to accept her connection: she couldn't order him into wakefulness. Eventually, Enzo calmed and returned to his former serenity, and when he woke, he had no recollection of his dream.

'Why hasn't Jovana contacted us?' he asked.

'Nobody can reach us.' She reached for his wrist and studied the fading red mark. 'We're supposed to wait. It will be okay.'

'We've been here nearly two days, Inès. They've forgotten us. I'm so bored.'

She laughed at him. 'We're supposed to relax; can't you understand that? You know how busy we're going to be. You didn't integrate the skills for the nursery work when you had the chance. You're going to struggle to keep up.' Enzo screwed his eyes shut and turned away from her. 'If you don't learn it you won't survive in the Threes. Let me teach you. People don't want a displaced grass worker on their team, celebrity or not.'

'You think I'm in trouble.' He welcomed her hand on his body and sighed.

'I'll look after you. Don't worry for now. Go back to sleep.' She knew he was tired, and like her, he needed time to recuperate. Inès thought about the tiny human *ungbörnir*, neatly protected in clearfibre eggs. She was looking forward to joining one of the boutique gestoria and watching the tiny infants as they broke free to compete with each other. She thought about her first moments after hatching, the overwhelming smells from which she could never escape, the fear of the other *börnin* as they pushed past her and her prevalent need to survive. Perhaps she had started her life in K3 but been delivered into the Sixes as a punishment of sorts. There was no way to know for sure. A low chime sounded, and the door swung open. Joaquín rushed in, breathing heavily.

'Wake him,' Joaquín panted. 'There isn't much time. Everything's changed. Jovana's not coming here.' He looked around furtively. 'Hopefully, nobody will.' Inès shook Enzo's shoulder, unable to rouse him from his sleep. 'Odyssée's producers have cancelled the show—no one knows why—and you have to leave. I can't help you. My boss is furious. It's a good job she's unable to track you. Your inhibitors should last three more days, but she's the guarantor for the apartment and will almost certainly come here to find you.' Joaquín ripped the sheets from the narrow bed and tipped Enzo onto the floor.

Inès gathered up the clothes she had ordered and threw them at him. 'Get dressed,' she hissed, turning off the windows.

'It's an unimaginable fuck up. So much so there's a mandate confining information to its level of origin. There's a rumour it's a precursor to refusing all inter-level permits. You have to go now. I'll find you, I promise.'

Inès wanted to protest, but the words wouldn't come.

'Jovana was always my confidante,' Joaquín said, 'even before I came to Third. She was good to me and will be there for us once you're able to reconnect. I know she cares about you both, and your friend Hyun-jun, and she'll make sure nothing bad happens.'

Enzo pushed himself up and folded his arms, but made no pretence at getting ready to leave.

'Jovana's understanding of Tion is quite impressive.' Joaquín kicked Enzo's shoes across the floor. 'I'm sure she's already looking for you.' He could feel his frustration growing because he didn't have enough time to pander to Enzo's ego. 'You have to be strong because tomorrow isn't going to be the same as today, not any more. We all have to be prepared to transition.'

'But to what?' Inès protested. 'We don't know what to do. Who sent you? Please don't leave us alone. We won't make it.'

'The assizes aren't going to deport you since Fourth won't accept the transfer and you have no sponsor to pay for routeing back to your original levels. They'll cache you, Inès, or worse. Abeyance is the last hope of the unjoined because nothing follows death.' They were both finally dressed and ready to leave. 'Keep moving and try not to interact. I'll get you some staters by the time the inhibitor cuts out.' He hugged her lightly before he left.

'We should follow him,' Enzo said.

'Don't be stupid. He's right. We calmly walk through the streets and keep moving. Look for anything we can use, food even. We should be able to travel a couple of degrees in the time we have. No one will find us.' She reached for his hand. 'You have to trust me, Enzo.'

It was hard to determine if the Threes were less crowded than Fourth. Inès thought the number of people was about the same, but she couldn't tell because the skyplate was so much further away. Enzo had complained bitterly that the sky was too close in the K4 tiers and would probably say the same here.

Inès did not feel anxious. Nothing confined her to any one place, and they wouldn't starve. Enzo had talked endlessly about training his company within the grasses so they could protect Noemí and the other *eldri-fólkið*, but he was just a scared *drengur* who needed her protection. He would never admit the truth.

'Do you think much about Hyun-jun?' she asked as they wove their way between the masses.

'Always. Hyun-jun was a good friend when I needed someone. The rest of my group left me so that I could test Hyun-jun. Miyu persuaded me to look after him. He was so optimistic—' Enzo shook his head ruefully. 'But inexperienced.'

'He left his farm behind and managed to gain access to yours, Enzo.'

'Yes, but I captured him and held him until I was sure he wasn't a threat.'

She dug her elbow into Enzo's side. 'He's tiny. What could he do to hurt you?'

'Plenty,' he said. 'I love Hyun-jun too. Do you miss him?'

'Of course I do. I hope we find him soon.'

'When we return to Sodality, we'll look for Jovana and Miyu. They'll know what happened to him. Joaquín will want to help. These are *hjðirnir* who care about us. They want us to be happy.'

'Don't you worry that without Odyssée we're of no interest to them? That we were just the latest trend?'

'Not us. We were sensational.'

The technician had told him a series of appointments would be more comfortable than a whole-body recast, but it was taking too long. Danesh decided this was his last appointment until he ascended. He cancelled the outstanding revisions and assured the technician that there would be other opportunities to update his physique and become his future self. He remembered the man in the white suit. Was that really who he wanted to be?

Cristóbal flatly refused his request for a job but did connect Danesh with someone who might be willing to help him leave the Depths. Aikaterine J-Omega-Oo-Beta warned Danesh that all ascents were being closely monitored and asked him to pay two hundred staters before any further discussion. He knew Pazel would be monitoring every transaction and would be delighted that he had purchased an up-levelling. He agonised during his long walk through Seven's corridors before he realised his only practical evasion was offlining and stealth. An *eldri-kona* met him and insisted he should pay for both Lacuna fares and did not disclose their destination. She refused to engage with him for the duration of their transit.

He followed her from the car through streets identical to the ones they had left. 'Relax,' she smirked, 'we're not going inside.' Two customers had left the speakeasy when they arrived, and Danesh was glad that he would not need to have sex with either of them. 'Twelve thousand steps.' The woman pressed her hand against the bulkhead, and a small hatch opened. 'The door at the top of the *bogdo* will open in eight hours. It's a one-time thing.' She handed him a torch and pushed him into the triangular stairwell. Sodality evaporated as she closed the hatch behind him and he hopped up the first quintet of stairs. He had no way to judge the passing of each coming hour, but it did not seem to be an impossible target. By the end of the day, he would arrive in K4 and could make enquiries as to Cristóbal's whereabouts. Every fifteen steps was a full turn, he needed a hundred turns an hour. After twenty, he was exhausted. For a while, he pushed upward without thinking and was unconcerned about his disconnection. He thought it might be best if he did not reconnect when he arrived. Pazel would have to resort to conventional surveillance.

The staircase stretched endlessly into the darkness above and below him, and all he could hear was his strained breathing and faltering footsteps. Danesh was confident he had sufficient pace but was impossible to tell. Tion was full of unanticipated moments, but he had to let go to open his eyes. He wanted to learn everything he could about the world and was determined to use it to create his independence. Each set of steps was more difficult than its predecessor. Somewhere inside of him, Pazel had already provided the tenacity he required to succeed, and it would show him what to do. It didn't matter if he used the staters because Pazel had already bought him.

The ceaseless ascent necessitated his automated response. Danesh was mesmerised by each turn, and his body became so light that his movements were effortless. He began to worry that he had collapsed and was imagining his procession, but he continued in his dream state until the steps were no more. He no longer cared if he had reached his goal in time.

It was the rush of online that told Danesh the door had opened, but it wasn't until it threatened to abandon him that he made any effort to leave. The K4 air was fresh, and he blinked in the bright light as he rifled through the clamorous tagging. His suit was dishevelled, so he kicked it in the closing door and headed for a cleantube and clothing store.

Danesh paid for a ve-meeting with Aikaterine and pleaded with her until she sold him Cristóbal's location. He was almost eighty degrees away, and she recommended a roofcar service for his journey, which she said would take an entire day. The sixteen-seat carriage was suspended from the skyplate and made several stops before it attached to a long chain and hurtled across Tion's arcs. When he arrived, the Lisboa Pit's doorman app refused to admit him without a sponsor. Danesh had provided Cristóbal's TUID, but the sentinel software smugly informed him that his associate was not responding. He was about to look for somewhere to wait when he received a rating request for Aikaterine's service. Almost as soon as he completed the survey, he was admitted into the club. The atmosphere inside buoyed his spirits as he sought a secluded spot where he could survey the pit's clientele. He spotted Shu-fen immediately and could not understand how he had forgotten her delicate face. She was hidden within the arms of a capacious, dusky *eldri-kona* and appeared to be sobbing. He didn't know if he wanted to talk to her.

Shu-fen needs something to live for, he surmised, and it shouldn't be someone from her past. I have cast her aside, and I would do so again. He was sure she had always known this about him but loved him anyway. Pazel knew little about affection and had nothing to offer as advice. Danesh realised his existence was self-serving and he had no capacity for compassion within. These were things that he had, at some time, cut away, and he dared not reintroduce them. Shu-fen already surpasses me, he thought and made his way to the door.

Not yet, ný-maður. *You and I need to talk.*

He was herded into a private room and told to wait. He watched as the old woman passed Shu-fen to the man at her side and slowly ambled across the floor. She drew the curtains behind her and settled down opposite him.

'I watched you as you chose. Shu-fen is in my care now. I know who you are and what you've done because I was there. My name is Doha. Why did you come here?'

All he could glean from her profile was a close association with Cristóbal. 'You know why. Even so, I thought I used to need her, and that might still be true. I thought she needed me, but it's not the case, is it?' Doha offered no response. 'Where are the others?'

'I forget what happened to the *drengar*. The other *ný-konurnar* didn't endure, but Shu-fen was stronger.'

'Is she content? She's all I had.'

'Then you should have chosen differently. I'm not taking Shu-fen away from you, Danesh. You have already discarded her.'

He opened his *sikatā-ātamā* to Doha and dared her to look. 'Do you think I ever loved her?' He felt her push through his life.

Sometimes Doha smiled, as if what she saw validated her assumptions, or perhaps she could interpret the fragments of him that came from Pazel, yet her face was neutral as she lingered over Victoria's death. His capacity for ruin was immense. 'You mustn't let anyone remove this from you. One day you will require its strength. There was love in you once, but not for Shu-fen.'

'Please ask Cristóbal to speak with me.'

Doha completed her assessment and took hold of his hand, but he could not bear to close his *sikatā-ātamā* down. Danesh hoped he would one day feel about himself the way he felt about Pazel. He needed a way to become someone new. Doha didn't say anything when she left, and he watched her speak with Cristóbal on the other side of the pit. Danesh had no way to determine who had shown him a possible future on the day he met Victoria. It might have been a dream, but it seemed as real to him as anything else. The Pallium offered no clues.

When Doha returned, she was brisk. 'He has no interest in speaking with you unless you wish to pay for his services.'

'What does he have to offer?'

'Nothing you might require. Cristóbal thinks you have no loyalty and he will give you nothing in return. Before I left the magnificence of the Ones, I couldn't comprehend joy, but now it is my closest ally. I've seen who you are, and we will not risk you remaining here.'

Once he was outside, he wanted to weep, but his eyes remained dry. There was so little value in a man's trust. He felt Cristóbal's refusal keenly, but it forced him to leave Danesh behind, so he submitted his application to be *wiederholt*, to reinvent himself and discard his old identity. He would purchase a full recast, mould his *māsadā-sarīra* and employ a splicer to wash away his issues.

Months later, when he had finished everything, he resolved to rely on his own earnings. The last thing Danesh bought with Pazel's staters was his new TUID. Mike Dla-Dda-Lamda-Phi did not look back as he strode out of the Fours.

The dust from the giant culms lay thick in the weatherwell, and Lior could see that Hyun-jun had collapsed against the wall. He had never imagined the world beyond his grass farm could be so monotonous. Lior had spent less than ten minutes in the scalding light and followed the footprints to the service hatch. He decided a very mean *maður* had designed the passageway outside—a man who wanted to punish the residents. He wasn't sure which direction to take along the corridor and didn't hesitate to query the Pallium. The delay that preceded its response was longer than anything Lior had experienced before, but he thought nothing of it. Colourful telltales danced in his eyesight, and he jogged along in the cool air.

Lior had food and water slung between his shoulders, and his only concern was the monotony of this sterile environment. He did not notice the subtle features in the walls and might have run straight past the portal, but the intense light from the plasma network spilt across his path, and he stopped to investigate. A transparent gig was suspended between the fiery streams, waiting for him to take a seat. Lior climbed in, and the door closed smoothly behind him as the vehicle began to move. On the dashboard was a ve-package keyed to his TUID. Someone knew he had absconded, but he wasn't going to turn help away. It wriggled slightly in his hand and was hard to look at directly. When he was ready, it unfurled to provide him with inter-level permits, staters and example strategies for staying out of trouble. There was no mention of Hyun-jun.

The FMP presented him with a topological map of the plasma network. It looked like a spherical cage intended to shield the Fives from below, but as Lior zoomed in, he noticed the interplay of connections between the K6 and K5, which he presumed distributed produce from the grass farms. The permit would allow Lior to reach any part of Tion, although he had insufficient staters to survive above K4. One of the plans from the package looked feasible and would embed him in as a freelance worker in a Fourth community, so Lior made a wedge reservation. He was unprepared for the chaos at the terminal and was grateful he wasn't in a hurry to depart. A group of algae technicians at the end of their two-month shift took pity on him and showed him how to interpret the departure boards. After his seat enveloped him, he fell asleep unaided and only woke when the ve-attendant told him to disembark.

Lior was not curious about his benefactor. It seemed reasonable that someone in the vast world would want to help a lowly farm boy survive. As he pushed his way through the crowded streets, he coveted the clothes the local *sálirnar* wore, the premium information services they subscribed to and the items stored safely in their bags. Lior was unprepared for the barrage of targeted advertising and found it easy to succumb. It was difficult to remember the time before when nothing was his, and everything he used or consumed had belonged to his *samfélag*. His stack of staters seemed woefully meagre and hadn't lasted as long as he had expected. The permit would be a quick solution, but it felt foolish to sell, so for the time being Lior would have to find a job. Possessions were undoubtedly demanding.

Lior rented a cabin but had to sublet it while he worked. The Pallium efficiently managed schedules to ensure the two occupants didn't meet. The small room developed an unpleasant odour which Lior attributed to the discarded clothing regularly strewn across the compartment floor. There were communal cleantubes in the street outside, but his roommate evidently spent his staters elsewhere. Lior was determined to find a better job and live alone.

It was tough to form friendships. There were apps to connect with *þjóðirnar* which took him on surreal ve-dates, but more often than not, his partner would exit before any climax. When Lior tried to talk to *konurnar* in the arcades, they laughed at his unsophistication, and several had suggested he returned home. He sometimes thought about Milagrosa and Riley Sampi and Riley Khar and wished there was someone to talk to about his choices. One afternoon, skulking in a café trying to make his cappuccino last for an hour, Lior realised he had stopped thinking about Hyun-jun. Sodality accepted his request, and within moments, he had become engrossed in Odyssée. It was incredible that so many people in the Fours were interested in someone he had known from early-nonage. After a few hours commenting on his friend's progress, Lior had a sizeable following of his own. When the narrator announced that Enzo and Inès would leave Hyun-jun when they up-levelled to Third, he decided it was time to take his place at their side.

It was impossible to identify the team behind Odyssée. Lior repeatedly submitted requests to explain his relationship with Hyun-jun, but he did not receive a reply. He queued to watch Enzo and Inès leave the Fours but was unable to make anyone understand. Someone had to ensure the programme maintained its focus on its central character and his quest to preserve the empyrealodes. Ultimately, he decided to take matters into his own hands and paid twenty staters to a thoroughly dubious *eldri-kona* who promised she could show him where Hyun-jun was.

Lior awoke from an uncomfortable sleep at the insistence of a sensational alert: Hyun-jun was broadcasting from deep within Second. The old woman was right, his friend was somewhere above, and now Tion was watching his every step. Instead of rushing after him, Lior returned to his regular spot in the busy café and settled down to watch.

Hyun-jun's death shocked him deeply. He wanted to flee and return to their grass farm as quickly as possible, but the online consensus demanded retribution and told *þýðirnir* to prepare for an uprising. Lior knew Odyssée required a new hero and it could easily be him. An unexpected eloquence waited deep within him, and he pleaded with his followers to promote his stream. Slowly his audience grew. Much of the traffic contained supportive messages or indiscriminate marketing material. Occasionally, there was abuse. He kept blogging while sifting through his ve-box and shared some of the most peculiar communications. He published the Odyssée's demand for him to cease posting, and it achieved two hundred million dislikes.

His manifesto was simple. The *þjóðirnar* dwelling within the Pallium were responsible for the Decline, and Hyun-jun had exposed them. The *forfeður* had not intended people to inhabit Second, and it was time to eradicate them. Lior had become a hero in his own right, and the support was overwhelming, yet he tried not to think about the *fólkið* who followed him. His dreams soon became an intimate crush, until he finally requested a block from his oneironaut. The next morning, the Pallium roused him from the nothingness minutes before his roommate arrived and informed him he had lost his job. Lior shuffled out of his room and into a vacant cleantube, trying to decide if he was concerned. He had various offers of support in his messages.

He requested an extra cycle. The FMP stated there would be no benefit and suggested alternatives to help him relax. He snorted and re-issued his purchase. When the tube finally opened, he felt refreshed and did not flinch from the offered hand outside. It belonged to a man who looked like he had spent many hours in the tubes himself, scrubbing away at an unwanted life. His name was Joaquín, and he was unable to hide the unrest that stained his appearance. Even so, Lior had prepared himself to accept help from whoever was willing.

It is in our best interest that you spearhead the assault on Second. Joaquín didn't say anything else. He handed Lior some fresh clothes and pushed through the milling *hýðirnir*. When they arrived at the transit hub, Joaquín ushered him into a pod. The connectivity was exquisite. By the time they had ascended through the Threes, Lior had documented his thoughts about Second and released them into Sodality. Moments later, Joaquín intercepted his post and made a considerable number of revisions. Lior examined the updates, which left him feeling inarticulate, although he grudgingly had to admit he was a young farmer while his sponsor clearly had experience in these matters.

The pod's lights flashed from white to red as the FMP issued a series of warnings regarding their transit through the Twos. Joaquín waved the messages away and provided local routeing instructions. When the door opened, he shoved Lior out and handed him a small equipment bag. *They will come*, he said, and the pod flitted away.

Where am I?

[K2 location].

Lior was amazed the Pallium offered the data up so readily, but more astounded that he could request routeing to his location from anywhere in the spheres. All of the suggested itineraries seemed unorthodox, and he knew Joaquín was managing things. Lior signed into his presence, issued challenges to his followers to actually follow him, showing them how to gain access to the Pallium's infrastructure. He drifted into a light sleep, knowing that Joaquín was right.

His oneironaut agreed to elevate him to a celebrated speaker. In his dream, he was an *einstaklingur* who was able to rally the population to his desires, and he basked in universal veneration. Each oration was spectacular and eclipsed its predecessor, and an endless sea of adoring faces lapped at his feet. As he spoke, his focus flowed from individual to individual, celebrating their love for him and validating their devotion. Their uniqueness was in sharp contrast to his expectations, and sometimes he was nearly distracted from his message. He almost failed to recognise Milagrosa Ya-V-Pe-Three and had to check her TUID. Her burnt face scowled at him. Liar, she crowed and pointed her charred fingers at him. Liar, the people around her echoed as unseen flames consumed them. Liar, Liar, the people raged, even though he tried to reassure them. The FMP offered him a solution, but he had to be sure. He grasped the blue button and a deluge of oceanic ice-water crashed through the crowd and swept them away. Lior awoke to tranquillity.

The men and women from his dream surrounded him. They were crammed into the hot corridors and were ready for him to lead them deep into the Pallium, but his bravado was a fantasy, and there was nothing within him that approached governance. He was a fraud and could not understand how his friend Hyun-jun had matured so rapidly. Imagined chanting swelled around and threatened to overwhelm him. He could not afford inaction.

Lior brandished his air mask high in the air. 'Let's go,' he proclaimed and followed the path that Joaquín had provided. He was relieved to hear *sálirnar* trailing behind him because his insecurity had washed his confidence away. The only thing that kept him separate from them was the routeing data, and he refused to discuss it with any of his companions. Lior needed to maintain his authority as it was all he had, but he was not their leader, only their guide, and he knew they would abandon him when the time came. His promises were lies, after all.

There was a lot of excitement when they reached the rift in the pipe. No one mentioned it had tempted Hyun-jun to his death. The gap had been repaired from the other side using pieces of metal scavenged from the Pallium's endless racking. The bundles of fibres from Hyun-jun's follow'long were still there, undisturbed, as were the slender bags that had held his provisions. Some people had already started to dismantle the barricade, until one by one, they were able to squeeze through. Lior did not want to look through the tear in the bulkhead and found he had misplaced his desire for retribution. He slumped against the curved walls and dropped his head into his hands. Three *táningar* pushed by him, laughing as the floodgates opened. Hundreds of people swept past, *mennirnir, konurnar, ný-fólkið*, even young *börnin*, unending waves of *mannkynið* intent on vengeance. None of them cared if Lior followed, until eventually there were only two people left, staring intently at him. One of the men was not wearing a mask and was breathing easily. The other was Riley Khar.

'You have condemned these *þjóðirnir*,' the stranger said. 'We cannot welcome them into our community.'

Riley Khar removed his mask. 'What have you done, Lior?'

The *útlendingur* held his ground. 'Your friend's death was a mistake, but we have to protect ourselves from your followers.'

'These *þjóðirnar* are not responsible for the Decline. Or for what happened here.' Riley Khar's words were laboured, and he panted in the thin air as replaced his mask.

'You have exposed us to Sodality. There is only one punishment.' The *útlendingur* did not move.

'I will deal with Lior,' Riley Khar said, and in a single movement pulled his grass blade from his tunic and plunged it into the stranger's chest.

Enzo's inhibitor started to wear off first. Inès was asleep and huddled against him, and all he wanted was to reacquaint himself with Sodality's warmth; however, his access was still rudimentary while the inhibitor clung on. He wished he could summon the TUIDs of some of the *þjóðirnar* he had met. If he could remember Miyu's or Jovana's, he could message them and let them know he was back. He couldn't even remember Hyun-jun's TUID, although he thought it started with Ezh, the sound that bound the three of them together. Enzo wished he could find a way to connect.

Inès stirred and wormed her way closer to him. He liked the way she smelt, despite having no access to amenities. Joaquín had been right. It was possible to survive in K3 without anything at all, so long as they kept moving. People in the Threes did not seem concerned with their possessions, and it was easy to find food before it was auto-tidied away. He doubted the competition of the Depths would provide the unjoined with such choice in sustenance, clothing and entertainment, but they would have found a way to survive, even in the Greater Numbers. He remembered the lean years in his grass farm, the ballooning community unable to sustain itself and how their circumstances brought unrest. It was a glimpse of the future. For the first time, he was concerned for Tion and finally understood what Hyun-jun saw.

'Are you online?' Inès asked with a yawn. She started to plait her hair to keep it from her eyes. He nodded and then shook his head. 'Me neither,' she continued kindly. 'My connection keeps coming and going. Have you heard anything?'

Enzo didn't like her talking about his pathetic recall. 'I can't stay on long enough to get in.' It was almost the truth. 'Let's walk about a bit and see if it's better elsewhere.' She didn't need to remind him that coverage in Third was superior to anything they had experienced in the past. 'It might work,' he said glumly.

Inès didn't correct him; instead, she pushed herself to her feet and then hauled him up. 'Come on, Enzo. Let's find you a decent socket.' She had already sent a brief message to Miyu and Jovana, explaining where they were and what happened when they entered the Threes. Inès said they had no option other than to follow their escort and noted he'd not been unkind, even so, she had not disclosed his TUID. She also didn't mention Joaquín's insistence on leaving the rented apartment but inferred they had nowhere to stay. There were hundreds of *Þjóðirnir* who Inès had met in K4, although she didn't want to risk any additional inter-level communications, besides it was unlikely that anyone from other levels would be willing to assist them.

There were people everywhere in the streets where they had slept. Before she had decided which way to go, she spotted a *miðaldra-maður* walking purposefully towards them. He looked dangerous, like a mid-life man who had survived terrible things and enjoyed the experience. Enzo immediately knew he was coming for them and pulled at Inès to hurry her away, but he was too slow, and the *útlendingur* seized his forearm in his rough hand. 'For fuck's sake, Enzo, I'm on your side.'

'Ghost?' Enzo asked.

'Not exactly,' the *maður* said, holding out his hand. 'Joaquín. Or at least I am now.'

Enzo felt his heart rate ease and returned his handshake. He was still uncomfortable with the fluidity of the people in his life. He studied the *kona* standing quietly off to one side. 'You're Miyu,' he said, uncertain of his insight, 'or Jovana.' She smiled at his awkwardness.

'She's Jovana,' Inès said. 'These are real people, Enzo.'

'We always were real,' Jovana said, 'but now we're physically here with you.' She indicated they should keep walking. 'I up-levelled this morning and have been trying to persuade Joaquín to make a fresh start. I was staggered when he mentioned he'd found you, Miyu will be relieved. I've secured a facility here in the Threes where we can remain unnoticed, alongside a few other nonconformists.'

Inès turned to Joaquín. 'You don't agree.'

'It's not that,' he said. 'I don't have the experience to decide. I'm going to have to rely on Jovana just as much as you are. It's a remnant of the water mining which is now a cavernous, empty space waiting to be re-filled. The Pallium has marked it as a bad sector, and entirely disregards it.'

'There's some history,' Jovana said enigmatically.

'New arrivals will have to relinquish their resources, which will be used by the entire *samfélag*. Jovana has secured a micro-sequencer and some fairly complex templates. We'll print components for a full-size version, mostly using elements extracted from the air, plus a few specials.' He indicated the bulky pack slung across his shoulders. 'Once I have the replication running smoothly we'll have access to the energy and consumables we need. It's the same principle as pe-to-pe.'

'What if the Pallium decides to repurpose the space?' Inès asked.

'One thing at a time,' Jovana said. 'Please come with us.'

Enzo shrugged. 'We don't have any other option. Who are the others?'

'Four *þjóðirnar* aren't enough to build a new community. There has to be diversity as well as balance. I've placed an advertisement.'

'Is that wise?' Joaquín asked. 'What if Nikora comes looking for us?'

Jovana set off into the busy streets. 'Nikora used to frequent Eleven-Two. She won't return. The cistern contained a sizeable habitat before it burst. I suspect it is still there and might provide us with a good starting point.'

Enzo was frustrated by their leisurely pace. He thought they required more urgency, but neither Joaquín or Jovana seemed concerned. Although he was sure Jovana was online, she didn't appear to be distracted by data services and idly chatted to Inès as they walked. He fell in beside Joaquín and wished he still had his *hanbō*. The *miðaldra-maður* made him nervous. 'How old are you?' he asked.

'Twenty,' Joaquín replied and frowned, 'but this isn't my original *māsadā-sarīra*. I have no idea how old it is. Could be thirty, I don't know. I guess it doesn't matter, although I used to be the same age as Jovana.'

'What happened?'

'I was brought to the Fours and couldn't find my way back. Jovana says I've lost my body. It's hard to explain, but things feel distant somehow, as if it wasn't mine in the first place. I'm Joaquín Visarga-Dza-Ue-Hayanna now, assuming I maintain my connection with the FMP.'

'And if you don't?'

'The original psychic apparatus will exert control. If I join you, we have to maintain our connectivity, which means we could be detected. It's a difficult decision.'

'Who wants to find us? I don't understand what's happening. The inhibitor, the assizes, Jovana. Why is she here with us? You said she wouldn't come.'

'Things change, Enzo. What about you? Wandering around Third as though you belong here.'

'Except I don't. Despite everything that has occurred, we're going to hide away in a closed community, like my grass farm. I should have stayed with Noemí.'

Jovana and Inès were a few steps ahead and had stopped walking. 'We have to concentrate on what's to come. Together.'

Enzo looked away. 'Do you know where my friend is? He should be here too.'

'In a moment,' Jovana said. 'I've ordered a car.' They silently waited until it arrived and settled into its broad seats. 'Hyun-jun succeeded. He found a way into Second, and he was fearless. There are *lýðirnir* hiding in the Pallium, and they attacked him. I'm sorry, Enzo, but your friend is gone.'

'A caching?' he asked, his face ashen.

'No, they killed him without warning.'

Jovana had left the pod's windows turned down, and K3 appeared flat. 'This is your fault,' Enzo moaned. 'And Miyu's. You had no right to send him there.'

Inès wormed her arm around his shoulder. 'We all loved him,' she said simply.

'Not like I did. Hyun-jun was all I had once my *ný-mennirnir* and *ný-konurnar* left. I don't even know what happened to them.' He leant over and pointed his finger at Jovana. 'You see everything. What happened to Hyun-jun? To the other grass workers?'

Jovana calmly pushed his hand away from her chest. 'You should be grateful Odyssée isn't available in K3. You have better memories of Hyun-jun than I do.'

'You didn't let me say goodbye,' he accused. 'I can't rely on my memories. Why did you offline us?' Joaquín didn't respond. 'What became of my *sálirnar*, Jovana?'

She looked directly into his eyes. 'They were cleared away. We had to because it was a contractual obligation. Remember, we were trying to protect Hyun-jun. You have to understand that Miyu didn't have a choice.'

'You told me we always have a choice,' he spat. 'You should have stopped her. Who will be next?' He leant forward to grab her throat, but Inès held him back.

'You can't let it matter, Enzo. We won't survive on our own. Odyssée must have taught you that.'

The car was moving too slowly for Enzo. It was no better than they had achieved on foot. Pods surrounded them in a sluggish swarm of disparate, competing vehicle designs. Enzo wanted to rant at Jovana, rage about what she had done to him, but he was struggling to recollect Guðmundur or anyone else from his grass farm, almost doubting their existence. He wished Hyun-jun was there to encourage him and help him remember. 'It will always matter,' he said stubbornly.

Who will be next? Joaquín asked Jovana.

She didn't outwardly acknowledge him. *It was a job, just like yours. Didn't you ever have to do something you regretted?*

Of course not. Joaquín felt unsettled by her question and realised that despite their ve-time together, they did not know one another. He trusted her because of their relationship but was unable to measure its veracity. He knew nothing about these people. Jovana had taken him away from Nikora, just as Nikora had torn him from Friedrich and his other friends. He still felt like an idiot.

You have to convince him it's okay.

How do I know that, Jovana? Just because you say so? I should leave Enzo and Inès to you.

Are you abandoning Eleven-Two?

He turned to face Enzo. 'What matters is that we have somewhere to start afresh.'

Enzo and Inès nodded yet they both looked defeated. Jovana

smiled briefly and closed her eyes. He summoned the address key for Nikora's TUID and wondered if he should call her. She was sure to want her rental back eventually.

At least forty people were standing in the dark whispering to one another and wandering about, unconnected and disorientated. Joaquín had purposefully distanced himself from the others without straying from the meagre lanterns. The portal into Eleven-Two had shut almost an hour ago and Petrişor, who appeared to be in charge, said no one else would join them for several months. Jovana had deferred to him immediately, and Joaquín realised she was no longer the architect of his future. There were a few pieces of equipment scattered around the group and off to one side was the shadow of the former underwater habitat. He suggested exploring the structure, but Petrişor was adamant: they would utilise it once they had established their own dwellings. There would be plenty of time once they were able to manufacture food and water.

The combination of damp air, rust and something he couldn't identify made the entire chamber smell bad. It was impossible to tell how large the cavern was, although Petrişor said it was a roughly a cubic kilometre and probably the largest unused space within Tion. He had only shrugged when one of the men asked why it had been left alone. The floor was damp, and some of the *lýðirnir* had slipped and clung to each other when they first arrived. They didn't fill Joaquín with confidence, but Petrişor had laughed heartily, helped them onto their feet and explained that it wouldn't take long to dry the compartment out unless they wanted to have an archipelago community. Inès volunteered to work with the micro-resequencers, and Jovana asked Joaquín to assist. He was sweating slightly and wondered how this had become his destiny. Joaquín didn't know how to refuse and was terribly concerned that Nikora would consider him absconded.

A carbon-wright worked in the twilight and bright, white lines burnt into Joaquín's eyes as he watched. He moved his head from side to side, and the afterimages ran across each other, weaving intricate designs. As quickly as the carbon-wright created panels, several *mennirnir* fused them to form small stockades, consigning them once again to enclosed lives. Joaquín would stay with the group long enough to watch them establish and then quietly leave. He did not relish a second lifetime of captivity, even though that was all he had really known. Nikora had shown him a better way.

Fólkið were busying themselves and appeared to be content, despite their lack of connection. Joaquín's head ached with data withdrawal, but there was no point in complaining. Jovana bustled around the micro-sequencer as components were printed and handed them to a *drengur* who deftly assembled a set of full-size models. Jovana made encouraging noises as she flitted about him, as if he guarded their very opportunities in his small hands, while Petrişor lingered away from the disorder with a slight smile on his lips. Joaquín was unsurprised he wasn't contributing, as he had the look of a man who had spent his life watching others labour for his benefit. There were packing crates scattered around him on the cistern floor, so Joaquín strolled over and started to organise them half-heartedly. Petrişor ignored him for almost fifteen minutes before interrupting.

'What are you doing? You should be helping the others. We have a lot to accomplish.' He waited patiently for a response, but was offered nothing. 'Jovana told me about her and how you became trapped in this *māsadā-sarīra*. I will make it possible for you to connect, so you don't need to worry about the ghosting.'

'I thought we were offlining?'

'There are *þjóðirnar* who need to be informed about our progress. They consider the repurposing of Eleven-Two an investment of sorts and will keep us away from prying processes, but you have to commit, Joaquín. You have no usefulness otherwise. You do understand we're creating a sanctuary?'

'Are we being held here?'

'We will eventually close the portal to the outside, but until then, it's not in our best interest for you to leave. I will not allow you to return to Nikora, but I promise to keep you safe from her. Now go and find something useful to do. Get the bioprinters working.' Petrişor deliberately turned his back on him and continued his vigil.

Joaquín picked up one of the containers and carried it across to Jovana. The reference to Nikora unsettled him and he doubted their exile would last. 'Petrişor mentioned you were looking for this,' he said, shaking the heavy box gently. 'I think it was this one.'

Jovana was feeding a clearfibre filament into the sequencer and occasionally reached to one side to turn a large spool. 'The metalloids?' she asked.

'I'm not sure. Nothing is labelled. I don't understand why we have to use raw materials.'

'It takes a lot of energy to run the sequencer. We'll use basic chemical processes for now. Petrişor will show you the plan if you ask him.' She opened the box and fished around with one hand. 'It's a carton full of catalysts. Very pretty, Joaquín, but not much use.' She pushed the container towards him with her foot and waved him off.

'Who is he, Jovana? Why should we do as he says?'

She continued tending to the sequencer and spoke without looking up. 'He's the one who's paying for all of this, or his organisation is. I have some funding, but not enough to support an entire community indefinitely. So I posted a request to Sodality, and the best offer came from an unlikely source. It practically guarantees that Nikora will be unable to find you because my patron is shielding Petrişor from her.'

'He offered me connectivity and has enough staters to guarantee access. Is Petrişor ghosted too?'

'There's nothing to suggest he is. I'm not surprised he has retained his access because we would need to know if anything threatened us. Anyway, all of my interests are within Eleven-Two.'

'Who is Petrişor working for?'

'Just find me the semiconductors, Joaquín, there should be a whole set of them. I need to print components for the tera-sequencer, and get them across to Hosniya so she can start assembling them.' She waved at a *kona* who was spectacularly wielding a spanner against a variety of bulky components. 'Be grateful that we're okay.'

Pazel considered very few *lýðirnir* to be his intimate associates. Each one of them refused to believe he was himself. It seemed more likely that they were the imposters and someone had entrapped him in a watered-down version of his own life. Mehdi tried to appease him with complex interpretations of his *sikatā-ātamā*, but Pazel said the wiring diagrams bore no resemblance to who he was and suggested the Curator seek alternative employment. Mehdi stressed that his behaviour only strengthened the case and continued to work. Neither of them could identify what Danesh had taken, other than a general feeling that something important was gone. Pazel was frustrated because the mapping was a finite task and, once complete, it should be possible to compare it manually with previous versions. Mehdi reluctantly agreed and showed him what had changed. Pazel was unable to interpret the differences.

There were several unopened messages from Nikora. She had been frustrated when they met in the taverna, and Pazel didn't care for her analysis. He was tired of her offers to track down the perpetrator and instructed Mehdi to tell her that he already knew who it was. He maintained he didn't feel anything was gone, and it was time to move forward.

When Pazel was on his own, he found it hard to adhere to his schedule. Had Danesh stolen his single-mindedness? The *nýmaður* had spent too many staters on his arduous climb to Fourth. That particular *bogdo* was rarely used for unrecorded up-levelling because those people who could afford to pay for a discrete movement could usually pay for it to be comfortable. Victoria had never charged anything close to two hundred staters. The door had opened on time, and Danesh had tumbled out.

Pazel didn't care to watch while the boy cleaned himself up. When he finished, he appeared fit and rested, and had removed every trace of his activities in K4. He had found a way to re-process all of his stater movements, and although Pazel could see how much Danesh had spent, he could not determine what goods and services he had bought. It probably didn't matter, and Pazel realised he might have started obsessing about the *drengar*.

Freja brought him some fresh coffee and sat down expectantly. She is far too generous with her own importance, Pazel thought, but she is willing to adapt.

'He intends to kill you, Pazel.'

'Yes. It doesn't matter.'

'He'll probably try to kill me too, and that does matter,' she retorted.

'I expect him to live out his life in the Fours, or even Third. He can do that as long as he has access to my staters. If he becomes a genuine threat, I'll cut him off.'

'Where is the little shit now?'

Pazel added her to his surveillance feed. 'With the traffickers. I've told Cristóbal to turn him away.'

Freja leant across the pit and peered through the curtain. She almost laughed: Danesh was sharing his *sikatā-ātamā* with an old, dusky woman. She grabbed a copy. 'I'll ask Mehdi to compare this with your archive. I'm sure he'll find what we're all looking for.'

'It won't be there, Freja. Danesh wouldn't expose himself if there were any risk. Irrespective of your wishes, we have to protect him because he's the only one who knows where it is.'

Freja sensed Pazel wanted to be alone. A few minutes after she had gone, he received a response from Mehdi. He left it in his queue and watched as the old woman told Danesh to leave. As far as Pazel could tell, the *nÿ-maður* seemed utterly unchanged.

Months later, when Danesh had become a new man once again, Pazel thought precisely the same.

REFLECTION
Pazel
অতীত

WHEN WATER MINING commenced, fundamentalists warned of the consequences of uncontrolled resource exploitation. There were comparisons with the global hydrocarbon crash, but most agreed the petroleum industry had collapsed under the abundance of cheaper energy, and the argument was lost. The world's vast expanses of ice had begun to melt at an alarming rate and threatened the land belonging to the three conglomerates. The oceans, rivers, lakes and seas were teeming with things that were of limited practical use. Water was no longer a precious commodity for sustenance and health; it had evolved into a global menace, waste product and dumping ground. Two-thirds of the world's surface remained inaccessible below the waves, which rendered potential real estate unusable. The detritus that had built up from the Industrial Age had decayed into an unpleasant slurry, poisoning most of the aquatic life. What was left was of little pharmaceutical, nutritional or practical value, but mainly it was just a lot of contaminated saline solution. They had to remove the water, and the technology was available.

Anyone could readily compute the burgeoning population's demand, and even accounting for luxury water, all that was needed was a thousandth of a per cent of the amount available. The people stored the majority of the requisite water neatly within their *māsadā-sarīra*, and Tion, their new world, maintained balance using an efficient recycling engine. To guard against error, the *forfeður* built storage reservoirs into the world's infrastructure, each cubic compartment as deep as the level itself and nestled into the Threes where the population was relatively limited. A handful of technicians monitored the tanks and occasionally pumped water between them to counter any echoes of tectonic drift.

Cistern 11,200 had burst a century after the Forming of Tion due to a minor failure of its convex base. Before engineers could seal the breach, a million tonnes of water exploded through the first eight decks of the level below. The Pallium had no appropriate reconstruction processes, so the Definitive Sitting assembled a specialist group to determine if the situation might be salvageable. There was considerable pressure to deconstruct the reservoir, but the engineers persisted, and repairs were made, despite the additional load on the other storage tanks. The team included an almost fanatical *maður*, Pazel Sad-Tet-Ain-Resh, who had a personal interest in disaster recovery. Within a few months, the engineers flooded the cistern again.

Something unexpected lurked within its depths, and it was entirely undocumented. Activists had conspired to construct an unobserved outpost, an overdue opportunity for insurgency, and hidden it within the water. They had created a covert habitat, isolated from the Pallium, and ensured it was immune to the influence of the masses beyond the cistern. Sturdy cables anchored it to the middle of the tank, but also allowed its careful repositioning alongside a portal resembling an obsolete Lacuna lock. It promised the possibility of a nonconformist life, of the chance to discretely rebel or to avoid the reality of the massively-populated world. Small groups would meet in secret at the gateway and enter the habitat for a quiet getaway. Once Eleven-Two had returned to its hiding place, where no surveillance could penetrate, they discussed their roles in Tion's future.

Pazel delighted in his time in Eleven-Two. He referred to the facility as his greatest achievement and said his only aim was to enjoy it. His associates regarded him fondly. Pazel's ambition had made the project a reality, and the K4 lives lost and the substantial expense incurred were probably justified. The habitat contained a few communal areas, a meeting hall and private spaces for the guests and crew. It was usually inert, forgotten and undetectable, yet for a few weeks in the year, eighty influencers, innovators and independent women and men enjoyed its solitude.

Pazel had insisted on embedding explosives into the rebuilt substructure of Cistern 11,200. He argued it offered an option to undo their repairs. The chief architect had ardently disagreed, but curiously did not arrive for her shift the following day and Pazel's modifications were incorporated. He never recorded the changes to the design.

Eleven-Two became a template for Tion's future, but Pazel wasn't particularly interested. He thought the machinations of his colleagues and friends paled alongside his achievements. None of them was capable of leading such extraordinary change, and despite demands that he take on their challenge, he resisted. He spent his days in the habitat's confined public spaces, assisting the maintenance crew and helping the temporary staff prepare meals. Occasionally, he would receive a technical problem, like the cumulative corrosion caused by the impure water outside, or a practical issue, such as how to make space for additional private accommodation. He approached every challenge as if it were more important than the last and continued to help his community grow.

During one of Eleven-Two's first summits, Pazel had obsessed over a woman, the only cultivator he had ever met. When Reihaneh announced she was growing a child for a prominent K1 citizen, he contrived to spend all of his spare time with her. Megagestoria manufactured the majority of Tion's people, and Pazel had never observed a pregnancy before. He was fascinated, asking a variety of questions that spanned medical, ethical and personal spectra until she eventually tired of his attention and locked herself away. She declared she should not be disturbed until Eleven-Two docked and its inhabitants could be released. Pazel was exasperated but not enraged. He said he respected her privacy and tried to apologise by cooking lavish meals and leaving them at her door. She told him he could not examine her more closely and left the food to waste, which deeply offended some of the other delegates. He discretely let the matter drop and spent the remainder of his time equally secluded.

An opulent celebration heralded Eleven-Two's centenary, and everyone who knew of its existence wanted to be there. Invitations were personal and scarce and brought together one representative from each year's assembly. Pazel was unsurprised that he was not selected as his popularity had waned in recent decades. For the third time, he negotiated a role as a sous chef and spent a chemically-stimulated month refreshing his culinary skills. The day before the conference commenced, he managed to obtain a copy of the guest list. He would not have selected any of the attendees to celebrate his achievement, and none would even recognise him for what he had done, except possibly Nikora. She anchored Pazel to Eleven-Two, and the slightest mention of her name summoned her pale, delicate features and the meadow-smell of her blond hair.

They had first met almost one hundred years before during Eleven-Two's third annual summit, and both recognised the wisdom in the other. She was a close secret, and he was terra incognita. They had enjoyed their fledgeling friendship, fenced long into the night, and the other delegates frequently accused them of derailing the entire project. Pazel could no longer remember what the group was working towards, and its goals were vapid and unworthy of his engineering success. He had built the most inaccessible, impenetrable and safe place in all of Tion and, to his dismay, nearly all of the great thoughts that occurred there were subsequently submitted to Sodality's online groups as soon as the session had disbanded. He decried the futility of it all and alienated his peers, and as the decades passed, they neglected him.

Pazel didn't mind. He had several other distractions, and his only reason to be in attendance was straightforward enjoyment. Eleven-Two was the one place he truly felt at home, and he had no urge to involve himself in the machinations within. It was his vacation from his life and a place of simple interaction, which he thought was essential for his sanity.

At the end of the evening service, while the antiquated crockery was being carefully hand-washed, Nikora bargained her way into the kitchen. Delegates usually paid their compliments in the dining lounge, as it was unseemly for the crew to mix with the guests. He was extremely pleased to see her, and although no one seemed to age these days, she looked significantly better than she did in his detailed, augmented memory. They embraced briefly and agreed to meet when his shift was over.

'Hard work suits you, Pazel,' she said.

He sighed. 'My days of pretending to think great thoughts in the intimacy of others were long ago. Now I prefer the galley's simplicity. I thought you had resolved to leave this behind.'

'You and I aren't going to agree, darling, but neither of us would side with these ineffectuals. Ever since you started prolonging, you've been different to them. Yours has always been a more sustained vision, but we've talked about it too much. I don't care that you're intellectually over-endowed and devoid of empathy, because you still promise a reasonable outcome, once we have cleared everything else away. I trust no one can observe us.'

'It's unlikely. There were no quantum services in the original specification, other than the operational requirements to keep everyone relaxed. We didn't want our thinking to be disturbed, not even by apps that might help order one's thoughts. Many regarded the lack of online as Eleven-Two's best asset. Personally, I think that's low on the agenda, and I may have kept a few things for myself. There's a place in the stabiliser room where you can catch up with occurrences on the outside.'

'You mean that while I was desperate for a little processing, all I had to do was hook in?'

'Would you have?' he asked.

'Did you?'

'Often. It helped keep things in perspective. The delegates are far too idealistic.'

She jabbed him with a finger. 'You cheated. I remember you extolling the wonders of a new society, uninhibited by the Pallium's vast information engine and able to think for itself while returning to the brightness like an addict. I'm amazed you kept it from them.'

He reached for her hand and traced the veins on her wrist with a fingernail. 'No one was looking for connectivity, except sometimes one of the crew. What they didn't know didn't matter. Do you want to use the line for something?'

'Not at all. I'm here because I would like your opinion about a couple of things I would like to keep private. The rest of the time, I'll enjoy the conference and do what I can to help them see reason.' She brushed his hand away. 'But before that, you've had a busy night, so we should do something to relax.'

They walked around the habitat like old friends. Pazel showed her his favourite parts of the facility, the safeguards against over-compression, carbon dioxide splitters that grew sapphires and rubies and lots of small places where he said he couldn't think of anything to cram in.

'I wasn't the principal designer,' he confessed. 'It was a group effort, but we had our differences, and eventually, they all left the programme. Exceptional waste of some spectacular talent, but I couldn't help it at the time. We stored everything on personal embedded alternates, so by the time I was the only one left, nobody could contest my truth. Only the financiers cared, and they got what they wanted from the process. I guess today's guests are their guests. Not to worry.'

'You could have achieved all of this on your own.' Nikora wasn't particularly interested in his response but was enjoying his company.

'I've been telling people this is all mine for a century, Nikora. Of course I could, and more. Now, I think it's time we refreshed their memories.'

CHAPTER ELEVEN
Grace
ভবিষ্যতে

THE SIMPLICITY OF the *raja'a* had endured for nine hundred and seventeen years, and consequently, Youssef had forgotten how to be bored. Each day, he longed for his daily reset. His overseer had abruptly ended his innocence with drudgery, and the new *tabi'a* unquestionably guaranteed tomorrow would be just as dull as today. He couldn't help but despise her. The notion had grown slowly over the first few months after his update, but as the months matured into an entire year, he became intimately familiar with his routine. Caitlyn muttered that all *þjóðirnar* survived from day to day on whatever skills they possessed and his pre-Forming life had been no different. He argued that she was misguided, that his twenty-one years before the building commenced were diverse and remarkable, and the subsequent pre-*raja'a* decade was full of optimism and wonder. She had never asked him about the mysterious task assigned to him by the *forfeður*.

Caitlyn's secret purpose consumed her. She didn't speak to him about her work nor did she offer advice as to his future, but devoted most of her time to Sodality forums. Youssef assumed Caitlyn had spent the past year preparing to sell the *tabi'a* and he wanted nothing to do with it. When she asked what was wrong, he told her he didn't understand why she had cached Freja but left Moshe alone. Caitlyn accused him of becoming surly and strongly suggested he find his own accommodation, just as Grace had done almost a year ago, but offered no help when he said he had forgotten how to survive on his own. Youssef knew she was hurting. He wished their relationship could return to how it had been when he could not recollect what they had said because whatever Caitlyn had previously felt for him had been lost. Grace was happily enjoying her newfound identity and always promised she would visit, but never arrived. This pain the *raja'a* would also have erased.

'I'm beginning to think that Rabindra is the least of your problems. Nikora has mobilised. I think she's starting to move people to the surface, and she wants us to join her. You have to decide, Youssef. She's made the same offer to all of my clients, except Grace. My guess is she plans to decompile the *raja'a* process at her leisure. Thankfully she has no actual knowledge of the new *tabi'a* bioapp.'

'Grace might be gone, but I'm not going to leave her here. I won't abandon her.'

'How can I help? I can provide you with staters.'

'I remain in awe of your financial independence, but I need time, Caitlyn, not handouts. Do not respond to Nikora.'

'I'll find something. Nikora remains susceptible to Pazel's influence, so if she believes she can demean him, there might be a way to delay her ascent. After Freja tagged Pazel, his only documented movement above Seventh was to purchase and repair a failed cistern in K3. I doubt he wants anyone to know because he also bought the transaction record. It might be enough to tempt Nikora. I'll speak to Kavya because she might be able to persuade the others to help me.'

'Is that wise? You always said they were cached to you.'

'Practically cached, it's not the same. Find Grace, but please hurry.'

Sometimes he thought about the bright, hungry flames that smouldered somewhere deep in his gut. The fire belonged to the years before the Forming and had always been his source of strength. They would one day ease out of his pores and dance over anything he handled, but Tion's sterile, artificial construction would no doubt endure. Yet somewhere in the levels below, there had to be a mass of energy, captured from the sunstar and locked into complex organic molecules, waiting for liberation at his touch. When he found them, he would release their latent power in an extreme conflagration, and he would dance naked in its glow. It was the only truth that mattered to him: in the end, when the swollen sunstar came to claim its legacy, its fire would destroy them all. The skin on his back was cold with the sheen of his sweat, and he hoped today was not that day.

The *tabi'a* had confirmed Youssef's lack of impetus. He had waited for Connor to rise up within Grace, so she could acknowledge the man she had been and Youssef could finally renew his friendship. Caitlyn's messages reassured him that the time would come, if only he were more patient. Youssef was concerned that without the *raja'a*, his distant future might flood his capacity to remember, and he would no longer be able to function. Caitlyn had said he barely used any of his native capability and showed him some metrics to support her case. If he was anxious, he could always use the FMP for additional storage, but she thought there was little reason because everything he did was so unremarkable that there was nothing worth recalling.

Caitlyn had suggested a project. She reminded him of his emotional outburst when Rabindra had abandoned him, days before the *tabi'a*. She described his forgotten chagrin and replayed his furious messages demanding her help, and eventually challenged him to track the foreman down. Youssef agreed to her suggestion without considering the consequences of success. He was unconcerned about trying to locate a single person because it was bound to be a protracted and repetitious task and seemed to be precisely the distraction Caitlyn presumed he needed. When Youssef had complained to Grace, she slyly said he had found Connor in a few hours. He was delighted she was starting to acknowledge who she had been but told her that Grace condoned Connor's capture. The conversation hadn't lasted long as they both tried to separate what they remembered from what they knew. Caitlyn had been very little help to either of them.

Youssef had concluded that Rabindra no longer existed. He was a rogue *sikatā-ātamā* lost in a mêlée of automatic weapons, and his physical form was nothing more than a pile of stinking meat. There was no conceivable way for him to have survived, saving capture, which would have led to a recorded caching anyway. If he had somehow escaped, he must have switched *māsadā-sarīra*, changed his identity or evaded pursuit through ways Youssef could not guess. There had been no sign of him throughout the year. Enough was surely enough.

Youssef spent his day sifting through endless records that were of no interest, and late in the afternoon, he decided he had finished. He composed a short message for Caitlyn and left it on a delayed delivery for her to receive once she returned to the apartment. He kissed her on the forehead and set off into the Fours outside. Grace had asked him to visit and gave him a keyed seeker to guide him to wherever she was staying. He hoped she would be delighted to see him again. There were more *lýðirnir* abroad than Youssef anticipated and he wondered if the online chatter was correct. He couldn't conceive of a population expanding so rapidly that the signs were visible to ordinary people. Sodality predicted Tion would reach capacity in the next two decades and he knew it would soon be time. Such growth! The *forfeður* anticipated it, designed the world for it, but he had never truly believed it would happen. The *tabi'a* scared him. He had closed his eyes, and the population explosion was instantaneous, and he realised it had passed over him without his engagement, although he could not be sure. Youssef's mind was filling with irrelevancies: the journey he took across Fourth; the blank *hjörnir* that sloughed past him and left bits of themselves lodged in his limited capacity; the constant nothing of online chatter, while day after endless day was unrecoverable.

'You came then,' Grace said as she welcomed him into her suite.

'I always said I would. Have you settled in?' He embraced her warmly but without lingering. Inside this *persónan* was his only friend and someone Caitlyn had helped him to recall. Youssef had not considered how he would respond to her as a woman with whom he could potentially cohabit. He hoped she had survived all of the change.

'Of course. Things are different now. The new *tabi'a* is a relief. How did you remain lucid in the barracks? I'd had enough of the remembrance problem after a few months.'

Youssef shrugged. 'What about your ghosting? Who are you now?'

'I'm not sure.' Grace paused, as if she was grappling with the issue. She still struggled to separate herself from Connor and wasn't sure she ever would. Grace felt disconnected from Tion, damaged in some mysterious way which left her orphaned from the world. She had become something she could not explain, a fighter, a killer, and someone focused on her survival. These were not traits that came from within; instead, she had learnt them from Nikora. 'Caitlyn insists the *tabi'a* is agnostic and doesn't care if this isn't my original *māsadā-sarīra*. I worry, so I maintain my connection to the FMP and everything seems constant. Caitlyn is adamant I'm okay to offline.'

'Possibly, but there's no need to take the risk either.'

'Can you feel the Pallium slowing, Youssef?'

He shook his head. 'I have little frame of reference. Is it true?'

'I'm not sure,' Grace said slowly. 'I've only had decent access for a year, I can't really say. Sodality is afire with speculation about its imminent collapse.'

Youssef grunted. 'We are well within the global design, Grace. I think the world will remain just as it always has.'

'Though you remember it before, don't you? Caitlyn told me.'

'Caitlyn Dzhe-Ta-Tse-Tsha talks too much.'

They stood awkwardly, as if they could not quite envisage each other within their discrete lives, both wanting to experience a feeling that didn't yet exist. Youssef wasn't confident he had enough time.

She took hold of his hand. 'There's a *miðaldra-maður* looking for me. He wants to know why Grace didn't return at the end of her contract. He is a suspicious man, and she was devoted to him. He's expecting her to return to him.'

'Were they lovers?' Youssef asked.

'Doubtful. I've found some of Grace's things, including a fair number of memories. Actually, it's difficult to separate hers from mine. Cristóbal probably wants to make sure she's okay, that I'm okay, and protect his reputation too. They were colleagues of some sort.'

'Has he come here?'

'Not yet, and I shift around a lot. A woman is trying to find me too. Caitlyn says she only wants the *raja'a* and I must avoid her at all costs. She mustn't know that Caitlyn has updated the bioapp. I think you know her.'

'You'd have to ask Caitlyn. She kept track of my activities before the interminable *tabi'a*. She told me about Nikora. I know what she wants, but we've had no contact. Are you concerned about the man?'

'Cristóbal? No. I can keep away from them both. It's not terribly hard to keep moving. I suspect she hired him to locate me. You and Caitlyn know how to find me when I leave. I suppose you didn't track Rabindra down.'

Youssef took a deep breath to steady himself. 'You're right. There are lots of ways to remain hidden. And I'm still angry. Rabindra used me to move through Tion, placing me in danger. I don't know who he was. He definitely wasn't the foreman we both knew. He decided I was expendable and I'd like to have a conversation with him about that. I suppose that appears foolish to you.'

'A bit,' she said, 'and maybe a little noble too. It won't do any good, though.'

Youssef laughed. 'It will make me feel better.'

'Who do you think he was, the ghoster?' Youssef shrugged and didn't reply. Grace pursed her lips and watched him intently. 'What if I tried to contact him instead? Using Connor's TUID. Invite Rabindra here?'

Youssef closed his eyes and put together a short simulation. 'It might work, assuming he survived,' he said, 'but I don't have a lot to go on. It's unlikely your hail would reach him.'

'We know he's not returned to the coalface, Youssef.'

'If I refuse, you'll do it anyway.'

She laughed and nodded and dived into online to create a suitable post. They waited for a little under twenty minutes.

'He's agreed to meet,' Grace said. 'In person and alone. I suggested one of the plazas a few DoAs from here, in a café or similar, and he recommended somewhere,' [K4 *location*]. 'I want you to come along and keep an eye on things.'

They endured the crush of the beltway and arrived a few minutes early. Grace requested a table in the small cantina and

Youssef wandered off into the masses. He purchased some surveillance feeds and circled the area, like a predator.

Stop pacing. You'll attract attention to yourself.

Youssef didn't bother to respond but took a seat in a bar opposite and ordered a drink. He received a message from Caitlyn but left it unread. *Þjóðirnar* milled along the arcade and obscured his view. He had a feeling that Rabindra would not arrive and started planning his evening with Grace. The local data rate was approaching zero, leaving most of the other patrons barely online and others trying to engage him in conversation, yet he maintained his vigil. When the *maður* asked to be seated with Grace, Youssef panicked.

Get out of there! It's not Rabindra!

Youssef was sure it was Cristóbal who had found her and assumed he would force her to leave. He divided his attention between the people that surrounded him and ensuring she was not harmed and pushed his way through as fast as he could. He watched as Grace acknowledged his warning and attempted to leave. The man sat calmly with his TUID suppressed, and his face obscured in the feeds. He held Grace in his gaze, whispered something that Youssef could not intercept and reached over to touch her chin. Youssef continued to jostle through the crowd and curses littered around his feet, but he could not reach the cantina before they left. The FMP held no record of their egress in its slow response, and he considered razing the eatery with his flames. Youssef had nothing to pursue and no frame of reference other than the assumption that Grace's history, which belonged to someone else entirely, had caught up with her.

He had let his friend down, but he would find her again.

Youssef went back to the bar to consider his options. The world was so full, and an *einstaklingur* could become lost in moments. Caitlyn had often mentioned that Grace was her own *alþýða* who was able to work through her problems, and if she needed him, she would request his help. Youssef was less convinced and replayed the data from her encounter. The stranger appeared to coerce her into accompanying him, even as she had attempted to flee, but Connor was an unknown and should not have been susceptible to his influence. It was his *sikatā-ātamā* that was dominant so Grace must have left of her own volition. Youssef wanted her to be safe. It had been a long time since he had really thought of her as Connor.

'Youssef Damaru-Da-Te-Epsilon?' Youssef nodded to the bartender. 'I've got a call for you.' His face glazed over and then brightened. 'Do you have any idea how much this is costing me? Why couldn't you answer my hails? I got your note.'

'What do you want, Caitlyn?'

'I can't believe the risk you've taken. Nikora has been trying to locate Grace for months, and you brought her out into the open. Where is she now?'

'Nikora didn't find her. It was someone from Grace's past. She went with him, and I lost them. You have to help me.'

'I'll find her, Youssef, and then you have to promise me you'll leave her alone.' The barman blinked twice, refilled the glass and mumbled his thanks for the call.

Youssef knocked the liquor back and requested another as he contemplated the last few months. If Rabindra had survived and wanted Youssef to find him, they would already be drinking together in a bar. He had wasted his time chasing the unassailable and achieved nothing. Youssef took another shot. From now on, if Rabindra wanted to talk, he would have to show himself. Youssef opened his public log, found his post about Rabindra's bloody disappearance and inserted a comment telling interested parties to contact him directly. He ordered another drink in the hope of finding his forfeited forgetfulness.

*

Grace was astounded by her response to Cristóbal's touch. He was mesmerising and utterly desirable, and she needed to accompany him. She couldn't hear Youssef's warning or consider Caitlyn's distant reminder because she belonged with this *maður* and felt entirely secure as they dashed laughing through the cantina's kitchen. A small part of her recoiled because her memory was at odds meeting him for the first time. Time attacked her and did nothing to heal the division between her two pasts, and her identity remained confused. She examined the longing that warmed her belly and was content that it was a simple thing with few facets. The words she had read as she discovered herself sprang to life, and she recognised he was made for her, simply and perfectly. She reached for his hand as they hurried through the crowded street, but he did not respond to her tentative tactile enquiry. Cristóbal pulled her forward and jabbed a fibre into her warm wrist.

I don't want to risk anyone intercepting our conversation. Who have you been working for, Grace? You've been away for too long. It must be important to keep yourself away from Sodality.

She hesitated and tried to separate lust from reason. It was too soon to tell Cristóbal who else she was as he might reject her or worse. *I'm looking for a man. His TUID is Rabindra Schwa-Rha-Ta-Te. A third party let the job, and I don't know who the client is. Rabindra's evasive but I thought I'd succeeded. I had no idea that you'd be here waiting for me, even though I knew you wanted me. You do want me, Cristóbal?*

Do you intend to deliver on your contract?

Another pause. *Yes. I have a reputation to maintain.*

Take some time out, Grace. Come back to the pit. People have been asking after you. In the morning I'll help you find this man. Assuming you need my help.

She laughed nervously under her breath, but the comms line

was not able to process her sentiment. *I'd like that*, she said and squeezed Cristóbal's hand one more time.

The Lisboa was precisely as she remembered. Her déjà vu was akin to a mundane documentary, rich with familiar detail but lacking a need for engagement. She descended its steps proudly and enjoyed the feather-touches of clientele requesting her TUID. A sparkle of associations radiated out as she reconnected with *lýðirnir* she had not considered for over a year, and she accepted several new invitations. These were her friends, her associates and she belonged in a way that Connor had never experienced. Youssef could never compete because his single brilliance was pale against this rediscovered firmament. There was a commotion around the central pit, but Grace did not read the lists. She needed to throw her arms around her friends and bask in their attentiveness before it faded.

She remained demure and took Cristóbal's arm as they approached the group. She wanted them to read her claim on him, even though it would not be acknowledged. Tonight, Cristóbal would play along, if only for Doha's amusement. Liang sat with disinterest to her left and a *ný-kona* to her right. The new woman was as indifferent as the bereft twin, so Grace did not waste cycles requesting her details. Doha took both of Grace's hands in her own, smiled and uploaded a series of questions with her touch.

Cristóbal pointed towards the pit. 'The *mennirnir* celebrating at the railing are Yash, Feliu and Oriol. They've worked a few opportunities while you were gone and won't stop hanging around. You could say that we've become used to them, especially since Doha stopped having the local assizes shoo them away.' Doha muttered something, but Grace didn't hear. 'She says they're not stylish enough for these surroundings and we should release their human capital. I don't know where she gets these ideas.'

A waiter brought her a long gin in an ice glass, and she enjoyed its forgotten taste. There was another commotion at the central pit, and one of Cristóbal's new acquaintances threw something in with the dogs. A klaxon briefly sounded, and all three came over and slumped at the tables.

'Fifteen staters on that shitty animal. I should wring its fucking neck.'

'You're a cunting idiot is what you are. We told you to back down.'

One of them slapped Cristóbal on the shoulder. 'At least Feliu is guaranteed to work your next job, boss.'

Grace could sense the warmth in their relationship as she savoured her drink. She did not mind them worming their way into Cristóbal's presence and preventing her from being next to him because she knew he would take her to his bed. He could sense the change in her, and finally, something about Grace Mu-Tlo-Ue-Jhan excited him. She remained aloof and impartial, laughing at their jokes and gambling with their stakes. Doha guffawed at the antics, but the *ný-kona* retreated further within herself. Grace maintained her countenance, waiting patiently for the evening to progress.

How is Liang managing without Bāo?

It's been hard for him. He won't acknowledge it and won't accept my counsel. He mostly sits with Shu-fen while they wait. I don't know what for. You seem different, Grace.

Is it that obvious, Doha?

Something has changed within you. You're certainly not who you were. Does he suspect?

Cristóbal? We've not spent any time together, other than the journey here. I've been working.

That's not the truth, is it?

Grace found herself unsettled by this *eldri-kona* who might uncover her. *I needed to change so he would see me the way I want him to. You can surely understand that, Doha?*

Oh, I do, I just don't believe you. Have your fun, but do not hurt him. Do you understand me?

Grace nodded and finished her gin. She waited for her moment and reminded Cristóbal she had nowhere to stay without being detected. He passed from man to man, hugging them, offering words of encouragement and gambling tips, and kissed Doha fondly. Liang did not acknowledge his employer, and Shu-fen remained mute but watched Grace intently, as if she could read Grace's manipulations. Even so, Shu-fen appeared distressed, not at what was to occur but with some loss of her own. The *ný-kona* looked wearily unsatisfied with her life.

Cristóbal took Grace by the arm and escorted her firmly up the stairs and out of the club. Outside it was warm and humid, a dramatic contrast to the over-oxygenated Lisboa Pit. Grace was uncomfortably hot and repressed and needed him now. She did not want to wait for them to negotiate their way across the arc and tugged at his arm as she muttered her urgency. Even though it had been over a year since Caitlyn gave her the cybercytes, her still-unfamiliar body ached with a longing she could not have predicted, and only he could fill her emptiness. Grace pulled him towards a speakeasy and shed her clothes at the reception, leaving them for the attendant to gather up from the floor. Cristóbal wore a suppressed smile, slowly undressed and folded his clothes neatly on the counter. He paid and followed her through to the lounge.

The front of the bar was a brilliant blue panel and lit the entire area. The barmaid kept the bar's ice surface clean with a large knife, which she also used to admonish her customers. There were several *sálirnar* sat comfortably around the room in various states of arousal. Some were engaged in elaborate foreplay while others sat quietly or idly chatted. Grace remembered her days in the barracks, where men spurned sensuality, and orgasm was sovereign and wondered if womanhood had changed her perceptions. The barmaid openly appraised them and pulled their preferences. Their drinks arrived in glassware that was warm to the touch but kept their contents close to freezing. Grace shivered and pressed herself towards Cristóbal, running her hand over his chest, his buttocks and legs. His awakening was gradual, and its slowness made her want him more. She reached up on her toes, slipped her arms around his neck and finally kissed him, feeling him rise against her. He lowered her to a couch near to the bar; his movements were fluent and unrehearsed. A *ný-maður* walked proudly across the room and sat at their feet, and as Cristóbal gradually slipped inside her, the stranger ran his hands over their ankles and lower legs. Grace thought the entering would not stop, somehow it seemed to continue forever, and she braced her feet against the young man's solid thighs as if he had joined them to provide much-needed stability. Cristóbal was hot against her, but his penetration was as cool as the drink that had lowered her inhibitions, and he majestically aligned his movements with hers. When Cristóbal could do no more, he asked the *útlendingur* to assist, while cradling her head in his lap. He quickly recouped and resumed his conquest, acknowledging the assistance he had received by welcoming the *maður* too. Later, after spending an hour in the soakroom, they left together, looking for somewhere in the daylight to sit and eat.

'You followed us,' Cristóbal said. 'What do you want?'

He was confident in his response. 'My name is Thibaut Kssa-Seven-Jia-Zeta, and I've seen you at the pit. I know who you are and have asked to meet with you on many occasions. When I saw you enter the speakeasy, I took the opportunity to become acquainted. I hate being an assize—it's been a hell of a *foutaise* year. I prefer to work for you.'

Grace was not impressed with his bravado. 'What can you offer us?' she asked.

'The same as everyone else. Loyalty, hard work and passion, but I will also do what it takes to get what I want.' He looked closely at Cristóbal, and both men glazed over as they started to negotiate. Grace felt refreshed and satiated but also detached from the night's experiences. She was uncertain how she felt about him now her most basic need had been met and felt unsettled at how easily she had allowed a stranger to distract her. She would forever be an amalgam of two genders and was incapable of understanding herself. The *ný-maður* straightened his clothing and shook Cristóbal's hand. He left without speaking.

'What did you agree?'

'He has some potential, but I'm not looking to add to my crew. He asked about Liang, and I said I would keep him in mind should I need to replace him. He wanted me to thank you for the opportunity to impress.' Cristóbal asked the waiter for some more coffee. 'Are you feeling up to locating this Rabindra?'

Grace nodded and granted him access to a sanitised copy of Youssef's search data. 'My client worked for him in Eighth, busting his *magairlí* in reclamation to create space for apartments he could never afford to rent, simply to ease overcrowding in K3. Not that anyone would willingly descend, no matter how fancy the neighbourhood. He thought that if he worked hard and gave a bit extra, he'd be able to leave the barracks behind and make something of his life. Rabindra was determined to prevent that and used his authority to justify his desires. In the end, my client absconded, but Rabindra tracked him down and did some terrible things to him. He needs to pay for his misdemeanours.'

Cristóbal studied her face. 'Sounds personal.'

'Yes. He was left in pretty bad shape and wants to talk to Rabindra about his actions. We're not sure he is who he appears to be and need to be certain that we're safe. It's very worrying.'

'It sounds personal to you, Grace.'

She picked up her cup and raised it to her mouth in an attempt to hide her nervousness. She did not know this man at all and had merely responded to the demands of her *māsadā-sarīra*. Her physical needs were a legacy from her body's past, and she knew there was nothing about her that was Grace Mu-Tlo-Ue-Jhan. Cristóbal had known that from the moment he met her in the cantina, and probably before. He had no interest in her and hadn't cared who had encroached on their intimacy. He would not keep her safe.

'It is,' she said. 'Will you help me locate him?'

'Of course. I said I would, and I have an excellent team. We found you.' Cristóbal held her gaze until she finally looked away. He had every opportunity to cause her harm, and while she was not frightened by him, she was worried about what he required.

'What can I do to thank you?'

'Nothing until you're ready to tell me what happened.' He got up without waiting for her reply and paid the bill. She hardly felt his lips as he kissed her cheek. It was a brief gesture that belied his earlier passion. She felt her stomach sink at the gravity of her situation.

I need you, Caitlyn. I have to speak with Youssef, and he's offline.

He's unavailable. Could I relay a message?

Tell him I'm okay. Tell him Cristóbal will find Rabindra, but he also knows that I'm impersonating Grace. I think I'm in trouble.

I'll send you an identity repeater app, hooked into a dummy TUID. Find somewhere to lay low.

How will Cristóbal contact me with his results?

Don't worry. I'll deal with it. You need to go.

*

The smell of blood was overwhelming. It sickened Youssef to his stomach, and he feared he would vomit again. He could taste its richness in the air with every breath, mingled with his bile. His throat was dry, and the pain that lanced through his head was consuming. His penis stung with the passing of caustic urine and something fierce stabbed in his lower abdomen. At least it was quiet, except for his laboured breathing and limping heart. For a minute, he thought the *raja'a* had reclaimed its supremacy and was tearing his body apart, and remembered nothing of who he now was. Youssef could barely move.

He was adrift in a vast space, dimly lit and warm. Everywhere he looked were three-metre long columns of meat, as thick as his waist, slowly twitching as they hung from uncountable racks. He lifted himself to his feet and raised one hand to his head, clutching at his brow in an attempt to soothe the dying brain within. Cautiously, he pushed his way through the farm as he tried to distance himself from the automated harvesters. He was amazed he hadn't been detected and bundled away.

Youssef had to be somewhere in K6, but he did not know how he had descended. His Pallial link was weak, and he was unable to sustain a decent data connection. Caitlyn would help him. She was always there for him, and he would be fine, as long as this wasn't the *tabi'a* failing. He remembered speaking to her through the bartender after his final pathetic attempt at luring Rabindra out. There were undoubtedly some strong drinks involved, but surely not enough to leave him like this. Youssef continued to work his way through the living muscle, throwing the odd punch as he tried to bring life back into his body. A warning light flared in his eyesight. He was dangerously dehydrated.

Some farms stretched for several degrees in both directions. With limited access, Youssef was unable to estimate how far he was from the edge of the factory, or even tell if he was circling himself. He threw one more punch and faced the meat. It felt like smooth clearfibre, yet it was alive, encased in a perfectly designed membrane that held the dense, expensive tissue inside safe from the air. It was taut, like the skin over a *tánin-kona*'s belly, and he could feel the solid muscle below. He removed his belt and twisted the buckle until it snapped. When he dragged the sharp metal across the suspended flesh, it oozed an emulsion of blood and a clear juice; he pressed his lips against it and drank greedily. A siren began to wail, and bright lights flashed, and Youssef sucked more of the noisome liquid down. His headache subsided, but nausea blossomed. He couldn't afford to lose the precious fluid and clamped his jaw shut as he pushed more furtively through the columns. It was impossible to judge how long it took to reach the boundary and embrace the cold wall, but as he did, online washed over him. Youssef was able to locate an exit almost immediately and requested a car to take him into the Lacuna.

In the stark, white illumination of the service corridor, he took stock of himself. There was dried blood on his shirt, and he suspected some of it was his. His face was tender and raw, and he thought he could feel a cut above his right eyebrow. As soon as the car trundled to a halt in front of him, he gratefully flopped into its unforgiving seat and requested routeing back to Caitlyn's apartment in the Fours: she would have to pay the fees. Youssef felt terrible but was not in any immediate danger. He drank from the straw at the headrest and stripped off his unpleasant clothes. Through careful inspection, Youssef found a fair-sized patch of the fabric that didn't smell too bad and tore it free. Once soaked, he used it to clean himself and look for other signs of damage because he did not want to succumb to the *tabi'a* just yet. Youssef was still somewhat uncomfortable with Caitlyn's revisions. The ability to restore his physical state without returning his perceptions to the day he signed up disturbed him, and he remained concerned about his mental capacity to retain everything that could happen in an unlimited lifetime.

You're still journalling your thoughts, Caitlyn messaged. *It's understandable. I couldn't trace you yesterday, Youssef, and from what I can see from the car's surveillance feed you've had a big night. Did you suppress the* tabi'a *before you went into battle?*

Youssef couldn't think. He wanted to remember commanding the *tabi'a* to remain dormant but did not remember how to give such an instruction. His headache was returning. He opened a call. 'I'm not sure what happened, Caitlyn. I need to talk with you. I'm having a difficult time ordering my thoughts.'

'You're hungover, Youssef, and you appear to have been in a fight. If you didn't consciously stall the *tabi'a*, then it must be something else. It hasn't been an issue before.'

'You damaged the *raja'a* with your tampering.'

'I probably need to do a little more debugging. I suspect the excessive alcohol has interfered somehow, which would be a small irony. Have you heard from Grace?'

'No. Is she okay?'

'For now. I've helped her disappear. Cristóbal didn't mistreat her even though he's aware she's not who she claims to be. Grace has persuaded him to find Rabindra for you. She must have traded something with him. When he tries to contact her, the FMP will patch him directly through to me.'

'Thank you.'

'I think she was worried about you. I was too.'

'Could you sponsor my up-levelling, please? I should be with you in a bit.'

The car was compact, and its interior quite restrictive. Youssef tucked his knees against his chest and hugged them tightly. For the first time in a millennium, he was uncertain and the days before the *raja'a* seemed distant. He was supposed to be a nondescript, inconspicuous man who no one remembered, but he had become too involved with his overseer. At least it was not an emotional arrangement.

Youssef was drunk the day before he had become a *konservator*. He loathed his colleagues, despised the leadership and had a sizeable disdain for the corporation itself. He knew the FMP promised an end to independent processing, not to provide the future population with an astonishing computational service but to halt the proliferation of currency mining. It was the first agreement between conglomerates seeking to monopolise the pre-Forming economy, so Yussef al-Qasemi toiled tirelessly to ensure only physical citizens could earn staters and not the software they might attempt to deploy. After months of failed testing and endless conflict within his team, he stormed into his boss's office and quit. A somewhat masculine woman from Human Resources took him to one side and said he was just what management wanted.

Weeks later, his newly-assigned warder had advised that the *raja'a* would not allow him to become intoxicated because the microscopic *vélarnar* would oxidise away any alcohol in the blink of an eye. He said it was one of the side-effects and Yussef tried to quit his job for the second time. Early the next morning, the breathalyser gave a positive result, so he was marched to the gym to sweat it out. He was the only person using the equipment, and the trainer beasted him mercilessly until he was sober. After he had showered and rested, an infoengineer took him to a compute lab, wired him up and pumped him full of technical wisdom. When he thought his skull would crack, he received several antibiotic, hormonal and antiviral shots and was sent to the *raja'a* bay to have the vesicle installed. After the surgery, technicians cleaned him carefully and erased his wounds, cut his fingernails and shaved his hair, then applied electrodes to tense his musculature. They silently left after they had finished before his warder returned.

'Are you ready, Yussef?'

'I guess.'

'We have given you all of the information required. You must not allow the Feynman Milburn Pallium to become self-aware.'

'I understand.'

Every sensation imaginable had crashed down upon him and forced his life apart as the *raja'a* was applied.

When Youssef Damaru-Da-Te-Epsilon came round, he was in an apartment overlooking an extensive park, which workers were ripping open as the tsunami of new construction progressed. Enormous machines were eating into the bedrock and extruding the vast vertical pylons that would one day hold concentric level after level. Youssef felt alive and optimistic about what was to come. He had traded his future memories for an eternal co-existence with Tion at the cost of a foolish errand, and he had the better side of the bargain. As the years raced by his warder's instructions had remained his freshest recollection until his very last overseer had released him from the *forfeður*'s bond. Youssef decided it was time to let go of his thousand-year designation and he should probably thank Caitlyn for his release.

The Forming had caused the world to stagnate. Youssef could, at last, appreciate the simplicity of the design, the legacy of two global organisations coming together to tear down their opposition and create a stable consumer environment of mighty proportions. Balance was inevitable and desirable, and the FMP stood firm to curb progress. Quietly, in the background, was Youssef Damaru-Da-Te-Epsilon, once called Yussef al-Qasemi, a reluctant *konservator* tasked with protecting Tion from itself.

He shivered and wished he was ready for the *tabi'a* to kick in. If Caitlyn's assessment of his hangover was correct, he still had several hours left until his vesicle's cybercytes went to work. He uncurled himself and drank more water, flexing his arms and legs as the car hurtled into Fourth. The transport expelled him at the plaza, and he walked through the dry heat of the confined streets. She was waiting for him with a kimono and a protein-rich fibrous gel.

'Cristóbal has already found Rabindra and is waiting to speak with Grace. I have no idea how he's managed it so quickly. I told him that you were her client and he should give the information directly to you. I faked Grace's authentication, so you're good to go. His simulacrum is in the other room.'

The sending was monochrome and appeared somewhat bigger than actuality. Cristóbal's clothes were sprayed on to emphasise his masculinity and the bars through his nipples were over-accentuated. Youssef found him neither intimidating nor appealing and sat opposite the image.

'I have what you want. In return, I would appreciate you telling me where Grace is.'

Youssef thought for a while and weighed up his options. 'She's gone. The woman you met was granted the *māsadā-sarīra* in fair exchange before your Grace consented to an unauthorised caching. I can send you a link if you wish. I'm sorry, but there's nothing left of your friend.'

Cristóbal leant forward as if to intimidate Youssef. 'How did this happen?'

'Grace's client wanted something I have, and she was using one of my associates in an attempt to expose me. It ended in an altercation between them.'

'I have a client of my own, and I want the body back. Unoccupied.'

'I'm afraid that's not possible. There have been some modifications, and the transfer is permanent.'

'Then ghost your associate out of it. I don't care. I want the *māsadā-sarīra* in exchange for Rabindra.'

'I said no, but I can offer you our technology instead. Is it what you want, *rajul dahkm*? The details are here,' [*data*]. 'We can complete the installation in the next few days. It will more than compensate for your loss.'

The black-and-white man sat back in his chair, and his eyes glazed over. Moments later, he returned and nodded. He reached inside himself, presented a small ve-package to Youssef, and slowly faded from the room.

Caitlyn had observed the exchange and reached over to Youssef for the information. 'I'll check it's clean,' she said, excusing herself.

The headache was just as vibrant as before, but the listlessness of the Sixes was beginning to wane. His outlook was indefinite and not for the first time he was concerned about how he would survive it. The *raja'a* erased the day's experiences to preclude a lifer's eternal drudgery, but Caitlyn had removed that safeguard, and he might remember it all. She had not enhanced the program; she had bastardised it. Long ago, he had committed to protecting Tion forever, and he only now realised what that might mean.

When Caitlyn returned, she was smiling. 'I must say Cristóbal has impressed me. Rabindra's hiding in First topsky. He appears to have purchased his privacy, and according to the ve-package, he is flush with staters. There's no way you'll be able to afford to get close to him. Youssef, there's something else. The combatants who came for you. I'm afraid Rabindra hired them. I have verified the transactions. He set you up.'

Youssef scratched his cheek while he considered his options. 'Make the arrangements for Cristóbal to have the *tabi'a* installed and thank him for his assistance. I'll need a decent rental as I won't get authorisation to ascend. Would you take care of the details, Caitlyn? I can pay whatever is required.'

'What about Grace?'

'I don't think she's safe from Cristóbal yet, but maybe he'll see things differently once the *tabi'a* is applied. We'll be spending a lot of time together, so we're going to have to find a way to get along.'

The button came with a disclaimer concerning processing delays. Youssef's ghosting was queued up for forty minutes before he was able to pour himself into the waiting *māsadā-sarīra*. The body was strong and healthy, and he felt instantly refreshed and well-rested. The log stated that this particular *māsadā-sarīra* was only available for a maximum of fifteen consecutive days in every month and was otherwise in maintenance. Youssef was unaccustomed to such vitality and wished his warder had adequately prepared him. The agency was almost five degrees from Rabindra's location, so Youssef headed for the nearest hub to hail a cab. There were only a few *lýðirnir* about despite it being early afternoon. He had forgotten the peacefulness of the most exclusive areas of K1, and once again berated himself for not choosing a more sophisticated level to see out his days.

Rabindra's apartment was a solitary, slender tower, glazed in the deepest blue. It rose from the groundplate on a point no larger than Youssef's rented forearm and widened to accommodate living areas in its middle. Further up it split into three transparent, azure ligaments that hooked directly into the skyplate far above. There were no obvious ways in or out of the structure.

Youssef paused to admire the tower and watched as other *sálirnar* did the same. He switched tagging on and was baffled by the commentary. The building was a prototype and apparently designed by the Pallium as the ultimate in segregated living. It was intended for installation in the Greater Numbers for habitation by citizens from any level and would protect and preserve its single occupant indefinitely. Each residence contained a fallback alternate and a pointport, plus power generation and recycling facilities, all protected by a centimetre of reconfigurable sapphire glass. It was unlikely he would be able to gain access. Youssef was disturbed by the independent compute capability, which was designed either for unspeakable pursuits or Pallial collapse. Neither did anything to assuage his nervousness.

A private chime sounded, and Youssef looked at the message header. Rabindra knew he was watching and had sent a warning. He opened it cautiously, and the world brightened to a startling white. Rabindra surrounded him in every imaginable configuration.

I know what you are, Yussef al-Qasemi, and you will not prevail. I shall not permit you. I have studied Caitlyn's prospectus, and once I've obtained the tabi'a, *I will come for you.*

The multitude melted away, leaving Youssef blinking under the skyplate. In front of him was Rabindra's donjon, sparkling in the bright daylight. As his eyes focused, a *ný-kona* emerged from behind its slender leg, walking purposefully towards him. Youssef did not recognise the new woman and had no sense that she was a threat. Her black jacket was open enough to reveal a string of stones at her throat, identical in colour to the donjon. She reached inside the coat, and with a single, elegant move, pointed a gun directly at his heart and fired.

Grace was there when he came round. She was sitting next to his couch with a large, steaming cup in her hands, staring into the middle distance. Occasionally, Grace took a cautious sip as though the tea within was still too hot. When she realised he was awake, she gently smoothed his brow. He flinched away from her fingertips.

355

'Caitlyn says the psychogenic stress will dissipate soon. Rabindra shot the rental, not you, Youssef. There was a pretty hefty fine from the agency, which she has paid. Caitlyn had to dig around a bit to bring you back because there was no way to execute the return protocols. You're fortunate. It's been several days.'

'Why are you here?'

'Cristóbal collected me after he received the *tabi'a*. He said there was no longer any reason for me to hide. He's still here. He helped Caitlyn retrieve you.'

'Ask them both to join us. Caitlyn's bioapp puts us all at risk.' He placed his hands on his face to be confident he had survived. He had felt the life escape from the rented *māsadā-sarīra*, and it was a death unlike anything he had previously experienced. Should Rabindra be able to decompile the *tabi'a*, he would ensure Youssef embraced death's full glory soon after.

In Youssef's opinion, Cristóbal seemed even less real than his simulacrum. When he arrived, there was something about the perfect hue of his skin that made him appear entirely artificial, and perhaps his earlier sending was the more faithful representation. He did not look like a man that Youssef could ever trust. He remained apart from the two *konurnar*, implying they were not worthy of his confidence and waited for the silence to become awkward before speaking.

'I have traded her life for mine,' he said curtly. 'I prefer to have both, so you remain indebted. *¿Entendéis?*'

'I can appreciate your view, but the situation is more complex. The *tabi'a* is easily traced to Caitlyn and then to us. Rabindra wants to unlock its secrets and exploit them for himself. Caitlyn, did you ever use the Pallium to work on the bioapps?'

She looked nervously at each of them. 'No, when I took you on, I received an alternate containing the bioapp algorithms. It's in here.' She patted her right thigh. 'Independent processing was an article of the contract.'

'Good. Then Rabindra can't find what he's looking for unless he comes for you. Cristóbal, you have to protect her.'

Cristóbal stepped forward until he was close enough to strike him. 'Why?'

'Because I said so. ¿*Entiendes*?'

The two men glowered at each other and neither backed down. Grace closed her eyes and waited for the tension to dissipate. 'You have to tell us what all this means, Youssef. Cristóbal has agreed to help you, but he's quite right to be angry at what happened and what I did to her. You need to remember that I didn't ask for any of this. None of us did. Why did Rabindra try to kill you?'

'Youssef is a lifer,' Caitlyn said quietly. 'He is a *konservator*.'

Cristóbal sneered at her. 'That's *estupideces*. It's a childish fantasy—the Forming supported economic development, nothing more. No mysterious guardians are protecting the *forfeður*'s intent. They were businessmen, just like me. I cannot accept this *maður* as a trustee of a long-forgotten aspiration any more than I believe that Rabindra will come for me. It's farcical.'

Youssef held up his hand and faced Caitlyn. 'What was your crew working on when it disbanded?'

She was clearly nervous about responding. 'Apart from being your overseer?' He nodded. 'I suppose Jovana Omega-Beta-Zha-Ge managed our elucidarium, and we were ultimately accountable for everything that happened in Odyssée.' He gestured for her to continue. 'It was a part of a greater project,' she said, 'one that we never really understood. Concerning the Pallial Decline.'

'And who was Moshe?' Youssef asked.

'At first, we assumed the FMP had become aware, and he was its representation.'

'Is that even possible?' Cristóbal asked. 'It doesn't sound credible.'

'Why not?'

'The Pallium is a thing, not an *alþýða*. Just because it's very complex and has unlimited access doesn't mean it is alive. It can't evolve because it only amasses information. Anything it does is an emulation of human responses. The FMP does not exhibit them. Why would you waste time on a bad assumption?'

'Because it commissioned us,' Caitlyn breathed. 'We had a lot of evidence to show that our original contract came directly from the Pallium. It was a logical response to the Decline. A machine could easily come to that conclusion. I don't see why this is relevant.'

'I don't think Moshe could have been its host,' Youssef murmured.

'Why not?'

'Because it's not Moshe who wants to stop me. The Pallial Decline isn't because Tion is finally in equilibrium or because Odyssée and Hyun-jun sparked an uprising. It's because the FMP's focus is its internal tasks.'

'So why did it contract us?' Caitlyn asked.

'That's something you should ask Rabindra,' Youssef muttered.

Grace held up her hand. 'After what he did to you?'

Caitlyn shook her head. 'The *tabi'a* would restore me just like it restored him. Youssef is suggesting Rabindra, not Moshe, is intertwined with the FMP. If that's right, the Decline was only a symptom, because the system stalled while its attention was elsewhere.'

'Creating Rabindra,' Cristóbal laughed, 'there's no way it could imagine such a thing.'

'On its own, it couldn't,' Caitlyn said. 'But we gave it the template after Moshe appeared, when we tried to prove he was the Pallium. I later theorised Moshe was a fragment of a larger *sikatā-ātamā* separated from his original host. It made the most sense, and it still does.'

Cristóbal turned to Youssef. 'Yet why would Rabindra want to kill you?'

Youssef cleared the decor from the wall and started arranging densely populated probability tables. 'The FMP is watching me now because I'm using its services. It's practically impossible to do anything without it being aware.' He zoomed in on an insignificant, modest possibility. 'This is my designation, and I suspect the Pallium knows.'

Grace pretended to study the data while Caitlyn slipped into Sodality and the two men continued to glare at one another. Inevitably, Youssef would carry out his designation, she knew he had to, but the consequences could be extreme. She refreshed the wall with archived pictures from the pre-Forming. 'If there's a remote chance that Rabindra is the cause of a processing crisis, then Youssef surely has to prevent him. We can't survive without the support it provides. It would be impossible.'

'And what if destroying Rabindra destroys the FMP as well?'

Grace made a small noise. 'I can't say, Cristóbal.'

'It's not much of a plan.'

'Perhaps we should gamble that removing Rabindra won't cause the FMP to collapse.' Grace squared her shoulders resolutely. 'We should do something.'

'And what if Rabindra's just a regular *maður*?'

Youssef made a fist and waited for Cristóbal to do the same. 'Then he'll be another unauthorised caching. Shit happens.'

Caitlyn had returned and cleared her throat. 'There is another way. It might be possible to design an analogous *raja'a* for the Pallium, which could constrain its systems to a point in time. If Rabindra is a part of the FMP, he'd effectively be restrained, which would fulfil Youssef's designation. I worked on the Pallial

Decline for months and have a reasonable grasp of its design.' She called up the footage of Hyun-jun's death. 'The *sálirnar* who lived in Second before the Odyssée uprising had damaged the FMP extensively, threatening its future operation. This man was responsible,' [*data*], 'and he remains committed to relocating a minuscule population onto Tion's surface. I think this would stop him too.'

'How credible is Pazel's plan? It seems unlikely to me.'

Caitlyn sent a series of infographics to their eyesight for them to review. 'It's hard to be sure. He's a lifer and has amassed almost thirty-four million unallocated staters, so he can afford for his records to be protected. His résumé is impressive. When Pazel was nineteen, he achieved moderate acclaim for an isolation environment within K3, and he has been a prolific segregation advocate ever since. I suspect Pazel has reassembled his people elsewhere in the Twos, causing more damage, and he intends to eradicate the levels below to secure his position. I'm afraid of him and have been for some time.'

The two *mennirnir* had stopped listening to Caitlyn, focused instead on planning another excursion into the Ones. Grace assumed they were going to ghost in and confront Rabindra, risking rentals and possibly another psychogenic episode. Their security didn't concern her because the impact on their future together, whatever that might be, paled compared with the possibilities Caitlyn had described. She continued to outline various scenarios without realising she was already alone.

Grace studied the spectres of her past and tried to quantify how she felt about both men. She did not want a relationship with either, nor did she crave the physical solace that Cristóbal had provided. Even so, Grace had not survived so that an *eldrimaður* with a messiah complex could mindlessly erase her. For now, she had no interest in anyone's safety but her own and refused to be trapped in the Fours when Pazel's doom arrived.

Youssef and Cristóbal had already reached the same conclusion.

'I'm coming with you,' Grace announced. 'Caitlyn, you should too. It's dangerous to stay here.' She spent ten minutes moving things around Caitlyn's apartment before she realised they wouldn't be taking anything with them.

An hour later, the four *þjóðirnar* closed the apartment's door behind them and prepared to leave K4. They planned to rendezvous in a hotel in First topsky, two degrees from Rabindra. When Grace had asked how they could transit so readily to the top of the world, Caitlyn had laughed and told her that her companions had earned the right to buy whatever they required. There was no reason they had not ascended earlier, other than finding the time to sort out all the little details. Grace had smiled at first but became annoyed when she considered the risks to her safety.

It's a delicate balance, Caitlyn told her. *We haven't attracted any attention in Fourth. Nikora would have come for you wherever you had been. From today, we will be more conspicuous, and although life will appear more comfortable, it will no longer be as simple. Please don't worry. We will take care of you.*

Their suite was going to be available in a few hours, and they drew lots for their various journeys. Caitlyn tinkered with their TUIDs, although she knew her adjustments wouldn't bear much scrutiny, particularly if passed from automated approval to a demarcator. Grace was given an itinerary and warned against requesting alternative routeing. She was excited about the pe-to-pe transit and reasoned she would be the first to arrive. Grace relished spending time alone, just as she had when she was Connor and worked at the coalface.

The pointport was nestled amongst eateries in Caitlyn's local marketplace, ominously opposite a cacherie. The smoked glass door was locked, and Grace had to wait for a full minute after identifying before it opened. The interior was a mottled, brown stucco, and although the polished surfaces reflected the glow from the tiny spotlights, the room remained unwelcoming. There were black couches against the two walls, long enough for her to stretch out on, and a high reception desk in front of a central, free-standing partition. She peered over at the diminutive, dark-skinned *ný-maður* who had unlocked the door. White e-tattoos covered his face and looked to her like crawling maggots. He appeared entirely disinterested in her, so she sat on one of the seats and idly tongued through Sodality pages while she waited. Eventually, she received infographic instructions to walk behind the wall for her transfer.

Beyond the partition, there were three cubicles, each closed off with semi-transparent metal doors. Two of the compartments were in use, and Grace thought she could see signs of distress twisted onto the passengers' lifeless faces. Sodality noted some users preferred to remain aware during the preparatory process, but Caitlyn had sensibly pre-ordered oblivion. A fierce, blue light swept through the parlour as her assigned cubicle went through its final bio-purge and the door slid open, bathing her in the smell of recently hatched *barnið*, which she found comforting. She removed her clothing and jewellery and placed them into the disposal hopper. The pictograms in her eyesight showed her how to stand, with her weight forward and her knees slightly bent. She gripped the smooth metal handholds tentatively, nervous at their warm tingling. Motile straps reached up to secure her feet and wrapped tightly around her ankles as a ve-indicator flashed green, amber, red, and she felt a needle bite into each calf. She tightened her hold on the rail as the ice-cold clawed its agony up her legs. She had forgotten to accept the first analgesic. She panicked, letting go and trying to shake the webbing from her feet, but bindings snaked down from above her and pulled her into position. *It hurts, it hurts, it hurts,* she screamed, but nothing heard her as the silence claimed her consciousness.

Once she was immobile and unaware, the point-to-point process steadily cooled her to halt the biological systems, before shunting antifreeze glycoproteins into her bloodstream and dropping her core a further forty degrees. Grace was dead, her neural activity ended, and her life gone. Her flesh was an almost-frozen effigy, which was ready to be analysed. Pumps droned for several minutes until they had extracted the frigid air from the chamber. An auric band descended from the top of the chamber and rapidly spun as it detected the first keratin filaments of its passenger's hair. The Pallium charted each atom, recording the states of its particles determined and relationships with its neighbours. It documented her body at an astonishing rate, identifying billions of discrete points per second and burning them away to reveal layer-after-layer of human structure. The disintegration slowed as the golden circle drifted towards the floor as if the demand for Pallial attention was increasingly challenging to meet. Grace's cubicle was the second to be emptied and sterilised, while what remained of the once-enormous physique in the third continued to be processed.

The FMP shunted Grace's data from buffer to buffer as she processed through Tion's levels. The transit commandeered vast compute resources to preserve the representation of the two identities fused into a single, delicate frame. Point-to-point was unchecked processing consumption that dwarfed all other Pallial demands and was singularly expensive. Caitlyn had paid one point seven kilostaters for Grace's journey.

The destination station was a bright parlour filled with flowering orchids and surrounded by a perfect cascade. Each transceiver was situated behind the flow of water, obscured from physical or virtual view. Occasionally, people entered the warm deluge for transit, or stepped out and were met by an attendant holding a soft robe. Youssef was lounging in the reception eating orange and grapefruit segments from a platinum dish. He smiled as each arriving passenger stumbled through the water, unaware of their surroundings and confused by their reassembly. Youssef hated pe-to-pe. Each journey since the *tabi'a* had left him feeling disassociated and emotionally disturbed at the destruction of his original essence. He hoped Grace would not infer the same and instead assume pe-to-pe had sent her from one cubicle to another. She did not need to consider the truth.

Grace didn't notice him when she arrived, but she looked surprised when she returned wearing a white lace dress. 'I don't see how you could get here before me,' she said.

'You've been in transit for five hours, long enough for me to pop across to check Rabindra is still where I left him and grab lunch. You probably feel like crap.'

She groaned. 'I've spent so much time in-and-out of different bodies I don't know who I am any more. I feel lousy though, nothing like I did when I entered that bloody thing.'

'It's the new atoms. They don't want to be you. They're rebelling.'

'Is that possible?'

'I'm fucked if I know. Pe-to-pe sucks. Come on. It's almost time.'

Youssef held out his arm, and Grace took it tentatively. She wondered if her feminine deference was a symptom of overcompensating, but she was happy to have someone steady her as she walked. Spacious gardens filled with flowering shrubs, glistening under the night skyplate surrounded the pointport. The plants looked impossibly alive, as though gardeners had carefully tended each leaf, deliberately placing drops of moisture on them for aesthetic purposes. She wanted to linger and examine each bloom, and it was a few seconds before she looked

364

up at her surroundings. It reminded her of the emptiness of the coalface, but this was not destruction for reclamation, this was a vast open space that served no purpose other than emptiness itself.

'How far?' she asked.

'The skyplate is half a click above us. I think there are two decks below here, before the Pallium. It's not the best view in the Ones, but there's a lot worse. We should check into the suite: the others are just ahead of us. Cristóbal has run some simulations and has a couple of options I support. It seems he is unexpectedly resourceful. Caitlyn and I will supervise the tech from the rooms, and Cristóbal will take care of the physical interaction. We've all agreed that Rabindra needs removing from play, except you.'

Grace tightened her grip on his arm. 'I have to trust that you've each considered the options. It's surely not possible for one *mannvera* to contain the FMP's knowledge. That can't be true. Rabindra did a terrible thing to you and you are entitled to retribution. We have to do this.' They walked through a series of interconnected gardens and courtyards and passed a few *hjðirnir* as they went, most of whom smiled or offered words of greeting. It made Grace feel uncomfortable, almost as if her boundaries were compromised. She was relieved when Youssef pointed to the two-story glass building Caitlyn had rented.

'We can live here afterwards if you want,' he suggested.

Inside the square structure was a large atrium, tastefully furnished to complement the floodlit gardens. Suspended above, in the four corners, were personal spaces overlooking the communal area, each with a graceful staircase. Caitlyn was stretched out on a thick black rug, blankly staring through the arched roof. 'She's already in,' Cristóbal said as he closed a large case and attached a shoulder strap to it.

Youssef shook his hand. 'Caitlyn's set up a secure compartment where we can talk to Rabindra, assuming we can get him to send over. We can't distract him from what we're doing so I want him to know why. Cristóbal's solution is fairly practical.'

'I've reviewed all the data I can find on the structure. It's called a donjon, designed to isolate and protect its user. When occupied, there's potentially no way in or out, other than pe-to-pe, which he wouldn't have long enough to use. If he ghosts out, there won't be a *māsadā-sarīra* for him to return to.' Cristóbal clasped Youssef's hand and kissed both of the women before he left. *Caitlyn, are you sure about the decompression?*

Yes. When the skyplate fails, there will be enough time before the structure reasserts itself.

'All I need to do is gain his attention,' Youssef said, leaning against the exterior glass with his eyes closed.

Grace would have felt abandoned, but Connor had been used to being alone and comfortable when his companions were online. She was determined to be an active participant, so she tried to relax before entering the vestibule. Grace had expected a harsh setting, probably a uniform white with austere features, but Caitlyn had created something impossible to comprehend. The dimensions were perplexing, and the colours and sounds and textures jarred against each other. When she looked one way, the organic intricacy was overwhelming, while the other was a lifeless technocracy, but when she looked back, she faced a quantum void, a barren waste ground, a serrated horror and so on. She couldn't see anything that resembled her friends, so she sat down on nothing, waiting patiently.

As she studied the turmoil, a sense of order coalesced. It brought calmness to the environment and caused the rapidly evolving notions to become apparent. She wanted to rush forward into the serenity, but somehow she knew it was

Rabindra. In that instant, she recognised him for what he was, the very heart of their lives, capable of interpreting everything. She was intent on the destruction of the only comfort of endless billions of people. Something tingled at the base of her spine, and she preserved the moment. Grace decided to force Tion's evolution.

There were two subtle changes in the setting, but her awareness of her non-physical surroundings made it hard to understand their position concerning Rabindra. Grace couldn't identify them but decided there was one for both of her companions, and probably something that represented her. She imagined they would surround him and squeeze him until Rabindra could not escape Youssef, Caitlyn and herself. All Cristóbal needed was a minute to break Rabindra's structure from its moorings to the ground and skyplate. So she held onto every bewildering feature of her ersatz world and encouraged them to develop. As she took control, the calmness gave way to a furious disruption, and she grasped that as well. Colours swirled, temperatures plummeted, and her balance was in disarray. Eventually, the environment assaulted every sensation she was able to process. She was burning with pain and terrified by what might happen. Grace held tight and ignored everything, bedlam gave way to blankness and then she was back in the glass apartment.

Youssef and Caitlyn were standing hand-in-hand at the widest window. Grace did not know what to say when she joined them and moved to Youssef's right, but he took her hand too and squeezed it while she looked. Grace felt emotions rise in her throat as she realised what they had done.

In the twilight outside, ruination had devoured serenity. The manicured shrubs in the gardens were withered, their branches stripped of foliage, and many ripped from the ground. There was debris everywhere, and unidentifiable things smeared the windows. Grace became aware of the klaxons sounding beyond their rooms, and plate-by-plate, the sky lit up. The level had experienced violence that far exceeded anything it could tolerate, and the devastation was profound. As the light exploded across her view, she noticed the tear in heaven. It was a jagged rupture that had reached into the void beyond their true world.

'Did Cristóbal survive?'

'We're not sure. We can't obtain a connection. Cristóbal blew the anchors on Rabindra's donjon just as he breached the skyplate. The pressure differential was enough to rip it out of First. I imagine his fancy glass home is smashed somewhere on the surface.'

'Is that sufficient?'

'Cristóbal thought so.'

'How long until we can step outside?' Youssef asked.

'About twenty minutes,' Caitlyn said. 'Constructors have already woven a temporary repair, so it's just a matter of having adequate air pressure. Where will you go?'

Youssef didn't answer but calmly got up, holding their hands. An army of spiders and deliverers and other *vélmenni* swarmed across the grounds, and masked *sálirnar* finally started to appear. There was no order to the activity; it seemed each person or machine was abroad according to his, her or its agenda. It was a chaotic effort that did not promise the beauty of before. Grace groped for connectivity, but her familiar sockets were absent. They were forcibly offline.

'I saw what he is,' she said in a small voice. 'How can one man be the Pallium? Is that why it's failed?'

'You saw what he wanted you to see,' Youssef said. 'The FMP is probably unavailable because it diverted its resources for its restoration. There's no reason to believe it's unserviceable.'

'Things don't look that coordinated.'

'They're not,' Caitlyn said. 'The poor Pallial response is due to the *raja'a*. I inserted a specialiser into the bioapp to allow it to tailor its sockets for the FMP and gave it unfettered access. It was the only way I could think to distract Rabindra.'

'Why? I found a way to restrict him,' Grace said. What have I done? she thought.

Youssef let go of their hands. 'We all did what we felt would give Cristóbal his opportunity. Now we have to hope he succeeded. Caitlyn, you need to remain here to assess the damage. When you establish a connection, don't waste it on chatter. Grace should come with me.'

The air outside was frigid, and she felt lightheaded as they strode across the plaza. Close by, the individual clean-up effort did not appear disorganised at all, and Grace realised her initial observation failed to understand the arduousness of the entire operation. She could not comprehend what the *raja'a* might do to the Pallium and how the global processor would adapt it. Caitlyn may have given it something wonderful to incorporate into its quantum being, which would keep it from decaying, or perhaps it was a poison from which it would never recover. She hoped they had forced Rabindra out before the *raja'a* took hold, and that the future would once again be like the past. Grace noticed the tingle in her spine again, and its cold fingers crept up her back. She watched as a small machine that had been repairing the front of an apartment reached out for a deliverer as it passed and systematically dismembered it, discarding the whirring parts across the ground. Caitlyn should have kept the *raja'a* away from the Pallium because she had no way to predict how long its secret would be contained and remain unobtainable. The cutting chill in the air had given way to a dry heat that she found quite pleasant, but Youssef's shirt was dark with sweat, and he looked concerned.

'It's struggling with the new code,' he said. 'It will eventually settle down.'

Under a bench, two *miðaldra-fólkið* had tried to evade the outgassing. They were barely breathing as they clung to each other. Grace bent down to study their bruised faces. She hadn't anticipated that anyone else would be hurt. The fine network of broken capillaries on their skin looked like intricate ink work but provided little distraction from the cold reality of the decompression. She wondered if they had been lovers.

'What do you think happened? Was he killed?'

'Rabindra was fairly confident we would fail,' Youssef said. 'You were there.'

Grace didn't know how to respond. 'I couldn't make sense of the experience. All I could do was suppress what I thought was him.'

Youssef raised an eyebrow. 'I suppose our interpretations were all different. There's no reason why they shouldn't be, and it doesn't matter. Rabindra probably ghosted out, despite Cristóbal's intention. I can't predict what will happen to the Pallium, so we should get to the surface. It's what Cristóbal will have done.'

Grace could feel connectivity start to flow around her, although she was not yet able to sign in while the Pallium serviced higher-priority requests. She relaxed as her sense of well-being returned, realising that unlike Connor, she could endure any hardship as long as she wasn't isolated. Youssef was managing several low-level transactions, and soon they were standing outside a fashionable *kostym* shop. She was glad she did not have to engage with the attendant, holding her breath as the *kostym* wrapped itself around her. When she came round, Youssef had hooked them together.

The kostymer *have internal processors to enable them to operate in the Pretermissions or anywhere with degraded connectivity. They have an indefinite power pack and will outlast you and me.*

There were still few people in the plaza, and those they did pass may have assumed the *kostymer* were a precaution against further calamity. Youssef rummaged through the unattended debris and selected a sizeable panel. When they reached the former site of Rabindra's donjon, he detached a pair of compact resequencers from each of their *kostymer*, arranged them on the ground and balanced the metal plate on top. He motioned for Grace to step on, taking his place next to her before issuing instructions to the devices. Moments later, the platform began to vibrate before it shot up towards the damaged skyplate as carbon fibre pillars bubbled up beneath them. Youssef held her firm with one hand on her shoulder, and although she could not see his face, she knew he was concentrating on their ascent. He unclipped a cutter from his waist and wielded its disassembler in a broad circle above their heads. The temporary bulkhead gave way as they erupted through two metres of destruction and the panel plugged the fissure behind them.

Grace thought the *kostym* did nothing to lessen the impact of her fall to the surface. The black sky was awash with countless points of light, whites that were pure, yellow, red, blue. She wanted to peel the hood from her face and gaze at them with her eyes, but first, she had to locate Youssef and ensure they were both safe. Tion's regular surface was dark and scarred with small abrasions, but broadly featureless, other than the wreckage of Rabindra's donjon. She was wary of approaching it and hoped that Youssef had been thrown clear of the surface breach. She crawled towards the rupture and online washed over her as she peered down.

… has increased by almost twenty per cent but it's not typical of the degradation I've witnessed before. What if Rabindra's purpose was to obtain the raja'a *bioapp, so the Pallium can incorporate it and gain independence from us? It isn't its own entity yet, but I believe it is trying to establish itself.*

I've made a terrible mistake. Youssef, the Decline has increased by almost twenty per cent, but it's not typical...

Faint clouds caught the first light of the dawn. A brilliant orange crept over Tion's horizon, bleeding into the dark, boundless sky and threatening to burn everything away. Grace hoped Youssef could recognise what she saw, and he realised its fire was life and not destruction. As she watched an astonishing crimson blazed across the lowest clouds, the complexity of the colours rendered superbly by the *kostym*. Grace wondered if she could see more perfectly than before, if the unnameable hues came from beyond Tion, or if they were an artefact of her processed vision. The ambers and bronzes and magentas and violets were overwhelming, so she did not mourn the loss of the eternal, diamond stars. Connor would have been astounded by the sky's magnificence, but Grace had buried him in the Sevens and felt entirely detached from that past. Her transition was complete, the *tabi'a* had wedded her to her body, and she would live on the surface forever. A pale, almost-cobalt gap in the clouds promised the makings of a new beginning, and somehow she knew Youssef would find her. Cristóbal would eventually return to her as well because he too had unending time to devote to the future. Patience was still an unfamiliar ally, yet she had to embrace its serenity. Caitlyn's message rolled over her, its repetition as soothing as the waves that had once washed across the forgotten Earth kilometres below. Grace would not devote her time to Tion. Instead, she would claim Rabindra's buckled donjon for herself and watch the glorious sunstar rise each day. The sublime golds faded, and although the azure joy of the sky should have warmed her *sikatā-ātamā*, it promised only a distant relief from what was to come.

If you enjoyed *Tionsphere*, read on
for the prologue to *The Uprisers*,
Book 2 in the Tion series.

J.C. Gemmell

The Uprisers

Tion Book 2

Prologue
Freja
অতীতে

THE DELICATE SKIN on her ankle stung as Freja scratched away the fresh scabs. Mehdi was continually reminding her to take better care of her *māsadā-sarīra*, but she wasn't interested in protecting them. Each body itched as battalions of imagined things crawled over her. She knew the sensation was an artefact, but it didn't mean she could ignore it. Within a few months of joining Pazel's adherents, she restricted herself to one small area on which to attack the irritation and often she would lose interest before drawing blood. A sharp intake of breath and Freja caught herself, silently acknowledging she was again thinking about her own *māsadā-sarīra*, forgotten somewhere in the Fives. Maybe Jovana had sold it on, or perhaps Caitlyn. She hated the thought that someone was using her flesh.

Pallial services continued to degrade. Nothing was as noticeable as the sudden reduction Kavya had dubbed the Fall, yet people had forgotten how things had been five years ago. Pazel had been unable to determine what had caused the abrupt increase in the Pallial Decline. Although the FMP struggled against a slow, global cancer, Freja still worried that Caitlyn's request would eventually arrive. Mehdi was confident the Pallium would be unable to associate the caching with her endlessly cycling TUID, but Freja was not so certain. Pazel said she should trust the Curator and stop wasting precious compute time on an irrelevancy. After Odyssée's cancellation, she had been unable to track Caitlyn or the others. Freja hoped they were all lost, and Moshe with them.

She sometimes thought about Jovana languishing in Joaquín's arms, a childish lover who constrained her to a pointless past, and of Caitlyn fawning over Youssef and his improbable purpose. Miyu had been her closest companion until she tricked Moshe into accusing Pazel, and Freja thought she was surely responsible for their collective disappearance. Looking back, because the women's principal function was divining secrets, they had been unable to hide their private selves from one another. Kavya, the doyenne of data mining, understood the FMP better than any of them, and it readily responded to her encouragements. She probably spent each day ministering to its needs in the hope that she could prevent its deterioration. She could have stopped Caitlyn from using the caching voucher for the Odyssée contestants. Freja decided she loathed Kavya most of all.

The women had refused to believe Pazel wanted to protect Tion. They never considered his rationale, that preparation for a life without the Pallium was vital for their survival. Instead, they spent their days speculating about sinister motives and wasting their time trying to seek out wrongs until Hyun-jun paid for their hubris. Freja was glad she had left them and that Pazel had given her a new life.

Mehdi repeatedly questioned her about Moshe, who she thought he was and how they could locate him, but she was not interested in endorsing another rival for Pazel's attention. He cared little for his adherents' hierarchy, and Nikora remained his unending obsession. His confidants were his welcome distractions. Pazel often said that whatever her aspirations, he would not permit her to attain the surface. If she could accept that, she was welcome to stay until he ascended. Freja wanted to know what would happen once he was gone, but he never acknowledged her question. Mehdi informed her she was a replacement for Victoria and she should be grateful.

People had been telling Freja how she should feel her entire life. They sometimes asked how she was but never listened to her reply. They waited to pounce on her *sikatā-ātamā* so they could reshape it according to their agreed concept of acceptability. Even Mehdi offered to fix the unresolved issues he thought threatened her future viability. She had been wise to guard against splicing ever since she received self-schema access at mid-nonage.

Freja baulked when Pazel told her to facilitate an update to Danesh's persona. For an instant, she glimpsed the man her former associates shunned. He said she should appreciate why he had drained Eleven-Two, so she told him they were all ultimately fucked and he should add his worthless *māsadā-sarīra* to his ridiculous collection. Pazel forgave her when she returned and begged him for a new body that didn't itch. She eventually tucked the revision under her bed and tried to ignore its implication. Part of her wanted to hide the package and slip into the Ones to forget herself, but Pazel would send Cristóbal to reprimand her. He would not relent until he found her, despite their professional relationship.

It took a few days for Mehdi to locate the transformed *maður*. In the half-decade since his violation of Pazel's *sikatā-ātamā*, Mike had managed to ascend three times and was awaiting another recast to conclude his *wiederholt*, presumably before up-levelling again and enjoying his second life. Mehdi was amazed he had progressed so rapidly in the wake of the post-Odyssée prohibition. Freja used a rental to invite him to a dating shop where she tried to flirt with him. She was positive that he would not recognise her and Mike did not request her profile. They were comparing their compatibility scores when he said he had no intention of considering Pazel's offer. She informed him that his desires were irrelevant and infected him with the bypass for the remote install. She was simultaneously angry and indifferent. The next day she posted a reference to Victoria on his counterfeit timeline, and he replied using her former TUID. She deleted the thread and blocked his new identity.

About a month later she received a friend request from Danesh. It appeared to be a legacy artefact that had been languishing in the FMP since their very first meeting, but she knew what it meant. His original profile was very much in use and showed active connections with an extraordinary diversity of *fólkið*. Freja had facilitated his relationships through Tingting Kaf-Ayin-Beh-Keheh and wondered if Pazel was aware of the quiet movement to refute his ideology. Ultimately it did not matter because Tabitha's collection of dissidents were too self-absorbed to mount any kind of retaliation. Freja eventually recommended Mike to a successful K4 cachier in the hope that things would take care of themselves.

Whenever Freja challenged Pazel's relationships, he reminded her that he was responsible for a new Tion. He could not resist embellishing his words with images of his imagined future, which focused on the adulation he felt he rightly deserved. She knew he was entitled to everything he described because he worked tirelessly to meet his goal. It was easy to recognise the purity of his vision and accept it as the only viable response to the failure of their world. There was no other option for her because she had surrendered everything when she ghosted down from the Fives. All she could offer him was loyalty.

Remorse was Freja's unwavering companion. Mehdi offered to eradicate the memories of Danesh, which would leave her free to support Mike in whatever capacity Pazel desired. He said it would make her feel better, and it would be their secret. She didn't want to feel anything other than herself, so she quietly told him of her withdrawal following Victoria's death. He had smiled and said he had salvaged that particular situation.

'What will Pazel do with Victoria's *māsadā-sarīra*?' she had asked.

'He will use it for his ascent. The majority of people in Zero will be *konurnar*. At least to begin with.'

'A female ochlocracy no doubt. How awful.'

He had nodded his agreement. 'For those that must endure.'

Mehdi gradually became her ally and did his best to ease the pain. He built a simulation to show what would have happened to the four Odyssée contestants if they had been left alone. Their psychological collapse alarmed her. She occasionally spied on Mike as he settled into his new life and manipulated his environment to encourage some personality trait or other. Freja came to understand that *fólkið* were only the sum of their experiences and the Pallium was a tool they could use to shape people. She allowed Mehdi to suppress her desire to locate Caitlyn or the others only because he said it was a continual distraction, but she resisted any further modification even though he maintained a full set of backups. Once, she asked him if it would be possible to retrieve her *māsadā-sarīra* as there had to be records. He had shrugged and said she was being unreasonable.

Mike decided to meet Oskar in a quiet K4 coca house in a no-longer-fashionable arc in the hope they would be able to talk without interruption. This assumed he could stoically ignore banner advertising, unsolicited messages and people who claimed to know him through mutual acquaintances. Tion is far too connected, he thought.

Oskar was entirely without presence. A *drengar* in scruffy clothes that were too tight for him. His cheeks were slightly flushed, and his dark eyes cut straight through Mike as they shook hands. He was expectant but maintained an opaque countenance. Mike was pleased that this acquisition was progressing smoothly, now Oskar had come out of hiding. He wondered if he should have told him to clean himself up, but it was Mike who was probably out of keeping with his surroundings.

'I thought the numero-rep of your TUID was childish and quite a risk. What took you so long?'

Oskar shrugged. 'I was looking around. It'll be easier to get there with you, rather than going it alone. You interest me.'

Mike laughed, pleased he was right about him. 'I diverted you because I have some matters that would benefit from your flair for re-spinning facts. I hope that is of interest to you.'

'Who do you represent, Mike? I don't know if I can trust you.'

'I'm independent, but I'm creating a service for certain *lýðirnir*. Their world is a compact place where opportunities decrease with time. The Odyssée fiasco has made inter-level permits hard to obtain, and the Decline is a challenge in itself. What do you know about Tion?'

'That's not much of an answer.' Oskar paused for a moment, anticipating a response that did not come. 'I know about the tionsphere inasmuch as I could access from Sixth. My training suggested the Pallial Truth is susceptible to certain modification. It's not a big leap to presume they coloured my understanding in some way, so I'm happy to consider any insights you have.'

Mike rolled a dozen leaves together and popped them between his teeth. 'Stability is important, but so is growth. There needs to be balance without stagnation. Harmony has never existed, not pre-Forming and not now. Even as the three conglomerates competed to construct the new world on top of the old, there would always be a limit, and the rush to fill the empty places has its own legacy. We don't know how to stop, and people keep coming off the lines. I'm not sure when it will collapse, maybe it will be after I'm cached, but there is a notional ceiling, and we're incredibly close.

'The Pallium issues warnings which we quietly ignore. It's unlikely that one more person will break its systems, probably not a thousand or even a million. There is a danger of a crash, but we perceive the risk as slight. So what if we lend it additional capability to counter the Fall? Powerful alternates are easy to come by; it only takes fifteen years to create them in droves. We can harness all that raw potential in neat little compartments. They're much more efficient, and they could replace large FMP components in Second. Maybe release some of that space. System collapse isn't inevitable: it is desirable. In the meantime, there are a few opportunities for *bjórnir* like me and you to prosper from a world on the brink, as it were.'

The Forming of the tionsphere is, without doubt, the greatest achievement not only of the forfeður *but of all* mannkynið. *Our existence within its diverse levels remains an engineering marvel that few can truly comprehend, and should we have the need to Form again, we would fail. For a thousand years, we have coveted Tion's inexhaustible capacity, but now the world is full, and people must conform to survive. When you aspire, reach not for aggrandisement but contentment, and do not measure your worth in staters or status, because these things are ordained not attained. You must not despair in your isolation because Sodality will provide. We must meet our obligation to preserve the Pallium. This is our only purpose.*

Information is a fundamental right. I have dedicated my life to the FMP and advise caution, lest we are universally deprived of access. Nothing can be more critical to our reality. Without connection, we become nothing, and even blissful caching will be lost. While the Pallium regulates the population, it does not control. Its only purpose is to serve. Do not mistake the FMP for an engin-persónan, *it is a* vél *and has no life, although it is not unending. We have to reduce the demand on its systems to ensure its permanence; it cannot endure while it is threatened by deterioration. There is only one solution: the dramatic reduction in the number of staters in circulation to curtail our squandering of data.*

Fólkið *will rebel unless they are restrained. The tightening of Pallial services and the rationing of information guarantees continuity. The Decline is not the response of an individual or an assize movement. The FMP has itself reached this conclusion and is fulfilling its obligations through our suppression. Therefore Odyssée was incidental, and Hyun-jun was a bystander, but his uprising foreshadows terrible events yet to come. Hyun-jun was driven to expose the infestation within Second, but not by the Pallium. These were the tactics of* mennirnir, *perhaps the same men who have hidden Enzo and Inès away. We must accept an uncertain future where data sabotage is a way of life. The Fall was an attack on our continuation and aptly named, for we have lost so much of our global capability.*

It is time for mannkynið *to commit. We must halt the megagestoria and cache the non-contributors. We must redistribute the population and confine ourselves to our appointed level. We must restrict data access and cease inter-level communications. We must drive deflation and restrict the use of Pallial services.*

We must prepare for a crisis of evolution.

— Kavya Ngo-Dza-Ta-Thorn.

'You really botched the splice,' Mehdi warned. Psychic wiring diagrams surrounded them, masses of coloured lines woven through one another. Delicate flags were attached to nodes in their thousands, and their symbology indicated various states of Mike's well-being. Pazel had told her to review the *maður*'s development on a regular basis, and his personal need to maintain meticulous copies of himself made the task simple. Freja had come to Mehdi for help accessing Mike's private storage and with her initial interpretation of what she found. It had been her idea to hide Pazel's revision within Mike's backups and wait for him to have cause to revert.

'We should fix these inconsistencies before we do anything more creative. It's a wonder he has any semblance of sanity given the number of incongruous truths he supports.'

'It's the difference between Pazel and Danesh. I think Mike can tell them apart.'

'Unlikely. There's nothing to indicate any separation. Or duality. Just a jumble of conflicting crap. I can clean most of it out now and then add your update. I'll ensure he doesn't suspect.'

'Just like you could for Pazel. Why doesn't he let you?'

'He says he would know.'

'Then Mike would too,' Freja said. 'I did the best I could, and he survived.'

'You made him into a monster. That's what you told me. What if he comes for Pazel? What if he kills him?'

'Pazel would be fine. That's what you're here for, making endless editions of him and preparing them for Zero.'

Almost half of Mike's iconography lit up around her. 'See all of this? It belongs to Pazel, and it's pretty active. Danesh is a fucking shrewd *maður*, and he worries me. We should cut this away while we have the opportunity.'

'You mustn't. Pazel would be livid. He must have his reasons for keeping Mike alive.'

'Then he is a fool. Which means Mike is too.' Mehdi reset the schematic and added the new pathways. 'It's done. I've set a replication into future backups and an alarm for when he accesses them.'

She reached for Mehdi's tanned hand and squeezed it fiercely, gazing into his pale blue eyes. 'Why did Pazel assign this to me?'

He studied her face, remembering the other *ljðirnir* who had used the *māsadā-sarīra*. 'Pazel likes to unnerve people because it helps him establish his authority. You came to him troubled by Danesh's response so now you get to relive that every day. I can still help you forget.'

'I'm coping, Mehdi. There's no need.' Freja let his hand go and invited him into a fresh vestibule. 'Let's see what Mike's up to. Maybe we can exert enough influence to make him failover.'

GLOSSARY

abeyance: supposed place for separated *sikatā-ātamā* that are not cached in the Pallium

adherents: Pazel's staff

aðili: person (Icelandic), also *alþýða, einstaklingur, persónan*

afkomendur: descendents (Icelandic)

Afzal Eight-Heta-Heta-Pha: K7 prosumer plant manager (Arabic: عادل)

Ahmad Phi-Nn-Nu-Nje: K4 *stochastís* (Arabic: أحمد)

Akash Dv-Tse-Wynn-Pha: K3 experience artist (Hindi: आकाश)

Aikaterine J-Omega-Oo-Beta: K3 *stochastís* (Greek: Αικατερινη), refer to Kathy

amie: friend (French)

airdoors: sets of consecutive doors designed to separate areas of differing air pressure

alþýða: person (Icelandic), also *aðili, einstaklingur, persónan*

al-qahwa: Arabic coffee (Arabic: قهوة)

alternate: stand-alone processor, separate from the Pallium

annals: oral records maintained by chaunters

Annapurna: area of Bodem in K1 (formerly a massif in the Himalayas, Nepal)

apashabd: shit (Hindi: अपशब्द)

archivist: administrator responsible for data within Bagāla

Aryan Be-Zeta-Kappa-Delta: K1 media personality (Sanskrit: आर्य)

Ashraqat: K0 unjoined (Arabic: أشراقات)

assize: behaviour regulation worker

Atanas Five-Damaru-Ghha-Va: K7 splicer (Macedonian: Атанас)

atītē: in the past (Bangla: অতীতে)

Audrey One-N-Tshe-Tsha: K4 data engineer

awamori: rice liquor (Japanese: 泡盛)

Bagāla: the Bengal fan region below the K9 substrate ('Bengal', Punjabi: ਬੰਗਾਲ)

Bailey Xi-Omega-So-Tje: K6 grass worker

balaa: yeah, yes (Arabic: بلى)

balach mòr: big boy (Scottish Gaelic)

Bāo Tlo-Tsa-Gamma-Rho: K4 trafficker (Chinese: 褒)

baṛhiyā: good or great (Hindi: बढ़िया)

barnið: baby (Icelandic)

bartamānē: in the present (Bangla: বর্তমান)

bastardo: bastard (Spanish)

Beatriz Dha-Fa-Sharp-Tau: K1 housekeeper

Beurs, the: stock exchange (Dutch)

bhabiṣyatē: in the future (Bangla: ভবিষ্যতে)

bias tariff: standard charge for prejudiced behaviour

bila shaka: without doubt (Swahili)

bioapp: software to influence the way a *māsadā-sarīra* behaves

Bodem: the interface between old Earth and Tion ('bottom', Dutch)

bogdo: passageway used to move between levels without detection (Korean: 복도)

börnin: children or babies (Icelandic)

Budi Phar-Tet-Che-Thorn: K5 oneironaut

buffy-headed marmoset: small primate

cache: licensed euthanasia with online representation of *sikatā-ātamā*

cacherie: euthanasia store

cachier: euthanasia worker

caching voucher: authority to cache an individual by TUID

caching warrant: license granted to a cachier, required to trade

Caitlyn Dzhe-Ta-Tse-Tsha: K5 elucidarian

Caleb Qua-Phi-Heta-Ban: K9 assize (Hebrew: כָּלֵב)

Carl Shcha-Yat-Q-Eight: K0 engineer

carbon-wright: carbon dioxide artisan, able to fashion items from the air

chaunter: performer of the annals, often sung

chāy: man (Thai: ชาย)

chekidzhiya: wanker (Bulgarian: чекиджия)

clearfibre: plastic alternative, manufactured from grass farm waste

coextension: modification of a person's *sikatā-ātamā*

cojones: balls (Spanish)

compeller: *sikatā-ātamā* adjustment software

comprenez vous?: do you understand? (French)

Connor Va-Six-J-Jhan: K8 regenerator

coño: shit (Spanish)

cony: pussy (Catalan)

Cristóbal Hie-Ngo-Sharp-Damaru: K4 trafficker

cybercyte: non-biological cell, refer to *raja'a*

Danesh Ne-Baluda-Va-Wa: K4 *stochastís* (from 'Dinesh', Hindi: दिनेश)

dankie: thank you (Afrikaans)

data miner: automated process to locate information

datrix: embedded technology used to exchange data with nerve tissue

Dawn Zhe-Mo-Ne-Psi: K3 cultivator

default caching: euthanasia of a customer who has a zero stater balance

Definitive Sitting, the: sitting responsible for all assize sittings

demarcator: inter-level assize, border agent

Dens, the: communal sleeping areas

Depths, the: levels Five through Nine

desequencer: device to reduce items to elemental components

designation: task assigned to a *konservator* by the *forfeður*

disseveration: the division of a community into two

disunion: separation of the population from the Pallium

DoA: degree of arc (approximately 110km)

dòufu: tofu (bean curd, Chinese: 豆腐)

Doha R-Ta-Gim-Ta: K4 nonworker

Doină Ngo-Gimel-Tet-Rha: K9 chaunter

drengar: boy (Icelandic), also *tánin-maður*

duotenancy: two-person multitenancy

e: electronic (prefix)

early-nonage: first half of childhood

edition: aspects of an individual's *sikatā-ātamā* combined with another individual, not necessarily the entire persona, refer to imprint, mediary

Efstathios Resh-Bo-Psi-Delta: K3 actuary (Greek: Ευσταθιος), refer to Stathis

einstaklingur: person (Icelandic), also *aðili*, *alþýða*, *persónan*

Ekatommýrio, the: unjoined population from Kathy's gestorium ('million', Greek: εκατομμύριο)

eldri-fólkið: older people ('senior people', Icelandic)

eldri-kona: older woman (pl. *eldri-konurnar*, 'senior woman', Icelandic)

eldri-maður: older man (pl. *eldri-mennirnir*, 'senior man', Icelandic)

Eleven-Two: habitat in the Threes

elucidarium: group of workers who can be purchased to complete tasks (pl. elucidaria)

ēma: eh (Gujarati: એમ)

emalter: embedded personal processor

Emma Upsilon-So-Tah-Baluda: K3 charm therapist

empyrealode: K0 solar collection bands

engin-fólkið: non-existent people ('no one', Icelandic)

engin-kona: non-existent woman ('no one', Icelandic)

engin-maður: non-existent man ('no one', Icelandic)

engin-persónan: non-existent person ('no one', Icelandic)

entendéis (*entiendes*): you understand (Spanish)

Enzo Gim-Six-Be-Upsilon: K6 grass worker

epitome: quantum representation of a persona managed by the Pallium

Erica Ini-Rayanna-Di-Ban: K8 regenerator

estupideces: crap (Spanish)

Étienne Ya-Mo-Cil-Rr: K6 driver

Fall, the: a sudden twenty per cent reduction in Pallial services, refer to Pallial Decline

Feliu Tse-Koppa-U-Ka: K4 porter

Flemming Feh-Upsilon-Dza-Fa: K1 independent worker

FMP: Feynman Milburn Pallium, refer to Pallium

foda-se: fuck (Portuguese)

fólkið: people (Icelandic), also *lýðirnir*, *sálirnar*, *þjóðirnar*

fólksfjöldi: population (Icelandic)

Fonseca's Clash: a Portuguese bar in the Sevens

Foretokening, the: a *sikatá-átamá* applet

forfeður: forefathers, creators of Tion, demiurges (sing. *forfaðir*, 'ancestor', Icelandic)

Forming, the: the building of Tion

forsaken: a person who has never been connected to the Pallium

fount: water sequencer

foutaise: crap (French)

framer: cameraman

Freja Mo-Rho-Ef-J: K5 elucidarian

Friedrich Shcha-Nnya-Pha-Koppa: K5 router

fullorðnir: adults (Icelandic)

futon: mattress usually placed on the floor (Japanese: 布団)

geen: no (Afrikaans)

geen probleem: no worries (Afrikaans)

genorep: refer to genorepository

genorepository: genomic data library in the Tens (Southern and Northern)

gestorium: people factory or nursery (pl. gestoria)

ghost, ghoster, ghosting: refer to rehosting

gocco: *sikatā-ātamā* replication software, commonly used as part of a multitenancy (from print gocco, Japanese: ごっこ), refer to imprint

gōngjī xīpán: cock sucker (Chinese: 公鸡吸盘)

Grace Mu-Tlo-Ue-Jhan: K4 trafficker

Greater Numbers, the: levels Ten through Fifteen

Gregory Nine-Fi-Jia-Oo: K5 router

Grusha Mo-N-Mu-Ka: K7 Bodem maintainer (Russian: Груша)

Guðmundur C-Tau-Nnna-Zhe: K6 grass worker (Icelandic)

Haben Lje-Qua-Wynn-Mo: K4 cashier

hadal zone: the deepest region of the ocean lying within oceanic trenches, levels Thirteen through Eighteen

hanbō: half-staff used in martial arts (Japanese: 半棒)

Haziq Lla-Four-Ne-Te: K4 *stochastís* (Arabic: حَاذِق)

Heikapu Gamma-G-Po-Mo: K7 assize

hila'a: cloned version of the *raja'a* ('ruse' or 'trick', from 'hila', Arabic: حيلة)

hoofoo: human food

ho'ohiki: a pledge (Hawaiian)

Hosniya Gim-Ghha-Ll-Mo: K3 engineer

Hossein Di-Hayanna-Sha-Fi: K1 media assistant director (Persian: حسّين)

hugbúnaður: interactive software application (Icelandic)

Humaira De-Ko-Mo-Zayin: K4 *stochastís*

hypervirus: bioengineered agent targeting immunosecurity structures, capable of operantly reengineering itself, also mutable hypervirus

Hyun-jun Ezh-Wynn-Rr-S: K6 grass worker (Korean: 현준)

Ichirō Yat-Rha-Sigma-Kappa: K4 assize (Japanese: いちろう)

'īlio 'ino: ugly dog (Hawaiian)

imprint: a member of a group of individuals sharing a single, identical experience; the basis of multitenancies, refer to edition, mediary

Indah: a *hugbúnaður*, Budi's personification of the Pallium ('eternal' or 'abiding', Indonesian)

Inès Psi-Two-Zeta-Dha: K5 elucidarian

Interdiction, the: the inhabited parts of Second

inter-level permit: authority to move people or goods between levels, required to transit between non-adjacent levels

Ivor Tau-Rho-Nnya-Nyo: K4 waiter

Jack Ge-Tau-Two-Bo: K1 media technician

Jared Nine-Sigma-So-Zhe: K4 facilitator

Jeremy Alpha-Q-Nnya-Rayanna: K1 socialite

Joaquín Ghha-Qui-Baluda-Tlu: K5 router

Jovana Omega-Beta-Zha-Ge: K5 elucidarian

juncture: a discrete collection of ideas that form a segment of a dream

jaqsï: Good (Kazakh: жақсы)

Kahurangi Da-Rr-Dda-Lla: K3 driver

Kap: refer to Heikapu Gamma-G-Po-Mo

kararehe: animals (Māori)

Kathy: refer to Aikaterine J-Omega-Oo-Beta

Kavya Ngo-Dza-Ta-Thorn: K5 elucidarian

kay: one of Tion's levels, each a kilometre high

Kermadec: area of the Pretermissions, extending down to K17

kombu: edible kelp (Japanese: 昆布)

komurumurua: bollocks ('testicles', Māori)

kona: woman (pl. *konurnar*, Icelandic)

konservator: individual charged by the *forfeður* with a designation for the protection of Tion (pl. *konservatorer*, 'conservator', Danish)

kostym: protective suit (pl. *kostymer*, Swedish), refer to *stövlar*

kostyman: person using a *kostym* (pl. *kostymän*)

kweme: nutritious seeds grown on a vine ('oysternuts', Swahili)

Lachlan Jia-Tlo-Ban-Five: K7 Bodem maintainer

Lacuna, the: transport conduits

lalaki: man (Filipino)

late-nonage: second half of childhood

levels: separate tionsphere zones, from One to Eighteen, subdivided into tiers, refer to spheres

leysingja: free person, who has no role within Tion (Icelandic)

Liang Tlo-Tsa-Gamma-Rho: K4 trafficker (Chinese: 梁)

lifer: a person who has used technology to extensively prolong life

Lior Ka-Mo-Visarga-Omicron: K6 grass worker (Hebrew: ליאור)

Lisboa Pit, the: a gambling club in the Fours

Lockie: refer to Lachlan Jia-Tlo-Ban-Five

Low Numbers, the: levels One through Four

Lucas Visarga-Yo-Tsha-Tshe: K3 waste processor

lýðirnir: people (Icelandic), also *fólkið*, *sálirnar*, *þjóðirnar*

ma hi alllaena: what the fuck (Arabic: ما هي اللعنة)

maður: man (pl. *mennirnir*, Icelandic)

magairlí: testicles (Irish)

manngæska: humanity (Icelandic), refer to *mannkynið*

mannkynið: humanity ('mankind', Icelandic), refer to *manngæska*

mannvera: human being (Icelandic)

Mariana: Region in the Pretermissions, extending to K18

māsadā-sarīra: body or bodies ('flesh body', from 'māsa dā sarīra', Punjabi: ਮਾਸ ਦਾ ਸਰੀਰ), refer to *sikatā-ātamā*, *viakatī-pūrā*

mchumba: sweetheart, term of affection (Swahili)

mediary: an entire sikatā-ātamā suppressing the entire persona of some other person, the process used in caching and rehosting, refer to edition, imprint

megagestoria: factories to mass produce people

Mehdi Gim-Het-Fa-Feh: K7 *māsadā-sarīra* technician (Persian: مهدی)

mennirnir: refer to *maður*

merda: shit, bullshit (Catalan, Galacian)

Metztli: K0 unjoined (Japanese: 美智子)

Meyer Eth-Eight-Eight-Iyanna: K1 administrator

mid-nonage: eighth birthday

miðaldra-fólkið: mid-life people ('middle-aged people', Icelandic)

miðaldra-kona: mid-life woman (pl. *miðaldra-konurnar*, 'middle-aged woman', Icelandic)

miðaldra-maður: mid-life man (pl. *miðaldra-mennirnir*, 'middle-aged man', Icelandic)

Mike Dla-Dda-Lamda-Phi: K1 cicerone

Milagrosa Ya-V-Tje-Three: K6 grass worker

Miyu Che-Zeta-Phi-Ezh: K5 elucidarian (Japanese: 美結)

MoA: minute of arc (approximately 2km)

moji: characters from left-to-right and right-to-left scripts used in TUIDs and other tagging ('character', Japanese: 文字)

Moshe Nnna-Schwa-Sharp-Pha: K5 elucidarian (Hebrew: מֹשֶׁה)

mpendwa: dear or loved one, term of affection (Swahili)

mpenzi: sweetheart, term of affection (Swahili)

multitenancy: single experience shared by multiple users, facilitated through *sikatā-ātamā* replication software, refer to *gocco*, imprint

mux: combination of multiple sources into a single data stream (multiplexor)

mvulana mzuri: sweet (or good) boy (Swahili)

Myron Qui-Lv-Damaru-Zhe: K5 router

náungi: fellow (Icelandic)

ndiyo: yes (Swahili)

nenos musculares: muscle boys (Galacian)

Nergüi Ngo-Five-Gamma-Yayanna: K4 assize (Mongolian: Нэргүй)

newed: reached adulthood, fifteen years from conception

Nihilities, the: levels beyond the Pretermissions

Nikora Vayanna-Yayanna-Vayanna-Cheh: K7 Bodem maintainer

Nitin Da-Ezh-Alpha-Kssa: K5 router (Sanskrit: नितिन)

Noemí Na-Oo-Do-Ge: K6 grass worker

nonage: childhood, up to majority at fifteen

Nürasyl: K0 unjoined (Kazakh: Нурасыл)

nǚrén: woman (Chinese: 女人)

ný-eldri: new senior person (Icelandic)

ný-fólkið: new people (Icelandic)

ný-kona: new woman (pl. *ný-konurnar*, Icelandic)

nýliði: newcomer (pl, *nýliðar*, Icelandic)

ný-maður: new man (pl. *ný-mennirnir*, Icelandic)

Odyssée: a video programme

offliner: individual who practices disconnection by choice, not unjoined by necessity

Oliver Feh-Tlo-Epsilon-Eight: K4 artisan

oneironaut: dream auditor (from oneirology)

opinn-fólkið: people who live on the open surface of Tion ('open to people', Icelandic), refer to Zeroer

Oriol D-Digamma-Rayanna-Mu: K4 porter

Oskar Theta-Tau-Phar-Lv: K1 assistant cicerone

outrightsider: quadruple rightsider ('outright rightsider')

pacharán: liqueur made from sloe berries (Spanish)

Pallial Decline, the: reduction in global processing services, refer to the Fall

Pallium, the: global processing service

pas assez bon: not good enough (French)

Paul Iyanna-Keheh-Ta-Tsadi: K9 verderer

Pazel Sad-Tet-Ain-Resh: K7 industrialist

pe-to-pe: refer to point-to-point

perd skit: horse shit (Afrikaans)

permit: refer to inter-level permit

persónan: person (Icelandic), also *aðili, alþýða, einstaklingur*

Petrişor Va-Ya-Eight-Shin: K3 industrialist

piča: cunt (Czech)

podatram: land vehicle

point-to-point: quantum transportation of people or goods

pointport: point-to-point station with one or more terminals

politique: policy or politics (French)

pragtige: beautiful (Afrikaans)

pravda: justice (Bosnian)

pre-Forming: before the building of Tion commenced

Pretermissions, the: levels Sixteen through Eighteen

progenitor: base of a *sikatā-ātamā*, created at conception, may be
   used for identification purposes

Punim Iota-Gamma-Tav-To: K8 sex worker

puta: bitch (Catalan)

Puysegur: area in the Fourteens (formerly a trench in the
   Tasman Sea, situated between Australia and New Zealand)

Qióng Yayanna-Mo-Tlu-Pha: K6 *stochastís*

qu: quantum (prefix)

quibebe: Brazilian squash soup

Quín: refer to Joaquín Ghha-Qui-Baluda-Tlu

Rabindra Schwa-Rha-Ta-Te: K8 regenerator

raja'a: bioapp that restores an individual to a former state
   ('retrace' or 'return', from 'rajea', Arabic: رجعة), refer to *tabi'a*

Rajah me sauvera: Rajah will save me (French)

rajul dahkm: massive man (Arabic: رجل ضخم)

rehosting: overlaying a *sikatā-ātamā* on an alternate *māsadā-sarīra*;
   a mediary, refer to ghosting

recast: genetic update to *māsadā-sarīra*

Reihaneh Gamma-Oo-Ghha-Thorn: K1 cultivator

rightsider: person with a TUID containing right-to-left mojis

Riley Khar-Lla-El-Wo: K6 grass worker

Riley Sampi-Llla-Po-Da: K6 grass worker

Ruby S-Zeta-Iota-Omega: K1 makeup artist

Saburo No-To-S-Bāo: K4 porter (Japanese: 三郎)

Salik Dzhe-Nje-Kappa-Damaru: K7 purification plant worker

sálirnar: people (Icelandic), also *fólkið*, *lýðirnir*, *þjóðirnar*

samfélag: community (pl. *samfélögin*, Icelandic)

sato: rice wine (Thai: สาโท)

Sawyer Jeem-Psi-J-Rha: K1 assize

se presser: hurry (French)

shǐ: shit (Chinese: 屎)

Shu-fen Ma-Eight-Po-Na: K4 *stochastís* (Taiwanese: 淑芬)

shuō dé kuài: speak quickly (Chinese: 说得快)

şığıp keteyik: Let's go (Kazakh: шығып кетейік)

sikatā-ātamā: mind or minds ('psyche spirit', from 'mānasikatā ātamā', Punjabi: ਮਾਨਸਿਕਤਾ ਆਤਮਾ), refer to *māsadā-sarīra*, *viakatī-pūrā*

Smiž, the: short message service; local or remote radio connectivity ('wireless', from 'simsiz', Uzbek)

sitting: interface between the Pallium and assize community, refer to Definitive Sitting

SoA: second of arc (approximately 30m)

Sodality: online consensus or community

Sophie Sampi-Lv-Ta-Xi: K7 sysadmin

spheres: refer to levels

spider: fixing machine, a robot or *vélmenni*

splice: refer to coextension

splicer: coextension practitioner

spokes: inter-level Lacuna structure

Stathis: refer to Efstathios Resh-Bo-Psi-Delta

Stater (ꝯ): unit of cryptocurrency ('weight', Ancient Greek: στατήρ)

stochastís: data capitalist (pl. *stochastés*, 'thinker', Greek: στοχαστὴς)

stövlar: protective footwear (Swedish), refer to *kostym*

stúlka: girl (Icelandic), also *tánin-kona*

tā mā de nǐ: Fuck you (Chinese: 他媽的你)

tabi'a: version of the *raja'a* that does not reset an individual ('succeed' or 'follow', from 'tabie', Arabic: تابع)

Tabitha: refer to Tingting Kaf-Ayin-Beh-Keheh

tamaiti: child (Māori)

Tāne Six-Kha-Omicron-V: K8 regenerator

táningar: adolescent (pl. *táningur*, 'teenager', Icelandic)

tánin-fólkið: younger people (Icelandic)

tánin-kona: younger woman (Icelandic), also *stúlka*

tánin-maður: younger man (pl. *tánin-mennirnir,* Icelandic), also *drengar*

tier: discrete floors within a level, easy to move between

Teva Ban-Tau-W-Schwa: K0 comms operator

Thibaut Kssa-Seven-Jia-Zeta: K4 assize

thráfstis: encryption hacker ('breaker', Greek: θραύστης)

threader: threading practitioner

threading: surgically attaching two or more people together (conjoining)

three-to-one: enforced caching submitted by three people for matched staters

TUID: Tion unique identifier, comprising a names and four mojis

Tingting Kaf-Ayin-Beh-Keheh: K7 sysadmin (Chinese: 婷婷)

toku hoa: my friend (Māori)

tömsög: testicles (Mongolian: томсог)

topsky: the uppermost tier in a level

Toshi Dzhe-Mo-Cheh-Qua: K1 publicist (Japanese: トシ)

trips: people with three right-to-left mojis in their TUID

Tyler Pha-Pha-Gim-Lla: K7 Bodem maintainer

Ulyana Shcha-Omega-Nje-Khar: K5 oneironaut

ungbarn: infant (pl. *ungbörnir*, 'baby', Icelandic)

unjoined: someone does not have a Pallial connection

unko: shit (Japanese: うんこ)

uprisers: people who force their way up through the levels without authorisation

uprising: mass migration of people to higher levels, including the mobbing of the Interdiction following Odyssée and the subsequent exodus to Zero

Uthman Ini-Upsilon-Dzhe-Pi: K6 *stochastís*

útlendingur: stranger (pl. *útlendingar*, 'foreigner', Icelandic)

Uxío Tse-Jia-Nnna-Kssa: K8 datrix technician

valse huise: false houses (Afrikaans)

Vasco Di-To-Jeem-Fi: K5 oneironaut

ve: virtual (prefix)

vél: machine (pl. *vélarnar*, Icelandic)

vélmenni: robot, or artificial epitome (pl. *vélmennir*, Icelandic)

verderer: officer charged with protecting Bagāla

viakatī-pūrā: entire being, the sum of *sikatā-ātamā* and *māsadā-sarīra* (from 'person full', Punjabi: ਪੂਰੇ ਵਿਅਕਤੀ)

Victoria Qua-Za-Jia-Ya: K8 courier

Vihaan Nje-Ka-Jia-Qui: K7 Bodem maintainer (Sanskrit: विहान)

Vínculo: isolation area in K4 ('bond', Galacian)

visionär: visionary (pl. *visionäre*, German)

Votaries of Quín: community of zealots

voucher: refer to caching voucher

Walloppong Iota-Ta-Yayanna-Chin: K8 regenerator (Thai: แสดงกระทู้)

wapenzi: darlings, term of affection (Swahili)

warrant: refer to caching warrant

Wayland Wo-Sha-Tsv-Schwa: K3 assize

wiederholt: second chance, repeat life ('retry', German)

Wiesław Tshe-Ge-Zha-Jia: K0 engineer

wit fokker: white fucker (Afrikaans)

Xin-yi Nn-Fi-Omicron-Psi: K8 demarcator (Chinese: 心怡)

Yash Wo-Khar-Jia-Tsv: K4 porter

Yasuo Zha-Rha-Zeta-Ban: K4 porter (Japanese: やすお)

Yo: refer to Lucas Visarga-Yo-Tsha-Tshe

Youssef Damaru-Da-Te-Epsilon: K8 regenerator (Arabic: يوسف)

yuddh: war (Hindi: युद्ध)

Yuuto Zhar-No-Wo-Epsilon: K4 cachier

Zara Ne-Zayin-Ngo-Lamda: K4 *stochastís*

Zejneb Jia-Delta-Nu-Feh: K6 *stochastís* (Arabic: زينب)

Zero: the external surface of Tion

Zeroers: people who live on the open surface of Tion, refer to *opinn-fólkið*

Zoe Mu-Qua-So-Beta: K3 life stylist

þjóðirnar: people (Icelandic), also *fólkið*, *lýðirnir*, *sálirnar*

The Visionary
A Tion Story
J.C. Gemmell

At the beginning of February 2060, Mount Erebus erupted, the first of a chain of Antarctic volcanoes that forever changed Earth's future. Within days, sea levels began to rise, until sixty metres of water claimed coastlines worldwide.

Twelve-year-old Xin-yi and her mother fled their home, surviving amongst a community of rice farmers. A year later, a chance conversation with international census officials prepared her for a new life.

Now fourteen, Xin-yi commences her training as a visionary. It is her task to imagine a new Earth, rising above the drowning waters. Thousands of young people strive to design a world in which the displaced millions can live, and engineer a solution that will take a millennium to populate.

But Xin-yi's challenges are more personal: coming to terms with the loss of her brother and unexpected feelings toward a friend. She has to choose between working to benefit humanity and her internal conflict with love.

Set over three decades after the 2060 flood, *The Visionary* combines dystopian, future and science fiction, and introduces J.C. Gemmell's *Tion* series.

"Drawing attention to society's pressing issues such as climate change and rising sea levels, J.C. Gemmell gives us a glimpse of a terrible future that's more of a possibility than anyone credits. *The Visionary* also showcases humanity's brilliant innovation under pressing needs of survival… A perfect blend of futuristic gadgets and dystopian society, *The Visionary* is a must-read!"

— Readers' Favorite

The Uprisers
Tion Book 2
J.C. Gemmell

The elimination of Earth's excess water was crucial to building a better world, providing access to real estate and raw materials. For a thousand years, the ejected ice remained safely stored in Tion's orbit, and the human population soared.

Mike has a licence to move tourists through Tion's spheres, despite new restrictions in the movement of people and data. His latest clients know nothing of his previous life and relationship to Pazel, or of the voice from his past, tempting him to return.

When Mike discovers scattered communities across Tion's exposed surface, he knows he must confront Pazel. As they descend into the Depths and beyond, the crisis facing Tion becomes clear: the oceanic ice starts to bombard the world. Their journey becomes one of survival, not just theirs, but for hundreds of thousands of billions of consumers.

The Uprisers follows desperate people as they are forced to leave the safety of their connected lives behind and rise up toward the surface of Tion.

Demiurge

Tion Book 3
J.C. Gemmell

Desperate people will do anything to survive. Could a new god be enough to save them?

The world survived for a millennium without gods until the devastation and disconnection became unbearable.

Heikapu has attained Tion's surface but needs biotechnology to preserve the behaviour regulators who live there. There is only one guaranteed source, but she cannot locate it in the barren wasteland. In the levels below, an army of fanatics seeks the same thing, but they may have a way to recreate it for themselves.

The flood has devastated Tion's infrastructure, and the central processing facility has failed. Billions of people are disconnected for the first time in their lives and have lost all sense of hope. One faction has a way to provide data to the masses, but it means exploiting the people they depend upon; they have no choice because, without a replacement processor, they cannot recreate Caitlyn's bioapp.

Somewhere on the surface of Tion, a new god is protecting the uprisers. His power may be great, but is the price too high?

Printed in Great Britain
by Amazon